Magdalen's Way

A Journey With Mary of Magdala,

Bride of Christ

And Keeper of the Way

By Arlene J. Colver

For

Mervin "Beaver" Colver

To "Beaver", my soul mate and husband, best critic and ever present companion, thank you, dearest. Thank you for being there when I woke to the present and for lying beside me as I lived in the past. Thank you for listening to me rant on about my journeys and for reminding me of who I am, for pushing me forward when I was shy and for standing on my feet when I was anxious. You are and always have been my Love and my Light.

In an open hand you have held my heart and with an open mind you have received my dreams. Thank you for every fair exchange and for honoring me with your love.

Acknowledgments

My prayers of thanksgiving go out first to the Spirits of Mother Mary and Mary Magdalen who have shared so fully their wisdom and wonders.

Special thanks to Linda Rush and Melinda Colver for editing in a hurry what it took me five years to write, to our Cable Postmaster Dick who put up with the many manuscript mailings and return postage calculations and kept smiling every time I came in and to my dear companions on the Way: my son David and friends Scott, Mary, Cathy, Bethany, Jo and so many others for listening to my stories, dreaming my dreams and helping me to find my muse.

I must also thank all of those who have supported my work by reading and re-reading, editing and encouraging me to continue this five-year journey. Faithful friends, there are too many of you to mention, but please know that you have contributed fully to whatever success this work achieves.

May your hearts be visited by Faith, Hope and Charity

And may your souls find Peace to be their home.

So Mote It Be!

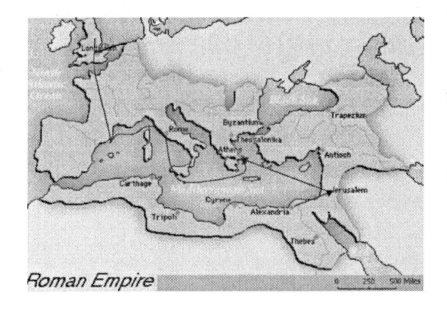

Magdalen's Way

Author's Note

Several years ago I undertook an awesome project. Through an incredible dream sequence, I was able to access the life of Mary Magdalen as the bride of Christ and later as a woman of philosophy and spiritual endeavors. I am aware of the emotional set, psychological profile, and spiritual belief system of this woman. I became, during my sleeping hours, totally immersed in her identity to the point of living within Magdalen.

There are literally thousands of people who claim to have been Mary of Magdala; I am not one of them. I have, however, moved into her entire consciousness. Unlike past life recall in which the re-caller sees him or herself as if watching a movie, this was a true regression in which I was not observer but participant in the drama of that lifetime. I believe that all things are happening within the same frame and that what I was able to do was to move my awareness to Magdalen's life and time.

I diligently journalized the days of Magdalen's life with Jesus as well as after His ascension. This book was developed from that journal and long hours of research to prove the value and truth of the stories to myself.

The story is sometimes heart wrenching, sometimes humorous and always inspiring as Magdalen's ministry after the Master's ascension and the birth of the couple's daughter, Sharon, takes her from the Celtic tribes of Gaul to the shores of Avalon and the County of Holland spreading her Way throughout the Roman Empire.

Curiosity over the supposed celibacy of the Master and the place this woman of the night played in his life has given rise to many other writings but none that I have seen expose more fully the possibility that our true Christian legacy might be in our human experience rather than a separate spiritual search.

I feel that Magdalen's Way has given a stage and dramatic setting to the life of the Master Jesus and His soul mate. Living through my dreams as Mary Magdalen has put historical perspective and understanding to what seemed dry scripture to me before. It also has given personality and reality to the Master and His associates.

I have come to love Magdalen and want to share her message with everyone who has an open mind and heart regarding the gospels and their connection to us today.

TABLE OF CONTENTS

Chapter 1

The Resurrection of Life and Love

The bed seemed cold without Jesus beside her, and she pulled the blanket up around her neck trying to ward off the chill. In the darkness Magdalen's eyes followed the drifting shadows created by the fluttering flame of a single candle in the next room. Emotionally exhausted and unable to sleep, she awaited the dawn and her future by focusing on the past. Her mind sifted through memories, thrusting out temptations to despair and embracing comforting recollections to cling to through the night.

"Once", she thought, "I was young and innocent, a Priestess of the Goddesses Mari, Anna, and Ishtar, living in the triple towered temple of Magdala. Look at me now; I, Mary Magdalen, live in the modest home of my Jewish mother-in-law and sleep on a mattress filled with straw."

Magdalen shuttered at the thought. Once the Sacred Virgin of the Goddess's court, she now was the prostitute bride of an executed criminal. She of the High Place, the Magdalen, was now looked upon with scorn and pity. When her father, Syrus, and her mother, Eucharia, sent her off to the temple, they had thought that she would be a fitting gift for the Goddess, a beautiful child with position, intelligence and wealth. They had been sure that devoting a daughter to the Goddess' temple would bring them favor and boons beyond their wildest dreams.

They believed Magdalen would benefit too. Being raised in the temple she would be educated, protected and trained in the ritual arts of priesthood. Her status in the Roman community

1

would be raised to a level far beyond other women. She would have the blessing of the Great Mother and the community.

"Some boon," she thought, "now I'm separated from my parents by death and from my own home and wealth in Bethany and Jerusalem by a marriage scorned by many. Now the cross has widowed me and the most precious union for which I gave everything is lost." Magdalen pulled the covers tighter as if to protect her from her own thoughts.

"The scriptures of Judea promise that it is lost only until the morning." She tried to control and direct the mind chatter in the direction of hope. The very scriptures that condemned her to her present misery were now her hope for the future. It seemed ironic and strange to have been so close to the Goddess and now to be subject to the whims of this nameless patriarchal God and laying here feeling so much alone.

The temple had been communal; she had never been lonely there. As the High Priestess she had other women with whom to share her burdens and her joys, her thoughts and feelings. For a while she tried to concentrate on the comfort she had known.

She remembered the lamps in the darkness, with sweet smelling oil that scented the women's quarters with the aroma of lilacs. She imagined the virgins moving quietly through the corridors and meeting secretly to tell tales and gossip, giggling and huddling together in warm down filled beds. Like sisters they shared everything, jewelry, clothes, hopes and dreams. She missed them now and said a small prayer to the Great Mother for their safety. "Mother cloak them all in comfort and Divine Innocence, for I miss their love."

The love of the virgins was not the only thing that Magdalen missed. It was also the temple's warmth and security, its feelings of home and hospitality. Widows with children and aging parents to care for, those who had been divorced from their husbands or abandoned by poverty stricken parents, everyone living under the protection of the Goddess was made to feel useful, safe and secure within the temple walls.

She remembered how the women banded together to care for and educate the children, to keep public records and to learn and teach the written languages of the Roman Empire. Magdalen could see in her mind dreamy images of the green and golden fields, the full to bursting grain bins, the piles of dried figs and the vats of olive all stored for the security of the people. In the dim glow of the candle, she could visualize the traders coming and going, bringing with them the richly colored ribbons that she still adored. They traded their trinkets and brass, gold, and silver for the fine wool, cotton and linen that the women produced.

This wealth and guarantee of safety were the reasons that gentile and Jewish parents alike gifted the Goddess with their daughters. Her own parents had found it easy to follow the God of Judea and then imagine the Goddess of Rome as his consort. By offering up their daughters, they were assured popularity within the Roman community and the girls were given a future of security and comfort. Some of the young women were eventually given in marriage to prominent and illustrious traders, priests, and nobles. Magdalen was aware that this was the kind of arranged marriage that her mother-in-law, Mary, had with Joseph.

Magdalen, however, had been singled out for the position of High Priestess. Upon reaching the age of puberty she had undergone the initiation rite of defloration at the hands of her gentle sisters. She was not to take a husband but had many lovers, those men who came to the temple to honor the Goddess. They were Roman soldiers, Greek traders, and nobles from around the world. Not one of them would have thought of her as anything but a Priestess, until she left it all for her sweet, eccentric and loving prophet. Not one would have dared to dishonor her in word, deed or omission, not then. "In honor of the Goddess." She whispered to the darkness. "I give my whole self and yet remain untouched."

She had learned the art of Sacred Sex and the rituals and rites of the Mother Goddess. She spoke four languages and could communicate with her sisters telepathically. She interpreted dreams and visions, her own and those of great noblemen. She could ferret out truth from any consciousness and had been of service to those in power more than once. Now Rome and its Goddess found her to be the street tramp, the whore, and the Jews and their God had proclaimed her a sinner once filled with demons but saved by the grace of Yahweh. Magdalen's positive thoughts were evaporating as her mind began to wander to her current circumstance and tears slid down her cheeks in a warm and silent flood of rejection.

Even those men to whom Jesus had entrusted her care thought of her as a threat. They were envious of her intimacy with the Master, of her understanding of his words and of their secret conversations. Now she awaited sleep in this darkened room all alone, save for Mother Mary.

"Thank God and Goddess for my mother-in-law." She thought out loud. "Having her has been like keeping a part of the temple with me."

The thought of Mother Mary sleeping just a few feet away brought Magdalen a feeling of gratitude and love. Her mother-in-law referred to Magdalen as daughter, sister and friend. The two were deeply bonded and always supportive of one another. Mother Mary was filled with quiet wisdom. Her soft brown eyes had a look of compassion for everyone she met and her hands were always ready to help. Healing came easy for Mary and many had seen the miracles that she had done, but she always stood in the shadow of her son. When they were alone together she shared stories with Magdalen both of Jesus' childhood and her temple experiences. Magdalen was always curious about her husband's past, but she truly enjoyed the temple stories more.

Strange, Magdalen thought, that remembering the temple and her childhood was such a comfort. It seemed so long ago. She had left the temple and inherited her home when her father needed her to care for him after her mother's death. That was, under law, her first obligation. She had not given up her position as High Priestess but remained the personification of the

Goddess, the Mother, even while living in her own house. Then her father too passed from this earthly life. She was alone and seeking solace when she had heard of her sweet prophet, the Master who healed and who was said to baptize. It was a fateful day when that charismatic teacher approached her assailants and silenced their anger. It was without a doubt the most powerful day in her life and until yesterday the most frightening, but she didn't want to think about that incident just now. Instead Magdalen drifted off with thoughts of the love that had changed her life and conceived the child within her. Tomorrow, she prayed, would bring a resurrection of that life and its love.

Rising early, even before the darkness had lifted, Magdalen washed the tear stains from her cheeks and quietly combed her hair. Long, thick cascades of curls fell in gentle drapes to frame her face. Jesus, she thought, would not want her to cover her head or braid her tresses today. He so liked the softness that free flowing hair brought to her face. She looked at herself in the polished brass mirror and wished she had berry juice and indigo to color her eyes and lips and conceal the redness and pain that her tears had left behind. Careful not to awaken her mother-in-law she moved out the door and into the streets of Jerusalem.

There were few people on the streets so early, and without incident or questioning she soon was through the city gates. Despite the purpose of her journey, Magdalen was enjoying the walk. Spring had broken early and birds were just beginning their song of awakening as the sun broke the horizon. Somehow she felt that the beauty of the day was an omen of good fortune. Jesus had vowed that today he would rise, and the sun's return in such a glorious display of rosy light was a promise that he would keep his word.

Placing her hand on her belly she spoke to her unborn child. "Your Father comes home this morning, be glad and rejoice with me."

She approached the graveyard with some apprehension. It was believed the spirits of the dead were not to be disturbed. Otherwise they would become angry and perhaps, through the energy of that anger, keep her from reaching the sepulcher where Jesus would be waiting for her.

"Goddess of the Dawn, protect me and deliver me to him that I love." She prayed.

Joseph of Arimathea had provided a tomb for Jesus. It was Joseph that had procured the body and along with Nicodemus had arranged a burial for the teacher. He had purchased a new tomb, one that was not filled with the remains of some unfortunates who had died without means.

"Jesus," she thought, "will awaken to a clean and untainted room."

Carved into the rock of the hillside, the cave-like sepulcher had been sealed with a large rock. It had taken three men to put it in its place, the same three Roman soldiers who Magdalen would have to confront when she arrived there on the pretense of anointing the body of her husband.

But when she arrived at the tomb there were no soldiers at its door and the rock itself had been rolled away. Magdalen was aware that Jesus could have moved from the inside of the tomb to the streets of Jerusalem without the need to move that rock.

"He has left this as a sign." She whispered to herself.

Her heart leapt with joy and she felt a quickening in her womb. Jesus was alive and so was his child. She had brought with her healing oil, but she had more to offer Jesus now than merely comfort for his body. She carried within her a legacy of life and love.

"But where is he? Why didn't he wait for me?" Magdalen found herself thinking out loud again.

The sun was full now and the day was beginning to warm. Magdalen walked through the graveyard searching for Jesus. Another Mary, a student of the teacher, arrived to join her as a second witness and as a helpmate to nurse the ravaged body that they expected to find. She was almost hysterical with grief when she saw the open tomb and lamented Jesus' disappearance loudly with great shouts and wailing. Magdalen silenced her quickly.

"Stop that! You will wake the dead and those living that would force us into a grave of our own." Magdalen covered the woman's mouth with her hand.

When the wailing had stopped Magdalen released her, and she ran off eager to share the news of the teacher's disappearance with his disciples. Magdalen was glad to be rid of her, but knew that the news would soon become a myriad of rumors and gossip that would upset everyone.

"Nothing reaches the mind as it was when it left the mouth." She was talking as much to herself as to the child within her.

As she walked the road back toward the city alone, Magdalen pondered on what to believe. Had Jesus risen and then abandoned her? Had he been abducted, perhaps only to be crucified again? She couldn't believe either of these things. Jesus truly loved her and he was a man of loyalty and compassion; he would be anxious to find her. What's more he was a miracle worker and able to quell any attempt at abduction.

Then she heard the soft call: "Mary? Wife?"

"Rabbuni!" She ran to Jesus' outstretched arms.

She held him tightly, as if he would disappear if her embrace were not strong enough. Then the tears stung her eyes; being held there, against his chest, she felt a void that she had never felt before. It was almost as if it were a corpse that held her. Magdalen was not afraid of Jesus but for him. The crucifixion had been too much, she thought, he was entirely changed.

Jesus held her closer, "Do not fear for me, my sweet Magdala. Do not be afraid. My life is a new life, different from before, but still filled with love for you."

In that unyielding embrace, Magdalen realized she could not hear or feel the heartbeat that she had always known. The teacher's body was not functioning with human life. It was animate, seeing, speaking, walking, but something was wrong. His frame seemed smaller, and the whiteness of his complexion was much the same as it had been upon the cross. There was not the tan that the sun had brought him in life. Yet there was not the look of death about him. He lived, but he lived in a way unlike he had before. After a long while the couple released one another. Magdalen held his hand in hers and stepped back.

From this angle she could see that his aura, the energy that surrounded him, was the same as it had always been. It was only his body that had changed. Satisfied that in some way he was alive, Magdalen momentarily released herself from her fears. The tension in her face eased and she forced a smile as Jesus reached out to touch her.

"Our child will, indeed, inherit the earth." His hand blessed his wife's womb with its tenderness.

"I was sure that you would know before I could tell you." Magdalen's smile grew more genuine and warm.

Then she offered him the balm she had brought with her to care for his wounds. Jesus denied any pain but sat down on a rock and allowed her to caress his hands and feet anointing them with the healing salve. Her concern for her husband's well-being returned as she felt the absence of warmth in his body.

"I expected you to return to me as you were." The tone of her voice was both disapproving and demanding.

"All things will be explained, my dear Magdala, but for now know that my spirit is alive with love and light and its power controls this body." Suddenly Jesus' flesh became warm to the touch. His complexion glowed and was radiant with light. "This is the power of spirit, Magdala, to control all matter and yet remain without the need for it."

"You are more handsome than you have ever been, and warm and glowing like the sun!" Magdalen had shock in her voice.

"It was your compassionate touch and your desire for my sake that prompted this transformation." Jesus stroked Magdalen's long hair. "You wear your feelings as you wear your hair today, Magdala, free and flowing, thick and without a veil. You are genuine in your emotions and that is one of the reasons that I love you as I do. Remain as free as you are today, and let our child grow in freedom from fear as well."

Magdalen pushed the hair from her face and looked up into Jesus' eyes. Those deep blue pools of light drew her into them. His gaze had always made her feel safe while yet vulnerable to his love. He bent to kiss her on the mouth with deep passion.

"Magdala, my sweet Magdala, you bring life to the dead and stir my heart as always." He kissed her once more.

"I am in no hurry to return to the others, but Mary has gone ahead of us with a zealot's need to stir trouble instead of hearts." Magdalen said it with a certain amount of disdain.

"Then let us not hurry," Jesus laughed a little. "She will learn the lesson of temperance when her zeal angers Peter."

"I love Mary, but her hysteria can be overwhelming." Magdalen defended her prior judgment.

"She is a good and loving woman, a fine example of the human need to be loved." Jesus winked at Magdalen to assure her that in some way he did agree.

Hand in hand they left the graveyard and walked through the olive groves. No more words were spoken as Jesus and Mary of Magdala made their way slowly back to the city. There was a light scent of blossoming trees, the sun was warm as it filtered through the branches, and for a little while the couple could savor the love and light that had been resurrected on this spring morning.

As they neared the city, Jesus' body waned its brilliance and returned to the way Magdalen had found him. But without haste or reluctance, they journeyed to the place where the apostles and Jesus' Mother Mary were meeting together in prayer for his safe return. Entering through the city's gate they walked along the narrow cobbled street to the house where the group had eaten their Passover meal. As they entered the upper room Magdalen felt a bit of nostalgia. The lamps had been extinguished with the rising sun and the coarse gauzy curtains allowed in just enough light to see by, still keeping out the insects that buzzed outside them. The long trestle table with its cedar couches and stools had been set with cups and bowls. Beside the place where Jesus had eaten his last meal was set a measure of wine and upon the plate that once was his rested a loaf of bread. Although the apostles, now only eleven, and her mother-in-law were reclining for a meal, no other food had yet been placed on the serving table. It looked and felt much as it had on the night of Passover.

The news of Jesus' disappearance had been received, and the men were in heavy debate regarding his whereabouts. The din of conversation and food preparation kept them from hearing the door open or noticing the couple's arrival.

"Peace be with you." Jesus called them to awareness with his greeting.

Mother Mary rushed to her son and throwing her arms about his neck she kissed him on each cheek. "God has blessed me again. Praise the Lord in the heavens!" she shouted her prayer of thanksgiving.

She turned then to Magdalen and hugged her too. The men watched this reunion in awe. Jesus was, indeed, among them once again. The room's energy changed completely from what it had been. Now fear filled the upper quarters as it emanated from the eleven apostles. Each one's reaction to Jesus' presence was unique to his personality.

John cried so violently and inexhaustibly with relief that he wet himself. He was the youngest among them, barely able to grow a beard, but he loved the teacher with a loyalty and depth that could one day cost him his own life. Jesus often let the boy rest his head upon his chest while they talked. He saw in John a prophet and philosopher with wisdom far beyond his years. Because of this the teacher spent long hours alone with John, seeing him as a prodigy. The others objected to this special treatment and looked at John now as a weakling who could not even control his own bodily functions. Jesus did nothing to quell their contemptuous remarks today. He was mute as he stood near the doorway.

Thomas, strong willed and skeptical of all of Jesus' works, had boasted that he would not believe in a resurrection until he had put his fingers in the holes of the nails and his hand into the side where Jesus had been pierced by the sword. Now Jesus stood before him, and in the light dimming cloud of Thomas's doubt he became a glorified figure of a man. His wounds were open but they were bleeding light. Brilliant warm rays of illumination shot from his hands and feet toward the mystified men. Even Thomas, the man who robbed the others of their dreams with his skepticism and critical thinking, began to weep silently. When he was told to touch the wounds of Jesus, he refused, and then believed. Once again, the others mocked the weakness he displayed and his boasting became a subject for jest among them.

Brash, bold and always quick to anger, Peter shouted demanding silence in the Master's presence. Peter was the name Jesus had given him; his birth name was Simon. The name Peter meant rock and the man truly was a rock of faith, but a more hurried person Magdalen had never known. Peter moved quickly, spoke quickly and often ended up with his foot in his mouth. This time it was James who brought him back to reality.

"Dear James," thought Magdalen, "he is always so sure, calm and collected."

James could bring reality to every situation no matter how emotional it was. His mother and Mother Mary were close friends so he knew Jesus as a child and the two were often thought to be brothers. Magdalen liked James and his attitude as he held up his hand to end the arguing.

John's brother, the other James, went to his sibling's side. He was embarrassed by his brother's reaction, but he had a need to comfort him too. When the two were together, Jesus called them the sons of thunder, for they preached loudly and with strong voices. John, of course, took his courage from James, but his faith was his own.

Philip, who had three daughters and a wife at home, was quiet. Magdalen could see the fear he held in his heart for his family's safety during all this chaos. Her silent prayers went out to him.

Andrew was Peter's brother and like Peter he was a fisherman by trade. He slapped his brother on the back and motioned for him to sit at the table. There was a hardiness to both of them and as the huge hand met with Peter's back in a firm but loving blow, he followed Andrew's directive.

Thaddeus, sometimes called Jude, was a brother of the first James. He had some of his steadfastness and calm running through him, but not the courage. Thaddeus moved as far from Jesus as he could get and Bartholomew who was almost always silent moved to join him.

The Zealot, whose rightful name was Simon, was just about to express some of the zeal for which the others had named him, but Matthew stopped him with a shaking finger. Matthew had been a tax collector before he joined Jesus. He now held the purse that once Judas held. His mathematical mind made him a good choice as Judas' successor.

Eleven men's minds then moved to a cowardly space, inwardly they all but denied Jesus, as Peter had just a few short days ago. They were about the business of finding ways to keep themselves in the good graces of the Romans and Jews alike. This would not be an easy task. The Roman government was always on the alert against its foes, feigned or real. Jesus' resurrection would be seen as possible insurrection as far as Caesar was concerned. The faith of the Jews was firm in its expectation of a savior, a Messiah, who would one day come to be King. They believed that on the day of the Messiah's return all Jews buried within the walls of Jerusalem would rise from the dead, filled with life and light. Those buried elsewhere would tunnel their way through the earth to take part in this universal resurrection.

"For heaven's sake," thought Magdalen; "in their folly they even bury sticks with those outside the walls to help them tunnel through, yet now they do not believe."

Magdalen was psychically reading the men's thoughts and perceiving their fear. Despite the Jewish tradition and faith, it became apparent that the apostles never really believed that Jesus would live again, and that they felt his arrival would jeopardize their position and lives in some way. Jesus said nothing, only stood at the end of the room by the door and looked on almost sadly. Then they began to openly question Jesus. Peter asked about the coldness of his body.

"When the body of Lazarus was raised, it was warm, as life had made it. Master Jesus, you are cold and white and look like the walking dead."

Jesus said rather matter-of-factly, "Lazarus still needed his body, but I have no need to live within the limitations that a living body would put upon me. My time here with you will be short so do not waste it with questions of no concern. Soon I will leave again, this time without returning and I have only this short time to explain important things to you."

His admonition stung Peter's ego and pierced Magdalen's heart. She was expecting their lives to return to what they had been before these past days of anguish. He had not mentioned to her that he would leave again, or that the leaving would be permanent. Tears came again to make little rippling brooks down her cheeks as she turned to Jesus' mother for comfort, but Mother Mary cried too. The disciples exposed their fear and pain through the aura that surrounded them.

Magdalen knew that Mother Mary felt, as she did, disappointment in these men who had been instructed to be their protectors and the bearers of responsibility for the continuation of the work and Way of Jesus. They all shared the sadness and fear brought with the realization that Jesus would leave again. There was a sick feeling in Magdalen's stomach; but even as her emotions were swelling and her tears were about to drown her, she said nothing. She had said very little at all since they had left the graveyard. It seemed an eternity before Jesus finally led his mother and Magdalen down the outside stairwell and along the back streets to Mother Mary's home.

Many had heard of Jesus' return. People kept coming to the door, and to most he instructed Magdalen to say that he was not there. Keeping her honest, he would disappear and reappear only moments later. There were chuckles and grins exchanged among the three as the day progressed with these repeated comings and goings. Jesus' lighthearted attitude toward it all gave the family a much-needed respite from the somber and solemn procession of events over the past three days. Despite the stream of seekers and Jesus' good humor, the question still came back in Magdalen's mind. "Is he dead yet, or alive still?"

Behind her, Jesus reclined on a couch of stone that was ornately carved. He said nothing for a long time, only watched Magdalen work, and she felt his eyes follow her every move. Then in a low and sober voice he said. "Could you come here and make love with what the cross has returned to you?"

Now his body became illumined as it had when he had kissed her back at the graveyard. Magdalen turned toward him and looked at his brilliance in delight. Jesus burst into laughter that made her laugh too, releasing all of the tension that had built through that day. Mother Mary giggled a little and left. Their lovemaking was as it had always been, passionately strong but warm and soft. It was truly a homecoming and, for Magdalen, Jesus was again alive.

Later others came seeking him and again he eluded them by his disappearing act. Night came, but Jesus had no need of sleep. Supper had passed, and he had had no hunger. Before supper Jesus had toasted his return with the women and three others who had joined them for the meal. But that single sip of wine was all that he had taken into his body since before his death. He seemed to have no need to carry out the every day activities of life, but was obviously capable of doing so when he desired. Magdalen's confusion returned, but tonight there was a peaceful sleep that overcame her questioning mind as she spooned into her husband's body.

Chapter 2

The Living Dead

Disciples came in pairs and by threes until there were assembled some thirty men and women awaiting the arrival of the Master Jesus. When they reached the house Jesus looked to his wife and mother to be his heralds. "Go up and tell them that I am here."

Silence fell as the two women entered the room. The group watched almost reverently as Magdalen escorted her mother-in-law to a couch and made her comfortable there. Mother Mary was still a young woman really, but the events of the crucifixion had weakened her constitution and not even the return of her son had been able to completely restore her to vigor. She walked slowly with her head down and her hand to her chest. Once she was settled Magdalen turned to the others.

"Peace I offer you and good news, Jesus is arriving even as I speak."

She proclaimed her husband's return just in time, for the door had not opened but now Jesus stood in their midst.

"I am with you and bring you peace."

His greeting seemed to be an enchantment, like that of a magician; it triggered a transformation in his body once again. He glowed with light and the aura that surrounded him was golden and alive with powerful energy. Peter looked at Jesus in amazement.

"Master, how are such things possible for you?"

"One day, Simon Peter, you too will move by the power of Divine Will and not by human energy." Jesus responded.

"Teach me now, Master, so that I can serve you better now." Peter was always in a hurry and over-zealous in his approach to learning.

"One day, Peter, I will teach you, but today you need answers to deeper questions."

Jesus' tone indicated that he would not be moved, and with a disappointed look the apostle became quiet. Then Matthew questioned him.

"Master were you dead, really? Are you alive now? Help us to understand clearly the ideas of life, death and resurrection."

"The life that is mine now is not the life of a man, but the Source of all life. It is the life of the Spirit within. You have enough of a mind to understand this much. Understand me now and listen."

Jesus paused to see that they did, indeed, understand him. Magdalen looked back at her husband with perfect understanding, but knew that the others did not comprehend as much.

"Husband, explain for us the process of physical creation from the Spiritual Source, please. For these matters require deeper questioning."

Jesus knew and appreciated her desire to make simple what could not be made easy, and so he continued with his explanation.

"The Divine Source is like a father and the seeds within the Source's groin are the souls of people and the spirits of all living things. The Divine Source impregnates the Divine Mother, which is the earth, with these seeds of life. Like a mother's womb, the earth carries and sustains life for her children."

He looked again at the group of listeners for a sign of their understanding.

"Mother and father must come together before a child is conceived. The woman cannot conceive unless a man's seed is placed within her."

This they clearly understood and responded with affirmative nods, but they murmured as they looked to Jesus to explain what that had to do with the creation of life through the Spiritual Source. He saw their pondering and went on a little more.

"The man's seed is the source of life, but cannot sustain a child during gestation. For this the mother is needed."

Again they nodded and murmured. Of course they understood how babies were conceived and grew within the womb, but Jesus was not certain of their understanding.

"The soul of a person is the seed of the Divine Father. Just as a man's seed is alive within him, souls live within the Divine Father as his seed and manifest no earthly body because the seed for a body has not been sown within Mother Earth. This is the life that I am now. I am the Living Seed; I live within the Source of life, the Spiritual Source or Divine Father."

There seemed to be more understanding and yet the concept was not clear to them. Some shrugged their shoulders and others sat down on the floor in contemplation and a few in boredom. Jesus decided to go on despite their confusion.

"The fact is, all shall live again as I live now. It is only that you might see me that this body is walking with you. It is only that you might believe that I talk with you and explain these things to you. So hear me and understand.

"The source of the soul is the Divine Father. And the soul knows the Divine Father, because within the Father, the soul lives. But once the soul is sown in the womb of the earth and takes a human body, it knows only earthly life. Only after the soul has matured through earthly experience and escaped the limitations of life here can one see the Father in one's image. Just as any child cannot know its father's face until it is born, you cannot know the face of God until you have a change of heart and are born again in Spirit."

John now exhibited his need to know about all spiritual matters.

"Master, suppose one does not come to know God in this lifetime but dies in ignorance, what of that one's soul?"

"John, your question reveals your fear of damnation." Jesus responded quickly.

"When one dies in ignorance of the Father, the Father returns the soul to his groins and strengthens it. Then the Father sends the soul forth again to impregnate the earth and grow into spiritual adulthood." Jesus felt the question had been answered, but John asked again.

"You mean to say that we will live again as we do now? Again we will become children and have to grow to adulthood seeking knowledge of our Source?"

Magdalen had to smile at the young man's question. Certainly she was not in complete understanding of how the Source worked, but she had believed in reincarnation from childhood. It was obvious that John was still burdened with the Jewish concepts of heaven and hell as the wages of life paid by God after death.

"These things sound strange to you, but know that you will live again on this earth in a new body and then again you will sometimes live without a physical body. This is how we live, some within the Divine Father, some within the Great Mother, and some that have come beyond the womb to know both Spirit and Matter. This is how I have lived among you, knowing both the Source and the place where the seed can grow. I have been both the Son of God and the Son of Man."

Jesus answered his young apostle's question. Philip, still filled with concern for his family, spoke to Jesus in a low tone.

"Jesus, Master, does death then separate us from our families and expel us into oblivion?"

"Fear not for loneliness Philip." Jesus tried to comfort him. "Death of the body separates bodies but it is a great reunion of souls. You and all those you care for will one day be reunited within the Source. The body dies, the son of man returns to spirit and the soul lives forever within the Father.

"When you live as I live now, you will have come to know eternal life. You will no longer fear or face death, because it will no longer be real to you. You will live within the Divine Father and not within the womb of the earth. You will know the Divine Mother from the experience of life here and the Divine Father you will know because you will have left the confines of the earth behind you. I have come beyond the womb of the earth. And I see my Divine Father and know my Divine Father by my likeness to him just as a son recognizes his earthly father by his likeness to the man. That is, I see my Source and know my Source by the fact that my works are the works of the Source.

"This is the way of life for all people. It is not my way alone, but the way of all who are the sons and daughters of the Divine Father. As death of the body came to me, no life left me, for I am yet the Living Seed.

"And I am your brother, for there are many seeds. And all the children of the Father are loved and so what is for me shall be also for you, but only by your choice and your free will. The Father cannot live for you but his life is extended by the life of his children. The family of God remains a family. But one brother lives yet another life than his sibling, for no two are alike in their life, but all are alike in their Source and in their likeness to it. You know the sons and daughters of a man by the resemblance they show in their faces to their father's face. Know then the sons and daughters of God by the countenance of their minds and spirits, for their Source is the Greater Mind and the Greater Spirit that is God."

Now it was a woman's voice that came from the crowd. "We must then see all people as brothers and sisters and be aware of the Divine Seed within them from which they came. But not one of us can be greater than the Father that is God."

Jesus nodded a denial and held out his hand as if to silence her.

"The father is not greater than the child. You revere your father because he is the source of your life. You do not revere him simply because of his adulthood, one day you also will grow to be an adult. So it is with God. What God is, you are also, but you have not yet manifested spiritual maturity. When you have done this, you do not cease to revere the greatness of God, but you come to know your own greatness as well. You do not fully understand, but the day is coming when people will turn to you and know that you are the Father also. You are the Father of the seed thought that will turn people to the understanding of God and knowing of God will no longer be enough. That day comes. And the day comes too, when all these things will be understood by many people and you will have been the husbands of that understanding."

James spoke as Jesus paused. "Master, I understand then. The Divine Father impregnates the Divine Mother, our earth, with the souls of many and the earth is pregnant with Divine Life and we are all brethren. We can know the earth and its ways because we live within her as an infant within its mother's womb. How then can we ever know the Divine Father if we are yet trapped within the earth and its ways? What religion or theology will give us this growth? In what way can we come to know God as our Father and grow to be like God?"

Jesus was glad for a question that came from some understanding. "I speak to you of knowing my Father. I speak to you of knowing God, that is the Source. You know of God as a man knows a woman because he has lain with her. He knows her body, but the woman's true self he does not know. So you know God. You have come to religion as a man satisfies himself with a woman. He has no knowledge of the woman's need for him. And you have no knowledge of God's need for you. You have no concern that your intercourse with God is satisfying or pleasing to God, only that it pleases you. That is how you know God, you know God by that act that pleases you.

"To understand a woman, one lives with her, fathers her children and lays with her while she brings forth life, not only while she accepts the seed. To understand a woman, one talks with her, one shares with her the feelings that life gives to you both. That is the way that you must come to understand the Father. The way one comes to understand a wife. And still, even then, there is the mystery that surrounds a woman. That mystery is one that can only be answered with the passing of time and life experience with that woman. It is the same with God. It is the mystery, perhaps, that drives you to understand a woman better, to be with a woman more. It is the mystery that makes it exasperating and frustrating, so it is with God also. God and man come to intercourse first, and then to a marriage, but to the oneness of knowing - this takes the eternal life of a person."

Now James began to scribe what was being said, but Jesus stopped him. "Do not write my words. For it is not for you to know what I have said, but for you to understand what I have done and why I have come. Because my reasons are your reasons, my thoughts, your thoughts, my words, your words. Do not be writing down the words of a man, but instead turn your attention to the understanding of the word that is God. Do not be like the man who ravages woman, rapes and thereby injures her love. Be instead the good husband who comes to understand the wife and lays with her in more than intercourse and hears her feelings and what she means to say. Do not listen for words of love like the man who finds a whore whom he pays to say these things. The Pharisees are like that man. Be instead the man who finds a lover who he can come to know in more than body, and whose words are truths and not the words that he has paid

22

for. Put away your stick and your tablet. Listen and know me, for I will not be with you much longer. I will return to the Father and the earth I will leave behind for the sons of man to care for. For the earth requires yet the deliverance of humanity. And in turn the earth nourishes the growth of humanity and teaches them to know the likeness they have to their Father God.

"And I leave you now to ponder for a little while the things that I have said. I will come again as you see me now, but soon I will not come again, so be careful in your thoughts and in your words with each other. There is but a little time for you to question. And there will be many questions. Even after the spirit has come upon you, you will question."

And as Jesus walked toward the door, without having benefit of opening it, he disappeared.

Chapter 3

A Day to Savor Life

When Mother Mary and Magdalen arrived at home, Jesus was waiting for them. The evening passed and then the night with a steady stream of callers from all walks of life. The next day, however, belonged to Magdalen and Jesus alone.

The Master seemed pensive as the couple strolled along the rocky and uneven shores of the Sea of Galilee. His gait was slow and his gaze was ever on Magdalen as she skipped on ahead of him. To her the walk was an adventure. Magdalen found shells hidden within the stony beach and showed each one to her husband with enthusiasm for the beauty and energy of her small treasures. Jesus smiled at her childlike display of pleasure but remained remarkably quiet. By noon Magdalen was hungry even if her beloved wasn't. They reclined in a grassy spot a few yards from the shore and she munched away at dry fish and cheese. Jesus looked on as if he had never seen her eat before.

"Why are you so still and preoccupied?" she questioned him. "Do I look different today, eating my fish, than I have before?"

"I am savoring your beauty, my Magdala. And realizing that soon I will not see with eyes or hear with ears the glories of the earth and the people I love ever again."

Jesus' realization didn't come as a surprise to him, but to Magdalen it was a reminder that he would soon be returning to what he had called the Kingdom. She coaxed him on excited to hear tales of the holy realm.

"When you reached the Kingdom what was it like? Did the angels sound their trumpets? Was the music beautiful to hear? Is the throne that you said God had prepared jeweled, or is it a couch like you have here? What was it like? Why must you go back? Tell me about the kingdom of heaven and how it looks and sounds and smells."

"I was as much on a throne hanging upon Golgotha or sitting here as I am now, as I have been with my Father, Magdala. In spirit, there is no need for a seat upon which to rest. In spirit, there is the knowledge of the Kingdom. That is the throne upon which my spirit rests. And the jewels, the garnish of beauty, is the awareness of the exquisiteness of the earth's raiment in every creature, be it animal, vegetable or mineral but especially in humanity."

Jesus' arms went out in a gesture that pointed to the beauty that surrounded them at that moment. Magdalen looked at her little collection of shells and other treasures. Sifting them through her hands she had to agree.

"Yes, darling, the beauty of the earth is without measure. These are jewels of the sea I would suppose.

"So, to be crowned and enthroned is simply to be made aware by the spirit, then. But there are angels, Jesus, I have seen angels and I know that they do exist. Was their song as beautiful as the psalms describe it?"

"Yes, my dear Magdala, there are angels, but they must be here on earth to be seen, and only here can their joyous song be appreciated. In spirit, dearest, there is no sound, only peace. The trumpets of angels call to you here, in your heart, and in the hearts of all people who believe in what I have taught them."

Jesus covered his chest with a large hand and light streamed from beneath it.

"Even in your misery, you sounded a note of joy upon my return. You sounded that note as much because it proved that we were right as you did because we could again make love. I know you. You are as pleased to be right as you are to be satisfied."

He grinned at his wife's flushing cheeks. Jesus was more than right about Magdalen's need for self-satisfaction and she knew it.

"Do not feel guilty or embarrassed Magdala." He cautioned her. "And do not pass blame to God for the human suffering of these past days and nights."

"God is not guilty, Magdala, of anything. No wrongdoing is the work of God. Yet all things are the work of his nature in people. It is strange, but anger and hatred, punishment, even crucifixion, come as the result of the plan of God for humanity. Not that God plans that people suffer, not that I, his knowing son should suffer, but that all people gain. You have gained; even Rome has gained from my resurrection, for by my coming you have hope. By my coming, you know that death can be escaped. It is not a thing of God. Death is a thing of the body. You know that and that too troubles you. I speak and you still question within you whether or not I am alive, you think that perhaps I am only a dream from which you cannot yet wake up. I am no dream. This is the spirit that drives the body. This is the living God. You are as I am now, only you do not think of it that way. The dream is that the body lives. The reality is that the spirit lives and the body is nothing but bread without it."

"Moses was said to have heard the living God. What did God have to say to you?"

Magdalen asked the question feeling she already knew the answer. If one could not hear the song of the angels in the Kingdom, then it wasn't likely that God had a voice either.

"There was nothing that the Father needed to say to me, for I am one with the Father, and therefore I know the mind of the Father. What is there for you to say to me when I tell you your thoughts as you are thinking them? My Father knows me, and all people, even better than I know you. And I am One with the Father, so I know the Father's thoughts and his ways.

"The way of spirit is a simple way and it does not interfere with the ways or laws of governments or religions. God is not the end of the way but the way itself. God is the Way. And I am One with the Father, so I am the Way." Jesus sighed with the thought of the misunderstanding among people regarding religion and its need to control.

"I say to you, Magdala, that what is, is God. The thing is that in life people are sleeping and in death they are awakened. But they can awaken when they are ready even before death, or one can shake them and wake them, as I have tried to do. And on awakening they do see God and they hear his words. Without eyes and without ears they see and they hear the sights and sounds of the Divine. I am awake and I will wake many to be with me. That is why I gave them bread and wine and the Rite of Remembrance. I have put spirit into simple bread and wine. I have put myself within them and as they consume the bread and drink the wine, they ingest my spiritual energy as well. That is the same spirit that is the Father. And they will do the same as they pass this thing from generation to generation, and they shall be healed of their guilt for all time by this one act."

Magdalen ventured to interrupt. "Husband, guilt keeps people from wrongdoing, doesn't it?"

"Guilt, my dear Magdala, is like a drug that keeps one sleeping. Do you remember how I took leavened bread into the temple? And how I ate from the grain of the priests of the temple? And how I instructed that the things one takes in are not sinful, but instead the things that come out of a person are to be challenged? Well, what comes out is too often guilt. People are guilty by the act of the heart not by an act of hand, or eye, or mouth. The Law of Moses gives people the drug of guilt and keeps them sleeping. It is not a bad or wrong law and had best be kept for now, but in other generations they will see my Way. They will know God, and there will be no guilt in the hearts of the people, because there will no longer be reason for guilt."

27

"Should all wrongs then be forgiven?" Magdalen asked yet another question to which she already knew the answer.

"I forgave while I hung. People will remember that. The apostles will teach such forgiveness. They will not let loose of all guilt or punishment, but they will create less reason for guilt. Not that man on the cross beside mine, or the Roman soldiers, or the Sanhedrin required my forgiveness, but I have set them free of guilt by my words. It is up to them now to remain guilt free. It is for the guilt of all people that I died and that on dying I forgave. I relieved people of guilt so that their hearts could be healed. How often have you been there and heard me say, your faith has saved you? Your sins are forgiven? And they walked away cured by the Father, by me I suppose, not by this hand but by the release of their guilt."

"If there is to be no guilt and all is to be forgiven, then why have laws at all?" She asked.

"People make laws. And only people can judge the unlawful. But it is no law that makes sin, or the act of unlawfulness. It is guilt that makes sin, guilt in the hearts of people who yet are sleeping and unable to see the spirit that is living within them."

"That doesn't answer my question. Why does God allow laws if God has no use for punishment or guilt?" Magdalen sought to bring her husband back to the subject at hand.

"No, I guess it doesn't answer your question." Jesus laughed at his own digression. "Laws do not represent what God wants people to do or not do. Laws represent God's need for organization in the universe. How we organize it is up to us but it must remain organized and stable. We accomplish this through lawmaking, government and religion. People believe what they see. They have only seen that guilt, punishment and fear and regret can create and control the organization that God demands. Because they have seen it work they continue to remain in the darkness. One day they will see the light. They will know that love is the key to organization of the universe. But for

28

now they know only what they can see in the dream state of living here."

"So, people are tied to faith in the dream and what it shows them rather than the reality of wakefulness in spirit." Magdalen stated her understanding.

"Yes, they believe only what they can see for the moment. They see death, and for them death is believable. They saw life leave me and it was believable to them that I was dead. Now I live, and perhaps they will come to see even in their dreams, and they will believe then in life after death as well. They will believe in the eternal life that God has given them. They will come to know, even while they live on earth, that the body is dead without the spirit and that the spirit does not die when the body dies.

"When I say to them or to you, I live, you think that I refer to this body, to the body of a man. It is not so. I am. I live. I, God, am in life eternal. For I know spirit and am no longer asleep or unaware of my life without the body.

"All of humanity sleeps for a time while they live on earth. And all people will be awakened when death comes to their bodies. I woke up while my body lived. It was by the will of God, the plan of the Father, that I woke up; as were all the works that I did here. No one is separate from the Father, but there are people who sleep through the Father's works and see not the power of God. These see only the laws of empires or of Moses, and they do not see the working of the Lord in their lives. These people are not to be thought foolish but are to be shown compassion, because for these the guilt is a heavy burden. These people punish themselves or wait on the law to punish them. There is no use for God to punish or rebuke. When people wake they are one in God and no longer seek to punish one another, but instead to love one another as I have loved them."

Jesus stopped to watch the waves and held out his hand in a gesture of awe at the power of the sea. A bird lighted upon it and he moved it to his cheek. "There is as much power in the gentle spirit of the bird as there is in the tumultuous storm on the sea. Love is the gentle power that can overcome the chaos of fear, guilt and blame." The little dove cooed and Magdalen took this as a sign that the bird knew love's power and Jesus' faith.

"Jesus, you have said that the commandment is only one, to love one another. Is it possible to truly live the way of love while we are yet asleep on this earth?" Magdalen looked into his eyes as the bird flew off.

"This is the only law, it is the way of God to love one another. This law I have given them, and this law too they will fear breaking, and from it create guilt and thereby sin. But it is closer, Magdala, to being awake than the way of eating or not eating, of dressing or washing or of not dressing or not washing. Fewer laws make fewer sins, I think. Yet they require a law. Be it then the natural law of God. Love is the only law that matters in heaven or on earth." Jesus stopped again and this time looked directly at his wife.

"Let us put this thing to rest then. Your true concern is that I leave you behind." He circled her body with his arms and held her tightly. "I will go to spirit, to my Father, as I have said. But for a little while I will be here with you. For a little while I will still be your husband. For a little while they will still call me Master. And I will use this time to love you as a man loves a woman and to speak in ways that even sleeping ones can hear. But soon I will go, for this body cannot live without the spirit, and my spirit has a need to be one with the Father. And now that I am awake and the work is ending, there is no need for this body. Yes, I will go and you will miss me, but you will do it in joy, because my suffering is over and I am awake and alive in God.

"This will be clear to you, and you will miss me in joy and not in sorrow. The sorrow that you and my mother have felt these past days will be remembered for generations, but you will forget the pain quickly. You will give birth to a New Way when I am gone, and the pain will have been forgotten as a mother forgets the pain of delivering her child. And you will remember my words and my works and think of me, but you will think of me in joy, and the trumpets will sound as if blown by angels within your heart. This I promise you."

"I have always known that the true Kingdom is joy and peace within your heart." She said as she bent and gathered up yet more shells. "Still, it is hard to comprehend life without ears to hear and eyes to see. It is harder still to comprehend for those who have waited so long for you to come and to save this nation of Israel. They are expecting a God and a Messiah with the same vision that they have. They want a kingdom that has a monarch who welcomes them body and soul. I don't think that they are ready to relinquish their notions of a spiritual world with all the golden attributes of the empire of Rome."

Magdalen took his hand as they continued walking along the shore.

"You are right, again, Magdala. I speak to these people in parables, for their understanding is only as complete as their knowledge of earthly life." Jesus shook his head again as if he were desperate for another way.

"I returned to find more ways to teach them. I said that for a little while you would not see me and I let the body die and the tomb hold it captive. And I also said that then again in a little while you would see me. And here I am again within the body that I might explain all these things to them. But my time is short and their minds limited."

Magdalen pivoted to stand in front of him and took both his hands in hers. "Indeed, you are here again, and I think your parable about the wife came from our own union and even our lovemaking yesterday." She squeezed his hands tightly and winked. "You have paid honor to our marriage and to me with your parable. What's more I think it worked."

Jesus returned her smile. "It will be up to you, Magdala, and the other apostles to teach the Way and to keep the Rite of Remembrance alive for them so that they never forget the eternal life of the spirit and the vulnerable and fragile life of the body." Jesus put his arm around her waist as they continued walking.

"Our child and our grandchildren will know the Way," she assured him. "And the Rite will be for them a reminder always of their heritage both from you and from God."

Then Magdalen's voice grew stern, "I will not however take joy in your leaving or in being without you, I am a woman as well as a spirit after all."

Jesus grinned at her indignation. "You are a woman like no other, a true Goddess in spirit." He laughed out loud.

Magdalen wasn't sure she liked his joke. She had always considered herself the likeness or personification of the Divine Mother despite the New Way that she followed and to her this was no laughing matter.

"Is there not a feminine nature within spirit? I believe there is." She voiced her opinion quickly.

"The Goddesses and Gods of the Romans are not the icons and idols that the Jewish people think they are." Her objection continued. "It is the Spirit, both male and female, that is portrayed in the icons that is the Divinity, not the idols themselves. You have said this yourself. I am not the Goddess but the personification of the Goddess. You are not the God but the personification of the God."

"You are right as usual, my dear Magdala." Jesus stroked her head. "You above any other understand the Way of Love."

And upon this the apostles and Mother Mary approached and began walking with them. Peter had heard Jesus' final remark.

"Do we not understand as much as she does?" His words revealed his distaste for the idea that a woman, any woman, could have more understanding that he did.

Jesus put an answer to the question. "She understands with her heart more fully the Way than your mind could ever perceive it."

His look at Peter was one of admonition and the subject was dropped for the moment as they arranged to remain together and to find lodging for the night. Matthew, who now held the purse, procured quarters for them by renting an upper flat with two rooms, one that allowed the women to have privacy and another large communal room where they could share their supper and sleep for the night. After everyone had bathed the meal was served up. James, always eager to eat heartily, was devouring his food with his usual zest. His boarding house reach and quickness to fill his belly were something that the group had become used to. Spoonful after spoonful of stew and rich gravy went down the man's gullet like oil being poured into a vat. He belched loudly and reached for more.

Jesus watched him eat for some minutes before the apostle realized that the Master's eyes were on him. Embarrassed by the teacher's gaze he defended himself with a question.

"Isn't it good to eat like a man before doing a man's work, Lord?" He asked.

"The work that you are all to do will require bread for both the body and the spirit. Let me tell you this. The food that is blessed holds more power for the whole being than food that is devoured without thanksgiving and praise." Jesus responded.

"Lord, then bless this food so that by your hand I will have power." James asked for Jesus' blessing.

Jesus rose and shared with them again the bread and wine and its Rite of Remembrance. He reminded them to do this in memory of their life here and in spirit. As he ate the bread and drank the wine his body glowed with brilliance once more. This time, however, the apostles did not question its beauty but prayed aloud in thanksgiving for his return.

When this was finished Jesus went off to be alone in meditation and begged them not to follow him. The men muttered and debated things of spirit and earth among themselves. Mother Mary and Magdalen sat together and listened. Magdalen did not want to join in this conversation for fear of still furthering Peter's injured pride. For this evening she would be silent and question nothing until her husband's return.

It was a long time before Jesus reappeared in their midst and blessed them for the night. The blessing was a sign that the evening had come to a close. All along the outer walls they unrolled the mats the innkeeper had provided and found sleep upon the wooden floor. Magdalen and Mother Mary stayed close to Jesus. Magdalen put her head in his lap and he stretched one long arm over his mother's shoulders to keep her warm.

Chapter 4

A Woman's Understanding of Fear

Magdalen awakened early to find that Jesus had already left. She gently touched the place where he had been and said a silent prayer for his safe and quick return. The others were all sleeping and the room was dark and quiet. She lay there a long time wondering where her husband had gone and thinking about the words that he had spoken the day before. Thoughts of a future without him plagued her mind with fearful apprehension. It was incomprehensible that she could find joy in his leaving as he said that she would. But he had been right about everything else, why not this too? Still, joy was not what Magdalen was feeling as she awaited his return. Her body was tense with fear and her heart ached as if pierced by the sword of ruin. Hoping to ease the pain, she prayed silently for faith and courage while she waited for the others to wake up.

Mother Mary stirred next to her and Magdalen reached out and touched her arm to let her know that she was awake. Quietly they left the room and went to wash and redress in private. The women talked as they had so often, as they braided one another's hair.

"How does he expect us to find joy in all of this?" Magdalen asked. "Certainly he knows how much I love him and that I could not possibly be happy about his leaving!"

She knew that Jesus understood her feelings, but his remarks left her wondering what he really thought. After all, this whole thing had gotten out of hand. The teaching he had done brought upon him the episode at Golgotha, and upon Magdalen the rebuke now of even the Romans. The Jews might be conspiring at this very moment as to what should be done about those that had followed him. Everyone was afraid. The disciples, the apostles, the Jews, and the Romans, were all afraid.

"Mary, are you afraid?" Magdalen asked his mother this question supposing that Mother Mary's admission of fear would somehow justify her own.

"Yes, I 'm afraid. I was afraid when he was born, and fearful when Herod sought to kill him. The King looked for a Messiah, and I held an infant. I was afraid again and again all the days of his adulthood. I feared when he left me that I would never see him again. I feared again when he returned, for his teaching in the public places gave way to all manner of scandal and hatred from so many sources. I feared when he was brought before Pilate, not for him, because I know that he always does what must be done and he is capable of things of which I have yet to know, but I feared for myself and for these men that he calls apostles. I wasn't afraid to die. Death is easy, I would think, but I feared living without the love that I have felt with him. Everyone needs to be loved. I have the same need as you do. And you know that it is for yourself that you are afraid now, not for the threats of the Pharisees or even the Romans. It is for his love that you yearn, even before he has left you. I know because I have the same fear. And the men have it too.

"People who think only of the comfort of wealth and riches, who are concerned with lust and no outlet for it, are concerned with death, because they fear the loss of treasures or of emotional satisfaction or physical affection. It is why they bury with them the assets that they have accumulated. It is why some bury concubines with their masters. But people who think of more than body, people who think of the comfort of mind and heart, these people fear the loss of love and belonging. Jesus says that this comfort is the eternal love of God, and that it cannot be lost. But to hear his words is easy, to know such love takes the holy understanding that put him on Golgotha and then brought him back to us after his death. Has he talked to you of Golgotha, of the crucifixion?"

"He has." Magdalen answered, unsure of what really was believable of what he had said.

"He said that he had no pain, except for that in his heart. He says that if he can now be walking and talking with us I should believe that he could control the entrance of pain into his body. He says that we inflicted our own misery, not by God or the doom that befell us were we injured but by our lack of faith in him or in the Divine. He was actually attempting to comfort me as he said all this, and it seemed as if he were more like a father than my husband. I don't know what to think these days since he has returned. Surely he has seen an unseen God. He says he saw God without eyes, but what has that vision done to him? One minute he is a glorified lover and husband, the next a mere shell of the past. He is less than human, yet more than a man. It is eerie, this new person that has come in the body of Jesus. I was hoping that perhaps you understood more than I; you have known him for all of his life. And I thought that maybe you could explain it to me in a way that I could understand so that some of my fears would be gone."

Mary answered but briefly, "I cannot explain what he is now, and the son I knew left me very young to come home a different man. I cannot explain, but I know that his love will force him to answer us both before he leaves us again."

By this time the apostles had been awakening, and the women returned to the room where they were. A servant girl brought in food and served them, but before anyone had eaten Jesus came through the door, again without benefit of opening it. Still bewildered by these acts of magical appearances, the apostles were filled with questioning.

James queried first, "Lord, how do you enter through the walls that were built to keep men out?"

"If, without life in it, I can move and use this body, then why cannot I do likewise with the wall? I place the wall behind me. It is not so difficult a task as it was to raise the body from its grave, or to hang it upon the cross at Golgotha."

Andrew spoke out then, "Jesus, this answer is not enough for us. Our minds do not understand these things. You are the Christ, and I believe this, and perhaps the Christ understands and can do these things, but for us, we do not understand."

Jesus answered with a slight smile, "I had a long journey to go today, and there is little time left here. If the land, the path, and even the door are moving as quickly as the body, then the journey could take half as long. So for me it is necessary to make these things move so quickly that you cannot even see the movement. You have more time now than I do. You don't need to understand, for there is time for you yet to enjoy all of your journeys and open all of the doors before you. When it is time for you to understand, you will understand and be able to do these things. For now, put it out of your mind. It is not why I came."

"Tell us, Lord, why then did you come?" This was John, the young one whose love was always so apparent. He hung on every word that Jesus spoke and held himself close to Jesus as if he were his true son.

"Go on and dine. Then we will talk, and I will tell you more of why I am here today." And he reclined as if he would dine with him. So Magdalen went there to serve his food, but he put up his hand to say no.

"I have no need of the bread of your life. But the rest of you eat or you will be fearing starvation the way you fear all other things." There was a bit of teasing in his remark. Magdalen could tell by the way his lip curled up when he was trying to hide a smile.

The large platters of fruit, cheese and bread were passed around and the apostles and Mother Mary and Magdalen ate until they were full. Then they dismissed the servant girl and she took with her the plates and the bowls and serving things. And when the room was clear the men reclined at the table waiting for Jesus to speak.

"I have far to go today. And I will move as quickly as I did this morning, but it will take you three days journey to go where I am going. So I have come to tell you to meet me at the sea three days to the south. You will find me there along the shore."

John was concerned, "Lord, how will we find you. You were in the tomb for three days, and we are in want when you are not with us. There is discontent among us without you. I fear that we will not find you and that we will become quarrelsome and lose our way even before three days have passed."

Jesus answered, "John, my son, my son, bring with you my mother and my wife. And trust in me, for if I say that you will find me, you will find me." And as he said it, he left as he had come.

The apostles prepared for the journey and together they started toward the Sea of Galilee to walk its shore for three days journey. They planned to stay close to the water's edge so that John's fears would not come to be true. If Jesus was to be on the shore, they had no notion of missing him.

On the third day they had gone their journey, and when darkness came the group rested on the sand and rock without blanket or cover and waited for the Lord to come. Despite the situation the warm breeze kept them comfortable, but Peter was fearful that John had been right. He built a fire so that if Jesus would come he could find them more easily. And he tended the signal blaze far into the night while the rest slept. Magdalen's mind moved from one thought to another as if it had wings. Where had he gone, anyway? And for what purpose? And why did they have to come on this journey? She went on thinking and wondering until she too slept.

When Magdalen woke, Jesus was laying beside her. He was not asleep but instead was watching his bride with a gentle and loving gaze. Peter had dozed off at his fire, the tender winds of spring had stilled, and the night was now cold. Magdalen kissed Jesus, wrapped her cloak a little tighter, and drifted off again. He lay there just watching them all without so much as a whisper. The apostles had not heard him arrive. At dawn Peter woke with a start to tend his fire again; he did not notice Jesus resting next to his wife. Magdalen was awake now but in a sort of dreamy state. The days before had been tiring and she would have preferred at that moment to simply stay warm and sleeping.

But now Jesus spoke to Peter, "What are you afraid of now, you wake with a start and don't even notice my presence. Your fear did you no good. You have no awareness or caution. Suppose I had been a robber in the night instead of your Master."

Peter was embarrassed. Jesus had caught him again being who he was. Without the boasting and without an audience, Peter was simply Peter and afraid of almost everything and everyone these days. But then, they all were. He was not embarrassed about being afraid but of having been so foolish and so vulnerable in his fear. Jesus was right again. What good was fear if it did not make you cautious? What kind of protection would it offer if you did not use your fear to be wary of the world and the people about you? It was already becoming obvious that fear was to be the topic of conversation for that day.

The others were waking now too. Peter had not answered Jesus and probably did not know what to say on his own behalf. The others came up, one at a time, and greeted him as he stood next to Magdalen. Andrew asked her why she had not alerted them all when Jesus arrived, and then there was the usual male laughter at which she blushed and Jesus retorted.

"You fear this too? That you have been cheated?

"Of what? My arrival? I am here and now you see and know it. Or do you fear that you have missed my affection for which you have so longed? Do not be reproaching her. If you had been watching, you would not have missed either my arrival or my affection! Now warm yourselves and find fish for breakfast. I want to eat with you."

Now that surprised Magdalen! He had eaten some since his return, but it had always been the ceremonious meal in commemoration of his death, or so she had thought. But this time he actually sounded as if eating had become important or perhaps that he was truly getting hungry. He should have been if his body was indeed as alive as hers. He should have been starving or at least showing some signs of his fast. But he did not appear paler, or waning, or thinner. He was the same as he had been since his return. He even wore the same clothing. It never seemed to be wrinkled or dirty from his journeys. Magdalen wondered again about Jesus' travels and where he had gone and for what reason. Now he stood warming himself at Peter's fire and awaiting the return of Andrew and James who had gone fishing at the shoreline. They stood up to their waists in the cold water holding nets that they had brought folded in their coats for exactly this purpose.

Finally they brought the fish, and Mother Mary prepared them over the fire. Magdalen set out the bread and the wine and cheese that had come with them on their journey. Everyone sat around the fire, even Jesus, and they ate. The apostles ate ravenously, as if they had had no food in days. Jesus ate slowly and with what appeared to be thought, but Magdalen knew it was not the breakfast about which he was thinking. There was a sermon coming.

Then he turned to Peter. "Peter, tell me of your fear this morning before the sun came up."

Peter was back to the usual nonsense that Jesus tried so hard to teach him to control. Now he had an audience and a need to defend himself in front of the others. "But Lord, it was not that I was afraid of man or beast, but only that you would not see the fire which had gone down in my sleepiness. We traveled far and fast yesterday, and my eyes were tired from the smoke of the fire which I had been tending all night for your arrival."

"Are you begging then my forgiveness for falling asleep, for letting the fire die, or for being afraid, Peter?"

This conversation would be another soft duel with words between the two. Peter always remained respectful and loving as he engaged in his excuses. He was like a child who was certain that he would win favor by his attitude, if not by his opinion or knowledge.

"Lord, I beg your forgiveness in all my frailties."

"Peter, you are without frailties in tongue or tale. These things are strong in you. For fear, you need no forgiveness. Fear cannot be forgiven; it can only be released. Guilt is erased by forgiveness. Fear on the other hand cannot be taken away by the words, presence, or penitence of another. If my being here can make you unafraid, then how is it that you were afraid when I was right here among you?"

Andrew spoke up in defense of Peter. "But, Lord Jesus, we did not know that you were here. We thought that you had not yet returned from your journey. We must know you are here for our fear to be gone."

"Then know it." Jesus spoke rather gruffly just then. It was as if he were becoming impatient.

"I heal the sick, bring sight to the blind, but your fear I cannot take from you. Your doubt I cannot erase. Your cover to the sight of God, I cannot lift. You must do this. Alone and together, you must do this. I have told you many times that when my body leaves my mind and my spirit are still with you. Do you believe that it is with this frail body that hung upon Golgotha that I have and will yet protect you? Have you heard nothing in all this time that you have spent with me? The Pharisees and the Romans and the Jews, they all have all been driven by fear. With fear they have walked all the days of their lives. They have feared God. They have feared punishment. They have feared each other and even themselves.

"Fear is like a whip that drives the donkey forward only to ruin the animal before the burden reaches its destination. Where have these taskmasters then driven their people but to rude awakening, shattered dreams, and sleep that is never quiet or sound?

"You cannot lead people by fear; it is by love that people are led. Put the carrot in front of the donkey and it will move forward willingly and in hope and joy and good humor. It is led by its desire to move toward the beauty, smell, and taste of its food. It is by love that people are led. Hold it in front of them, show it to them, and they will follow it throughout the journey of life. It is by being drawn to the beauty and light of love that people find God.

"God is like the good father. You do not fear the good father, but instead respect him, knowing that his wisdom and love determine his decisions. You do not fear the decisions of the good father; you respect them. But it appears that you fear the decision of God when you are awake all night for no reason but to make sure that someone else can see you so that you will be protected by that person's presence. You fear the wisdom of God when you think that if a robber came it was not for the good of all to share your goods with that robber. You will always be afraid while you lack faith.

"Think about it. When you are unsure, when you do not know, that is when you are afraid. And even when I tell you a thing will happen you are afraid, because then you know something will happen only because I said so and not of your own mind. You have no faith, and so you fear that I could be wrong, yet you know that I have always been right. The thing that can erase your fear is the knowledge of the presence of my Father as your Father. It is the knowledge that the wisdom and love that are present in the good father are present in God. There is no sense to fear. It drives you to discontent. What will you do when I am gone? You fear that also. You are to lead people by the love that is yours, and not drive them with the fear that you have adopted from others.

43

"To know, my dear Peter, is to be alert. To fear is to be unconscious. You cannot sleep and yet lead people. They will not follow you through your dreaming. You must be awake, all of you, all of the time, to the hungers of humanity. Did I not know the hunger of your stomach this very day? Or the hunger of the many on the mountain? There are other human hungers. Did I not know your hungry desire for knowledge when I enlisted you to follow me? Have I not satisfied the hungers of your mind each day that has passed? Have I not known when you wished for home and family? And then gone with you so that you could have their affection? Did I not know the need of my mother for a son, and then provide in John, my beloved, a substitute for myself when I died? If you know the hungers of humanity, then you can satisfy those hungers, and in feeding the hungry no one has anything to fear.

"If fear blinds your knowledge of any person's needs, then that person will be like the hungry dog who bites the hand that feeds it. If, though, you know the needs of a person, then that person is like the dog that is thrown food for the first time. You throw out the food far ahead of your steps so that the animal doesn't need to come close enough to do you any harm. But the next time the dog can come closer, for it knows that you will feed it, and it waits for the food, and no harm but only affection comes to you then from the animal.

"But be careful to hold honor in your dealings. Do not start off knowing their needs, gaining their trust, and then turn away without satisfying their hunger, for like a hungry dog people will surely attack you then, and once again fear will be yours. Always you will be looking behind you, and jumping up to tend a fire. Always you will be mistrusting and expecting doom and the anger of those behind you. Only what you know can be trusted. Know this, what is in front of you can be seen and known. What you turn your back on in hatred, judgment or deception, these things you cannot see as they attack in the form of people, or in the form of those people's thoughts which will come from behind to bite at you in a haunting that will make you eternally the fearful one.

"Are you understanding? Feed the needs of every person, no matter what those needs are. And know those needs and what they are. Let a person's fulfillment go before you. That is, answer to a person's needs before you approach them with the truth that is what you are teaching. They will come then, the next moment, close to you and eat your truth as if it were a fine feast. They will do you no harm if your truth is the savory meat that you have promised. But if you have in you deceit, or malcontent, or fear of that person, then your truth smacks of the taste of those things. That is, if you are judging this person, then the person will know it. And when you turn away from them, you had better be afraid of that one's hunger, which will make them mean and without care for the pain that they can and will then cause you.

"If you are afraid of the dog, the dog knows it, and he will use your fear against you. So it is also with humanity.

"If you have tormented, deceived or burdened or demanded too much from the dog, the dog will not trust you, and in its mistrust it will protect itself and so by cause you harm. So it is also with people.

"If you tend to your dog, giving it what it needs and showering affection upon it, and giving it always good food instead of the rotten meat of deceit, then the dog is ever faithful and caring and is more protection than harm. So it is also with humanity.

"And if you think that the dog will not know the good meat from the rotten, then know this, no dog eats willingly the meat from a sepulcher! So it is also with humanity. They will know the truth from the deceit. They will know the ripe from the rotten. As the dog feels the pain of having eaten even the slightest taint within the meat, people will know the leader who has given them something that they themselves would not have eaten. If you lie and believe your lies, then the lies become truth. If you lie and deceive others with your lies, in time there will be known the taint that came with the meat. Like the dog, the thing must only reach its entrails before it comes to light. It is painful, but it is vomited out and stinks all that it touches and all that is surrounded by it.

When the lies of a leader are taken in, when they reach the inner knowing of a person, then they too are revealed and bring back upon their giver the stink of deceit that will tell all that surround it that this person is filled with fear.

"Fear not any person, and give no person reason to fear you. Be as you are, not as you purpose to be. Love one another and all people as I have loved you. Even as I have fed you well, so feed others also. From this day to the coming of generations, my word will be truth. The words of some others, they are like the tainted meat. There is some part that is good, and there is some part that is distasteful and even sickening to the heart. Be watchful for yourselves and for the hearts of others whom you will lead, so that by swallowing the truth that is tainted you do not become so sickened as not to recognize the need for pure truth again.

"You are not here to poison the pack, not to test the truth for them. You are here to provide for its needs and its hungers with the purest of truth that is their spiritual meat. I charge you with this duty as I go before you to the kingdom where you might see and know the truth and no longer have fear.

"You do not fully understand, but understanding is coming. Think as you walk and tonight before the fire you can question me again."

Everyone rose to follow him as if it were his intention to lead them to some new truth and, thought Magdalen, it was. She and Mother Mary hastened their step to catch up with Jesus and walk beside him. No one talked, but Magdalen knew that Mother Mary was thinking about their conversation before this journey had begun. They had both been afraid; both of them who knew him so well were filled with fear. How could the apostles, who knew very little really, about him or his Way, be expected to be fearless enough to convince others of his teachings, when he would no longer be walking among them or working wonders and miracles? How could they possibly know the truth from the twisted truth? The Pharisees and the Sadducees obviously did not, and they were learned men. How could these fishers and carpenters and field hands and tax collectors, who knew nothing of any foreign land, or any religion, or any literature, or any kingdom, how could they be expected to know and not be afraid?

Magdalen was still fearful, only now she was not sure what she was afraid of. She decided that she would have to give that some real consideration before discussing it with Jesus. She did not want to be caught in her own trap the way that Peter always was, and she did not like dueling with words. Magdalen decided that her own questioning would wait until the morning. Let him answer the apostles this night, and perhaps she would learn something and have no need to ask questions for which she should already know the answers.

They walked until nightfall exchanging only meager conversation, and then they stopped to eat and camp for the night. Jesus celebrated the Rite of Remembrance with them but this time he ate nothing more. With the heavy drone of muffled conversation around her Magdalen fell asleep at the fire. She never even heard the questions, let alone the answers.

Chapter 5

Everlasting & Escene

When Magdalen awoke, Jesus was gone again. Mother Mary was already awake and some of the apostles had gone to find breakfast in the sea. It did not take Magdalen long to realize that she had missed the evening's conversation and then to seek out her mother-in-law in order to find out what she could.

Mother Mary was at the shore washing wooden bowls and Magdalen joined her at the task. "Mother, what did they ask him last night? Did he tell them that he would be gone from us again today? Where has he gone anyway? I don't understand all of this secrecy."

"They asked about the law. And he did say that he would be gone for a while today, but he didn't say where he goes, and I think that they were afraid to ask. For myself, I felt that if he wanted me to know he would have taken me aside and told me. And you should probably feel the same."

Magdalen countered, "I have held my questions this long because I felt as you do. But now it is bothering me. How can I feel peace when he is disappearing all the time and not saying where he goes or why? I know that all of us would always do as he asked, but why did we come on this journey?"

"The apostles did not ask, Magdalen, and neither did I. I think that they are afraid that he will be disappointed in them, or disgusted with their failure to understand his Way, especially after the words that he used to poor Peter last night. No one wants to be embarrassed in front of the others. I think though that he is waiting for them to ask. That is why I have not publicly asked him that question myself. And, like you, I have had little time alone with him."

Mother Mary had begun to comb Magdalen's hair. Fixing each other's hair had become some sort of nervous pastime. The women talked of the apostles' need for Jesus and their constant fear. They talked of what Jesus had said the day before and then Magdalen asked what he had said about the law. "When they questioned him," Magdalen voiced a questioning comment, "It was as if they were looking for a reason to rebuke or rebuff the Pharisees, as if they needed his permission. And too, it was as if they were looking for something they could fear, without feeling guilty about having such fears."

Mother Mary responded, "He said that the Law of Moses and the law of Rome were not to be abandoned, but were to be obeyed. He said further that even the law that had caused his death was a law that was good for the manner of people that had made it. And he said that the reason for law was humanity's reason and not God's reason at all.

"He told them that the law of whatever land they were in was the law that they were to obey, even as they taught his Way to the world. The traveler, he said, is subject to the law of the country through which one journeys, and that the citizenship of the traveler was not to one's homeland until they returned there. Some questioned that. They felt that a person should retain belief in the law of his or her own nation, and that if one retained such a belief, the traveler was subject only to that law. And Jesus said to that, that if a person followed the law of one's own nation when in a foreign country, then that person would end even as Jesus' life had ended. That he could see no reason for most people to die for a belief rather than going home to it."

The conversation continued as they debated their own feelings on this matter. The catch was long in coming that day, but when the fishers returned they ate breakfast. Then together they waited for Jesus' return. It was many hours, and the time was spent in little talk and much thought. The apostles pondered on the things that he had said, and Magdalen wondered again where he was at that moment and for what reason. It was not until after the evening meal that he returned.

"Greetings." He said. "Are you still pondering on obedience to a law that you do not understand and why you have come here to this place?

"You came here, without question, and in doing so you obeyed my law. Without understanding, you obeyed it. You are not here as a person subject to a nation because of citizenship. You are subject to me only because you have chosen subjection. You are subject to me because you have entered into my Way and now it is best for you to trust in me for I know the Way and you do not. It is the answer to your questions concerning obedience to the law of foreign lands as you journey. It is better to trust in the law of the land and find your way smoothly with the help of those that know the way than it would be to mistrust, doubt, or even disobey the law and find yourselves concerned for the right and wrong of every move and always defending yourself against those that would enforce the law.

"It is not by obedience that you say a law is right or wrong, but it is by ascription to that law that you say these things. It is not by being with me that you choose the right or the wrong where I am concerned, but it is by your teaching and preaching that you make these judgments." He reclined as if to sleep and the others did the same.

Magdalen was not about to sleep so quickly this night. She had to know where he had gone and for what purpose. Her own feelings of fear or guilt were far surpassed by her need to know if he had lost faith or trust in her since his return. It was not enough to know in her heart Jesus' love. She had to hear the words. He lay there quietly at first, but Magdalen knew that the question would not have to be asked this time. He would know her need to share her feelings with him and he would know her thoughts, as he always had.

He explained to her then, "Wife, I do not go away to avoid you or the men. I go to the places where others meet in my name and then defile the love of God by their own laws and the fears that go with all law. I go to meet with the Escenes. These people meet in the darkness of the world even now as we speak. They are a group whose meetings take place in the holes of darkness under the city and in the empty sepulchers of those that yet live waiting to die. I want you to promise me that you will have nothing to do with these people or their meetings after I have left you. I do not want you to be in the darkness. It is light that I have come here to bring and not the black hole that results from the fear that is both the cause and the result of law. Stay away from all this and keep the others away as much as you can have an affect upon them. These Escenes are strong in their faith and their law, and that strength could overpower the faith of many a disciple in the name of love of Jesus instead of the love of God. What I have taught and come to bring is the word of peace and love, not a new law, but instead a new spirit. As you sleep remember this and find its value in the morning when you are refreshed. You know, because I have told you, that those who are busy meeting during the night, when the sun cannot shine on them, will have no refreshment from sleep nor from the acts and words that they practice under the cloak of the night.

"Sleep now in peace, and I will still be here in the morning."

When Magdalen awakened, Jesus was at the shore. She went to him as the others still slept, and they walked slowly and silently for some time along the water's edge.

"I will send you all back again today, and I will go to where I have been most useful these past days in the hope that I will be heard and understood. These people, though, have little understanding. It would have been better for some of them if they had never met me. They have set me up as the Egyptians have set up their Gods, as a protector and a doer of evil toward those who oppose them. But the time left is short, and I must do what I must and then leave them to their guilt."

Magdalen offered the thought that perhaps he should stay longer. Of course her motives were very selfish ones, and he only laughed a little and shook his head to say no. After they had returned to the apostles and joined them in eating, Jesus spoke to them about the Escenes.

"Not even the adulterer is more filled with guilt than the one who deceives by way of distorted truth, or who enslaves by way of affection. These are the things that will keep this cult alive. These are the things that will breed trouble for them and for you if you put yourselves among them in thought, action, or home. Do not be in their meeting place, and do not give them approval by your words or actions. Answer their questions in the truth that I have taught you. Be careful that you do not fall into the trap that you set yourself when you think that by living among a people you can change that people. It is by knowing what motivates and what stimulates. It is by knowing what fears are theirs and what joys are theirs. It is by being within them, and not within their meeting or their homes, that you will bring them to hear you and to see your works. For in the darkness that these inhabit no one can see, and only by bringing them into the light will you help them. So don't go there, leave this to me. That is where I am going now. But when I am gone, move into their hearts and yet away from their homes. Preach to them only in the public places in the light of day, and express affection for them without judging but without condoning their fear and guilt. Remember all this as you find yourself journeying homeward."

As he finished, he again disappeared. The group proceeded on their journey and retired for the night on the rocky shore of Galilee. They had traveled for the remainder of one day and on through two more. This was the middle of the fourth day, and they arrived home to find that Jesus was once again ahead of them. The Master sent them all home to their families. Some of them were surprised to hear that Jesus was going to send them away from him, when he was to be with them for such a short time. He did not tell them when to return or why the trip they had taken had been necessary, he only repeated himself once more. He told them that no one was to remove himself from his family for the sake of anything but its welfare. He told them that he was always aware of their needs, and it was because he loved them that he was sending them to their homes. Again he reminded them to stay clear of the Escene systems, and to show their love for their families until he called them to him again.

They left and Mother Mary and Magdalen prepared food. They were hungry and tired from the journey. Jesus, of course, required neither sleep nor nourishment. He watched in silence as they made their way about the house putting things right and wiping and washing the sand that had accumulated upon and in everything.

As Magdalen turned the bed out and prepared for sleep, she turned and asked him if he was really that concerned about the Escene movement. He said that he was concerned for those involved and for those that might succumb to their teachings of evil and darkness. He explained to her that while within the Law of Moses there was indeed fear, this movement did not fear God. They took pride in that. However, they feared the devil or demons, and that fear instilled in them loyalty to the law. Not loyalty to a saving God, but loyalty to the law itself, which was bent on controlling evil rather than on pleasing God. So while it took some steps toward the betterment of attitude, it in essence replaced one fear with another and gave evil the power that only God deserved.

Magdalen lay down to sleep with every muscle aching and tired from the journey and from the work of the day, but she wanted him to go on talking. Jesus knew that and so he continued his discourse.

"My Magdala, you are wondering as much as they why I sent them back to their homes this day. Family is important. You might call it the heart of the living God. It is the thing that keeps humanity from loneliness and it is the thing that comforts them in their sorrows. Family and its responsibilities are overpowering to people sometimes, but the duty is forgotten when the love is experienced.

"There is no prayer that can be said, no meditation that can be done, no place on this earth that is as peaceful as is the result of the smile of a child that you have borne, or the feeling that man receives from a woman, not in lust, but in love and living. There is no wealth that takes the place of family. There is no law that is as easy, or just, as the law of a good father. There is no friendship that can ever take the place of a mother's understanding and knowing of her child.

"Wealth takes you further from your soul. Prayer takes you to trust in God. Meditation puts your body to rest and your mind in heaven. But family, it brings you to God and unites you with him. Everyone would find the search for heaven easier if they looked in the first place within the closest place, at home."

By this time Magdalen was feeling very drowsy and almost asleep. But she noticed the change his voice took and she saw once again the contemplative and compassionate personality that she had known before the crucifixion. She supposed, out loud, that he was right, because just the tone of his voice had put her at peace even then. And as he brushed her hair back from her face, Magdalen closed her eyes to sleep.

When she woke, Jesus was out in the yard. It was as if he were seeing the world for the final time, as if he could absorb it all better by his staring. Magdalen elected to remain silent and to simply go on about the work that needed to be done after their journey and absence from home.

Mother Mary baked and Magdalen went to wash clothes. Of course, Jesus had none to offer her. This was something she kept forgetting to ask about. He was always clean, even after his long journeys into the desert. He was never soiled and the need to bathe or to launder his garments no longer existed.

The women both spent a great deal of time and work in the re-establishment of cleanliness within the house and were ravenous as night fell. Jesus had remained silent almost the entire day speaking only briefly and only when spoken to. He had watched intently as they busied themselves and watched in a way that Magdalen had not seen since his resurrection. He was emotionally moved by their work. His eyes were dewy and filled with the glance of love for their efforts.

As he reclined on his couch, watching as they cleaned and cleared the food, he began a conversation that Magdalen thought was more a discussion with himself than it was with her or Mother Mary. Mother Mary seemed to sense that too, and she retired to her own room and, Magdalen supposed, to sleep. It had been a long day and the work had worn on them both.

Jesus talked as Magdalen too prepared for sleep. "The time comes soon when I will no longer see the beauty of this world. Each tree, and every camel, each child and every man or woman is a monument to the love of the Father. It is in these things, and all the things of this world, that one might find heaven, and still instead they build their own monuments. I will leave, and the body that is here will leave with me. And humanity will build me a monument of law.

"They will seek God in a man that has gone from them, and they will erect to that God a monument of law to honor a body that has died. Why can't they see that the living monument is God itself? It is seen in all the wonders of this world and it breathes with their breathing. How is it that I have loved them as my Father loves me, and still they seek the law that will take that love from them?

"It is only within this world that there is the vision of love, the feeling of love, the sound of love. Here is beauty. Here is affection. Here is laughter. It is these things that are a monument to love. It is these things that are the monument to the Father who is that love. It is these things that are the icons that depict me as I am.

"The law brings fear. It brings evil and guilt. It brings people sin.

"Where I am going, I will not miss the world and its wonders, because I have known it well. But I am yet seeing, hearing, and feeling these things now, and within this time that is left I have a yearning for the continuance of this heaven here, and all of its pleasures.

"You will miss me, but I will not miss your presence. I will no longer yearn for you, because still I will know you, and still I will live within you. When I am gone, Magdala, look for me. Look for the love that we have shared within all the beauties that I will no longer see. Remember that I do not leave them, but instead become one with them. See me in the beauty of the land, feel my touch in the wind and the water, hear my voice in the children's laughter. Know me then even as you know me now. Do not erect an icon to me, but instead recognize my image in the things that surround you. I will be the husband of your spirit. We will be one in mind and vision as we have been one in body. You will not be lonely then.

"The men will be lonely, but you will not be lonely. They will pine for me. They will seek a vision of me. And they will often be disappointed. They will give in to the temptations of the law, because they are disappointed and lonely. But you will not seek me, for you will know me within yourself. You will be able to recognize the sound of my voice within your mind.

"But right now you do not know how right I am. For now, you are lonely before you need be. Come, lay here with me, love me as you have before, and as you find peace in my arms know that you will find peace in my heart after I have gone."

They made love with passion and the graceful movements of a couple whose affection had been life long. Jesus held her tightly against his chest as their satisfaction came, and Magdalen listened again for the beat of his heart. It was not there, but in his embrace she knew his love for her, and she found peace in sleep.

Magdalen left the house in Nazareth alone. But as she walked the path leading from town suddenly Jesus was beside her. By this time his appearances and disappearances were becoming commonplace, but still it startled her. The couple laughed at her surprise and hugged each other in delight of the joke. With a loving hand Jesus slid the veil from his wife's head and became quiet as he took her hand to lead the way. They walked together, Jesus and his Magdala, in a silence that was a special kind of communication.

This was a well-traveled road. Carts came and went past them. They met the boy with the privy jars twice, once as he emptied them and again on his return. This slow pace made Magdalen wonder how long it would be before someone would notice Jesus, and if that someone would be a disciple or an enemy. In either case, the results would surely have been chaotic. That was why Jesus had elected not to make his present teachings a matter of public knowledge. He no longer went to the synagogue or the temple. He no longer gathered the groups in the desert. He simply appeared and disappeared at will, where ever and whenever he felt that his presence was needed or useful. He had done no healing since his resurrection, as healing was a sure way to gain public recognition and reprisal.

The carts and people kept moving. Each cart was laden with goods to sell or treasures that had been purchased and were now being brought home. The people carried nothing it seemed. Beasts of burden pulled the carts along or walked behind their masters with the baggage and baskets that had been secured to their backs by ropes and harnesses. More often than not, the stick or the whip was prodding the goats, camels, and horses and asses. The animals didn't seem to rebel, and Magdalen found nothing particularly unusual in all this, but she found the patterns of Jesus' thoughts unusual.

He was reacting each time an animal was struck. He was feeling animated compassion each time one of the heavy carts passed them on the road. It was as if he had noticed for the first time that these things were happening. He had always had a special kind of communication with the animals, and he owned no beast of burden himself. On occasion he had ridden, but he had never secured his goods to the back of an animal, and he had strong feelings about the use of animals by his apostles.

But he had never reacted to the employment of animals the way that Magdalen knew he was that day. It seemed to eat at him. Although he said nothing to her about all this, she knew what he was feeling. And before too long those feelings were to surface in an anger that Magdalen seldom saw in him.

They were approaching a goat cart that had stopped along the road. The owner of the cart had laden the already filled vehicle with a purchase of jars that he had made from a passing merchant. Along with the jars, he had placed the pack from his back inside the cart too. The little goat quite obviously could not move his burden. The goat was small and young, unused to the yoke, and it was apparent that he was straining under the whip and that he could not move for the sheer weight of his load. A crowd was beginning to gather as the master of the cart stomped his feet, shouted and whipped and prodded at the animal. Some in the crowd began to jeer. The man did look rather ridiculous standing there exasperated by this little goat. The hecklers were suggesting that he find himself a new animal or that perhaps he carry the weighty cargo and let the goat drive him. The scene made Jesus move closer and then to speak in an infuriated tone.

"God has never given you a burden that you could not bear, yet you set yourself above the Divine and put the goat to a task that cannot be done! You are not only foolish, you are cruel and vengeful."

He took the whip out of the master's hand and with an irate and sudden move struck him once across the backside as if to drive him forward. The blow was an angry one, but it was not hurtful to the man's behind.

"It is the way of you and of all your people to take vengeance upon the animals for the slavery that you once suffered. You are cruel but more importantly unjust, for this animal has done nothing but serve you. You cry out in indignation at the behavior of the Pharaoh in Egypt. You shout freedom in the face of Rome. You demand from all the obedience to the law of the Sabbath. And then you put behind an animal a burden too heavy to move. It is not by some manner of superiority that humanity is put over the animals, but by the love that is extended in fairness and just behavior. You are not superior but stupid when the burden does not move."

He cut the straps from the animal as if they were ribbons and then lifted the tongue of the cart and overturned its contents upon the ground. The goat moved only to the side of the road where it found some weeds upon which to nibble. The frustrated and angry master shouted out at Jesus, saying that he had no right to interfere with him or his animal. And Jesus answered, "Then God had no right to bring the plagues upon Egypt, and Moses no right to lead you from the bondage of the Pharaoh." Some of the crowd murmured in agreement, others in jest and disagreement, but Jesus and Magdalen simply moved on.

"It is the way of humanity," he said, "to find a place to put their anger and discontent. They say that they have left these things, but the reality is that they are yet venting them upon something or someone. Too many use the creatures of the world as their whipping boys. These creatures are grateful for their ration, and they are eager to please, but they cannot do what is beyond their limit. No whip will make it happen. No starvation will make it happen. No coaxing or prayer will make it happen. It is with animals as it is with people. There is the limit that is reached, and no more can be done. It is not wise to expect more than what can be given from man or beast. It is stupid to think that you can change the limitation by breaking down the body or the spirit."

Magdalen didn't answer. They walked on passing more carts and more people. When there seemed to be a time of solitude, he disappeared again without saying anything. Magdalen went on her way to the market in Jerusalem and then back again to home and the work of the day. She retired for the night without him and lay wondering if she too was venting her angers and hatred and judgments upon som
around her. Certainly the cart owner had no
wielding a temper with the Pharaoh against

Magdalen too could be wielding such a temper against someone without being aware of it. The thoughts took her to sleep.

The next morning she was alone in the house when two men stopped by looking for Jesus. She said very little, but only listened to their request. They asked if she knew where Jesus was; she denied, and rightfully so, that she had any idea of his whereabouts. They asked then if she knew when or where the battle would take place. Magdalen queried with some upset as to what battle. They responded as if, of course, she knew that Jesus would have to come to battle with Satan before he left, and that his fight would be the end of evil upon the earth. They told her that they were praying, not only to God for courage and patience, but also to Satan himself, for mercy and for the length of the battle to be short. For they believed that the powers of good and evil were equal upon the world of the earth and that only Jesus' good could be sure to win over Satan. They believed that the battle would happen in the sky over Jerusalem, but wanted to be sure by asking Jesus himself so that they would not miss the day or the place.

Magdalen almost laughed, but it really wasn't funny. These men were the Escenes that he had talked about, and Jesus was right. These people were surely worshippers of evil and fear, without even knowing it. Thinking herself quite clever to use Jesus' metaphor, she sent them away, saying that they would have to "seek him out in the sun". He was usually in the desert when he was not at home. She had remembered what Jesus had said about bringing them out of the darkness in which they preferred to meet, and she hoped that her suggestion might help. Moreover, she wanted them gone. They made her very uncomfortable, somewhere between frightened and amused.

Shortly, Magdalen had a third visitor, a Roman centurion. He had come to be baptized, he said. She knew the man but only slightly. He was seeking the forgiveness that John the Baptist had promised by the ritual of baptism in the Jordan. Despite the rumors, Jesus had never baptized anyone as far as Magdalen knew. He had made some comments about being baptized in water, and had been baptized by John himself. He had explained baptism as a ritual or sign of forgiveness, not forgiveness itself. The real forgiveness was to take place inside, within the hollow place of the being that is filled with the reflection that water gives. It is inside, he had said, that baptism works out the fears and guilt of a person's mind. The water of John, he had told them, was the water of sight and touch. It was the ritual that could symbolize for a person the washing of one's soul by the drenching of one's body. Everyone was born and raised in guilt and fear, he had told them, and those things needed to be washed from people's minds. Faith in the act and ritual of John's baptism would enable one to move from a faulty beginning to a new beginning within the soul that would be free of sin, guilt or fear. For in forgiveness by God, people could be assured that the remainder of this life would be worthy of God's acceptance and praise. It was only a ritual. What baptism was, was changing your mind about yourself. Magdalen decided not to try to explain to the centurion, but only to tell him that some of the disciples were baptizing. And that their baptism was the same one that Jesus had talked and taught about and even received himself. She sent him to the river to seek out the group and told him that Jesus might even be with them. He went on, and Magdalen sat to meditate at the doorsill.

Soon Jesus appeared behind her in the doorway. Magdalen then saw the apostles coming down the road toward them. Eleven men walked toward her with haste to reach the Master who had sent for them. As she watched them walk, Magdalen wondered what had ever happened to Judas Iscariot after his betrayal and resulting suicide. She decided that she would ask the very first chance she got. She wanted to know if the man had been punished, and what feelings, if any, Jesus had now about this cowardly apostle. Magdalen knew that Jesus was aware of what Judas was going to do before he did it, and it seemed odd that it should happen as it did. Once again he must have known her thoughts, for as the disciples came closer Magdalen's questions about the eleven became the sermon of the day.

61

"Have you thought about your numbers? Have you thought about the task that I have given you to teach all nations, when there are only eleven of you now? This is a job that not twelve, let alone eleven, could accomplish by themselves. You are not to be eleven for long. It will be after I've gone that you will replace the one that has left you because of his fear of failure. Once again there will be twelve. Twelve is a number that is significant. Numbers are a truth to all people. For in no country in the world, within no religion, within no government, is there an argument that one is not one or that twelve is not twelve. In numbers humanity can see that what God has produced is what is, and that it is truth. The numbers and their patterns are undeniable and without change.

"In the heavens, you have seen the patterns of the stars, the constellations that have been deemed Gods by the Greeks and the Romans and other foreigners.   These constellations are twelve, as you are twelve. Some the astrologers have not seen yet, but believe me. There are twelve. Each of the stars, says scripture, is set as a sign in the heavens as to the works of God and the patterns of humanity. The signs under which the time came for your birth are the patterns of your mind. The truth is that the patterns of the numbers are also the patterns of the skies, and these determine the patterns of the minds of all people. Each tribe of Israel, being twelve in all, was given a pattern, not a region, but a pattern in which to work their way. In all the twelve made the whole of Israel, and these parts together made a complete society in which all work could be done with the greatest expertise and craftsmanship.

"You, too, are of the twelve signs. Each of you within himself is lacking in some knowledge and ability, but these things another has because of the pattern set by the stars that have molded the pattern of your mind. Together, there is no thing that is not worthy of the whole. There is no task that is too great or too hard for you. Separately, you are minuscule in your effect upon humanity; together you have the power to change the minds of nations. Together, you are a complete cycle of learning.   It is as if you were one person whose lifetimes numbered twelve and whose soul could not rest at ease with its worldly knowledge, and its knowledge of spirit and its own mind. You are one, but you are one made of twelve. Know the days of your birth and the constellations under which you breathed your fist breath, and you will know that each of you is different yet each of you important. For in completion of any cycle is the whole. In any part of the cycle, there is no completion and yet a ways to travel. The traveler cannot come home before the journey takes its full turn. That is the way that the patterns of the numbers work. That is the way that the patterns of the stars work. That is the way that the mind works. Each person is the traveler of this circle of living that brings one back to the Source, that is the Father that is my Father that is God.

"Many lives you will live, as Elias is now John, and in each of these you will learn the pattern of a sign within the stars. And when you have learned all of the things that this sign controls, you will then come home to the Father. But not until those things that you are sent to learn are learned, not until those things of the pattern are complete, for until the circle is joined, there is no coming home.

"Keep all this in mind as you meet all manner of people, and know that they know some things and are learning others. And you, too, are learning. And you are not whole without the eleven that are your completion. You will come to see other sacred numbers, patterns and cycles to life, but it is not important that you study each one. It is only important for you to know that they are there and that the works of God proclaim the harmony of the world. Like the music of the minstrel in the court, or the words of the poet, these things are beautiful to the one who is aware of their harmony and pattern. And they are uncomfortable or even boring to the one who has an ear of tin. But most people know that the harmony of poems and music is there, and for that reason the words of the ode and the music of the lyre are beautiful to you. You need not study music to appreciate its harmony. So it is with the patterns of the world and of the works of God.

"There are twelve constellations, twelve tribes of Israel, and you were twelve and will be twelve again. These things are the pattern of something that can encompass this earth. From the shore to the shore and the mountain to the mountain, the constellations can be seen, each in a different place, at a different time, so it will be with you. No matter how distant from one another you are, you will be there as the completion of the whole thing that shall reach forever in distance and time. That is the word of God's love and the truth of my life.

"These things I leave you to talk of, and to think of, as I make my way to rest. And you do the same, for tomorrow we will go forth to heal the colony of lepers that is outside the farthest city to which you can walk in one day. There is much there that you must come to know before I leave you to do the work that has been mine."

He went inside and the eleven looked at Magdalen as if they expected some sort of explanation. She shrugged and went in too. They left, murmuring among themselves. These men knew nothing of astrology or the metaphysics of numbers. They had heard that the Pharisees talked of these things in the temple, and that Jesus had talked with them, but they had no real knowledge. The stars were so far away that to them it seemed impossible that they should be controlling their minds. But then again, the Roman's and Greeks felt that these constellations were Gods to be worshipped. Magdalen knew they were wondering how Jesus could be a believer in the one God, and yet have faith in the stars and their power. She was sure he would give them deeper answers one day.

Chapter 6

Leper Colony

Even with Jesus as their protection against contamination, the group was fearful of approaching the leper colony. This highly contagious disease was a death sentence to be sure. The vicious leprosy or "first born of death" as it was referred to in scripture, had no mercy or prejudice. Rich or poor could be stricken with its ravaging sores. It was believed that the Divine used it as punishment for sin, that it could be inherited along with the guilt of one's parents. Jews were told not to eat shellfish or fish from the river Nile for fear of catching the disease.

Jews and Romans alike shared their fear of contamination. At the first sign of illness, usually a sore or white spot on the skin, a person was required to show the entire body to the priests. It was the priests who looked for the living flesh within the lesions of the supposed leper. These open ulcers indicated true infection and when they were found the person was diagnosed and declared unclean. The leper's head was shaved and kept shaven. The unfortunate one was made to wear loose fitting clothes, keep the head bare, the mouth covered with a cloth and to cry out that he or she was defiled and unclean. As long as the disease lasted the leper was to dwell alone and away from the city.

If the disease were to be cured by miracle or method the sufferer appeared once again before the priests. It was only by the judgment of the priests that one could reunite with the community. Jesus was always sure to remind lepers he healed to show themselves to the priests before returning to their families, else they might be put to death for breaking Jewish law.

For those that could not prove such a miracle of healing there was nothing left to them but the leper colony outside the city's walls.

The colony was not a colony at all, not as one would think. It was a deserted gravel and sand quarry. The hole in the earth's surface was about fifty or sixty feet deep and the sides of the pit were of solid rock. The workers had deserted it when the loose sand and gravel had run out. Within the sides of the walls were carved, either by people or by nature, many caves and shallow tomb-like openings in which the lepers were living as animals would live. At the bottom of the quarry, water was coming up from the earth to form a small, muddy lake used as a pitiful source for water to wash the lepers' sores.

There was little sign of civilization equal to what you would find within the city. There was a central fire, and some smaller fires at the cave openings. Around these were some cooking utensils and a few people who appeared to be tending the fires and preparing the food. These that you could see from where Magdalen and the others stood, atop the pit wall, were not the severe cases of leprosy. These were those who had only recently discovered their plight by the appearance of one or two open sores upon their bodies. They had voluntarily committed themselves to life in the horrible circumstances that Magdalen could see from her perch. These new residents seemed to be in charge of whatever organization there was among the group. Obviously, those who were further along in their illness were incapable of helping or had become uncaring of their lifestyle and the everyday existence among the rocks and filth that surrounded them.

Magdalen had seen lepers begging in the streets of Jerusalem, but she had never been so close to the people or their suffering. It was horrible. Some moaned as the sores were deep enough in their body to cause terrible pain. Others prayed to their God or Gods, begging forgiveness and healing. Others wailed for the loneliness that had taken over their minds. In the streets of Jerusalem, the lepers kept their sores covered with rags and garments, both for personal comfort and for the protection of those who approached. Here there was no embarrassment; the bodies of these people were visibly covered with open and running sores, the sight of which made your own body crawl and ache. Magdalen hated being here. She wrapped her own garments closer, as if to protect her from the highly contagious disease. Jesus took note and established for her the fact that without touching these people and their sores, one could not catch the illness. She let loose of her clothes, more out of shame for her ignorance than real confidence in her continued health.

The lepers saw them at the top of the pit and began to gather below. They were accustomed to the wealthy penitents from the temple that often came to the top of the colony to throw down food or clothing as a way of giving alms and doing penance for their sins. They came out expecting this group to do the same. Jesus moved down the side of the pit to a flat place where he could sit, and there was room enough for all of them and for the lepers that now approached. He didn't speak at first, he only made it very obvious that he had something to say, and that their approach was welcomed rather than shunned. Many gathered, and soon it seemed as if the entire side of the pit was covered with these poor people.

Some of them had large grotesque tumors on their faces and necks that made them look more like mythical animals than people. Their lips were swollen with fatty tissue and often as their lower lip fell with heaviness drool ran down their chins and caused their skin to be chapped, red and raw. Children approached whose fingers had dropped off from the debilitating disease. Where their fingers had been, blackened stubs of bone peaked out through sock like coverings of worn rags. One little girl walked on two stumps where her feet had been leaving bloody tracks behind her. Many of the poor sick creatures held out a claw like hand in begging. Leprosy had taken away their ability to grasp and they needed help even to eat.

There was quiet moaning and desperate crying and hoarse coughing in the group, but there was no conversation. The people just watched the disciples and their Master as if frightened by their very presence. Their eyes showed little light and their heads all seemed to be bowed in depression and fear. Magdalen realized that the presence of anyone who was clean was odd, but why should they be afraid? Jesus told her that the people feared that the crowds would find it to be in the best interest of the community to put them to death and to burn their bodies as they burned the unclean fish that were taken from the sea. Tears burned her eyes and her heart was filled with sorrow for these poor unfortunates. Magdalen wanted desperately to make these people see and know that they had not come to harm them, but she really didn't know why they were there. Jesus had not healed since his return, and he had not been public in any way. Why was he here? Was he going to heal them all, and then let it be known that he was alive and walking among his enemies? Magdalen waited to hear him speak and soon he did.

"Do you know me?" He stood and spread his arms wide in order to be seen well by the crowd of nearly one hundred. "By my word and their faith, many have become clean. And I bring you now my word, but faith I cannot bring you. This you must find within yourselves. Your body is unclean, not because of your sins, but as the result of your guilt. You have no trust in the forgiveness of the Father, and so you manifest your disease to punish yourselves. Those who have gone away from me clean have come to me in trust. I say to you that all people who cling to guilt are unclean, whether in their bodies or in their minds. I say to you further that what is sin is the guilt you feel for your actions, words, or omissions. You are not being punished but find yourself deserving of punishment. When you can say to the Father, 'I have done what I knew to do,' then you will also say to the Father, 'There is no punishment deserved by the person who is just in mind.' It is not by what you have consumed that you are scarred. It is not by what you have done, or the battles that you have fought within yourself, but by the relinquishing of your mind to evil and guilt that you have wrought this fate. Trust in the goodness of the Father. Know that the good Father, that is my Father and your Father, would not punish the servant or the child whose intention was for the Father's own good. When you know that you are the faithful people whose intention was for the good that is the Father's, then you will trust that no punishment will befall you. I say to you, only trust in the goodness of the Father, and you will be healed." And he began to move among them, and to touch them on their sores, and Magdalen and the disciples waited for the many miracles to happen.

But many moved away from him. They were convinced that he was mad, or they found his words beyond understanding. Others stuck out their hands as a threat to the entire group. That was something that they had learned from their exposure to begging in the city. It was a sort of extortion that they used, a kind of blackmail that got them the financial support they required. They were said to have sworn to sleep in a man's bed, or to make love to his daughter, or to in some way touch him and bring upon a person the disease that would then make them equals in health, as well as in wealth. By these threats they found the money to survive.

Jesus had no fear of their touch, and the apostles took his lead. Although Magdalen knew that they were wondering inside whether or not the Master knew, or cared, what he was exposing them to. Still, Jesus continued, and soon the harassers among the lepers went away like the doubters who had left first. But there were a few, only a handful, that came close. Some fell to their knees, and others actually prostrated themselves before him. Some kissed his feet, and others reached out to touch his garments. These were cured. And they were not surprised at the miracle. It was the faith that it would happen that made it happen, that much Magdalen had learned from times before.

And those that were cured sang praise to Jesus and said they would tell all that they met that God was among them and that they had been saved by his goodness. But Jesus raised his hands to indicate to them that he did not want this. "It is by your faith that you are made clean. It is by your knowledge of the

Father's goodness, and not by my hand. Say then to those that you meet, that the love of God has made you clean. Do not mention my name, for I have no name now to mention. My name in generations will be revered as the Lamb. But who I am now, is the Shepherd, and the Shepherd is nameless. Go now in peace. Wail no more. Be lonely no more, for with you is always the spirit of the Shepherd. Go and show yourselves to the priests." And they moved away and went ahead into the town.

But the apostles questioned Jesus. "Why, Lord, were not all made clean by your power, and the power of God that is your Father?" asked Matthew.

Jesus answered. "The Father's responsibility is to raise responsible children. It is not the Father's responsibility to do the work of that child. God will not give to the child who is unwilling to do the work of learning the reward of knowledge. So it is with these that still ail in their bodies. They will not learn by hearing, so they must learn by experience. And knowledge does not belong to a person until he or she has learned the lesson set before them. They have heard, but they have not listened. They have suffered, but have not seen. So yet they are ill, until the time comes that they will learn and see and know the Father's goodness instead of only the wrath that they still desire.

"They will live again in bodies that are hurting and unclean by the presence of disease. They will live again to learn, and someday, at some hour, they will come to know. It is then that they will be healed. I am not the mind of any person. I am the soul of all people. So are you."

Jesus disappeared and went ahead of them into Nazareth. The rest of the group walked slowly back to the city questioning one another regarding Jesus' message to the lepers.

"Does he mean to say then, " asked Peter, "that all manner of illness and misery are the result of the mind, and that there is no other Source that guides our destiny? Just the other day he spoke of the stars as the map of our fate. And he says too that all things come from the Divine. Am I the only one who does not see the confusion in all of this?"

"Hold on, Peter." said James. "I can hear the anger in your voice. Your lack of understanding is not the Master's fault. You mix one lesson with another like soup in a pot."

"Well, if your understanding is better than mine, share that wisdom with us." Peter was hoping to call James' bluff.

"Jesus said that the Way is written in the stars for each of us. He said that we are responsible for our own guilt, which causes us pain one way or another including illness. He said that we could heal the body by healing the mind through forgiveness. The stars do not give us illness nor does God. God gives life and love and the stars show us the Way. If we use the guidance given we have no reason for guilt. If we do not use the guidance and do what causes us guilt or shame then we get sick. We can heal that sickness and help others to heal it. I see no contradiction here." He was firmly finished.

Some of the others nodded in agreement with James, but John could see that they were merely covering up their own confusion. "The Master has explained to me that the astrologers can predict the future for the earth and for people only so far as what will happen not how they will react. Getting sick is a reaction, just as healing is a reaction. The first reaction is the result of negative emotion. The second is the result of leaving that emotion behind. The stars give energy, humanity chooses their emotional and physical reaction to that energy." John felt he had defended the Master and at the same time established that he was wise as a result of his private time with Jesus.

"He spends too much time alone with you and Magdalen and leaves us in the dark." Peter was envious of John's relationship with Jesus as well as Magdalen's.

"Jesus does not slight you, Peter." James came to John's rescue. "He explains things to us in good time and he will explain all this further, I am sure. Besides John and Magdalen are willing to share what they understand with us. You have only to ask."

"It is humiliating enough to ask this beardless wonder about such things, let alone a woman!" Peter said it too loudly as they were approaching the house now.

"Hush, Peter." James warned him. "Your voice will be heard and you will have opened yourself to yet another chastisement."

Peter took James' caution to heart and became quiet as they walked to the door. By the time they had eaten and accomplished the Rite of Remembrance under Jesus' authority it was late and the apostles left the family alone. Magdalen welcomed this private time with her husband.

"So what a person constructs through guilt can be undone by forgiveness." Magdalen was examining again the nature of healing. "The ugly energy of guilt, blame and regret creates the ugly disease of leprosy. The beautiful energy of forgiveness and love destroys what guilt has made and returns the body and the mind to its beautiful and innocent nature." She thought for a moment. "What makes you feel sad makes you look bad; we always said in the temple." She smiled at her reflection in the mirror as she prepared for sleep.

"My Magdala, one day you will heal the lepers in heart and soul. You will awaken minds that I have left sleeping." Jesus offered something more for her to think about.

Chapter 7

Trines and Goddesses

Some thirty-three disciples sat in a more or less barren field, where the goats had been making what grass there was short, stubby and stiff. It was uncomfortable to sit on and Magdalen had to fidget attempting to soften the vegetation beneath her. Only some of the apostles had arrived with Jesus, the others were still on their way. The sky was rather gray and the weather cool for this time of year. Watching a cold and cloudy sky was somehow restful; the air felt like rain was coming and filled her with the expectation of refreshment. Jesus sat next to his wife upon the ground and spoke again of the patterns of the things in the world as it had been created.

"I have called the Father that is God, the Essence of Life. And you have come to understand that meaning. I have said that I am both the son of man and the Son of God. And I have said, too, that I will send upon you a visitation from one who is the spirit of both the Father and the Son. This Holy Spirit, the Paraclete, will dwell within you forever, and its presence you will know and recognize.

"These things I have said that you might understand the Trinity within the presence of God. But you have not understood. You have, instead, accused me in your mind of worshipping like the pagans a multitude of deities. You have thought that I am the God that you seek, and I alone. You have found me to be secretive, and confusion has been within you.

"Can you not understand that from one root come three branches? Can you not understand that from one stem there grow three leaves? Is the leaf possible without the stem, or the

73

branch possible without the root? Understand me now; God is the root. Its branches are the Father, the Son, and the Holy Spirit. So it is with the God that you have worshipped and found nameless among you. There is but one source of life that is manifested in three ways. Just as the root sends forth the branches one at a time, God sends forth these manifestations only one at a time.

"The first is the Father. It is by this branch that humanity first realized, by its own existence and life that there is a root. For the root is buried and unseen until the first branch appears. This person of God, this branch as it were, is the Divine Father whose energy came forth and displayed physical life.

"And before the first branch can whither, there emerges the second branch. This is the Son. This person of God is the Greater Mind, the pattern of all life, for it stems from the root and is seen after the Father. The essence of life has now shown its beauty by its manifestation of life two fold. And humanity knows by this that the root of life is a good and healthy root. It is the Son of God that is the mind of the Divine Root.

"And then the third branch appears. It is the branch that ensures humanity the fruitfulness of the root. It is the branch that is the Holy Spirit. It is the guarantee of fruitfulness and the assurance of growth. This branch is the final one, but it is also the one that is for humanity the guarantee of success. But for you, in your knowledge of what I say, this final branch is the indication that your life will be fruitful. This Holy Spirit comes forth and is visible when humanity has been enlightened to its power.

"You begin as a shoot from the Divine Father, but you also are the result of the single root that is the source of your life. You are the Father also, because each branch is joined at the root. You are the Son and the Holy Spirit for the same reason.

"You are dependent upon the plant, and if you sever yourself from the root, you have no more life. But remaining with the root, you are living and are one with the other parts. You will understand now. You will know that I have said that there is but one God. And all are the parts of that life. And the Father and the Son and the Holy Spirit are the branches from which spring forth the leaves that you see as parts of your life and your world.

"Each leaf is a person that is perceived different to the eyes of humanity, individual and separate, but not possible without the stem itself. Understand me now; I am one with my root. I am one with my stem. I am the leaf and the branch. And you also are part of my life. No leaf is better to the stem than another. All are nourished through it. No branch is barren as a result of the root; all have the gift of life that it gives."

As Jesus paused looking to their faces for understanding, Magdalen put her hand upon his knee. "You do go on, husband." Her eyes pleaded with him for some simplicity once again.

"God is Father, Son and Holy Spirit. One Source manifesting three Branches resulting in many leaves. The root is the One God, the Source of all life. The Father is the manifestation of physical life in all its forms. The Son is the Greater Mind that shows the pattern of life through the manifestation of all patterns and all thoughts. The Holy Spirit is the enlightenment that creates understanding and assurance of your purpose and power coming from your Source." Jesus concluded, looking to his wife for approval.

Magdalen wanted to relate the whole thing to something more than a plant. This was exactly the way that she had come to know the triple Goddess of the Temple at Magdala; she had to share her awareness.

"As mother, daughter and grandmother remain the same woman, each aspect of the woman's mind is different and her thoughts take many shapes and her body makes many changes. So the God of Abraham grows through the presence of its manifestations. Or the Goddess of the Romans grows and shape-shifts to display all the forms of beauty in nature and all the emotions too." She was suddenly sorry she had not chosen to ask a question. "Is it correct then to say, Teacher, that the human mind and body reflect the same aspects of God, growing into godliness?" Magdalen was satisfied to have saved herself from the apostles' verbal attack by finding the right question to ask.

Jesus smiled at her knowing how she had attempted to save herself. "The three persons that are one God is a pattern. There is a pattern to all things. And the pattern of three is the pattern also of the mind of a person be it man or woman. The person has one mind, soul, that is the seat of life. There are three parts to this single life also. There is the mind of body. It is here that there is the knowledge of life. Again, it is like the first branch springing from the root. It is the consciousness that you are alive, and that you live because you think. Then there is the second branch of the mind; this branch is the manifestation of feeling. It is in this part of the mind that you feel, you desire; you know and are convinced that life is valuable. The first branch brings to a person's mind the knowledge of life; the second brings knowledge of its value and protection of its existence. The third branch is the consciousness wherein you come to know that life brings forth fruit.

"Each branch has many leaves. These leaves are the things that you think. They are the things that you do or do not do. These leaves are the life that you live right now in all its beauty and, too, in its withered places. For some leaves turn brown and fall away, and others remain green and beautiful. And eventually there are flowers and fruit that come from the branches and these are the things that you call knowledge. These are the things that you will keep and find worthwhile.

"And in the field, when the farmer cuts the plant to the quick, that is when your body dies. The root is not dug up. Life is not gone from you. But you cannot see life, until once again there is the upcoming of the first shoot, and the second, and then the third. And life begins again, and you can see this life. But the root knows always that it is alive. But people do not know that life is there until there come forth the branches. You do not die. You are the life that is the root. And your mind stems forth also from that root, but it can be cut away, and the consciousness dies, but the being, the source does not. And a new life, and a new consciousness appear to have come up again in the spring. So it is that I have done this for you to see. And you too will do this time and again, for you are the root of all life, and you are also its branches and its leaves, and I with you.

"Think on all this now as you leave me. Think on the patterns. For like numbers, life is truth. Think on the three persons that are one God. Think on the three parts of your mind that are one thinking mind. Think on the leaves that are the things in your life, and the fruit that you may reap as a reward for tending well the branches. As I leave, I will come to you in your minds and hearts. For I shall never forsake you, but instead become one with you.

"This trinity of existence is there, within you, within all people, because it is the pattern of things. To do what I have done, you must come to know the whole self and all of its parts.

It was beginning to rain, and the wind had stopped completely. In the stillness the rain was soft and cooling. Magdalen opened her mouth to welcome some sweet refreshment from the sky. Jesus had stopped talking and the silence and the wetness were delightful and she smiled to herself wishing it would go on a long time.

Murmurs brought her back to the present. The apostles had noticed that they were receiving visitors, and were talking among themselves. The two Escenes, whom Magdalen had sent away just a few days ago, were approaching the group's position. Jesus rose to his feet and went to greet them. Somehow everyone seemed to know when Jesus' words were not meant for public knowledge but only for the ones to whom they were spoken. This was one of those times and the band of disciples followed at a distance. As he approached the Escenes, they hailed him as Rabbi and Master.

They asked him, as they had Magdalen, when and where the battle of good and evil was to take place. They asked also if there were preparations that they should make for that time and for the hereafter. They wanted to know what stock they should put up for themselves and for him. Jesus laughed a little at first, and then he spoke loud enough for them all to hear.

"If you put up for me a sword of finest metal and a shield of the greatest strength, I would not wage a war for you. If you put up for yourselves the foods that the body required for a million months, still you would be starving. The time that will come is now. The place is where you stand. And the battle is yours not mine, for I am at peace. Satan, therefore, does not know me as his enemy, but knows me instead as the victor without battle. You cannot see these things, no matter how plainly I put them, but you can see them, perhaps, in thoughts that are your own."

Jesus' tone had gone from that of laughter and empathy to one of frustration even close to anger. He continued, "I have said to you, Satan is not. I have said to you, love is the law, and war its reverse. How can there be then a battle? There is no enemy, no weapon and no war. You step out into the sun, and the rain falls. You are the carriers of a darkness that is filling the world. You are the seed of a fruit that cannot be eaten without the fear of death. I say to you, think again. See this that I am, as I am and not as you would wish me to be in your search for a God that lives within a single body of meat. You know the bitterness of the seed that is the life you lead. You know the bitterness of the fruit that comes from that seed. Go from me and let the light again shine upon me and those that are with me. I cannot reach you in the darkness."

It was as if he had not said anything at all to them. Even if they had heard the sermon that had gone before, they would not have wanted to understand or change their minds. Magdalen knew that. They made murmurings about the Master. They were sure that he was simply unwilling to tell them what they wanted to know. They did not lose faith in his goodness by all of this. They only saw and heard what they chose to see and hear.

As they walked away the sun erupted from behind the clouds and warmed them bringing brilliant light to the countryside. And even this small miracle of life did not arouse in them the knowledge of what he had said.

Jesus disappeared then. Magdalen knew he would be home when she returned there, and he was. He said little and Mother Mary and Magdalen went through the usual routines of the house and the body before they retired. Jesus sat on his couch in meditation and Magdalen watched him until she fell asleep.

The next day, the apostles questioned Jesus regarding the place of the Pharisees and the Sadducees as leaves upon life's branches. They had seen that Jesus had often tempted the Pharisees with logic and truth and had tested their knowledge and ability with words. He had challenged everything that they stood for in the Law of Moses over the days of his teaching, but little had been said as to the position of the Sadducees. These people were a sort of freethinking group that had been almost as challenging to the Pharisees as Jesus himself. However, they had never been quite as successful in their approach or the outcome of the verbal games they played. Many of the Sadducees were now joining the Escene movement and that knowledge was what prompted the apostles' questioning.

"These people think." Jesus said, "That fate alone stands in their favor. For if a person is thinking about his or her actions and his or her truth, one will in time and trial find the one truth, that is the love that is God. The Pharisees do not think their own thoughts, but are provoked to thought by the mind of Moses. They have no opinion that has not been stated before. For this reason, they will always remain blind to truth, for truth is learned by thought and error and thinking again. They acknowledge no error on the part of Moses, and so they acknowledge no thought of their own to be in error either. These others, these people of thought, they know that in the past there has been error, and they are open to that possibility again, however remote they now think that it is. They will see their errors, and they will change their minds about many things. This is their salvation: that they think and then believe. Damnation comes in the belief without thought and the determination to allow no other to think.

"Those Sadducees that have joined the people in the Escene movement will now have two choices. They can remain people of thought, and learn from where they are, or they can become Pharisees of another kind. They can find no error possible and cease thinking turning to the ways of the worship and promotion of the establishment of evil among them and others. If they remain people thinking to learn, they shall come away from this thing, and once again change their minds to goodness and love of God. If they cease to think, they too will find themselves in the darkness both day and night, and will soon see nothing. They have come to tempt themselves by reason of the very thing that will save them from evil -- thought. But they are not lost forever. They are only floundering now to find the truth that they know exists somewhere, and they shall, most of them, succumb to no one's truth but their own. For those that are not strong, the idea of thought will leave them, and faith will be to the thoughts of another. These will perish from the earth like withered leaves. But someday they shall spring forth again parts of the same root and will be fresh and new and more nourished than before. For the leaves that they were, will act as mulch and fertilize the root of life. No life is wasted, and none is without attachment to the God that is the source of life.

"Remember always that you, too, are such a leaf, and such a branch. You too can find yourselves tempted to avoid thought and go forth to teach only words. My words, indeed, but words only nonetheless. Teach what you think. Live what you think. Be what you think. But do not cease thinking, for in that state you will lose your mind and another possesses it. It is by this means that demons and evils come to possess the mind and the body of a person. Think, always think, about what you say and what you are. Do not be quoting me, when you have not yet come to understand me. Think on that then."

And he disappeared quickly.

Magdalen ventured a comment. "The truth must then evolve with knowledge." The others left with grumbling about her attitude of superiority and her connection with the incredibly sinful Goddess and her temple.

Chapter 8

Awakening to Spirit

Through all Jesus' preaching it became clear to Magdalen that God could never be seen or perceived, except through its manifestations. The Father was simply the first knowledge of an unseen force or source. The Son was the knowledge of a personal part in that source and spirit. This Paraclete, or Holy Spirit, that Jesus was to send was a new knowledge; the Holy Spirit was the knowledge of Divine Power within. God was the source of all people and of everything that stemmed from people. Humanity could worship everything that stemmed from God, but no law or religion really worshipped God at all. These only held holy the manifestations of God. It sounded blasphemous, even more obscene than anything that Jesus had been accused of. Her blasphemy, though, was clearly in line with the ideas of the material personification of the Divine that she had learned in the temple. Magdalen was not denying God but attempting to find God and Goddess within life. Her mind was crazy with attempted rational. She had to ask Jesus about this and many other things, silly things, she thought, like why he didn't get dirty and about the lepers who were not healed and how the Paraclete would come. Magdalen needed time alone with her husband, and it arrived with the morning.

The dawn had come while she lay awake thinking about all of this. Jesus was there beside her appearing to sleep. Somehow everything was mere appearance to Magdalen now. She didn't know what was real and what was not. Anyway, he appeared to sleep beside her. She knew that he needed no sleep, so it was mere appearance. Magdalen rose and prepared for breakfast. When her husband got up there was silence between them at first. Jesus went outside and she went about her chores within the house. Then he came in and sat himself down, his elbows on his knees and his head turned upward toward her as if eager to listen. Magdalen knew that he was waiting, but didn't know where to begin with her multitude of questions. Jesus broke the silence.

"Let us take care of the easy things first," He said. "I am not covered with the dust of the earth any longer for a very simple reason. It cannot cling to me because of the strength of the light that you see coming from this body. The strength of its force is greater than the strength that dirt has to cling to anything. So even when the wind pushes the grime against me, it is forced away again by my light and falls quickly to the ground. It is as simple as that. You see it happen when you see the light that exudes from my body. Simple."

"All right," she countered, "Then how does the body go on without nourishment or heart beat?"

"I am more in control of this body than when I lived within it as you live within yours. It is by my will alone that it continues to be animate and appears to live. For you, and for me before resurrection, life was a thing that was subject to the events and circumstances of nature. Life in this body now is the result of my will, not my willingness. That is the difference. It is not something that you can totally understand now. But understanding will come in time, the understanding of this thing that you call life. I have come to see it as mere animation."

Magdalen was quiet then. These questions regarding God were the ones that really mattered to her, and yet she was embarrassed or even frightened to ask. There seemed to be some sin in her discovery.

"God is the root, Magdala. You cannot see the root until the branches spring up. You are right in your understanding. God is unseen and shall never be seen by anyone. The Father is seen in the eye that is the eye of the mind. It is a third eye that is in the center of the forehead and people cannot see this eye yet.

Coming face to face with the Father is the knowledge that you are one with the root. Coming face to face with the source of life, the root as I have said, is not possible. You cannot even know where to look for that source until you have seen its manifestation, only under the manifestation can you be sure that you will find its source. That is, you look beneath the branches for the root; otherwise, you can search in vain forever. You look beneath the branches; that is, you look beneath or within yourself, for you are the manifestation of the source that is God. It is really simpler than one perceives. It is really not blasphemous at all. It is the truth. Do not be ashamed of knowing the truth; instead acknowledge what you know and endorse it when you are confronted."

The silence in the room did not reflect the pondering in Magdalen's mind; it chattered on. She wanted answers to other questions that she was not sure that she could verbalize. She had to think. She had to know how to ask before she did the asking. As she formulated her questions the answers came.

Jesus said, "With this new knowledge, Magdala, one gains something precious. You have seen the Father and the Son, and the Holy Spirit already dwells within you, and you are aware of its presence. In time to come I will make known the presence of the Holy Spirit within the apostles, all of them, and they will know this power only because of what I will have done. You know already, by your own mind. You are a woman of thought and for that reason, and not for having known me; you have saved yourself the agony of life and the distress of disease. The Holy Spirit will come as a great light unto them, and they will feel as if they have always known me and understood my Way. But they will know these things by what they consider miracles. You know these things by the nature of who you are. It is grand that your heart is filled with such knowledge. Do not be ashamed or frightened by your own power. Only know that what you know is the truth and that I share that truth with you. You are not alone. I know that you fear loneliness and you fear the way of life here. It is frightful, indeed. But it is only those who live in no fear that have peace, so be not fearful. There is not one thing in all of

Nazareth or Jerusalem or even Judea itself, there is not one thing in all the empire of Rome that can harm one hair on your head if you know the truth. It is things unknown, it is the things hidden that are fearful. The things that are known and seen in the light of day are not things to be feared. You, my dear, can see all the things of your life in the light and the goodness that is the source of all. You can see the root because you have found the branches and seen beneath them the Source itself."

All this reassurance seemed to have little or no value on one hand and an undetermined amount of worth on the other. Magdalen's heart was rejoicing in her knowledge. Her body and her mind wept on the inside for the lack of courage that she felt regarding her future. She asked no more questions, and no more answers were offered.

The day wore on as any other might have before the crucifixion, and they went about the tasks of life and its pleasures. Evening came and went. Meals were served and eaten. Lovemaking began in an embrace and ended in sleep.

Jesus was gone when Magdalen awoke. That seemed just fine, because for now she wanted to talk to Mother Mary, to have some helpmate in her emotional state. She wanted to share her enlightenment, but more than that she wanted to find out if her mother-in-law felt the same as she did.

" Misery loves company," she mused. " Or maybe, we all have a need to know that we are not alone in misery or joy, either one."

Magdalen dressed somewhat elegantly for an average day. The blue dress was silk and draped her form in a clinging that revealed her body's beauty. She fastened her hair on top of her head with a silver clasp and, throwing a light white veil over her tresses, went out to find Mother Mary. She was hanging rugs and blankets on the side of the house.

"Mother," she said. " I need to find your counsel. I have been talking with Jesus and his words say that there is nothing to be afraid of, but yet I know that he knows how frightening all of this is to me. Are you afraid of your son's leaving? Have you found that you are sometimes frightened even of your own thoughts? Because I have."

Mother Mary went on working. She was quiet, as she usually was. Magdalen shouldn't have expected anything different. But somehow, this day, her attitude made Magdalen almost angry with her. She wanted her to demonstrate some of what Magdalen knew she had to be feeling. More importantly, she wanted Mother to admit that she felt the same way she did. This would justify her personal fears. There was so much to be afraid of. As if Mother Mary had just picked up Magdalen's last thoughts, she began.

"Magdalen, there is so much to be frightened of right now that I can only say that I am frightened of everything. I am frightened of the Jewish upheaval that could result if he should be discovered. I am frightened of the upheaval among them if they know that he has been with us and that we have not admitted his presence to the Pharisees or the Rabbi. I am frightened of the Roman guard that will surely strike out against us if they come to think that Jesus or the apostles or the disciples themselves are a threat to Caesar. I am frightened that he will leave and we will be left penniless and without comfort or protection from any of these things. The apostles are only with us now because Jesus is here. When he is gone I fear that they, too, will forsake us for others and other ways. Their loyalty is to Jesus and not to the mother that bore him. I even fear that you will go. I fear that Joseph will not return this time. I fear so many things, yet I fear nothing. I know how strange and incomprehensible that sounds, but I have, long ago, discovered things and thoughts within me that say that there is nothing at all that can hurt me really. There is everything to fear and nothing to fear. There is everything to learn and nothing to know more than I do. Of course, you are fearful. Of course, you are distraught. I do know your sorrow. Just as I know that you once feared barrenness."

There was a twinkle in Mother Mary's eye as she spoke of Magdalen's most personal fear. Of course she knew that her daughter-in-law was with child. Magdalen, though, wasn't ready to announce her pregnancy to anyone. Her flush, however, revealed everything.

"Now you fear bringing a child into this life without a father's presence. It is understandable and expected, and Jesus knows all this too."

"What will I do?" She asked, almost as if she needed an answer. "Where will I go? What of the hatred that has come between the men I once served and me? What of the love that I have shared with Jesus? I will never forget that! I can no longer find it within myself to be of service with the same body that has been with him. I cannot go home; my house is empty and all but demolished. The worst of all my fears is that I may be wrong about my faith. I have discovered that no one can see God or arrive in God's presence the way they have an audience with the king. Jesus says that I am right, but what will others think? The Jews, my mother's people, will not find this truth of mine acceptable. What of the Romans from which my father came? They would say that only a God that can be seen is a true God. What of the apostles, even they feel as if they will one day see and know God in a sort of way that I know to be impossible. I am beside myself with questions to which there are no answers. I am frightened of things that I cannot change. I am frightened, and I am at the same time eager and curious to know more of the truth about this God that can never be known."

"Magdalen," Mother Mary responded. "You never have to leave my house. Together we will create safety and security right here and now. We will find a way. The apostles will come to their senses and bring us comfort, or we will find comfort in each other. Don't worry about that any more. As for your house and your things, why worry? If they are gone, they are gone. Forget about them. As for Jesus' leaving, this loneliness I cannot erase for you, but I will suffer it with you. You know I will miss him too. As for knowing God, we will share this too. We can share the loneliness and the unity between us. That is more than many people ever have to hold them together as a family. These things we will share."

Magdalen hugged Mother Mary tightly and told her that she loved her and that a better mother no daughter ever had. She meant it more than she ever did before, but still they both worried and were frightened. It was a time of fear, but it was less painful knowing that they had one another to lean on.

The day went on and occasionally they spoke of the things that they knew and questioned the things that they didn't. It wasn't as if the women offered each other any answers. They simply shared their knowledge and the lack of it. It made them closer. It brought them to hold each other and sleep together when night fell. In Magdalen's mind she prayed that morning would bring Jesus home with some new form of hope for the future.

After finishing her laundry by the shore, Magdalen's morning walk finally brought her home. There was a conference going on. Jesus was home with Andrew, James, and Matthew, along with John. But John wasn't part of the conversation. He sat alone looking quite forlorn in the corner against the wall. He sat on a stool that had a straight back, but somehow he managed to sort of slump backward against the corner.

The three other disciples had been teaching in some of the cities near by, they were questioning Jesus as to what to say about some of the things that they had been asked. Did God really want them to follow the Law of Moses? Did it matter if you fasted or sacrificed? Was there a law that they could obey under this new doctrine that would ensure them that they were pleasing the Lord? Magdalen could hear the answer coming even before he spoke.

"There is no law that God has given that humanity can follow. There is only the natural law of love that exists between God and humanity. That is to live in fruitfulness. The sacrifices and the fasting and the ritual and routine of religion are mere modality used to control society in the name of God. These things have nothing to do with the true God. They are mere exercises in self-chastisement. They are ways that people use to achieve superiority and holiness in the eyes of others. Would God have asked you to kill a thing merely to give it back to God? This is foolish. What would God do with two turtledoves or one lamb? These things cannot be of service in the place of pure spirit. What good is a dead sheep that is burned? It cannot even be eaten. What good is killing two birds? These are of no value when consumed by flame. It is folly, indeed, to waste the miracles and wonders that are the result of God's goodness. The only good that comes from such a thing as sacrifice is the good that it does the mind to have given up something. You are human, and you perceive that suffering results in purging the soul of guilt and gaining God's forgiveness. The truth is that you are doing the forgiving and the purging. You gain, in your mind, by these things that you do, but God gains nothing from any of this.

"As for the fast. It is the same, really. You give up something and you feel that you have done this for God's sake. You feel that you have done this for the sake of the sins of which you feel that you are guilty. But the truth remains that the fast has done nothing but make your belly swell, and later you will curse God for having given you such a rigorous task as fasting. You will use fasting to show others your holiness. You will use fasting as something to complain about. What good is all this? God has put on earth everything that you need to provide you with food in abundance. There is no gain from fasting except that you find yourself in high esteem among others and perhaps within your own mind. Although, seeing as how you know the truth about why you fast and also know that you are doing it for reasons that are not of God, you do not even gain personal pride. You only gain in the minds of others and by that you feel that you are better and more holy and gain greater respect, wealth, and allegiance. You do not fast for God. You fast for these other reasons.

"Sacrifice, if you will. Fast, if you will. But do not put upon God the blame for your suffering and your lack. It is your own doing. If you do these things that they might remind you of the presence of abundance in this world, then fast. Fast in silence and in private. If you give to the temple the means to support the priests, then sacrifice, letting the animal live until it can be of use to those who require its flesh for food. Do you not remember thou shall not kill? There is no law that is God's law that would break the Ten Commandments given to Moses. There is only the law and religion of humanity that would do such a thing.

"Keep all this in mind. But keep also in your mind what I have told you about the nature of travel and the responsibility and wisdom to live within the law of the land through which you journey. Do not teach them to fast. Do not teach them to sacrifice. Do not even teach them to seek me, the man whose love has brought you to this place. Teach instead that they are in that love and that my love is the love that is God's. My Way is the way that is without law, but is not breaking the law. My Way is that I am, and here in my being I am without blemish. That includes the blemish of sin against the law of governments and of Moses."

They absorbed all this and they went out leaving John behind. Magdalen offered to feed him with Mother Mary and herself, but he declined. He was so sad, this boy. He was so very confused, not about what Jesus had just said, that he understood better than many who were much older than he. He was confused, as Magdalen was, about the future and the responsibility and the way of things to come. Jesus went over and touched him, and there was a tear that streamed down John's face. The Master only smiled and stroked his head as a mother might comfort a child. Then Jesus disappeared.

John didn't question that any more. They were all getting used to his coming and his going. Instead, John made himself useful quite obviously not wanting to leave. He worked with the women as the day went on into night. The next day they met again in a rented room in Nazareth at Jesus' direction. He appeared as he always did now, suddenly and yet expectedly. They were here at his request, so there was silence until he spoke.

"In these final days, I have no more to tell you, but perhaps to explain what I have said before. For you are hard put to understand some of these things. You understand the life of humanity because you are human. You cannot yet understand the life of spirit because you do not yet know that within each one of you there is the spiritual person also.

"I am not alone in the works and wonders that I have done. There are others who have gone before me who have done these things. There will be others after me, including some among you, who will also do these things."

Peter interrupted, "Tell us Lord, who it is that can equal you. Am I; is Andrew or John, to be a worker of such miracles as only God can do? Let me be among them, Master, and I will do well by you."

Jesus laughed as he so frequently did at Peter's remarks. Then he answered in a serious tone of voice. "Peter, the person who is so engaged in being the duplicate of yet another person will not know spirit but only humanity. Those that will do as I have done must first come to leave my miracles behind and then come to know the power that makes miracles possible. That is the person of spirit within you, each and every one of you. When I say to you that I shall send the Paraclete, the awareness of Holy Spirit within is what I send. I send this thing, this sign, because you are yet but people, and people require the symbols, the signs, the works and wonders before they are convinced. But if you are convinced only by the miracle and not from faith in the truth, then you are still a person without knowledge of the spirit within you. You only see spirit within me. You call me friend, Rabbi, Lord and Master. Forsake these names. I am not above you but with you. It is not by my spirit that I have done these things, but instead by the Holy Spirit that dwells within the minds and hearts of all.

"There is no way that you can find that spirit without going within. There is no way to recognize that spirit until you have recognized yourself. If you are still asking my permission, my approval and direction to be spiritually aware, then you are not aware at all. I will send the sign, but the spirit is already here. I can, as I have said, light the way. This is why I have come. But I cannot walk the path for you, nor will I carry you. You must move through this learning of yourself, by yourself, but within the light that I have provided.

"And I give you yet another sign so that you will know that what I have shown you will light the world. Know that your light also can shine as brightly as you walk among the people of all nations and preach to them love that is warm and bright and alive as the sun itself." And as he stood there the room was flooded with a golden light that was coming from his body as if he were the sun. And his clothes became white as snow, and then he disappeared as he had come.

Andrew was the first to speak, "How can we do such a thing? My body is not the sun of the sky, and there is no fire here. And Jesus is filled with a fire that seems overwhelming to anyone else who would see what we have seen here."

Peter responded, "If the Lord says that we shall shine, shine we shall."

Then John spoke with a quiet and somewhat doubtful tone, "Jesus said to find the spirit within. I think he is suggesting that we are without understanding yet and the light from him that illumined the room comes from full understanding. What do you think Peter?"

John was obviously trying to soften his thought with a question to which he needed no answer. Magdalen could see that John, as young as he was, did not need the approval of any one of the others. He was coming to a deep understanding that he was already endeared to God and that the understanding that he had must be felt and not known the way one knows mathematics. He was a precious child to her until this day.

Somehow he was more a man than any of his elders from this time on. Magdalen had talked with him before, and she knew that he felt deeply everything that he had learned. She had suspected that there was more to his learning than he had ever before expressed. Now he was beginning to openly share that learning. Magdalen was sure that just as soon as these others got the jealousy and envy out of their minds they would see and hear John as a man, a holy man of great knowledge.

They all left and went out into the street. Jesus could not be seen anywhere around and so in pairs they went on their way to teach in the neighboring towns. For this had been what he had prepared them for all the time that he had been with them. Magdalen went home and Mother Mary went with her. Magdalen's feelings for John were now added to all the other emotional upheaval within her. There were good feelings, bad feelings and feelings that could not be defined as good or bad. She simply felt and felt deeply everything that had been happening and what had not yet come to be. She fell asleep that night trying hard to sort out her emotions and to come to some peace that would allow her rest. Only physical fatigue was there to carry her to her dreams.

Chapter 9

A New Ordination

When morning came, the feelings that Magdalen had taken to sleep with her were still there and they were even stronger than before. She stood in the window looking out and wondering if she would ever be what she had been before Jesus' death. She wondered if she was capable of understanding or if her mind was only fooling her. She wondered what it would be like after he was gone, and she wondered which of her thoughts or emotions were responsible for the tears that were now running down her face.

It was a quiet sort of weeping at first, but then Jesus came up behind his wife and encircled her in his arms. His touch was all it took to turn the quiet weeping into uncontrolled sobbing. Every feeling Magdalen had came gushing out in the sobs until she all but lost her breath. These things had all been bottled up for so long that her crying was an emotional explosion, and she simply could not stop. Jesus said nothing, but only held her and allowed her to cry.

It seemed that it was a very long time, but eventually Magdalen quieted and the sobbing went back to single tears and they ran slowly as she turned again toward the window. She didn't know what to say. It seemed useless. If she had unanswered questions, she surely didn't know what they were. If she was feeling badly, as obviously she was, she didn't know how to describe her reasons. A steady stream of tears kept running down her cheeks. Jesus wiped two or three away, but when they didn't stop he reached for a cup from the shelf that hung above the kitchen workplace. He held the cup to

Magdalen's cheeks, one side at a time, and caught the tears. She had to laugh.

"What do you save them for?" Magdalen asked with a gentle smile.

He reached out to her face with the cup and caught another.

"Feeling is a precious thing. It is something that too few have found really. They feel fear or anger, but these tears are tears of love. There is as much compassion here as there is fear. There was no anger in you when they crucified me. There is no anger in you over my leaving. There is wonder and awe. Yes, and I know that there is fear. But the fear is only for the body, and there is more fear there for my mother and our unborn child than there is for you.

"Crying is a cleansing of feeling as well as the expression of it. To cry is to express the good feelings and to cleanse us of the bad ones. I have caught the good feelings. These were the quiet tears that were there after you had cleansed yourself of the negative ones. I know because I felt that as I held you. I caught the good feelings because these are the feelings that are to be treasured and used. But even these must be expressed to be of value. The expression of love gives the same good feelings to those who would otherwise have missed them. They are like fertilizer on the field. The expression of good feelings nurtures and feeds the minds of others."

Magdalen smiled brighter now and felt better about her outburst. She went to take the cup in order to wash it with the other dishes from the morning, but Jesus did not give it up. Instead he emptied the precious drops of love out the window onto the ground.

" My Magdala will do great things. Watch," He said. "They are fertilizer for beauty." Then he set the cup aside and went to his couch.

Magdalen went about the rest of the morning and early afternoon as usual. She was fairly quiet, still thinking on what he had said and on what she had felt. Jesus was right, though, about the cleansing. She had needed to cry for weeks already and it simply hadn't happened until now.

As she prepared the evening meal, there came a knock on the door. She turned, expecting Jesus to disappear from his spot on the couch. He had not allowed himself to be put in any position of public exposure except for the time with the lepers. That, of course, was a safe place considering everyone's fear of contamination. But this time he only nodded that she should answer the door.

There was a woman there, young and obviously quite concerned. She carried with her an infant, not yet two. The child was covered with a wrap that only allowed the baby's eyes to show. She pushed past Magdalen and knelt at Jesus' feet. Magdalen was feeling again the deep and sorrowful emotions that had brought about her tears earlier. This poor woman was in fear of losing her child. She dropped the wrap from the child's head and there on his forehead was one lone mark of leprosy. She was begging Jesus to heal the child. Her pain was expressed in her face and her voice. The mother, fearing that she would have to give her child to the colony and that the child would have to suffer a long life, pleaded and begged. She told Jesus that she would not ask him to undo the work of God otherwise, but she could not leave her other children in order to live in the colony with this leprous one. She would obviously have been willing to do that, had she no other responsibilities. Jesus touched her hand.

"Give the child to my wife."

Magdalen took the infant from her and without thinking stroked its ugly sore. Jesus was comforting the mother and wiping her tears with his hand as he had his wife's earlier that day. It occurred to Magdalen that there were too many tears shed in this world. Necessary and good or not, no man or woman should have to feel what this mother was feeling, nor shed the oceans of tears she was sure had already been cried.

Magdalen's own troubles seemed so minor now. She held the child and sat down rocking her body to give the baby comfort.

After a while, when Jesus had finished speaking to the mother, he turned and spoke to Magdalen, "Let her take the child now."

She returned the baby to his mother's arms. As she did she meant to cover the child's face, as it had been when they arrived. The sore was gone. The woman began to sob in relief. Thanking Magdalen over and over, she kissed her hands and her head and her hair. Magdalen begged her to stop and told her that the healing was the work of God, and that the Son of God sat there behind her.

Jesus shook his head. "Look out the window, Magdala. Look beneath the window."

Magdalen was bewildered, but did as she was told. There, under the window in the twilight, bloomed a single flower. Its white head was on a single stem. There had never been a flower of any kind that would grow in the sand and gravel and heat beside the house. She went outside to look again, this time closer. Jesus motioned for the woman to go out ahead of him and sent her on her way. Then he went out to be with his wife.

He stooped alongside Magdalen to see the flower himself. "Feelings – fertilizer. They make happiness grow. It made the flower bloom and it healed the child."

Magdalen started to cry again, just a little, and then laughed at herself for doing so. Jesus laughed too. She picked the flower sure that the sun would ruin it in the morning. Once inside, with the flower safely in the same cup that had held her tears, she forgot all about the evening meal. But Jesus reminded her of the spiritual nourishment the flower had given her.

" My Magdala will do great things."

Jesus disappeared early in the morning and was gone overnight. Magdalen spent the time thinking about what had happened with the child. Whenever she spent time thinking Magdalen spent time sewing, and so she worked on one of Jesus' old garments, a white cloak. She had determined to finish her embroidery on it before he left and give it to him for his journey. Even though she knew that he would never need to change clothes again, she wanted him to take something of her with him. Rather a foolish thought, she knew, but nonetheless her own need to know that she would not be forgotten had more influence than real logic at this point. Besides, it troubled her somehow, to be with him as it was before, and yet not be doing any of the usual things to provide for his comfort. It seemed like she should be doing something just as she had always done, and this was all that she could think of.

Magdalen was using only yellow thread. It had come from Egypt or maybe Persia and its color was like sunshine against the white of the garment. She thought that the color would go well on him now with the aura that seemed to surround him sometimes. Before she had always liked to use red and blue on his clothes, the few that she had decorated. He wasn't much into the ornate things that Magdalen liked, and so even now she kept her design simple. It looked like wheat, and she planned it as she stitched.

As she diligently continued with her embroidery, she was thinking more and more about the healing that Jesus said she had accomplished. It astounded her to think that she could be capable of such a thing, and she kept looking at the flower in the cup where she had put it. She wondered about the flower too. She wondered how it had come to grow. Certainly it was not from her tears, not really. He couldn't expect her to believe that, after all she was not a child who believed in that sort of magic. And it couldn't have come from anything that she had done, because then she would have known.

Healing in the Temple of Magdala was accomplished by conscious thought and the use of herbs, potions and prayers to the Great Mother. There she knew that she could heal and did it through the power of the Goddess and the rituals of the temple High Priestess.

Magdalen thought hard about that. This time she didn't know that she was healing the child, and yet he had been healed. Could it be that she did things like this and never even knew what she was doing? Could it be that she had accomplished other things without even noticing that she had? This wasn't the first time that she had touched a sick child and felt compassion. It wasn't the first time that she had cried for the release that everyone needed at times like these. Were there other flowers, other children that she had affected by her feelings and emotions?

Now that she knew that she was capable of these things, what should she do about it? Women did not do preaching and teaching. And certainly she could not travel as he expected the apostles to do. Jesus would not want this; Magdalen was sure. But what good was it to know that you could do something if it was of no value to anyone? She decided that the last thought was a foolish one too. She knew that there would be other times like this, when without any need for preaching or teaching, she would feel and show compassion. And that there were always ways in which she could touch people to ease their pain. She didn't need to go anywhere. She didn't need to say anything. After all, that is how it worked just yesterday.

Magdalen really wished that Mother Mary, who had gone off to do the marketing, would come home so that they could talk about all this, but her wish was not granted. She ate some bread and cheese, swept a little and then was drawn back to her sewing. Magdalen supposed it was really her thoughts that drew her back and not the thread and needle. Thoughts of the healing that she had accomplished took her to remembering what her husband had done before and after that event.

In her mind's eye she could see again the gentle smile as Jesus had gathered her tears. Fond feelings of marital love and loving filled her heart. Her mind was full too, with memories of Jesus and how she came to know the love within him. It had seemed so unnatural to her at first, a man whose mind could work like her own. He was a man who thought as much of love as he did of lovemaking. She thought about how they used to play together. She thought about how he liked her hair, even seemed obsessed with it at times. He'd make a sort of rope by twisting its length and then wrap it about him as if to hold her to him. He'd comb it later and talk to her, just talk. Or sometimes he would say nothing, but allow her to go on like a magpie about everything and anything. And all the time there would be a smile on his face, a smile that told her that he loved her.

It occurred to Magdalen that even though he was alive she was mourning him. She was remembering him as if he were dead and gone. But these were happy memories, memories that made Magdalen laugh out loud at how they must have looked when they were together. He had been so filled with fun at those times, and she was filled with joy at his pleasure and happiness.

Magdalen decided that she had to make this garment really special, and one at a time she pulled a few strands of hair from her head. She incorporated the long silky hairs into the design that she was embroidering. That way he would take a real part of her with him, a part that he found special. The garment would be more than just handiwork now. It would be Magdalen, and he wouldn't even know it. She could hide the dark hairs beneath the yellow threads and he wouldn't know. She didn't want him to know how sentimental and foolish she really was, but she didn't mind admitting it to herself. Maybe she'd tell Mother Mary when she came home what she had done. She would understand. Something told her that Jesus would probably understand too, but she decided it was better left unsaid.

As for the power of healing, Magdalen decided that she would have to think more on it before deciding if there was anything that she should do about it. This she would talk to Jesus about. She wanted to know what he expected of her after he was gone. He was always talking to the apostles about what they had left to learn and what they should teach and even where, but he had said none of these things to her. She would ask as soon as he came back from wherever he was.

Magdalen lay down to wait for Mother Mary hoping to tell her all her tales, but her mother-in-law didn't arrive until she had fallen asleep. When morning came, so did Jesus. She didn't have time to tell Mother Mary about the day before, her thoughts, or the hair in the embroidery, but she did have time to talk to him.

She asked about the healing again. He responded that what she had considered something so special could be done by anyone who was in the place of true love for people who were willing to accept that love. He told her that there were many things that people did every day that they were unaware of that were healing to someone, gave someone faith, hope and the energy to come to health again. He explained further that there was little need for concern about how well she did or how many she could help. The only things that were to concern anyone were the things that enabled them to continue loving in the way that he had taught.

She asked whether he expected her to teach or preach as he sent the apostles to do. He answered that there was no need for her or for Mother Mary to risk the danger of travel doing what the men could do. It would be better for them, he said, if they remained in Nazareth and simply answered the questions of those that would come. For now it was here that they could be of the most value and it was here that they could keep their love alive.

"But one day, my Magdala, the Spirit will guide you to other lands and you will convert the world to a New Way. My Magdala will do great things."

She looked up into his loving eyes, "Jesus, I will wait for that guidance anxiously for I must do whatever God has ordained for me." She squeezed his hand in hers and looked away as if looking for direction.

Then Magdalen asked her husband when he would leave. To this he answered very directly, which was something that surprised her.

"I will be gone before two Sabbaths have passed, but my leaving will not break the Law of Moses." She knew that he referred to the fact that he would not travel on the Sabbath, as it was considered unlawful.

Asking where he was going seemed a ridiculous question, so Magdalen asked how long it would take. It seemed like it would be a short journey from here to wherever heaven was if it could be accomplished in less than two weeks time. And she had a hard time understanding where and why he had to go anywhere at all, because he said that heaven was here in your heart. Then why did he have to go anywhere?

He answered that it was time for him to be gone from this world of humanity and that the journey would be done before she could blink an eye. He said that the distance was something that could not be measured, for there was no measure of miles between this world and the world of pure spirit, the world to which he went.

Magdalen supposed that she looked perplexed, certainly she was. He responded that there was no way that he could explain to her this sort of journey into another place in time and space. But that it was sort of like changing your mind about where you want to live and then taking your body to that place. She still couldn't quite conceive of such a thing, but it didn't seem to matter.

Talking about his leaving seemed the perfect time to give him the garment that she had embroidered. She had finished it the night before and laid it under her sleeping mat in order to keep the stitches from puckering the fabric, and to keep the sand away until she could give it to him. She went to get it now and turned to offer it to him.

He smiled, and Magdalen remarked that she had wanted him to take something of herself with him when he went, and asked him to wear it on his journey. He changed then into the new garment, looked at her and laughed.

"I promise not to soil it until I leave." He knew that even though he had explained about the light that kept him clean, Magdalen still found it miraculous that any man could remain clean in the wind and weather for even a day, let alone thirty.

Then he looked at her and his smile became more tender. "You wanted me to take something of you, and so inside your stitches are the hairs of your head. I do not find it foolish, Magdala, only dear. Please remember that the most precious part of you I take with me has nothing to do with the garment or its threads. I take the joy and the love we shared. And I take it to be kept for eternity."

Magdalen was embarrassed that he knew. "Did you read my mind, or could you see the hairs there?"

He laughed again, "What's the difference? I knew. I know you, so I know what to expect. The rest is simply being sure. And besides, I know that they are missing from your head."

She put her hand to her head, unconsciously she was looking for a vacant spot, and then she laughed out loud. Even he couldn't see that they were gone. He was teasing and she was silly enough to have fallen for his joke. Jesus laughed loud and long shaking his head from side to side with merriment.

When Peter and Andrew arrived the merriment ended and the three men went off together. Mother Mary and Magdalen talked as they worked. The women laughed at Magdalen's foolishness and at Jesus' knowing all about it. But Mother Mary didn't laugh at her daughter-in-law's sentimentality or her superstition.

Magdalen shared with her mother-in-law Jesus' direction that they remain at home and teach through example and through answering the questions that others would pose to them.

She shared, too, his prophesy that she would do great things. Blushing a little as she spoke, Magdalen recalled the story of the flower and the child's healing and how Jesus had ordained her to see the world and to travel one day to spread a New Way among all people.

Mother Mary nodded as if she could see it all happening just as he predicted. "When the time for that is right, Magdalen, God will guide you to and through this holy destiny."

Even after they had eaten and laid down for the night the women continued to chatter on. They talked about their plans for the future and decided that in the morning they would see what few belongings Magdalen might have yet at her house. No matter how few or how worthless these things might be, they might also be useful to them later. It seemed like the time to begin thinking about a new life with hope rather than fear. Magdalen fell asleep savoring her own knowledge and power and trying to imagine what remnants of the past she would find in her house and what she would even want to carry with her into the future.

Chapter 10

Moving On

The women made the journey to Magdalen's home in Bethany as they had promised each other. There was little left to find, at least in Magdalen's eyes. Mother Mary found the fact that her daughter-in-law had so many books quite intriguing and even exciting. Most people did not own books. The libraries of the state or the temple were the source of all written information. But Magdalen had received books from many of her visitors to the temple and other friends particularly those in the government or in the army of Caesar. They knew of the Priestess' passion for learning and had always been extremely extravagant with their presents to her. They found the scrolls and slates now mostly crumpled or broken with pages scattered and missing. Together they gathered up what remained legible in the hope that Magdalen would somehow be able to reconstruct the missing pages from memory. She had read and reread everything, many times over.

Magdalen took two remaining gold cups from the cupboard in which she had kept her dishes. The goblets had been part of a set that, like the books, had been a gift. They were beautifully engraved with the symbols of the Goddess and little doves in flight. Her fingers ran over the small birds and she brought the cups to her heart.

"These I will keep as vessels for many memories."

She assumed the missing servants had taken the rest with them or sold them for the first offer. There was little else left in the cupboard. Most of her household things were made of clay and had been broken in what appeared to be an attempt to search for something. Magdalen thought that after the servants left robbers had come and gone through her things hoping to find some treasure that the thieving staff had missed.

She took a few clothes and some fabrics and ribbons that remained along with the cups and what books they could put together. There was a book of limericks that she particularly liked whose leather sheath was now gone. There was a brief little book that had been put together as an Egyptian history that spoke mostly of the lineage of kings and the division of properties and their inheritance. Magdalen liked that book because of its picture like documentary, and because it described the land by the mention and description of remarkable natural landmarks. It was always fun to read the descriptions and imagine what it would be like to be in the places that the people were describing. There was another work, written by Caesar about far off places and she gathered it up too.

There seemed nothing else to take that the women could carry. There was furniture, of course, too heavy for robbers and obviously too heavy for them. Besides, they had no use for the furniture at Mother Mary's home. They put the things in bags and secured them to their waists with pieces of the ribbon. Their dresses nicely covered the fact that they carried anything of value. Although Magdalen questioned the real value of any of this at all, even to her, they covered it over in order to avoid tempting robbers along the road back to Nazareth.

As they proceeded back, they took notice of three men. They seemed to be following them, but not eager to jump to fearful conclusions the women simply sped up their pace. The men too increased their speed. The women slowed down. The men slowed down. When the women stopped for a moment along the road, the men stopped too. Now both Magdalen and Mother Mary were sure that they were being followed, and now they were definitely afraid. Dusk was approaching and they had to lose these men or risk robbery and assault in the darkness.

Magdalen whispered, "There is a curve in the road ahead. We can hide in the reeds growing around the creek. But we can't let them see us leave the road."

Mother Mary pointed at herself and mouthed in silence. "I'll go first." Now she pointed to the north indicating the direction she would take.

Magdalen nodded. She would wait until Mother was well-hidden and then go off in another direction until the men had passed. Later the women would meet at this same bend that was to be their offing place.

They hurried their pace and then slowed down. They stopped and started several times. It didn't take too long and by their reaction the women could tell that the men were confused and didn't know what to do next. Somehow, they really didn't seem like robbers. Magdalen thought that they were not smart enough for successful thievery. As they began rounding the corner, Mother Mary darted into the reeds. Just a few feet after that, Magdalen did the same. The bend in the road and the height of the reeds had helped them to avoid being seen on their exit. The women stayed still, each of them quiet and statue-like. The men came to the turn and were talking bewilderedly about the women's absence. They asked each other if perhaps they had disappeared as Jesus had done so often. They decided that this must be the case. Then they doubted. Then they were sure. It was getting quite comical really. Magdalen had to stifle a giggle with a hand over her mouth.

After many minutes of this bizarre debate, the men went on their way. Mother Mary and Magdalen were quiet but moved closer together. In a whisper, they decided that they had better wait a while longer to be sure that the men were gone.

Once back on the road, Magdalen looked Mother up and down. Mother was obviously assessing Magdalen's appearance too. Now they had come to the creek expecting to get a little wet and dirty. But here they were, what seemed like an hour later, looking at one another as if they were both lunatics. This was ridiculous, after all what were they protecting? Not the few possessions that they had hidden. Their hair was full of grass pieces and their dresses were wet to the waist. Mother Mary looked hysterically like one of those Egyptian pictographs of a Jewish slave, a Jewish pregnant slave. The sack of Magdalen's belongings showed under her wet and clinging garments like a belly filled with child. She looked at Magdalen and laughed. Magdalen appeared to her as she did to Magdalen, absurd to say the least. They laughed and splashed back into the creek to wash off and then fell as they attempted to come out of the reeds with the sacks still attached to them but now filled with more wet and reeds than goods.

They joked like sisters, like young girls on some adventure. They walked onward as the darkness came, decided that the men had only been curious about their connection with Jesus, laughed again at their confusion over the women's whereabouts, but then Mother Mary began a serious conversation. She suggested that soon Magdalen should talk with Nicodemus about what to do with the remaining goods and the house itself. Nicodemus was a disciple, not a Jew, and not really Roman. The man was a fair and just merchant who was revered by all for his success as well as his honesty. He knew business in Jerusalem and Bethany and he would be able to advise Magdalen of the best thing to do about her real estate and other belongings.

The journey was too long for the night and they slept by the wayside hidden again but this time without the wetness of the creek.

Magdalen met with Nicodemus that very week. John brought him to her at Mother Mary's home. He said that he would find a way to settle her affairs. He knew of a family whose affiliations were neither Roman nor Jew who would be glad to find their home in Magdalen's house until she could dispose of things in a proper and profitable fashion. They would care for the house and perhaps be persuaded to put things back in order and good repair. The man was good with his hands and they were in need of a place to live before a child was born.

This was very much the way that Nicodemus always seemed to do business. He simply found solutions for everyone that benefited everyone. It was uncanny, his competitors would say, that he had been successful at all. Yet Nicodemus never doubted that true success could only come in this win-win fashion.

Nicodemus was indeed an example of living faith as Jesus had instructed. But he had been that way, as Magdalen understood, even before he had met Jesus. It was because of Nicodemus that Jesus had a burial. And it was because of Nicodemus that many of the disciples found homes. And because of him also that motherless children found themselves in the arms of barren Roman women who paid him the price of adoption. But he only placed children, never slaves. They were children that would be honored and respected as the heirs to the Roman legacy and a birthright that they would not otherwise have had. And he placed, not unwanted children, for he believed that children belonged in the homes of their parents. He placed only children that were homeless orphans, who would otherwise be raised on the charity of the multitude and live in the commons or in the streets.

He was going to look at the house and arrange the rent with the family. He would report back to Magdalen as soon as that had been accomplished. Another thing about Nicodemus was that you didn't rush him. Business took time, as much time as it required for honesty and clarity in all dealings. Magdalen didn't mind though. These things had been left this long, no need to hurry now. And Nicodemus would be responsible, that she knew.

He dined with the women and with John before he left. Jesus had not been with them all that day. Magdalen slept, but only after a long period of thought about where he was and when he would leave. Somehow the house really didn't matter any more.

To everyone's surprise, Nicodemus came the very next day to tell them that he had succeeded in finding the couple that he had referred to and that they would be moving into Magdalen's house even as they spoke. He assured her that while they were now unable to compensate Magdalen for the residence with money or gifts, these people would put the house back in order. This was essential, he said, because he had succeeded also in establishing a buyer for the house, a man and his family that were coming to Bethany from Egypt. The man was a treasury person for the Pharaoh who would now be working for the Roman government. He was a man of means and would be able to pay handsomely for Magdalen's house, but it was necessary that things be in order when he arrived. The couple that Nicodemus had found would be able to accomplish what needed to be done and at the same time wait out the arrival of their child. The man would be finding work with a farmer who was in debt to Nicodemus for his property. He was calling in another favor. As always, Nicodemus had accomplished the perfect harmony in his business transactions and Magdalen was to benefit along with everyone else.

After the evening meal, Nicodemus stayed for a while to talk. Everyone was curious as to Jesus' plans and all sat about supposing and anticipating. They all wondered, too, where he was now, for to their knowledge no one had seen him for several days. Magdalen mentioned that he might once again be with the Escenes, but Nicodemus said that he did not think so. Jesus had made mention to him that these people had come beyond listening even to him. He had said that they were the kind of people that heard only what they cared to hear and that there was no further use of words with them. The small talk went on for several hours, but nothing was said of any real consequence. They reminisced and talked about the past more than anything else. Then Nicodemus left and John, who had been there all evening, left with him. Mother Mary and Magdalen retired with new hope for a prosperous future.

The eleven were gathered at the house in Nazareth later that week. All of them had been waiting for the Master's return and wondering if he had left without warning or final good-bye. They were hoping that Magdalen and Mother Mary would know where Jesus was. Of course the women knew no more than they did. They sat about the room on the floor as they had done many times when Jesus was among them. No one had dared to sit on the couch that he so favored.

There was little being said and the feeling in the room was one of doom. Magdalen couldn't stand it any more, all this remorse and no one even knew why they were feeling so morbid. This was not a funeral. He wasn't dead, and she wasn't about to go through any more mourning. He would be back, she told them. He wouldn't leave without telling them and Magdalen sat herself on the couch with an attention-getting thud, as if she might end the lull or perhaps change the mood by filling the vacant space. She was angry inside, angry with these men for demonstrating such grief when she was so sure that there was no reason for it. Or perhaps she wasn't sure at all and what she was angry about was that they were raising doubts in her mind. She just sat at the foot of the couch and said nothing more.

Everyone seemed to be staring at her. Magdalen knew that they felt she was out of order sitting there. She knew further that they were expecting something to happen. They were superstitious beyond belief, and Magdalen guessed that one of the reasons that she had seated herself on the couch was to prove their superstitions invalid. But this time something did happen. Jesus appeared seated next to her cross-legged on the couch and resting against its back.

It wasn't a sudden appearance, the way he had come in through the walls before or the way he arrived after a journey. It was slow. It was as if he arrived a piece at a time or in some sort of degrees of being. He materialized as if he were growing there. It wasn't frightening or even startling. It was too slow and smooth to be a shock.

When he was all there, he laughed out loud. He laughed and continued laughing. Laughing at her, really. He knew Magdalen's ego had put her there, and that now she felt that the apostles were perhaps right in their superstitions and she was feeling embarrassed for being there in his place.

Finally he spoke, "You might have sat right on me, Magdala!"

Magdalen turned red. First the embarrassment made her too conscious of herself to think. But then it dawned on her. If he were teasing, all right, but if he meant what he said, then he must have been there before she sat down. Magdalen questioned him finally, and as he laughed he conceded that he had not gone anywhere but had been right there in the house the whole time that they were in search of him.

"I have been invisible to your eyes. But you have not been invisible to mine. I have watched, listened and took notice of everything. It shows me how you will be after I have left you."

Peter was the first to ask how this act of God was accomplished.

"It is an illusion, Peter, mere magic. All the things that are called miracles are nothing more than magic. These are not the works of God, but the works of humanity. The things that I have done in my name are the works of man. These things are the appearances and disappearances of my body and of my things, and even the things of others. They are the things of which scripture has written that Moses did or like the turning of a rod into a serpent by Aaron. The changing of water into wine that I did at the wedding at Cana was like this."

He took a pear from the bowl that sat on the floor next to the couch. As he handled it, he talked again.

"How can I explain to you that nothing is still? Everything of this world is moving. Some things move slowly as a man walking, and others move quickly as a horse that runs under the whip. The man you see clearly, the horse appears as a streak without distinct lines of demarcation. The things of the world, all the things of the world, move in these degrees. And all the parts of these things move this way also."

He took up a knife and cut the pear in half. He cut the half in half and that half also and he continued until it was all but juice.

"I can cut even these small pieces as many times as there are numbers to count. And there would only be an end by the fact that the pieces would be too small for you to see. But even these, within the mind, can be understood as yet smaller and smaller. This is how I disappear, by separating the body into the smallest of pieces and the pieces continue to move, but now move separate of one another."

Thomas asked him, "By what means to you cut the body into pieces, Master? Not by the knife as you have done with the pear. How then?"

Jesus answered, "It is by the power of will. The will of a person is stronger than the strongest metal sword. Remember always that this magic is just that, the will of a person It is not the power of God or spirit. It is the magic of humanity. It is illusion. With the right teacher, anyone can learn one or all of these tricks. They can be mere entertainment in the court and have nothing to do with spiritual knowledge or the knowledge of God. The fact that a man can work these wonders does not make him a man of God. This is not what I have come to teach you. Any teacher can teach the student these things."

Peter asked then, "Master, how is it that after the things have become many pieces, it becomes whole again, as you have appeared this moment before us?"

Jesus responded, "The pieces are still moving, even after they have separated, and the speed at which they are moving is the same as when they were moving together. You only need to direct them to themselves and the thing again becomes whole. It is simply a matter of learning and practice and anyone can do these things."

Peter, of course, was intrigued and wanted to learn to appear and disappear as Jesus did. Jesus led them outside. He looked up and there was a cloud set off by itself. He instructed Peter to watch the cloud, and it disappeared. He instructed him to watch the spot where the cloud had been and the cloud reappeared.

Then he told Peter, "Now, Simon Peter, you do it. Separate the cloud into pieces and move the pieces in separate directions away from each other. Imagine that you are within the cloud and dissipating it as you would the fog on the ground as you move through it. Where you are, the fog cannot be. Your mind is as powerful as your body. Do the same thing here."

Peter concentrated with everything that was in him. After about ten minutes, the cloud went away and the apostles laughed and Peter was triumphant and eager to continue. "Now the body, Master!"

"First, put the cloud back, Simon Peter."

Peter concentrated again. Nothing happened. He paused, as if to start over, again nothing happened. Jesus intervened after about twenty minutes.

"Simon Peter, when the cloud has been put back, then we can move to the body. I would not lose you to the four winds as you have lost the cloud."

Jesus laughed and the apostles laughed. Peter was as embarrassed as Magdalen had been sitting on Jesus' couch.

No one really understood all the things that Jesus had said. No one was sure that they could ever do these things. Always, there was superstition and faith in God, which accounted for the wonders that Jesus was trying to help them to understand as natural things, magical only in the sense that they required training. Magdalen certainly did not understand. Nor could she see any reason for understanding. She had no need to turn water into wine and no reason to disappear, at least not at the moment. Furthermore, she felt that if people could all do what Jesus had just done then there could be intruders in a person's home that you could not even see. She wasn't sure that any of this was worthwhile, and as soon as they were alone, she said so.

"Good, Magdala, then you know that what is worthwhile is the meaning of spirit, and the magic will never get in your way. Magic, superstition, tradition, and ritual are things that come as you search for spirit, but these are resting places for your ego, they are not the destiny of humanity. Humanity's destiny goes far beyond magic. I have used magic as a means to raise the attention of the multitudes. I have used magic to instill faith in my words. Now I use magic as a way to teach you how very little the magic itself means. You have learned; pray then that they learn with you before I leave them to their production of illusion. There will be magicians among the children of God. Pray that there will also be children of God among the magicians. Let my passing be the beginning of spirit among people of all nations. And let my passing also be the end of illusions that deceive people into believing that spirit is only within those who work wonders and words but still do not know the Father from whence they have come."

Magdalen asked him when he would leave, and he responded that it would be soon. She asked him if he were going to disappear now and he assured her that he would remain whole from now until his leaving. She gave a great sigh of relief at that promise. He laughed again, but it was a gentle and understanding laugh.

When morning came, Jesus sent Magdalen to find John and send him to the other apostles to tell them that he required their presence. She didn't have far to go. John was on the road coming to the house. After she sent him on his mission, Magdalen returned home. Jesus was outside the house looking up at the sky and thinking deeply as he did. She found Mother Mary inside.

Jesus' mother said, "He will leave us today."

Magdalen felt tears well and her heart pound as if in fear. She went back out and found him just as he had been when she arrived. But he turned and held her then.

"Magdala, there will come a time when you will understand that going is not going at all. This body will leave, but this man is present with you always. And the spirit that has grown in this body has outgrown it as a child outgrows his clothes and must take on the cloak of a man. I have outgrown my use for this world, but its need for me is filled by the presence of my spirit. My love for you in body, that you will miss. My love has been more than that. It has been a love of the spirit that you will never be without. Do not be sad in my leaving, but instead be joyful at my growth and at my life. I do not, this time, die. I live eternally with the Father and know only love and light, not the darkness and emptiness and forgotten memories of the sepulcher. Do not be afraid, for you will come to no harm. I promise you that ever I will watch over you and over my mother from a place where I can be of more service to you than ever I could as a husband with a body. I have outgrown this world, but I have not outgrown the love that we have shared. Instead, I have become that love and on my leaving love is all I shall be. And you will see, love is eternal. It will be known by every person that walks the path of this world and my memory shall be forever."

"Love lives eternally, but remember, husband, I am with child, your child, who shall now be born without the benefit of an earthly father."

Magdalen didn't know that she was angry with Jesus, but there was anger in her voice and in her heart just then. He could know the hairs on her head and yet seemed unaware of her needs now.

"My Magdala, my sweet Mary," Jesus held her tightly to his chest and kissed her forehead.

"You hold within you the future for the world. You hold within your womb a future faith. You hold love within your womb, Magdala, and a glorious love it shall be."

Jesus motioned for her to sit with him upon the grass.

"Wife, you have told no one of your pregnancy not even my mother, yet you know that she is aware of it. I felt it best to let you be the first to speak of it. It is a mother's right to choose her time for telling such things. Tell her now so she can rejoice with you after I am gone."

There was a grin that emerged from Jesus' lips. Magdalen smiled wide too, but only momentarily.

"How can I rejoice?" The anger was unmistakable.

"Magdala, rejoice with me for our child who will bear the truth into the future world. Rejoice with me that her Father and mine have sown their seed and brought forth such a lovely flower. Rejoice with me that together you and I have conceived the child of love, for love, and to love. She will be, indeed, a flower of the Divine."

Jesus' head was raised as if he were giving praise to the heavens.

"Know that I will never leave her, but remain with her in visions and in dreams. She will know me as dearly and as deeply as anyone but you, my Magdala. Know that. Know too that she will be filled with your fire, your desire for exploration and your search for knowledge, but she will bear my moods and my need for solitude and for jest. Expect this child to make the remainder of your life a journey of unpredictable roads that will take you far from hearth and home."

Jesus knew that she carried a girl. Magdalen couldn't talk. She couldn't say anything at all. If she had, she would have wept for reasons she was unsure would be spiritually valid.

Jesus now placed his hand upon Magdalen's belly and blessed his child. He promised again that his earthly family, while they would have to endure the circumstances of life, would never want for support and love. He called upon his Heavenly Father and then upon the Goddess that Magdalen knew so well to be

Grandfather and Grandmother of his offspring and to bless and care for their daughter all the days of her life. He ended the blessing by kissing Magdalen's abdomen and stroking her hair for the last time.

"I will not say goodbye, my Magdala, but only that I love you and will be with you both always."

The apostles began to arrive and he asked them to wait outside as he went in to his mother. Magdalen didn't know what he said to her. But she was sure that Mother Mary was feeling all the same things that she was, and that he responded to them with the deepest love and respect that he had ever shown her. She was wiping tears as they came out together.

He began to walk out into the fields and they all followed in anticipation of his next words. When he had found a grassy place in the sun, he sat himself down and began to speak as if each man and woman were the only one there. It was the most personal feeling and yet the thing was becoming very, very public. Disciples began to arrive, one at a time, in couples, and in small groups. It was as if someone had sent them the message to come. It was as if they were told to be there, but to Magdalen's knowledge no message was ever sent. Seventy to seventy-five people, all of them disciples of Jesus during his lifetime, gathered together. Each one felt a personal presence with the Master. Magdalen could see it in their eyes. Each one was not surprised to find the others there and each one knew that in some way they had to be here at this time. It was sort of a strange scene really. All these men and women were mesmerized by the words that now came slowly and methodically from Jesus.

"Brethren, what is a disciple, but one who learns? You have been students to this teacher, and brothers to this man. In my life, you followed me as your Rabbi and your Master. In my death, you mourned my going and awaited my return. You believed in my promises, and in your faith you were strong, even in your doubting, you found new faith. And I kept my promises. For the love of a disciple is met by the Master with love. And there is no finer love than the love that teaches; this is the love of the Father that is God.

"And what I have taught you is all that you can understand for now. There is nothing more that I can do for you in this world. But from another place, from the place to which I now depart, I can do much for you. I cannot take away your pain. I cannot find a home for you. But from my home, I can show you the way to do these things. Through the Paraclete, the holy one who is spirit only, I can reach you and secure in your head thoughts that will ensure your victory over the evils that humanity has conjured into this world. Is it not better then that I leave you now and go to that home that will enable me to do more for you? Is it not better upon a path of darkness to have a light than a leader? For in the darkness, even the leader cannot see. But with a light in your hand, you can move freely in the darkness. You have no need for a leader to show you the pitfalls and the sand pits and the rocks and the crevices. I am that light. I have been the leader whose light was too dim sometimes to show the path to those behind me. But now I am the light itself and there is no shadow of my humanity to cloud your vision of the Way any longer.

"Your way has been my Way for as long as I have lived. Earthly life in awareness of God has been my way and yours. Now though, I am the Way itself, for there is no body to encumber me. I cannot fall into the pits, nor stub my foot on the rocks, nor find myself caught in the crevices of life. I am the Way, and not merely the traveler upon it. And what I have done, I have taught you to do also. The truth is that I am. That truth is the only spoken wisdom ever arrived at by humanity.

"You are, just as I am. That truth is the only truth that exists. It is everlastingly truth, for when you are - you are. Of this there is never doubt. You are, not because of God, not by way of your mother, not as a result of the seed of your earthly father, you are - because you are. That is the only truth that cannot be disputed. I am is the truth of God. And I am is the truth of humanity. I am the truth, the way, and the light. These things you believe. These things I have taught you. These things are the legacy that I leave behind for this world. Learn that you are these things too, and you will join me in my home. By the presence of the Paraclete, you will understand and accept these things. For it is by that spirit that I have come to know the Father. It is by that spirit that I have come to know myself. It is by that spirit that I have come to know you. It is by that spirit that I have come to have your love.

"My going now is the prelude to the coming of Christ among all people. I have come as the Christ in man, but in the time to come Christ will live among the human lot. I have been the leader and now I am the light. Watch in the light and find yourselves secure in your travels through this world."

At this, his body began to rise above the earth. He floated just above the heads of the tallest men and he raised his hands in blessing with the sign that he had shown to Magdalen as the nature of humanity's connection with God.

As he said, "In the name of the Father, there is found the source of life and the light of the world, In the name of the Son, there is found the way to everlasting life through the body of man. In the name of the Holy Spirit, is found the knowledge of single truth that unifies the source with its body and its mind."

And his hands moved in the sign and his body began to dissipate slowly, very slowly. He disappeared into the air just as he had appeared that day upon his couch.

There was no weeping. There was no discussion. The apostles had been given instructions to teach and to preach the way, the truth and the light. They had been told that the Paraclete would come to them, and that they were to remain together until the spirit had visited them. Mother Mary and Magdalen moved to return home, but John stopped them and asked what they intended to do. They told him that they were unsure but knew that everything would be all right. Magdalen said that Jesus had not left at all; it was only his body that had gone. John seemed to understand what she was saying and then left the women to themselves. The apostles remained together as he had told them to. The remaining disciples left as they had come; very little was being said among these men and women. There was a reverent sort of silence. There was no grief. Magdalen felt as though the grief would come later. As a matter of fact, she knew that it would. For now though she needed to return home and find space for her own feelings.

When they arrived at the house, Mary and Magdalen sat together on the couch and said nothing. The emotions of the day and the journey itself had tired them. They had nothing to share in words just then, and each of them knew the feelings of the other. They fell asleep in each other's arms.

Chapter 11

The Paraclete

Both Magdalen and Mother Mary knew that Nazareth was not the place for them just now. They made the journey to Jerusalem and arrived at the inn where the apostles were gathered together. Nicodemus was with them, and Martha, and Joseph Justus, and Matthias. Joseph of Arimathea was there too with his two daughters. The apostles had gone directly to Jerusalem after the Ascension, as Jesus had instructed, to wait for the Paraclete. They had met the others at the temple where they had gone to pray.

By the time that the women arrived every disciple in Jerusalem knew of the Lord's Ascension and of the presence of the apostles within the city. Everyone had been instructed to hold this information in complete secrecy. There was still fear among them that the Romans or the Jews would take some sort of action against the disciples of Jesus in order to protect themselves from the public opinion that this Master was the Messiah who would return to be king.

The feeling in the room was one of apprehension. Everyone awaited the arrival of this Paraclete, yet unsure of what or who the spirit would be or how it would come to them. No one knew when or in what way to expect this arrival of knowledge.

It was past mid-day when Magdalen and Mother Mary arrived, and the disciples and their families were leaving to arrive at their homes and hotels before dark. The dark streets of Jerusalem were not the place for disciples to be these days. The apostles had taken up residence together in this single room.

The women elected to stay with them, both for the financial reasons and for the safety of male company.

The eleven apostles and the two women were left with Joseph and Matthias who had been with them from the beginning; and a discussion began about the obligation to fulfill scripture by replacing Judas Iscariot. There were a lot of strong feelings regarding Judas and the betrayal that everyone knew he had committed. There had been little conversation about him, however, until this night. Now they had to replace him and it seemed as if they were fearful that they would choose wrongly as they felt Jesus had done. But Magdalen knew, as they all did really, that Jesus had almost dictated to Judas the act that he had carried out. Judas, of course, followed the direction of the Master that had been given verbally and also the one that Magdalen knew had been given to him within his mind, the way Jesus had sent messages back and forth with her when Lazarus was about to be buried alive. Judas, though, obviously could not live with the outcome. Magdalen thought that he felt Jesus would save himself and that his act was one that would only help prove the divinity of the Christ that he knew Jesus to be.

Judas had been in charge of all the financial matters, the purchasing, the hiring of rooms and servants. It was because of their common interest in finance and business that he and Nicodemus had been together so often and had been such good friends. Nicodemus had a hard time accepting the betrayal of Judas. He had a harder time accepting his fate to suicide.

Peter was the first to suggest that the position be filled remembering distinctly that Jesus had left this instruction and somewhat concerned that the thing be done before the arrival of the Paraclete. It was decided that these two men were the best selections and they drew lots for the position of Judas. Matthias was selected, congratulated by Joseph, and quietly accepted what he obviously held to be an honor. Joseph left then feeling that he would be intruding on any other business of the group. Peter had rented the room and the meals and now called down the hall that the servants might begin preparation for this evening's supper.

As the men, each in his turn, were offered basins to cleanse themselves before the meal, they began to talk of the coming of the Holy Spirit. Peter and Andrew recalled the baptism of Jesus by John the Baptist, who by this time had been beheaded after a long imprisonment.

Peter said, "Our Lord said then, after John had performed the rite, that it was good to be baptized, and that unless a man be born again first of the water and then of the Holy Spirit, he would not enter into the kingdom of heaven."

Andrew responded, "John had not wanted to baptize the Lord Jesus. He said it was Jesus who should baptize him. But he followed the Rabbi's instruction and carried out the thing despite his apprehensions. It was an emotional scene for John, and for anyone that watched him. It was because of his display and because of his apparent lunacy that we questioned the rite at all. I remember that Jesus remarked privately later that the lunacy of John was to be his earthly downfall. He was frightening people and the wife of Herod most particularly. The man went about screaming and shouting. He was quite mad, really. Jesus knew it, too. But he didn't seem to care about that. He said that what was written must be done, despite the current circumstances of John's mind. I think that John even frightened himself."

Peter offered yet another idea, "Perhaps the Paraclete will come to baptize us, as John baptized the Master with water. Perhaps John himself will come again to do it. Or Jesus will appear as he has done before. No, I don't think the Master will come, but perhaps John. Jesus said that John was the reincarnation of Elias. He said that men live many lives in many bodies to complete the work. Perhaps John will come in another body to do the bidding of the Master and baptize us now with the spirit."

Peter was getting carried away again. John knew it and he spoke up.

"There is no call for anticipation. The spirit will not be the ghost or the body of John. The Master explained to me while we rested that the spirit works within the mind and that there is no need for the element of water. The spirit is symbolized by the element of fire. If anything at all, the spirit will descend upon us as fire to purify us in mind, the way that water purifies the body that is bathed in it."

Mother Mary spoke then about something she had not even told Magdalen. She spoke of Jesus' return home after his long absence. She told how he came to her for the first time after his return and how she all but failed to recognize him. He had been gone a long time, yes, but a mother always knows her son. But Jesus was different. He was not the man that she would have expected him to be. He seemed meek in some ways and strong in others. These things in him were beyond the point of moderation. They were traits that contradicted themselves, and made him appear almost melancholy, or sometimes apathetic. Yet she knew that he was neither of these. His traits displayed themselves as something that they were not.

When she questioned Jesus about it, he had responded that he had received the initiation of water, and later of fire. He had told her very little of what had occurred on his journeys, but this he had told her. He explained that with the initiation of water he had come to know his manhood and to control his body within the world. His temper, his fear, his love and compassion had become pure and were things that he controlled outwardly and inwardly, and that was why he appeared sometimes to be apathetic. The initiation of fire had instilled him with the desire to teach, and to preach and to share his baptism of water. It was the fire of initiation with the spirit that had coaxed him back to Nazareth and to the needs of the world. It was the fire that burned in him that made him love all things and all people enough to serve in the way that even then he knew he would. He had about him a feeling of melancholy displayed that was

125

really a meditative state that enabled him to see the need and fill it for others. He attributed this to the fire. He had not said what either initiation had consisted of but only that he had gone through these things as rites, or rituals, or a religion of the true God.

The apostles had a great interest in the time that Jesus had been here before them, and they had a great respect for his mother. Magdalen's position among them was something that they had always felt was less than admirable. They tolerated her presence more than respected it. From the very beginning, they had felt that the Master was less than wise for having concerned himself with this woman. They met his demand for her acceptance with a cordial tolerance for the most part. And Magdalen wasn't sure how they would feel now. They knew that Mother Mary and she had become close, and that if they wanted Mother's presence, they would have Magdalen's with it. She was thinking about what Jesus had told her of all these things of water and fire, baptism and the spirit. She wasn't sure if she should impart her information or not. John, her one friend among the apostles, looked at Magdalen with anticipation and with his eyes encouraged her to speak.

"Jesus spoke to me, as he did to John, about the working of the spirit within mind. He talked also of the baptism of water that purifies one's emotions and feelings. He said that baptism rids a person of his sin, which is really the guilt that one has attached to all the thoughts, words and actions or omissions of one's life until baptism. It is after the person accepts water as the symbol of purification that one can begin anew without guilt or blame, fear or regret. Because with the symbolic cleansing of the body, comes the cleansing of the mind of the past. The spirit, he said, is something that comes later. It comes at a time when people are afraid of the future, as we are now afraid. The spirit is something that can bring presence of mind in the here and now and then one does not anticipate or fear the future. It is a burning desire that is left by the spirit to show its presence to others. He said that the fire of the spirit would some day bring to all people on earth the desire to share their love and their knowledge of God, which would then establish them in a kingdom of heaven."

The conversation went on as they ate and then lay down on mats to retire for the night. John held Magdalen's hand as he lay next to her like a child securing himself next to his mother. Yet he was like a brother in another way, telling her that she did well to speak.

In the morning the still fearful men and women remained in the room that sealed them from the outside and banded them together as a spiritual community. They were in prayer, even meditation, when the spirit came.

The room was filled with the sound of a great wind and yet they could not feel a breeze and not a hair on their head was moved. An unexplainable glow suddenly lit the upper quarters like many lamps. Sweet smelling perfume permeated the air and everyone fell to their knees. There were many spirits in the room with them, faceless people who said nothing but seemed to be attending, reverently and with love, this ceremony of light. Tongues of fire appeared over each one's head seeming to consume their thoughts with its blaze. The Paraclete was burning away apprehension and mistrust, fear and doubt. It came to them all. Not one person or spirit was immune to its dazzling brilliance or its profound affect upon the consciousness. It was as if some great honor was bestowed upon Jesus' band of followers and one could almost hear legions of angels singing their praises to God. It was an awe inspiring moment that left each one of them filled with devotion and unexplained rapture. Magdalen knew even in her current state of ecstasy that this would be a change in consciousness that would enable and empower them to carry out the work of Jesus from that moment on.

When the enlightenment ended everyone felt secure, confident and right in their truth and their ability to teach that truth. Now there was an unspoken pact among them of loyalty, trust and service. They saw fear as its useless self. While they vowed to practice wisdom in their daily affairs, they no longer feared the teaching that the apostles were sure they must and would do.

That teaching began immediately as the men moved together to the streets, taking up positions so as to create a forum of sorts. They were eloquent orators now with exactly the right words to express humanity's need for freedom of thought and unconditional faith in spirit. They were calling the people to baptism and to a change of heart. They were commanding respect and demanding acknowledgement as they began to speak. Their mouths opened and they began to talk in other tongues, a language that was unique from any other yet understood by all.

There were Jews and gentiles dwelling at Jerusalem, devout men and women out of every nation. And when the noise had been heard many people came together and were confused, because every person heard the apostles speak in their own language. The crowd was amazed and marveled at the eloquence of these men from Galilee. Parthians, and Medes, and Elamites, and the dwellers in Mesopotamia, and in Judea, and Cappadocia, in Pontus, and Asia, Phrygia, and Pamphylia, in Egypt, and in the parts of Libya about Cyrene, and strangers of Rome, Jews and proselytes, Cretes and Arabians, all heard them speak in their native tongues about the wonderful works of God.

Some questioned the meaning of what was happening before them. Others mocked the apostles and their words saying that perhaps they were drunk. Peter, standing up for them, raised his voice and spoke.

"Men and women of Judea, and all of you that dwell at Jerusalem, listen to me.

"These men are not drunken, as you suppose, remember it is still morning. They are fulfilling the prophecy of Joel. God has poured out the Holy Spirit upon our flesh and upon your flesh the power to see and to dream and to believe.

"Men and women of Israel, hear these words. Jesus of Nazareth, a man of God walked among you doing miracles and wonders and signs, these were works of God, as you know for yourselves. He was crucified at the hands of those that feared him and were arrogant enough to think they were righteous. But the Father raised him up as your scriptures predicted. And he walked for some forty days among us and told us all manner of wisdom. This is the power by which we speak to you now.

"Have a change of heart now, and be baptized every one of you as Jesus requested and release your guilt and your fear, your regret and your blame. Let not the laws of religion shame you any longer, but instead bask in the love that has brought you here. Then you too will receive the gift of fire in your hearts and you too will shine in the presence of all people."

Many people accepted all this and had a change of heart. They found hope in the words of the apostles and moved to the river to be baptized by them. They gathered around the men and listened to their words and took instruction as to how they should pray and how to participate in the preparation and reception of the communion meal that Jesus had prescribed. The day was long and the apostles were wet to their waists from immersing so many souls into the river of baptism. They were cold to the point of numbness and they had not eaten since before their enlightenment. Magdalen and Mother Mary knew that it would soon be time to return to their room of security, their safe place, and to make plans for the future. Surely this day of miracles and mobs of baptisms had to end soon.

The women had been helping all day. They walked into the water with the infirm and the elderly holding them steady and drying them when they emerged cleansed and relieved of the past. They had carried heavy water jars so that the apostles and the crowd could drink freely and avoid the effects of the hot sun. Together they had borne litters for the sick that wanted healing. Now they were tired too. The energy that the Paraclete had given empowered the spirit, but all of their bodies were filled with fatigue. As the long lines of spiritual aspirants began to shorten and the crowd of onlookers dwindled, Mother Mary and Magdalen returned to the rented room and ordered that food be prepared for the returning men.

When the apostles arrived wet and weary they were conscious men who were more eager for discussion than food. Peter began his recollection with questions.

"Did you see the dove? It was suspended there in mid air at the ceiling when the wind came."

Mother Mary and Magdalen both proclaimed a vision of a dove within the room. But after considering this, Peter assured them all that the dove must have been there in the physical sense, since more than one person beheld it. His logic was not well accepted. Some of the others grumbled about his comment feeling that the dove was indeed a sign of the peace that they now all felt within their hearts.

John had new found wisdom falling from his mouth.

"Be the dove real or imagined, it is a symbol of what we are now and shall remain if we refrain from argument."

The others nodded agreement as they were reminded of the profundity of what had taken place that day.

"Magdalen and Mary, Dear Mother of our Lord, what did you two perceive? To me the light was blinding and I saw nothing but the brilliance of its golden rays."

James the younger questioned the women for he knew that they were far superior in their ability to perceive the things of spirit than the others.

"During the presence of the Holy Spirit, I felt and saw light energies as if they were smoke around us all." Magdalen spoke in response. "It was sometimes difficult to know the difference between energy fields and true smoke from the fire and lamps. Color and light made the difference, however, and after some readjustment of my vision the distinction became clear. There seemed to be a slight fogginess or smoky aura around the spirits too. It reminded me of the smoke of incense created in the temple. The smell was much the same too."

They all agreed that the sweet scent of the room commanded the same reverence as altar incense. Mother Mary offered her comments.

"I could see a large vortex of light at the crown of each person's head. They were like tornadoes of bright white light and within the center of each vortex was a flame, like a tongue of fire. I believe the flames were the source of the change within each one's mind. They were purifying us, ridding our minds of the debris of fear, guilt, blame and regret. It put me in mind of the alchemist's fire of purification that separates the gold from other minerals less valuable. We have been alchemically changed, I think."

"We have been altered, indeed." Peter responded.

And the others bowed their heads in thanksgiving for this great event and change of heart within them. When this moment of prayer was over James voiced his ever present need for food. There was a relaxed laughter as the servants were called to serve the meal.

After they had eaten and once again shared the Rite of Remembrance that Jesus had ordained, the apostles decided that they would leave Jerusalem as he had instructed them. They would travel again in pairs and preach the word of God to the entire empire. They would ask for alms on which to survive and they would take their meals with those that would listen to them.

"What of the women? They must be cared for. Jesus' mother and his wife were left to our concern. It is not right for them to travel with us and not right that they be left here to fend for themselves."

James spoke up quickly to answer John's question.

"Then, John, you and I will remain here in Jerusalem. This shall be our post and here we will continue Jesus' good work as well as look after the women."

Everyone seemed to agree that this was a most practical idea. Surely Jerusalem could not be ignored and surely John, the youngest, and James, the strongest, should be the ones to remain behind with the women. Magdalen thought this to be rather absurd really, for Jesus had promised that the spirit would always protect her and his mother and their unborn daughter, but she remained silent.

Chapter 12

A Broken Promise and an Injured Heart

Magdalen's faith was soon to be shaken. After the moment of Pentecost and the bonding and association that resulted, it hardly seemed possible that a day of tragedy should follow, but this day would be the worst in her life.

Mother Mary had gone to do laundry. Magdalen was alone in the house when a visitor came to the door. He was someone that she recognized as a disciple of Jesus, but whom she did not know by name. There was a second man who remained on the road, but she didn't recognize him at all.

The man at the door inquired of Magdalen as to the whereabouts of Jesus. He had heard, he said, that Jesus was still alive and walking about town. She assured him several times over that Jesus was no longer among them but that after his death he had returned for a time. She even began to tell him something of yesterday and the Paraclete, but he seemed not to believe her as he continued to walk about the room and look in every corner. He proceeded to enter her mother-in-law's private room and here Magdalen drew the line. It became obvious that it was not Jesus that he was looking for.

When she stood between him and the door to Mother Mary's room, he began shouting about a child. He was really looking for a child that it had been rumored Jesus had fathered. He was sure that Magdalen was hiding that child here. She tried to insist that no child existed and he began shouting obscenities and he struck her. Magdalen was stunned, but not unused to the temperaments of men she continued to argue. He struck her again and she fell to the floor.

The man continued to beat her and to tear off her clothes. Eventually Magdalen lost consciousness for what turned out to be only the first time. When she regained her senses she was on the frame of Mother Mary's bed. Trying to sit up, she realized that her hair was tied around the frame and as a result any movement of her head was near impossible. Her hands and feet were bound with ribbon. The intruder stood over her again shouting his vulgar oaths and calling her whore, temptress and Satan. He vowed to show her, he said, what she was and what she was made for. Magdalen tried convincing him that she would cooperate, that it would be more enjoyable that way. It made him angrier and with one hand he stuffed something into her mouth in order to silence her while the other he shoved far inside of her. Magdalen writhed and screamed in pain. She could see the man from the street watching in the window and her anger made her fight even harder. How could he watch and enjoy her pain?

The assailant urinated on her as he handled her body and then slapped her face from side to side. Somehow the ribbons came loose in the struggling and Magdalen began to kick violently at him. He hit her hard and again she passed out. This time she came to as she felt her hair being handled. Suddenly his knife passed the side of her face and her head was free. He had cut her hair at the scalp and Magdalen lost consciousness once more.

Now she was on the floor and her legs were spread wide. He had secured them this time to a yoke. The length of hair that had been cut from her head was wrapped around her neck and he had hold of it as he sat her up by pulling from in front of her. Magdalen's hands were free now, but she realized that there was no sense to struggle. He could strangle her with the hair he held in his hand. He pulled her head down under the yoke and secured the hair. Now he tied her hands to her feet and tipped her backward. When he finished, Magdalen was unconscious again.

Once she stirred as she felt a burning pain on her hipbone and again when she vomited as the gag choked her. It was getting dark when he put her back on the bed. The other man still stood in the window. Then just once he stabbed Magdalen with his knife. The pain of the blade was under her rib cage and severe enough to jolt her head with a lightening bolt shock of energy. This time unconsciousness was brought about by relief as the man escaped through the still open door.

Mother Mary's face was the next thing that Magdalen could recognize. Through teary half-closed eyes she looked at her mother-in-law thinking that she must have come back soon after the man had left because she had not bled to death. Then she lost consciousness once more.

Mother Mary was appalled but not panicked by Magdalen's condition. Once she was sure that her daughter-in-law was alive and that the pool of blood beneath her made the situation look worse than it was, she covered Magdalen's naked body with clean linen. Her hands went to the stab wound in Magdalen's side and with little pressure she created a healing just as Jesus would have done. With the bleeding now stopped, she called out silently for the Goddess to continue working through her hands. And then again she called out this time aloud to her son.

"Jesus, heal the wounds of her heart, for only you can do this. Show us the reason for this crime so that she will not be filled with fear or consumed by anger."

Satisfied that her son would send healing of the heart from heaven, Mother Mary turned her attention to the burn on Magdalen's hip along with three others that she thought must have been made with either his sword or the poker from the oven after the assailant had heated it in the fire. When Magdalen stirred from the pressure of her hands Mother Mary only asked if her daughter-in-law knew her attacker. Of course, Magdalen could not name him and shook her head to say no. Mother Mary proceeded to bathe her with water and olive oil. She stroked Magdalen's now cropped hair and shed tears for the pain of mind and spirit that she was going through. Mary placed a veil around Magdalen's head and covered her with warm blankets. Finally she forced wine that had been drugged into her and Magdalen fell asleep without ever telling the tale of her attack.

Every time that she awakened there was more wine and more oil for her body and then sleep again. She listened to Mother Mary sing children's songs as she dozed off. This went on for more than a week. Then one morning, Mother Mary helped Magdalen to bathe and dress and to eat. The poor woman was able to walk about a little that day, but she had so much bruising that the pain drove her back to her bed quickly. She kept wondering how someone could be with Jesus and know his love and then be so crazy and cruel as to assault his wife. She wondered, too, about Jesus' promise to protect her and where his loving heart was when this was happening. Magdalen held her hand to her belly and hoped to feel life within it. She was afraid that her unborn child had suffered because of her injuries and she wept bitterly at the thought.

As the days went on Magdalen had more hours of consciousness. There didn't seem to be any need to talk about what had happened, and Mother Mary did not coax her so Magdalen remained silent. She soon gained awareness that her mother-in-law had cleaned up and arranged things since the incident because the house and its furnishings seemed to be in pretty much their usual order. It was reassuring and yet scandalous that life could go on as normal after such an ordeal. By this time Magdalen felt more anger than pain and more doubt in the future than she ever knew possible. She was afraid, but even her fear could not keep her awake long. She dozed frequently through the days. There were a lot of tears when she was awake, usually when she felt the shortness of her hair. Somehow that hair was who she was, and it was gone. Evening would come and more drugged wine that clouded the memory of her assault and brought her to fitful dreams.

Weeks went by and Magdalen's wounds continued to heal. Her grief subsided but was not gone for the new mother's greatest fear now was that the rape and violent bruising of her body had affected the child within her. She was sure that Mother Mary knew that. She of all people could see the light of her child's life within Magdalen's eyes, so there was no reason to discuss her fears.

Mother Mary had confided in James and John, as well as Peter when he returned from a mission, that Magdalen was with child and about her assailant's reason for coming to their home. The men had heard that others suspected that there was a child to inherit the holiness of his father. With a blank stare Magdalen listened to their discussion and the news that someone might be looking for Jesus' daughter at that very moment.

"Little do they know that the child is yet within me," she thought, "and for the moment is safe from their envy. And she is a girl."

The men, though, felt this safety was not enough. It was not enough for the child or for Magdalen. The discussion of a safe haven for mother and child continued and James looked to Magdalen's face for some sign of agreement or disagreement. It seemed that now they were more willing than ever before to listen to Magdalen's words and she had none to share. Perhaps this pregnancy had brought them to truly see her as the Bride of Christ.

This made little difference to Magdalen for they were speaking of moving the women to Egypt or perhaps further east. Now she broke her silent stare with pleading.

"James, to Gaul. I want to go to Gaul. My dreams tell me that they would not search in Gaul."

All heads turned to hear what she had to say.

"Jesus comes to me in my dreams. He carries me off to Gaul, to a place filled with peace and understanding. He sets me upon the ground to deliver my child into the womb of the earth and she is safe."

Magdalen drew a deep breath.

"To Gaul, James, to Gaul."

Mother Mary remembered her prayer that Jesus would heal Magdalen's heart and believed that her dreams were his way of accomplishing that. She was sure that they should move to Gaul before the child was born. But the men argued against it. Gaul was a land of unknowns and they were convinced that Magdalen's dreams were the result of the drugs rather than intuition or guidance. Magdalen attempted to listen to the conversation but the apostles' words were drowned out by her inability to focus clearly, and Mother Mary again helped her to lie down to rest. Several times more she awoke that day and several times more dozed back into her stupor. Pain and exhaustion kept her from being fully aware of what was going on around her.

"Perhaps it is better to sleep than to be aware," she thought.

At least for now Magdalen would let these men take charge. The decision was made to remove the women to Egypt. While Mother Mary would have preferred Gaul, James, Peter, and John felt that going to Egypt would in some way fulfill the prophecies. Mary agreed that it was more than ironic that Magdalen would flee to Egypt to protect her child just as she had when Jesus was but a baby. Finally, everyone agreed and was content with the decision, everyone but Magdalen. She knew that she was too weak to win an argument with the determined apostles, yet her heart told her that the dreams were indeed a message from her husband. Silently she prayed and silently she prepared for the trip with Mother Mary's help.

The journey ahead would not be a comfortable one. Peter had called on Joseph of Arimathea, Nicodemus, and even Lazarus to help with the packing and with the financial needs of the trip. Joseph and Nicodemus were eager to share their wealth with the Master's family. Magdalen had to wonder now if some of her feelings of insecurity were reflected from the past and if perhaps there was some true friendship and respect developing with these men that was not there before. She entered in and out of sleep as the day wore on and the activity escalated around her.

The journey to Egypt began the next day at dawn. James and Lazarus drew the lots that gave them the honor and duty of escorting the women. A single ox pulled the cart upon which Mother Mary, Magdalen, and their precious belongings road. It was hot and windy and Magdalen tired easily yet; Mother had promised that she would not have to take any more of the herbal mixture that so clouded her mind. This meant that there was more pain but she endured it for the sake of keeping a strong mind as they traveled. James and Lazarus stopped frequently for her because they were concerned about the welfare of the child in her womb. She had felt a quickening soon after stopping the drug-laden wine and the movements of the infant made Magdalen feel more assured of her daughter's future. Mother Mary told her over and over that there was no reason for concern, but Magdalen was now a mother herself and filled with the anxiety that is common to pregnant women. She began to look forward to their arrival in Egypt and to the safety that it promised. Both James and Lazarus spoke continuously of that promise in an attempt to ease the women's minds.

That first night of the journey the group stayed at an inn, dining on hot food and sleeping in comfortable beds. Then the men decided that it would be of benefit to take roads less traveled and to stay clear of the crowds that immigrated on the main road. Many days and nights passed with little event. They slept by the side of the road and saw few strangers as they traveled. Each day Magdalen sat upon the cart in contemplation of the future. The wheels turned on the dirt roads and made noises that were almost hypnotic and this put her in a good place for pondering.

Mother Mary was concerned about her daughter-in-law's lack of zest and encouraged her to sew.

"Prepare a gown of ultimate beauty for the Princess when she arrives."

She handed Magdalen a sewing bag. As always, embroidery and sewing put Magdalen in a more positive frame of mind, and she began to heal more rapidly. Her appetite improved, and soon Mother could see a sparkle in Magdalen's eye when she spoke of the child and her arrival. The apostles were glad to see this positive change and never failed to look for ways of encouraging the little mother's growing enthusiasm. Soon they would arrive in Egypt to what end no one really knew, but the group, even Magdalen, was beginning to see it as a true haven of safety for her and her child

Each stitch put into the baby's new dress was a triumph for Magdalen. She was beginning to look forward to the child's arrival with anticipation as if she would be receiving a wonderful gift. After she had finished attaching bright red and yellow ribbons to the bodice she held up the dress for Mother Mary to see.

"I will present her in the temple as a Goddess is presented to the throne of the Almighty."

Mother Mary smiled a great grin. Magdalen was herself again, and it pleased her to see the light in her eyes.

"It is a wonderful gown, fit for a Princess indeed."

She touched the hem of the little dress as if to bless it and Magdalen returned her smile.

It was twenty-one days before they reached the ferry point on the banks of the Nile. The water was low and poles alone propelled the flat-bottomed cargo boat across this great dividing point. Carts, animals and travelers crowded the many boats that were coming and going across the river. Children clung to their mothers and to the wheels of the carts to keep from being lost in the crowd. Magdalen put her hand to her belly and whispered to her daughter.

"You will be safe once we reach the other side, my love."

Across the water Magdalen could see a small community with shops and fires from which the smell of cooking food drifted to entice travelers into the restaurants and inns that welcomed them. The idea of a new home and a city full of new and interesting people began to intrigue her. The notion of a marketplace with fresh fruits and vegetables, with ribbons and brass pots called to her senses. She was eager to disembark as the boat pulled into its slip. James lifted her down from the cart to the bank when they had safely moored.

"It will be safe here." He said reassuringly.

"It feels warm and wonderful James, thank you for keeping us safe."

Magdalen had not expressed her gratitude for any of the apostles' endeavors before now and James was glad to be acknowledged. Somehow his relationship with Jesus' wife had grown to be the love of a brother for his sister. He knew that her pain both in body and in mind had awakened him to her true value. The thought of losing her had shown him how much he cared and how much she had contributed to the sanity of the apostles as a group.

"I will ever keep you as safe as I can. This is a promise, Magdalen, from your brother James."

He wanted to bind the relationship and proclaim his love. Magdalen gave him a gentle hug and touched her belly.

"This will be home, little one," she said. " At least for a while."

She hugged James again this time more tightly.

Chapter 13

Life in Egypt

In the days that followed, the men found a permanent home for their little family. It was modest but comfortable and soon furnished fully with Magdalen's few belongings and items from the Egyptian marketplace where she loved to shop. The colors were magnificent and the textures beckoned her to touch every fabric and fixture. The fruits were just as delightful and Magdalen ate of them all. It seemed that coming to Egypt had been the right decision after all.

Magdalen wondered, though, about Jesus' words and instructions. He had thought that Mother Mary and Magdalen would be better off in Jerusalem or Nazareth than traveling off like this. But then he had also promised her protection and look what had come to pass only hours after he gave her his word that she and her child would be safe! Putting those broken promises out of her head was not easy, but Magdalen used the gaiety of the market to improve her mood. The melancholy was gone, and she once again found her zest for life and its future.

When the women were settled James left to join the other apostles in teaching across the empire. Lazarus worked as a harness maker and Mother Mary and Magdalen were involved only in the daily activities of women as they waited for the arrival of the child. It would still be three or four months before that happened. Mother Mary said that after the baby arrived she would return to Nazareth, her home was her home forever. Magdalen still wondered what lay to the west of them and thought that there would be a reason one day to travel to Gaul as her dreams had indicated.

Magdalen had interpreted dreams all of her life. To her they were meaningful ways in which the spirit world communicated with those on earth. Now her dreams were calling her to a new life, but not until her daughter was born and presented in the temple at Jerusalem. Sometimes she wondered which temple was the proper place to present such a little Goddess. At Magdala the girl might find true happiness, but that would not be Jesus' Way. At the Jewish temple of Yahweh she would only find guilt and fear. In her imagination Magdalen constructed a new temple for the Way that Jesus had taught. Then she mentally tore it down.

"God is Love, and requires no housing," she thought.

Once again her thoughts turned to her unborn child and the safety she wanted to provide for her.

The months that followed began to fill with the joyful anticipation of the baby's arrival. The little girl continued to move and Magdalen felt more confident of her health every day. The women waited without patience, as Magdalen grew larger and more uncomfortable. Her back ached with the weight of her body. Her skin was dry and cracking. Her arms looked like the back of some wild creature from the desert, and she began to shun the sun whenever possible. Mother Mary consoled her with tales of the beautiful and unique effects of child bearing.

"Magdalen, birthing is a mystery that cannot be solved but only experienced and only by women. You will find that when all this is over the life that you will hold will far outweigh in value the price you paid."

Mother Mary didn't want to sound admonishing, only informative.

"Women forget all this, my dear, or else there would be no people born to inhabit the earth."

She laughed at this and stroked Magdalen's hair which was now growing back profusely. Magdalen prayed that she would be renewed when the child arrived.

143

"God and Goddess let me endure with gratitude and rejoice in the greatness of a woman's body, but please give me back my senses and my waist when this is over."

The two women laughed until tears came to their eyes. Catching their breath and regaining composure took a few minutes. Then Mother Mary rubbed olive oil on Magdalen's parched skin and swollen belly.

"To care for and honor a pregnant woman is to care for and honor the creation of life. It is important to honor yourself now, Magdalen, because in so doing you honor all of creation and its cycles. Jesus would be doing this for you if he were here; I know he would. He was terribly excited about the child, you know."

Magdalen now asked a question of her mother-in-law that she had kept within for months.

"Why did he allow me to be raped and his daughter be put in danger? Why did such a loving husband abandon us when he did? Why could he not keep his promise of safety for us after he was gone?"

Tears flowed and where there had been joy moments before there was now deep sadness and loneliness in Magdalen's heart that could not be consoled. Mother Mary held her gently rocking back and forth to comfort her.

"I cannot answer your questions, Magdalen, only God knows the reasons and the purpose behind such pain. It is for us to trust that it is all done by God's will and according to the Way of love."

Magdalen continued to sob as her mother-in-law hummed the tunes of psalms of faith from scripture.

"Think about it Magdalen," Mother Mary interrupted her song. "Perhaps you can learn something here in Egypt that you would not have learned any where else. Perhaps your daughter must be born here so that you and she can have a point of departure on a special journey. I don't know, but your dreams might tell you, or even just someone in the marketplace that you meet by coincidence. Jesus always said that he would guide our Way, maybe this whole ordeal has been guided from beyond."

Magdalen raised her head and stopped her crying.

"Mother, I will be more open to the people I meet and more aware of the places I go. My dreams though call me always to Gaul. It is as if I have a great mission there that must be completed for my daughter's sake."

"Pay attention, Magdalen, and be aware. Keep on dreaming, but focus on honoring the life within you first and foremost. After the child is born it will be revealed to you, I am sure."

Mother Mary cautioned her about getting too carried away with destiny and neglecting the present.

"When your day of delivery comes, you will have great joy. Jesus will rejoice with you, as will I. For now, find peace in knowing that what ever comes God has his purpose."

With that Mother went back to her chores and Magdalen picked up her sewing once again.

"I will wait for the child's arrival focused on honoring the life within me. But when that day comes, life will be revealed to the world and answers revealed to me."

Magdalen made this determined affirmation as she took another stitch in the small garment she was preparing for her daughter.

"That will be the day of deliverance in more ways than one."

Delivery approached quickly now and Magdalen anticipated that each day would be her daughter's birthday. Mother Mary giggled at her impatience with understanding. Together they prepared a layette of clothing and linen for the little girl. Lazarus built a cradle and bought a down comforter to put inside it. The three immigrants to Egypt had become a family of love and familiarity in the midst of foreign languages and cultures.

Heavy and clumsy with the burden of life, Magdalen went to the marketplace everyday. She loved the activity and the colors, they raised her spirits and the new awareness she had vowed to was always present. One day as she passed through the aisles of shops her attention came to a young woman leaning against the wall apparently with no interest in what was going on around her. She looked rather lonely and sad. Magdalen approached the dark skinned woman with no apprehension.

"Are you alone?" she asked.

"I am always alone these days." Came the reply.

"Have you no family then?"

Magdalen was curious that a woman so young would be on the street alone.

"I have no one. My family was killed on the battlefields, and I am forced to support myself. You look as if you could use a good mid-wife, by the way. I can do that for you, for a price better than most. Simply give me room and board and I will help bring your child into this awful world."

The bitterness was obvious, but Magdalen knew that she must have this mid-wife and no other. She had been sent and Magdalen was sent to her too.

"You will come home with me this hour then." She took the woman's hand in hers and led her toward home. "What are you called?" Magdalen decided introductions were necessary.

"I am Sara." The woman offered no more information.

"I am Mary of Magdala. Most people call me Magdalen. I am a widow and live with my mother-in-law Mary and our dear friend Lazarus. You will like them. They are both very kind and warm." Magdalen was trying to warm the conversation as much as possible.

"Your time is very near." Sara attempted to change the subject with her observation. "I know these things. Your child is eager now."

Magdalen's hand went to her belly as it always did when she thought of her daughter. "Everything is ready now that God has sent me you." Magdalen looked into Sara's deep brown eyes that were now filled with curiosity.

"What do you mean, God sent me? You picked me up on the street and took pity on me, I think. But I'll take pity if it feeds me." Sara was curious about Magdalen's theory but skeptical to say the least.

Magdalen opened the door ahead of her new employee. "It is the Way, the way that God works. God sends you just what you need when you need it. It is what we believe."

"Well if that's the case then this God didn't send me a moment too soon. Your child is ready!"

Sara said it with conviction that she knew what she was talking about. Magdalen made the introductions and Mother Mary and Lazarus immediately opened to Sara despite her sarcasm and bitterness.

"She does need us and the Way of Love." Mother Mary whispered in Magdalen's ear as they set the table for supper. "Perhaps Sara is the reason that you came to Egypt, Magdalen. You can both benefit from this I am sure."

It took only a few minutes for Sara to acquaint herself with the little house and its cupboards. Then she motioned to Magdalen to sit down.

"You shouldn't be doing all of this. It is my job now. And you, mother-in-law, simply tend to her needs. It won't be long now."

With that Sara prepared a wonderful meal, served it and cleaned up the kitchen. Lazarus looked at the two bewildered women.

"She may be a dictator but she can cook and works hard. I like her." He said.

The three laughed and Magdalen grabbed her belly with both hands.

"What's more I think she's right, my daughter wants to meet all of you tonight." Magdalen announced her labor with joy.

Sara and Mother Mary made her comfortable and Lazarus left the house instructing them to bring word when the child arrived. This was a woman's moment and he went to wait with his male companions.

Through the night Magdalen's labor continued and with each contraction she whispered the name of Jesus. Mother Mary and Sara held her hands and kept her warm. It was evident that Sara was adept at what she did and knew exactly what Magdalen required for comfort and ease of delivery. She took care of every possible need.

The child arrived with the dawn. Like the first rays of light, she promised a new and better day for all. Magdalen named her daughter Sharon. She was small but strong and immediately suckled at her mother's breast. As Magdalen nursed for the first time, Sara put things back in order. She took away the soiled linen and the basin that she had used to wash the infant.

"This Way you have, I am sure it works for you. I have a way too."

She put a small bowl on the table next to Magdalen's bed. Inside of the bowl lay the umbilical cord that had nourished Sharon within her mother's womb.

"This is a gift from Isis, the Egyptian Goddess of Love and Fertility. It is said that kept in a place of the heart the cord will bind mother and child together for eternity."

"Then where will I keep it?"

Magdalen moved to get up but Sara restrained her.

"You have time to decide. It must dry up first anyway, rest for now."

Sara looked pleased that Magdalen had accepted this gesture with such graciousness.

"She will learn her father's Way from her mother and her grandmother, but she will always have the blessing of the Goddess Isis and a sacred bond with you that will live forever."

Sara put another blanket over Magdalen as if to say that the subject would now be dropped. Mother Mary had gone to fetch Lazarus and the family was soon reunited in celebration. That night Sara became an adopted child and seemed quite pleased with her new home.

At first light Lazarus sought out a courier to send word to the apostles of Sharon's arrival. The courier's journey had to begin right away, for although he could travel quickly to Jerusalem there was no time to waste. Magdalen would have her rite of purification in just seventy-two days when she would present Sharon at the temple.

Lazarus, anxious to immortalize mother and child, hired an artist, an Egyptian man, to paint a portrait of them. He promised to finish his painting before Magdalen would leave for Jerusalem. Magdalen found this artist and his ways extremely fascinating. He painted on a thin sheet of stone using vegetable dyes and oil to create his work. Mother and child didn't sit for their portrait. Instead, they went about their daily routine and the artist watched them intently and put on his "canvas" his impression of their likeness. He wore thick bands of gold about his arms and ankles and many chains of gold around his neck. It was apparent that he was devotional about doing this painting and that he has some deep feeling for Sharon. He painted her thick hair with such care and put so much beauty and age into the picture of an infant that she appeared much older than she really was.

Sara, too, became devoted beyond the usual expectations of a hired nurse. She tended to mother and child as if she knew the connection to Jesus and to the future, yet Magdalen was sure that she had not been told. Everyone around her knew that this child was indeed her name's definition - Princess, the daughter of a King and Queen.

Soon the courier returned with word that James and John were on their way. A feast and warm welcome were prepared and the day that the apostles arrived was filled with celebration. They were delighted, not only to see the precious heir to Jesus' holiness, but also to be reunited with one another. John hugged Mother Mary and Magdalen with great strength and embraced Lazarus with open arms. James gingerly lifted the infant from her cradle and held her close to him.

"She is as lovely as her mother and as divinely sent as was her father." He kissed the baby's face and handed her to Magdalen. "I have brought a gift from Jerusalem."

James opened his bag and reached inside. "It is the cup from Our Lord's last supper before his death. It is the cup he used to give us the Rite of Remembrance." Removing the linen cover that surrounded it, he set the cup on the table for everyone to see.

"I think it should be Sharon's one day and used only for the sacred Rite of Remembrance until then. It was Peter who saved it and kept it all these months after Joseph of Arimathea placed it in his care. He was most eager that you should have it, Magdalen."

"Oh Sara, that is where I will put the cord, in a true place of the heart!" Magdalen rushed off to retrieve the umbilical cord that Sara had dried and put in a small linen bag with a red ribbon to keep it closed. She put the little bag inside the cup and wrapped it again in its cover.

"Thank you, James, and my gratitude to Peter and Joseph for this gift. We will use it tonight when we share the Rite together again."

Sara and Magdalen then explained the blessing of Isis to the men. The entire household celebrated Sharon's birth with the sacred Rite that evening and then talked until just before dawn. They shared stories and remembrances with the new members of their spiritual family. James and John told all of them tales of the apostles' adventures as preachers of the Way.

After two days of resting in Egypt and catching up on all the news and gossip the disciples, John, James, Lazarus, Mother Mary and Magdalen set out on the journey back to Jerusalem for her purification ceremony. With them went the mid-wife Sara and even the artist whom Magdalen had come to call Michael because she could not say his Egyptian name or write it either.

Once again the cart had been loaded with belongings, but this time it was being pulled by two horses and each member of the party had a steed of their own. The journey would definitely be less strenuous now. They could stay at inns along the way and take well-traveled roads. No one was concerned now for mother or child as far as attack was concerned, because what the enemies of the Master's movement would be looking for was a male child. Sharon and her mother were safer for her gender. No one expected that the heir to the throne of Israel would be a girl. The Princess and the Queen were treated as such by those who traveled with them.

Chapter 14

Purification and a New Way

According to tradition Magdalen would take the place of Mother Mary as head of the household as soon as her period of purification had come to pass and Sharon had been presented at the temple as her firstborn gift to God. Women were considered unclean for seven days after their usual menses and an additional thirty-three days after the birth of a son or sixty-six days after the birth of a daughter. No one was ever able to tell Magdalen why there was this difference in the time for purification, but she had been repeatedly assured that it had nothing to do with a girl being more unclean than a boy since all children were considered innocent and pure by Jewish law.

Presenting Sharon at the temple was not necessary. It was only demanded by law that the firstborn male child be given to God. A daughter was presented only by the choice of her parents. The presentation of the firstborn was an ancient ritual based on the recognition that every life came from God and all things in life. The Jews offered their first crops, the first wine, the first domestic animals born. All things were from the Lord and so the first of everything belonged to God and God alone. Before the sons of Levi had been given the place of the priesthood, the firstborn sons of every Israelite family had become priests, servants and ministers of God. Magdalen had decided that presenting Sharon in temple would ordain her as a Priestess of the Way for the future.

They arrived in Jerusalem early in the day. It was not yet close to sunset but Magdalen decided to go to the baths to do her libations. She bathed, plaited the hair that had grown back thick and curly and polished her teeth with sand and salt. She wanted to appear fully purified and clean before her ceremony.

"It is not that I think I am unclean." She told Mother Mary as they bathed. "It is only that I want the dust of the road removed from me before I present such a wonderful gift to God."

The next morning Magdalen bought her offerings, two birds and a small goat. She felt somewhat dismayed about the end that these animals would come to, as she knew that either their necks would be wrung or their throats slit only to be burned in sacrifice. She wondered if she could even go through with this ritual, but she approached the temple nonetheless.

Magdalen walked up the very long flight of temple stairs holding the small birdcage in her left hand and leading the goat by a tether in her right. Mother Mary walked with her carrying Sharon adorned in the dress that Magdalen had prepared before her birth. Through the doors of the temple of Jerusalem, Magdalen found a new insight. She looked about her in awe and reverence, but then found herself upset by the very intention for which she was there.

To the surprise of Mother Mary and those who attended, including the priests, she released the two birds she had so carefully carried with her up the stairs. Then she unfettered the goat and released him also. The birds flew about wildly and the goat made a hurried escape outside. As she took Sharon from her grandmother Magdalen made an affirmation.

"My child and I are pure enough. There is no sacrifice that can cleanse a person of inequity or blame unless it is a productive sacrifice. This ritual is nothing but destructive. It serves no God and no person. Certainly it does not serve a woman to bloody the ground upon which she walks in order to make herself clean of the blood of the womb. This is foolish. I will not, God wills not, that I do this."

Holding Sharon high above her head and facing the temple altars she presented her gift.

"I present to the Lord God a great gift, a Priestess of the future, my first born daughter Sharon –bat-Jesus. Her gifts are many, her face beautiful and her soul as white as snow."

At this point she left the temple and returned to the house of Nicodemus where they were staying.   There was no real discussion of her decision to forego the purification ritual. It seemed that the apostles and her friends and family were in agreement that she and Sharon were indeed pure in the eyes of the Lord.

James though was concerned that she had named the child and given her a surname in front of so many.

"Why did you do that, Magdalen? You have called attention to her and risked her safety once more."

"There are many named Jesus in Jerusalem these days." She responded. "Few would think that I would dare, but she has been given her father's name in the temple and presented as a firstborn, a gift to and from God. This is her destiny and I know that Jesus smiled as I raised her up in his place."

In the weeks to follow Magdalen and her supporters were more than welcomed into Nicodemus' household. Sara took care of the new mother's every need. Mother Mary indulged her mind in the books and scrolls that her host had within his library. She had not had that kind of opportunity for a long while and it delighted her. Magdalen looked after Sharon and enjoyed watching her mother-in-law rest so completely with her reading.

James visited everyday but went to his own home in the evening. Lazarus, too, found a new home and new work in Jerusalem. Michael, the artist who had become so devoted to the Way and to Sharon, left to be with Lazarus who wanted to support the man's talent in whatever way he could. Magdalen suspected that one day Michael would paint icons of the Gods and Goddesses of every religion.

Some afternoons Magdalen would nap on the veranda holding Sharon close and dreaming about the west and the place called Gaul. Those dreams became more and more frequent and alluring. One day she asked Sara about Gaul and related her dreams.

"You can interpret this for yourself, Magdalen." She coaxed her mistress. "You have been an oracle. You know that the dreams are telling you that you will find safety in Gaul and that Jesus is setting you there himself in the dream means that this is what he desires. Things change, you know, maybe when he said you should stay here he didn't know something that he knows now. It is my guess that if you don't follow your heart and your guidance you will be in danger."

"She is a girl, Sara. No one will ever suspect and we could stay here or in Nazareth with Mother Mary. I should become head of house now and relieve her of the burden. It is my obligation, really." Magdalen was arguing against herself.

"I thought you told me that Jesus directed John to care for Mother. Sweet woman that she is I could hardly think that she would want you to do anything that would jeopardize Sharon's future safety. She would want you to go." Sara was acting like Magdalen's altar ego.

"There is no need for all this discussion." Sara pointed out. "Go to the marketplace. You love it anyway. Ask the fortunetellers there. I've been told most of them come from Gaul. They can tell you what to expect, I'm sure. And I will watch Sharon so that you can go unnoticed."

Magdalen decided to take her nurse's advice. The next day she sat at a three-legged table in the marketplace across from a bizarre looking woman bedecked with gold jewelry and colorful scarves. Magdalen related her dreams and her draw to Gaul being careful not to reveal her identity or relationship to Jesus. The old woman looked at Magdalen as if she could see right into her soul.

"In Gaul the Celtic women bear the truth and reveal it to the men. Go there and go soon for the truth I bear is that your child is envied by the dark ones that roam these streets."

Magdalen had not said a word about Sharon. This old woman was truly an oracle, another gift from God to serve as guidance. She handed the woman ten shekels and was about to walk away when her reader reached out to stop her.

"Go soon and a Goddess will greet you there with further direction. Go soon." She repeated her warning. "Go soon."

When Magdalen arrived back at Nicodemus's home she sought out Mother Mary.

"I have been given the guidance you once said that Jesus would send."

Mother Mary set down the scroll she held in her hands.

"Are you sure that it was guidance?" she asked.

Magdalen told her all about the fortuneteller and the words she spoke and how she knew about Sharon. Mother listened intently to her story before responding.

"Dream on it once more, Magdalen. Perhaps Jesus will come to you again and reassure you that this woman speaks the truth."

Magdalen agreed that sleeping on this decision one more night would be a good idea. But as she drifted off she wondered about the need for haste that the old one had shared and whether she could wait much longer. She wondered, too, whom these dark ones were that might even at this moment be plotting against her child. Dream or no dream, Magdalen made up her mind to move. Guidance had been given and she was going to accept it. A visit from Jesus in her dreams would surely make telling the others easier though; but no dream came.

There was a great deal of discussion, even heated argument, when Magdalen revealed the decision to follow her heart and the guidance she felt she had received. The announcement that she was taking Sharon and moving to Gaul came as no surprise to Mother Mary. She understood but felt some sorrow on parting from her granddaughter, for this was not a trip that she would share. She fully intended to return to her home in Nazareth as she had planned. John, having been told by Jesus to care for and protect his mother, would go with her. Sara, too, had decided to follow with Mother Mary and learn more about the Way.

It was James who objected most strongly to Magdalen's decision to go west. Until this day she had always turned to James for advice and counsel. Now she was balking at his concern for her safety and her responsibility to the Jewish community. Magdalen felt more strongly than ever that both she and Sharon must remove themselves from such a community filled with disturbing memories of the past and its current religious violence. She would go to Gaul one way or another. While his mind told him otherwise, James gave way and knew that where Magdalen went he would go. She and the child should not travel alone.

Once James had committed to accompany them on the journey, Magdalen took over. She laid out her plans, settled her financial affairs in Jerusalem, bought a few supplies and booked passage to Greece. They would leave in just three days and Magdalen was filled with zeal and zest for bringing the Way to Gaul. There she knew in her heart she would find her parish, her priesthood and her purpose. She would also find a safe place for Sharon, a place where she would grow in freedom and come to know both the Way and the Truth.

Chapter 15

A Greek Wedding

There was a good Roman road from Jerusalem to Joppa. The thirty-mile journey wouldn't take more than a day by cart and horse. From Joppa they would sail aboard a merchant vessel to Athens. The captain had assured Magdalen when she booked her passage that the voyage from Joppa to Athens would be easy as the weather and winds were with them at this time of year. It would only take three days to arrive in Athens. There the group would stop and visit with friends. Magdalen had been to Greece before. When she was yet a young girl in the temple she had the opportunity to visit the markets and temples there in the company of an elderly trader and his family. No coincidence, she thought, that his daughter was to be married or that she had stayed in Jerusalem long enough to hear of it. Now, with fair weather and calm seas, Magdalen would arrive before the wedding celebration.

The group set out early that day heading for Joppa and one night's stay before they set sail. The weather was bright and so was Sharon's temperament that day. Magdalen was sure that the trip would be enjoyable. James on the other hand was grumbling already. He had never been to Greece and wasn't at all sure that he wanted to visit Magdalen's past or the temple city itself. Still he rode beside the cart with a stance of pride and confidence as they traveled down the well-paved road. Joppa he had seen before, there he would know his way around the harbor and the markets that they would have to visit before they set sail.

Magdalen had confined her store of supplies to what they would need for the road in order to keep the cart light and the horses swift. She was eager to get where she was going and saw no point in making the burdens of travel any heavier than they needed to be. James, of course, always wanted to be prepared for anything. He made no excuses for his need for hoarding supplies or over-supplying the portable food cupboard in the cart. Magdalen decided that it was time for her to start her preaching career right here and now. With James her target audience and the baby ignoring her mother's words in favor of chasing flies, she reminded the apostle of Jesus' words concerning abundance and supply.

"Jesus said, 'Take no thought for your life, what you shall eat; neither for the body, what you shall put on. This life is more than meat, and the body is more than its garments. Consider the ravens, for they neither sow nor reap and neither has storehouse or barn; and God feeds them. Are you not as worthy as the birds of the air? Consider the lilies how they grow. They toil not, they spin not; and yet I say unto you that Solomon in all his glory was not arrayed like one of these. If then God so clothed the grass, which is today in the field, and tomorrow is cast into the oven how much more could you ask for yourself? O ye of little faith! Ask not what you shall eat, or what you shall drink, never doubt the goodness of the Father. All have the same needs and the Father knows that you have need of these things. Seek instead the Kingdom of Heaven; and all these things shall be yours as well.'

"Those were Jesus' words, James, surely you remember them. Surely you have not misunderstood! What we need we will have by the very goodness of God. It is good to be prepared for a journey, but it is a doubtful faith that leads you to put up more than you know that you can use. Be cautious with your goods, but be more cautious with your thoughts, for these will cause you spiritual starvation and eventually your faith will be lost to your concern with your bodily needs and die out leaving you without soul. Take heart James and have faith, for I say to you that we shall always have an abundance of what we need. We will travel, not only this short journey, but also the journey of life, without any lack of prosperity. You will see, James, just as soon as you believe."

"First I will see, then I will believe," James retorted.

Magdalen wasn't ready to give up so easily, besides this rhetoric was making the journey go quickly, and she went on.

"Jesus explained it all to me, James. God has created great channels like aqueducts that we cannot see but are filled and flowing with light and love and continuously bringing to us what we need, everything we need. But when we think negatively or put our hearts in a place of lack, then we put up a dam of thoughts that keeps prosperity from flowing to us. You put up a dam each time that you fear lack. You put up a dam each time you hoard or are greedy or gluttonous. Your dams keep building higher and soon all you have is what you fear. I don't want your dams to keep my child from having the gifts of her father."

"I am neither gluttonous or greedy, Magdalen. I am practical and cautious. Be grateful for that! If the Master had been more like me, perhaps you would not have suffered your ordeal and the child would be safer right now."

Magdalen had to admit that her husband had broken his promise of safety and she fell silent for a while. The wheels of the cart made familiar clicking noises as they moved over the brick road and the repetitious and rhythmic sound soon lulled both mother and child to an afternoon nap.

The baby woke as they entered the gate at Joppa and Magdalen nursed her while she waited for James to arrange a room for the night. She couldn't help but think again about what James had pointed out, Jesus had broken his promise of safety and now, perhaps, she was going directly against his wishes by leaving Judea behind. Maybe her fears and her apprehensions had built dams that kept safety from flowing to her. Of course, she was just as guilty of dam building as James was.

"No more dams," she vowed. "No more fear and we will all be safe."

She was eager and excited to point out her self-discovery to James when he returned, but he was more interested in herding his little brood into the upper room he had rented for the night. Magdalen had to be satisfied with expressing her thoughts to Sharon and getting only soft coos in return.

The innkeeper provided them with an evening meal served by slaves. Eating fish, cheese and bread was beginning to bore everyone but the vegetable gruel and legumes reminded Magdalen of the days before Jesus' death, when she would prepare their meals and serve them with her own hands. Then they always had fresh vegetables from Mother Mary's garden and legumes from the market. She could almost smell the steam from her pot and taste the savory soup she had served him then.

"Soon," she thought, "we will dine that way again."

Magdalen emptied the portable cupboard and placed Sharon inside it to sleep. The morning would come early, and this time James would be an asset to their marketing. He would know better than she what to take with them on the next part of their journey.

"Although," she thought, "the voyage will be short and James is not going to build any more dams of fear to get in our way."

When the morning came it was off to the marketplace. Joppa was a busy port and the crowds were thick. Women pushed their way to the carts laden with vegetables and fruit. Some were dark skinned Ethiopians with colorful wraps and headdresses. Magdalen envied them the colorful garb, but she settled for a ribbon or two as usual. James made more practical purchases and frequently checked the purse to see that they had not over-spent or been shortchanged. He bought some leather bags in which to keep their store and a small flask into which he put fresh water from the well. Although the ship would be fully supplied with fresh water, James wanted to make sure that they would want for nothing. Too often ships' captains lacked scruples and promised more than they would deliver for their passengers.

Crossing the Great Sea from Joppa to Athens was not the adventure that Magdalen had anticipated. The sea was calm and the weather as fair as the captain had predicted. James had no use for his store of food and water; everything was as the captain had promised. Everyone aboard the ship welcomed two and a half days of uneventful travel.

Once in Athens, Magdalen sought out the home of her old friend Paul. It was his daughter, Cymene, who was to be married and she looked forward to the gaiety of a Greek wedding. Paul was not at his home, but the slaves told her that he would arrive within a day or two in plenty of time for the wedding that was yet three days off. The household staff led the group to guest rooms in which they had placed large baskets of fruit and bread. Paul and his family came from wealth and this wedding would display all of their prosperity and generosity as a sign of their gratitude to the Gods.

Magdalen gladly helped with preparations for the celebration. Weddings, especially Greek weddings, marked great social and economic changes that should be appreciated by anyone involved, whether guest or family. For a young girl marriage marked a rite of passage. She grew from being a maiden, to a nymph, a married woman without children, and then finally to an adult woman when she bore her first child. The entire set of marriage rites focused on the bride and her relocation to a new home and family, the most important transition in her life.

Cymene was spending a final few days with her mother and female relatives, friends, and servants preparing for her wedding, which would take place at her father's house. This pre-wedding ritual was one of the few events in which women were allowed to participate and celebrate actively. Magdalen was pleased to have been selected to help with these preparations. Even though her hands were sore from shelling clams and oysters until the many baskets were full, she enjoyed the company of the women joining in these pre-wedding arrangements. She thought again of cooking for Jesus in Nazareth and mourned a little over not having had a wedding when they were united.

Theirs was a practical marriage that did not require an actual wedding ceremony and was called a usus. The only requirement for a usus marriage was that the man and woman cohabitate for one full year, traditionally in the home of the groom's mother. Usually the woman would then pass into her husband's guardianship. But Magdalen's had been a free marriage. She retained her independence as heir to her father's fortune and therefore her father's rights. Since her father was dead, and had so stipulated in his will, she remained responsible for herself. She could then manage her own property and even initiate a divorce. There had been no celebration or ceremony and Magdalen indulged in every wedding she attended as if it were her own.

Cymene's wedding would last three days and on the first day a ceremony and feast were held at Paul's house. The bride made offerings, including her childhood clothing and toys, to the Gods. This signified the separation of the bride from her childhood, freeing her to enter a new life; and it established a bond between her and the deities she hoped would provide protection for her during the transition. Sacrifices to Artemis, Goddess of virginity and of transition, included locks of hair in the hope that she would ease the bride's first sexual experience. The bride and groom both made offerings to Aphrodite for a fruitful, child-rearing life. All of this was done with great pomp and circumstance until evening fell and the bridal party celebrated the goodness of the Gods far into the night.

The actual wedding day followed and began with a nuptial bath in the women's quarters. Water was drawn from a spring. A specially appointed child, Cymene's cousin, carried the bath water that was thought to provide a purification of the bride as well as to induce fertility, showing that the bride and her sexual initiation were the focus of this aspect of the ceremony. Cymene then dressed for the ceremony.

The gown Cymene's mother had made for her was exquisite silk and draped over her shoulders was a cape of fine wool. Cymene adorned her throat with a golden necklace jeweled with a single ruby. This was a gift from her father and something she would always treasure. The most important part of her costume was the veil, which symbolized her innocence and would not be removed until she was handed over to the groom. The fine silk folds covered her from head to toe and the wreath of flowers and ribbons crowned her like a queen. Cymene had selected Magdalen as her bridal helper, and with the bride's mother and other women she presided over the preparations for the meal and sacrifices. Now she would accompany the bride to the banquet hall where both the bride and groom would offer sacrifices to the Gods of marriage. This was, indeed, a great honor.

Magdalen had prepared everything for the ritual sacrifices. Flowers, candles of bee's wax in brightly polished holders, incense and aromatic herbs bedecked the household altar as well as the wedding table. When the sacrifices had been offered the wedding feast began. While this was one of the few public events women were permitted to attend, men and women sat at different tables. Delicacies, such as sesame seeds mixed with honey, were available as well as large portions of meat, fish, bakery and fruit. Food, drink and entertainment were lavish and abundant. For every song there was another glass of wine with a loud toast. Magdalen laughed as she watched James indulge in the food and drink like any Greek.

"He puts his prejudice aside at the sight of gravy and ale." She pointed out to one of the women.

Towards the end of the meal just as evening came the most important part of the ceremony began, the unveiling of the bride. First everyone lined up for the processional to the groom's home. A boy cousin of the bride was chosen to escort her. He represented prosperity and good luck for the couple, and symbolized their eventual child. The boy distributed bread to the guests; the bread was another symbol of the final product of this union, a child; and the basket in which the bread was carried represented the baby cradle. The child shouted the words "I fled worse and found better," and he wore a crown of thorns and nuts to remind the couple of how close and threatening our wild nature could be.

Guests were offering wedding gifts as the procession went along. Each gift recalled Demeter, the link between agriculture, fertility and social life. Friends and family handed their offerings to the bride and groom as they walked by or threw them into the empty cart that went ahead of them singing and shouting remarks of sexual anticipation and good fortune in life.

The procession was like a Greek play, a drama of the pain the bride felt leaving her family. The groom grabbed her wrist while Paul delivered her to her husband's control saying "in front of witnesses I give this girl to you for the production of legitimate children." Cymene was treated as a symbolic captive and the procession became a mock predicament that needed to be endured and overcome, as it was her final passage from childhood to marriage.

The groom tore the veil from Cymene's head and threw the crown of flowers to the crowd. He lifted up his little captive and handed her off to the waiting best man in the back of the cart. Then he boosted himself into the cart and gave a call to speed up the procession. Cymene's mother ran along side the bridal cart carry flaming torches to ward off evil spirits that might try to harm the innocent bride. All of this was set to wonderful music and choreographed with perfection. Magdalen was proud of her planning and participation as Cymene's maid of honor.

Finally the wedding chamber door was shut and remained guarded throughout the night by a friend of the groom. Friends of the bride sang outside the room to reassure the bride as she journeyed to womanhood and to encourage the couple in their attempts to produce a baby boy. Magdalen listened to the singing for a while until she was sure that her duties as the bride's attendant were complete for the day.

The final day of the wedding ceremony was called the epaulia. The day began with waking songs by the maidens who had been awake all night, and certain men who returned to wake the couple. The focus was still on the bride, as she received yet more gifts. These were not gifts for the household but personal items to be enjoyed by the bride alone. Magdalen gave Cymene a scarf of light blue silk that she had embroidered just for her. Cymene wrapped the fabric about her neck smiling and bowing in gratitude.

Life had been so somber until this wedding. Now it was filled with jubilation. Magdalen's joy over the celebration was only surpassed by her eagerness to create her new life in Gaul. Paul had been there many times and she was sure that he could now, since the wedding was over, share much information about the people and culture there. He might even be able to help in their traveling plans and put Magdalen in touch with someone there who could be of help with a place to stay and a way to get to the Celts. She would talk to Paul tomorrow, after he had ample rest and her own mind was clear. Everyone had an abundance of wine and food but very little sleep.

Chapter 16

Disciples and Thieves

When Magdalen approached Paul in the morning, she was met with his huge grin. He was obviously pleased with his showing of affluence and generosity at the wedding and with his daughter's selection of a husband. Paul was a free man with an attitude that regarded his daughter as a free woman, much as Magdalen's father had in his later years. Magdalen knew that his attitude toward women and their rights to property and decision-making was in her favor.

Paul agreed to help in whatever way that he could and together they looked over the charts and maps he had available. Paul said he would allow Magdalen's little group to travel with him but they would have to wait. He would not be leaving Athens for at least a month. Magdalen was not willing to wait. She drew an intended route across the map that Paul had given her and made a large star where he said the Celts could be found.

"That is where we will make our new home," she said. "Tomorrow we will gather supplies at the market, book passage on the next ship available and maybe even start out the following day."

James started to object to the haste in her decision, but Paul knew that Magdalen's mind could not be changed. He shook his head back and forth as if to warn James of the folly of trying to dissuade her.

The market at Athens was much larger than the one at Joppa, and James seemed rather confused by it all. Magdalen, though, had no hesitation in moving about. She pushed and elbowed her way to each vendor. This time she wanted as much as James to have everything she needed or might need.

"This isn't fear", she thought, "this is just accepting the fact that we have needs and our needs will be met."

This would be a three part journey, twice by sea and finally over land. She bought her supplies, and James carried her packages and possessions in both arms as he followed along behind her through the crowds.

She was forced to book passage on a slave ship with galley slaves at the oars. From Athens they would go to Sicily and from there to Rome. Once there Magdalen hoped to find passage on another sailing vessel, perhaps a merchant ship. But for this first leg of their journey home she would need to pack food, clothing, diapers for Sharon and plenty of fresh water.

Stopping at one vendor, Magdalen put Sharon into a covered basket making sure that she had plenty of room. Satisfied with her choice she purchased the basket and a new blanket too, warm and soft. The baby was quite content with her new cradle. The cradle basket reminded Magdalen of the wedding ceremony and the basket the bride received just for this purpose. Sharon was getting big, she thought, perhaps she would soon be in need of another sort of bed. For now, though, this would do nicely.

They arrived early at the dock; Magdalen wanted the best place possible aboard the ship. This first leg of the journey would take a minimum of ten days barring any bad weather or misfortune. She settled in as if she were creating a nest for Sharon, James and herself. Magdalen found a place on the second deck where there would be equal periods of sun and shadow to protect the baby and her own skin from over exposure. The entrance to the inner cabin was close in case of a storm or other need for shelter. It was a beautiful day as they set out and Magdalen appreciated the excuse to sit still and enjoy the sea air. She thought she would have plenty of time for prayer and meditation when she was not tending to Sharon.

James decided to walk about the deck and get a feel for the ship and its crew. Magdalen settled back to meditate on the future and was interrupted by four women passing by her little nest and giggling quite loudly. They stopped to coo at the baby and introduce themselves.

Magdalen instantly knew these women would eventually become her close friends on this journey. Sarah and Ruth were young, Jewish and filled with curiosity for the world. They would surely add joy to the journey. Carmel was dark skinned, from Ethiopia, more Magdalen's own age. She was enthralled with Sharon. And then there was Polaris, the Greek woman and grandmother/sage who asked as many questions as she answered. Magdalen was careful to reveal nothing yet of her past or her plans.

She spent this day making new friends, tending to Sharon and enjoying the weather. The women spent a lot of time playing lots or dice as they huddled in Magdalen's little nest. They ate small bits of cheese, bread and fish throughout the day and shared their stores with one another. Magdalen washed the soiled linen from Sharon in a barrel on the deck using water taken from the sea and Polaris helped her to hang the diapers over the ship's rail to dry in the cleansing sun. There was little meaningful conversation, but Magdalen felt certain that these women were meant to be her first true disciples.

Very strong winds rose up the next day. Other voyages had kept the ship close to the coastline, but out in the midst of the Great Sea winds like these created large waves and the ship rocked about like a child's toy in the bath. Nausea hit Magdalen hard. Although the crew was not frightened by the storm, passengers were hanging over the rail and retching violently. Everyone was sick it seemed but the baby and the galley slaves who were used to the rocking of the ship. The wind calmed at nightfall and it was easier to move about. Magdalen could even eat something again and keep it down. No one played lots this day and there was no conversation either, they were exhausted from the constant vomiting and retching. Magdalen tended to Sharon and dozed off when the baby slept.

The next day she and the others rose with the sun, and it was glorious. The sky was a brilliant blue and the water looked so deep and dark and it extended to every horizon. The ladies gathered together in their place on the upper deck, but mostly they napped still recovering from their seasickness. It was a quiet and pondering day for Magdalen. How should she open up a conversation with them about the child, the Master Jesus, her mission? She didn't know where to begin or even if she should. So the topic was left for another day.

Another day passed without event. Magdalen did play dice again and chat with the ladies, but still she didn't know where to take the conversation. She washed linen again, and as she did she pondered on how she would speak to them.

They would arrive in Sicily tomorrow but only for a brief stop to take on water, then it would be on to Rome. If she wanted their support Magdalen would have to talk to these women about her plans before they arrived at the capital. There they would spend three days before setting out for Massilia, and she knew she might be recognized during their stay. Magdalen decided to invite them to dinner in Sicily where there was real food and not the simple meals of the sea – fish and cheese and bread. They would dine together, break bread and be able to talk without fear of the crewmen overhearing. She certainly couldn't risk Sharon's safety by revealing to all these men where they were from and why they had come. Jesus aroused a lot of turmoil and the new religion was arousing even more in Rome. The women accepted Magdalen's invitation and were excited about the brief but pleasurable stop in Syracuse.

When they arrived in Syracuse harbor the women were amazed at the activity and variety of fare. There were what seemed like hundreds of fishing boats docked in the harbor. They ate a wonderful meal of goat and lamb and drank wine at an outdoor café. By breaking bread together they formed a true and intimate friendship. Magdalen told the ladies everything about the Master Jesus, his healings, miracles and teaching, about Sharon and how the Sanhedrin and the Roman's would like to end her life because they felt she would carry with her the abilities of mastery that Jesus had. She explained that they were convinced she was a male child and were not as likely to recognize her as she matured because of her gender. Magdalen told them how she intended to minister to Gaul and share the Way with the Celts and maybe even the Druids.

Carmel was the only one who was reluctant to believe in all this or to get involved with Magdalen. She had been born in Ethiopia but home was Hispania and she missed her family there. The others wanted to know more and to learn to use the power of mastery for themselves and to heal and work wonders. Magdalen told them that the Celts had healing powers too and that for those who knew the truth that power could be developed and harnessed to achieve true miracles. She convinced them that the women of the world knew as much or more about healing practices than their male counterparts and that they could join her in this journey and learn as much as they cared to about all these things.

Carmel said she had to think about it and was not yet convinced, but the others began looking at this adventure as the opportunity of a lifetime. They talked about bringing women together in circles to form communities of healing and spiritual teaching. Magdalen was sure to tell them that they could not speak of Jesus when they returned to the ship but that she would teach them about it all once they left Rome, when they would be on a sailing vessel where they didn't have to deal with centurions and slave traders. The environment would be safer and there would hopefully be more privacy.

James had dined with the women and then went off to the market in search of food for their journey. As he walked away from them he slipped something into Sharon's basket. Curious, Magdalen looked beneath the blanket. She couldn't believe it but James took a cup from the café, like a souvenir she guessed. This didn't seem like James at all and it concerned Magdalen. To make up for the pilfering she tipped the restaurateur handsomely, glad that no one else had noticed. Magdalen vowed to ask James about it when they were alone. She was sure that there must be a rational explanation.

When they returned to the ship the ladies were anxious to hear more and Magdalen tried hard not to allow the conversation to suggest anything that might incite trouble. But then trouble came through no fault of Magdalen or her band of new disciples.

A fight broke out over a man's purse. Each one accusing the other, both men were taken to the galley in chains. No purse was found. Magdalen knew that this was a scheme on the part of one man to appear to have been wronged in order to extort money from some of the others who pitied him. She told the ladies her theory and they gossiped unceasingly about the incident. Magdalen soon stopped this as she was ill at ease with condemnation and she set out to know why this man did what he did. She decided to take the prisoner some water and outright ask him. Being highly intuitive she could see in his eyes his first attempts at lying and she could also see some wounded pride.

The man was bankrupt because a merchant with a get rich quick idea swindled his son out of his birthright. It took all the money he had left to book this passage for the two of them to get to Rome and start over. Now he was out of all funds and had the attitude that he would give to the world what the world had given him – extortion and thievery. Magdalen reminded him that what one contributes to the world's agenda would multiply seven fold and soon become the way of life for everyone.

"You trusted," she said, " and you were betrayed. It has made you fearful and it has left your heart cold. When you betray another, you create within them the same coldness of heart as you have suffered, and the light in this world is dimmed. We are all less fortunate because of the thievery of another."

In an effort to undo the misfortune the man had contributed to creating, she handed him three gold coins. This she said was her contribution to affluence within society.

The man, being impressed with Magdalen's wisdom and generosity, asked for her forgiveness.

"The Father forgives," she said. " I act only as the Father's purse keeper for this one day. Because you have found goodness in your heart, the Father has allowed me to have funds to share with you. He has forgiven you already and now expects that you, like a good steward, will make use of these funds to find the way to heaven."

The man kissed Magdalen's hand and gave thanks to God.

Magdalen then found the other man and silently handed him three coins also. No words were exchanged but the man squeezed her hand as she held out the coin. That was his way of silently admitting his need and his appreciation.

"He too," Magdalen thought, "must have a heart of goodness hidden only by his fears."

Back on deck she relayed what had happened to the ladies. They were astounded. Why would she give her money to these troublemakers? Why give them something that they were ready to steal from one another? Magdalen answered simply.

"So they will not have need to steal."

With that she walked off to nurse her child. Nursing was as comforting to Magdalen as it was to Sharon. Somehow this intimate sharing with her child brought her calm and stillness, even on this ship of thieves and barbarians. It was a time when she would be undisturbed and could ponder and contemplate both present and future. Right now Magdalen was thinking deeply about these two episodes of theft. James, who had no reason for thievery, had taken that cup from the café. The man who had stolen the purse had a reason to steal; he feared his poverty and inability to provide for himself. Was one man right and the other wrong? Did it matter to God what your reasons for dishonesty were?

She had not had the opportunity to ask James why he had stolen the cup. Magdalen knew that there had to be a reason, but she wondered now what reason was good enough to validate a dishonest act. Jesus had reminded many that the basic Law of Moses had remained valid - do not steal. Could you make excuses before God, she wondered? Just then James rounded the corner and sat himself beside her somewhat oblivious of the nursing mother. Now was Magdalen's opportunity to investigate James' motives and true self.

"James, I know about the cup." She began with a tone of vengeance. "What were you thinking? Why did you take it, and why, in the name of almighty God, did you put it into Sharon's cradle? Think of the danger that you put us in!"

"It was but a prank, Magdalen. The cup is not worth more than the gratuity that you slipped to the slave girl."

James was not even making excuses. Instead he was giving reasons why this was not a crime at all. Magdalen couldn't let go of this bone. She had to gnaw at it until it was completely gone from her mind and she had changed James' mind about honesty and integrity. This, by Magdalen's idea of righteousness, was no prank. It hurt the café owner and it endangered everyone in the group. She was angry now and eager to put James in his rightful place of repentance. James could feel another sermon coming on, and he wasn't eager to hear Magdalen throw at him the words of the Law, the Way or Jesus. But the agitated woman used her own words, and even an unremorseful James had to take heed.

"James, the man who caused the raucous over the purse, he was stricken with poverty. Someone he had trusted had abused him. He is destitute and unable to care for himself when he arrives in Rome. That is why he was trying to extort money from the others. I believe that the Way says that God's heart goes out to the man's despair. Still he is not excused from his deception until he has righted the wrong and asked for forgiveness. The Father forgives all those who ask and gives each a full measure of opportunity to find again the Way. When I explained all this to him, the man found a light in his heart. He realized his stewardship over righteousness had been tested and that he fell short. When he asked for forgiveness I gave him three gold coins to make his way easier, they were God's gift to him and he was forgiven.

"You are a steward, James, not only of our goods but also of your soul, your mind and your body, to say the least of Sharon's and mine. Your stewardship was being tested when you were tempted to take advantage of the trust of others. When you succumbed to that temptation you created a lack in someone's heart if not their purse. You took from them a measure of trust and another measure of safety and security. You contributed to the creation of chaos and hate, bigotry, blindness to the light. Your "prank" cannot be excused, but it can be forgiven and you can gain the opportunity to right the error and find your way again when you find the purity and goodness in your heart that enlightens you to the truth. The Truth is Love, and love causes no harm, no matter how small it may seem at the moment."

"So, I have dammed up the flow of prosperity again, this time by instilling a small fear and mistrust within the innkeeper and within you, right? And now the world and its people are more fearful because of my act?"

James was now concerned about his responsibility. Magdalen knew that James would always want to be considered the responsible person and the one that could be relied upon to protect lives and goods without concern for his own betterment.

"What can I do? We are far from Sicily now. How can I make it right?"

"Give the cup with a full measure of milk and honey to someone who is in need, James. And you will have given a full measure of hope to the world, this will open the channels of prosperity for the world again."

James took the cup from Magdalen, filled it from their store and headed for the lower deck where the less fortunate passengers made their beds. Magdalen was pleased to see him move so positively toward a resolution. She was equally pleased that James' practicality had allowed them to pack a reserve, because suddenly there was a lot of sharing going on. She chuckled a little to herself and gave a silent thank you to God for having provided both their goods and James' presence on this journey.

One day seemed like the rest until they arrived in the Roman port of Ostia. The shoreline near Ostia offered no natural protection to ships. Small boats could sail up the Tiber to Rome without difficulty. But for large ships Ostia and its harbor were dangerous. A saving grace was offered these large vessels that was its lighthouse. The five-tiered structure was a guiding beacon for navigators. Slaves kept the fire burning day and night. During the day they covered the fire with wet straw, the resulting black smoke directed the sailors into the harbor. At night they could see the flames burning high at the tower's top and navigate quickly to mooring. The lighthouse was just a few miles north of Ostia, and when it was in full view the crew and passengers alike gave a shout of gratitude to the Goddess, the Great Mother. Magdalen hadn't heard such a cheer to the Mother in a long while. It took her back to yearning for the temple and the festivals of thanksgiving and honor that she had so often officiated at.

Once their vessel had been secured, Magdalen and the other passengers were allowed to disembark and made their way along the main street of Ostia hoping to find and inn or tavern that would have them. It was a busy town and within its walls was a huge mercantile exchange. There were groups of oil-importers, grain-importers, wine-importers, ship-builders, and rope-makers doing business as usual. On festival days they took their clients here to the taverns for a cup of wine between plays at the theatre nearby.

The theatre held over three thousand, and as long as there were empty seats admission was open to everyone. Rich and poor alike were free to partake of the drama offered in honor of the Gods and Goddesses of Rome. Tragedies bored Magdalen. She liked the comedies because of the jokes and brightly colored masks and costumes the actors wore.

Beyond the theatre were the apartments; the places weary travelers could spend a night before entering the capital city of Rome. Beyond that were the meadows and the umbrella pines that made this port look like an oasis that it truly was not. Green and cool in the summer, the countryside was inviting, but the town itself was raucous and dangerous for strangers. Sailors were noted for their violent nature and caution would have to be maintained.

Magdalen wondered if she and her group should rent one of the two-wheeled carts that moved commuters between Ostia and Rome instead of spending the night in this atmosphere. James, however, led the women into one of the largest taverns. It was dark and smelled badly. James assured the women that it was only the smell of cooking spiced sausages and honeyed wine. Hungry as they all had become, the prospect of such a supper enticed them to put the stench aside and find a bench in the courtyard upon which to eat and rest. The place in the courtyard they had chosen enabled them to be in the shade and to watch the ferry going back and forth across the mouth of the Tiber River. A beggar boy came by and Magdalen dropped a coin in his filthy hand.

"May the Goddess Mother make you fertile," he gave her his thanks.

After they ate, James ushered the women to a single-room apartment on the upper floor. There they would spend the night. Magdalen had considered visiting the baths at Thetis. Fires burned day and night there heating the water and the air beneath the floors to keep the baths at their warmest. Though it sounded inviting she decided it too dangerous and opted for a basin produced by slaves who had come to the apartment to serve them all with towels and water. Tomorrow she would be in Rome where she knew more what to expect at the baths and how to conduct herself. After she had bathed Sharon she washed her own body and then retired for the night. Soon she would be able to begin her true mission, she thought, she would begin walking the Way and leading others on their path of light.

In the morning children filled the streets playing their games of stickball and merchants set up temporary shops along the wooden sidewalks that lined the avenues of Ostia. After a breakfast of fruit purchased from one of these vendors, Magdalen and her entourage went back to the harbor and found a merchant vessel that was taking on passengers. They could leave from this same port in three days.

Once passage was contracted, the group went to the ferry landing. There James rented one of the four wheeled carts that carried passengers and merchandise alike aboard the ferry and up the Tiber to Rome proper. In a short time they were through the Roman gates and Magdalen was filled with excitement and nostalgia. Now she could go to the baths as she had done many times before. She could take Sharon with her and enjoy the atrium and the company of the other women as they shared their time and talk in the women's quarters.

That first day in Rome was relaxing and a much needed respite for body and mind. The next day, however, there was much that needed doing. Magdalen spent most of the day washing clothes and tending to a reorganization of sorts, but she did talk a good deal with the women about the Celts and how they were supposed to have a deep understanding of the link between earth and heaven. She had been told that while they seemed to believe in multiple Gods much as the Romans and the Greeks did that they had a special bond with the wisdom of earth and the love of heaven. They were also supposed to have a unique way of treating women and spirituality and were aware of the soul within all things.

The women were nearly as interested in the Celts as they were in learning more of Jesus, and Magdalen had all she could do to keep from beginning her tales. Rome, though, was not the place to bring up the movement of the New Way. The women would have to wait for her stories until they were aboard the merchant ship and safely assail bound for Massilia. That was only a day a way, she told them. Patience was hard but everyone decided to keep their word of allegiance to Magdalen's need for silence.

When they arrived back at the harbor, they were allowed to immediately board the ship rather than finding lodging. They would leave with first light so Magdalen sent James off to do the shopping alone. The baby now had two teeth and was fussy most of the day requiring all of Magdalen's time and energy. The women all loved Sharon and each took turns holding and rocking the little darling to give Magdalen a mother's welcome relief.

While Sharon finally napped and James was off, Magdalen was coaxed by the women.

"Tell us how you met him, Magdalen, please," pleaded Sarah. "It couldn't hurt just to tell us of your meeting."

"Yes," Ruth begged, "Please, just a romantic story among women. No one will be the wiser for that."

Magdalen was about to give in when Polaris, in all her wisdom spoke up.

"Don't be begging for tales that could cost you your own," she said. "You are both too young to appreciate the danger of being suspect of this New Way. I have only heard a little, but it sounds as if Jesus was considered an enemy of the state, and any mention will bring suspicion upon us. Wait as you were asked until we are well on our way to Gaul."

Carmel was disappointed, but she smiled in agreement anyway. Magdalen thanked her friends for their concern and the conversation went back to the Celtic culture and religion. No one knew much. Even Magdalen was mostly going on hear say. As the chatter continued, James came back, sacks of leather filled to overflowing. They would have plenty of stores for the remainder of their journey.

So as not to use up their supplies, James took the women back to the tavern that had become his favorite and again they dined on the spicy sausage and drank sweetened wine. The innkeeper was eager to make them comfortable and everyone enjoyed the last of their hot meals for many days to come. The ship was under way when Magdalen arose and she waved a melancholy good-bye to Ostia and Rome.

Chapter 17

Stones & Rocks of Faith

Once they had eaten and Sharon was down again, the women began their coaxing once more. This time Magdalen decided it would be safe enough to tell them the story of how she met Jesus and how they became united. The women were eager to hear what they thought would be a romantic tale. Everyone was silent as Magdalen began.

"A Pharisee had come to my home in honor of the Goddess. This was somewhat uncommon because of my attachment to the Jewish community via my mother. It was mostly Roman men and foreign traders and merchants who came to honor the Goddess, so this Jewish man was especially rare to me. Some men find pride in their abilities with women, and so this Pharisee found himself bragging to others after he left me.

"This made the Jewish community angry over my position and my association with one of their own men. Now, a man who leaves his wife for another woman does not commit adultery. It is the whore or the other woman who is at fault, for man is said to be at the mercy of a woman's wiles and his sins are then hers. It remains her responsibility to protect the virtue of both of them. I've never understood that law, but still it remains."

Magdalen gave a sigh of exasperation as she went on.

"Some days after this man's visit, I was walking toward the Mount of Olives. I was actually looking for Jesus because my maids and slaves had told me of his miracles and that he could cure all manner of disease. A group of seven or eight Jewish people came upon me and seized me. They made their accusations and their curses, as was always their way. But this time, they felt that they had the right and the responsibility under the law of their fathers to put me to death by stoning. While they were yet talking this all over and preparing themselves in whatever emotional way was necessary, a man came down the path, a large man, whose demeanor seemed to be one that did not belong to such a large body, at least not at first."

"Tell us more about how he appeared, Magdalen."

Ruth was eager to find out why Magdalen had fallen so in love with Jesus. She wanted to know everything about him.

"He was beautiful, Ruth, absolutely beautiful. His face was fine and it was aglow with light. His shoulders were broad and very strong. The sandals on his feet were filthy from the road, but his legs stood straight and tall. He wasn't smiling as he approached, but instead he wore the countenance of peace. There was no knit in his brow as he held up both his hands and questioned the people, 'What has she done?' They proceeded to tell him of my lack of virtue and my influence upon the Pharisees as a whole. And they asked him, calling him by name, 'Jesus, Master, you are the teacher, tell us if it is just to stone this adulterous woman, for she is guilty by our word and by the sight of many.' There seemed a long pause as he squatted there in the roadway, scratching in the sand with his finger and then rubbing out the letters with his palm.

"As I said, I had heard of this man, Jesus, whom some called Master. He taught in the synagogues of the small towns. He was quite obviously on his way now to Jerusalem to be at the temple for the Feast Day of the Tabernacle. I had wondered before what this man was like and what he taught. I had heard of John in the desert, a crazy man whose sole purpose in being seemed to be to scare the Jewish people into some sort of repentance. He was baptizing out there, and some said that he was the cousin of this Jesus. I thought perhaps insanity was a family trait, and that now this man could vent his apostolic anger on me as I stood held there by two others. Surely he would be as rash as John, but somehow he seemed too soft and quiet, too thoughtful in his response, to be purely insane or even filled with hatred as the others were.

"The long time ended then and he spoke. 'He that is without sin among you, let him cast the first stone at her.' Guilt is a powerful tool, but even more powerful when it is substantiated. Jesus had been writing there with his finger the sins and law breaking of every man present with his name beside the wrongdoing. One by one they left at his statement and I was set free. He was writing again and there he had spelled my name. 'Where are they that accuse you? Is no one here to condemn you?' He asked me. I could not say a word. 'Then I do not condemn you or be your judge.' He erased my name then, and wrote - come. I was not quite sure what he wanted, but he looked up then and said, 'To the house of my mother, and with no other man be again. Your days of such things are over.'

"I walked with him to the temple and there waited outside. I had no desire to put myself in jeopardy with these people again. He went in and seated himself to teach and speak bluntly to them and to the scribes and the Pharisees also. I could hear and watch from where I was and that for me was close enough. I was not sure yet just how far I was willing to follow this man. After all, he had a crazy cousin in the desert and the rumors about him were everywhere. Rumor also said that he taught great truths, and this I longed to hear, especially then. He was just; there was no question that he was more just than the law. I wondered if he had a notion to have me in honor of the Goddess like the others, but it did not seem that way. And by then I had become a good judge of men's needs and desires. This man showed caring. He showed truth, not the deceit of most. He made no bargains or attempted no threat of mind or body. He was different from any man I had ever met.

"I listened as he talked to them, 'I am the light of the world, and those that follow the truth that I am walk not in darkness but shall have the light of life.' He said in a loud voice. The Pharisees, great philosophers that they are, spoke out. 'You give proclamation of your wisdom and holiness before the Lord, this is self flattery and not to be held as truth.'

"He answered them. 'Though my proclamation appears to be of my own goodness, my testimony is truth because I know from whence I came and where I am going. But you do not know these things yet. Out there, you judged, as always you judge, according to the ways of the body that feels anger, hatred and desire and jealousy. But I do not judge anyone, for these are false judgments. And if I say to you that something is truth, it is truth, because it is without the flesh that I say and know these things. It is for this reason that I have been sent, to teach you also that you are to judge no one. In your law the testimony of two men is truth, so it is as I have said, my judgment is truth for I am one with the essence of life that is the Father.'

"They asked then 'Where is your father?' And Jesus answered. 'You do not know me, and you do not know my Father, but you will. For if you know me, you know my beginning and my Father is the beginning. And if you know the beginning, you must also know me.' And they were confused and mumbled again about his craziness. I wasn't muttering, but found myself as confused as they were as I continued to listen to his teaching. 'Wither I go, you cannot come, but you will seek me and find me not, for I am not of this world. What am I, what is any man, but the Father within him? And you seek not where I am, but instead you seek in the world of which I am not a part. You have made the things of the flesh the father of your deceit. You lie among yourselves, and therefore judge the truth that I tell you to be lies also. It is because you are seeking truth in the way of the world and its demons and their power of which you speak so reverently and often. I am not of this world, I say again, but you are of this world. And here it is and why it is that you must die in the guilt of which you have not convinced me.'

"'You are the servants of the guilt that you are convinced of. I am the son and the servant of the truth. It is for this reason that I was sent. I say to you, he who serves the truth shall not perish but will live in the light of it, and that truth is the truth of the Father.'

"They accused him of having a devil within him. He denied such a presence. 'I have no devil, but you have a devil, for I honor my Father and you honor the flesh. I am, and before Abraham and before Moses, I am. Before even the beginning, I am the son and the Father before me.'

"They took up stones, once meant for me, and cast them now at him. But he fled, taking me with him and we hid at the house of his mother. And I went with him as he had directed me, and I dwelled with him as his wife for what remained of his life. I spoke little and asked no questions that day, for my mind was yet confused, and I did not know what I should ask."

Magdalen fell silent, but the women were not satisfied.

"What happened next? I want details, Magdalen!"

Now even Carmel was anxious to know more of this love affair. Magdalen was a little disappointed, her friends were eager to share her romance with her, but they were not asking about the Way or Jesus' teaching. Her disappointment was apparent to Polaris who, though she too wanted to indulge in the love life of a friend, was wise enough to ask the right question.

"Magdalen, what did he teach you that night? What did he share with you that made him become so special to you? Surely it was more than lovemaking, I am old enough to know that love comes from knowing each other fully. Tell us what he had to share, please."

Magdalen smiled at her new friend. She was well aware of Polaris' wisdom and knew that it would be a great asset as they began their circle of the Way.

"Well Polaris, like you, I waited for the right question to form in my mind."

She smiled again at the sage-like grace with which Polaris conducted herself.

"The truth is, there was no lovemaking that night."

Magdalen giggled at their disappointment.

"But I did find my tongue and asked my questions. I asked him first what he had written in the sand about my attackers. He answered this way, 'No person has a true secret, for the spirit within them knows the truth. The spirit is available to all and what I wrote is of no consequence to you because what the spirit shared with me was shared to keep the man from making yet another mistake in his life. Each one's spirit shared with me their darkest secret in order that they would be guided to learning from their past errors, not so that I might gossip in my bedroom about them. That is the Way, Magdala, the way of truth teaches the Law of Love. It was by loving you enough to protect you and by loving them enough to carry them over the ditch of bigotry that spirit empowered the moment with truth.'

Ruth now pondered out loud.

"You mean that my heart might reveal my sins to another? That anyone can know everything about me? Here and now, without a word spoken?" She was frightened of this proposition. "I don't like this Way, already, Magdalen."

"Do not do what you cannot reveal, and do not hide what you have done. For the truth is what sets you free of fear, Ruth. That was the biggest lesson that I learned that night. Believe me, I didn't like the idea at first myself. After all, this was my unus, my wedding night, and this man I had married could quite obviously read my soul as easily as he read those at that stoning."

"What a thought!" cried Carmel, "To have a husband that could read your mind. Could know all about you, your past and the thoughts in your head, every complaint and comparison!"

"If you have a thought that concerns you, Carmel, it is better to put it out there than to let it devour you from the inside."

This was Polaris' wisdom talking again. She was well aware of the silly deceptions of young girls. Young women were used to gossiping and to keeping secrets. They even paid the children with sweets and coins to get information by playing close to the adults, listening to conversations and extending their ears to hear what they should not. Women had too little to do with the affairs of life in Jewish society as far as Polaris was concerned, and should take some lessons in living their own life instead of living through the lives of others. But she silenced herself as the others begged Magdalen for more stories.

"All right," began Magdalen, " I'll tell you about one of my first days with him, when I was stricken with awe at his compassion and his confidence.

"As Jesus came down from his place of prayer and meditation, a place that he had found on the mountain side and was private, quiet and alive with wildlife, he was greeted by many people whom he called disciples, students of his word. In addition to the twelve, there were thirty more. They sought his teaching and his prophesy of future happiness. Some came to be healed and cured of their internal dis-ease of emotional and mental natures. The crowd gathered in a spot that was like most of that area, flat and dry, absent of trees and even grass. This crowd was seen to gather by travelers from all over Jerusalem and Judea and even those coming from the seashores and from Tyre and Sidon. The travelers questioned what prophet or madman was gathering his disciples in such a place. They lingered there to hear him, and they brought with them their doubts of his sanity, let alone his power. The disciples, as always, sought to touch him. They sought further to have him touch those that were ailing in order that they might be cured, and even before they had reached the Master, they were free of their physical ails. And those that were of a nature of being ill within heard his words and felt peace and contentment, some of them for the first time. And Jesus turned his face to the heavens, because he wished not to see the faces of those that might keep him from his thoughts and personal peace. And then he looked out at the crowd and his eyes met theirs, each of them with compassion, and he said:

'Dear to me are you that are poor, and have little in this life, for your search for the kingdom is free, and it shall be yours. Dear to me are you who hunger now for knowledge, for you shall be satisfied unendingly. Dear to me are you who weep now, your tears will end, and you shall laugh when you know God. Dear to me shall you be when men hate you, because you have come to know who 'I' is and have tied yourself to this truth. And when they shut you out, in their system of caste, and reproach you, and reject your name as evil, because you have found yourself with me in mind. Rejoice when this happens, for your reward is great even to the height of the heavens. For truth is the highest of high. And to those who come here in the deceit that makes them feel their human power, woe to them, for they shall suffer greatly here as they struggle instead to learn from the teacher called pain. In my words is the painless teacher. In other ways, in other Rabbis, there is the teacher that makes people suffer within the spirit and sets one person against another. But this truth cannot be changed. I am the son of my Father, and I live among the family that my Father has sired. I say to you, so be it.'

"Jesus held all people in high esteem. His term of endearment made everyone there feel Jesus' brotherhood with us, a family tie that was one of respect as well as love."

Magdalen added her appraisal of the situation before going on.

"There were great murmurings among the crowd as Jesus spoke, and many felt that they had been wronged or slandered for their position within the community. At a later time, Jesus was to explain that it is not in riches that guilt is found, or in laughter, or joy, but that we can have all these, and not touch the peace that is found in the truth of God. I will tell you that story another time. He was speaking to those who came in doubt, criticism, and testing not to humanity as a whole.

But that is enough story telling for today,"

Magdalen was eager to get on with her efforts at producing a true community among the women.

"We have a great deal to accomplish today. Let us go about the work of creating a new family."

The women began by establishing a small area as their own. They placed mats in a circle out of the way of the deck hands, and in the center Magdalen placed a single cup and a plate for bread.

"Tonight," she said. "We will celebrate Jesus as he suggested. We will share a communal meal of bread and wine and remember his words of Love."

The women were eager for this first Eucharistic feast and to learn the meaning of the ritual that was part of Magdalen's New Way.

As the day went on Sharon fussed over her tender gums and she was handed from one woman to another until her mother was free to rock her. At times the women whined about the ship although Magdalen thought it much better than the last vessel. James was feeling better because there were fewer unsavory characters to deal with.

After the evening meal, Magdalen announced that they would now sit in their circle and commemorate Jesus. She would, this first time, explain the ceremony and the power that it had.

"As I take the bread in my hands and break the loaf, I am to say: Take and eat, for this is the body. Then I pass the loaf around the circle and each of you shares a bit of the bread. When we do this we are sharing the life of the body, for Jesus said that the body after all is but the bread that we take into it. Yet we must share the life of the body with one another and with our spirit, for the Father has allowed us to be here with health and the ability to work and to enjoy the acts of our bodies. Then I raise the cup and say: Take and drink, for this is the blood that shall be shed for many. Wine itself is a "spirit" it can inebriate and it can change who we are. So the cup represents our fullness of spirit and our need to succumb to its goodness. When we do these things we are establishing within our hearts a new way of life. We are reminding ourselves that we are both body and spirit and we are awakening our minds to the power that spirit has over body. When Jesus spoke of the blood that shall be shed, he referred to the life's true blood of spirit being poured forth from within our hearts. The cup of wine represents the sharing of spirit. It is the pouring out of our true self, without deception or hesitation, for the good of all."

Each woman reverently ate of the loaf and drank from the cup, for to them this ritual of communion meant that together they would live life by the power of spirit. No one was ready to talk about the ritual, except to say that they felt the power of spirit living within them. This was a new feeling that seemed strange, for they had never believed themselves to have any kind of power in this world.

Then Magdalen agreed to tell them about some of Jesus' miracles, because they were eager to hear of his works and wonders. Like waiting for the telling of a ghost story around the campfire they huddled together to hear her tales.

For the final time that day, Magdalen began her recollection of Jesus' good news. "When Jesus had stretched out his hand to touch the leper, there had been great murmuring about the power of his hand. He spent several hours at Capharnaum explaining that faith and love cure and not the touch of human hands. He explained further that for this reason he seldom laid on hands to heal. The disciples continued to murmur and mumble about his humility and they thought that he was keeping a secret power to himself, which they much desired to share.

"Among the crowd was a Roman centurion. He knew of Jesus and his miracles through prior association with my household and me. He approached the Master in a way that seemed almost planned to prove the point that Jesus had been trying to make. As he passed by me, the centurion touched my shoulder as a friend would. His knowledge of me caused more mumbling among the disciples. They were reproachful of Jesus for our relationship and also had great concern about sharing the Master and his knowledge with a Roman. But Jesus was not concerned with their dissent and he looked to the centurion to explain his presence. 'Lord, my young male servant, so dear to me has fallen gravely ill. Say but the word and he shall be healed,' the man stated his request. Jesus saw that this man's servant was like a son to him, and that his concern for the child's health had brought him there at great risk of the rebuke of the apostles as well as the Roman governor.

"The soldier expressed his concern for his position and the possible outcome as he stated that he did not deserve to be sold into slavery by the governor for his faith and love for this boy. He expressed to Jesus his knowledge of God's power without the intrusion of human hands or presence and Jesus used this opportunity to enhance his previous lecture on healing power. Then he said to the centurion, 'By your faith it is done at this hour.' And he turned to the apostles and told them. 'Go and see for yourself.'

"When the apostles reached the house of the centurion later and discovered the cured boy, they believed that this must have been coincidence and that very probably the boy's fever broke quite ordinarily. They still believed that Jesus was hiding some secret and that he alone healed, they looked to touch his hands expecting to find more than human flesh. Jesus again spoke of faith and love. He reminded them time and again that it was for the world that he came and not for only the Israelite nation. In their selfishness, he said, they would only find darkness and he expected that most of Israel would not see the light of love because love did not allow for prejudice and judgment. With that he told them all to find peace in their dreams that night and he went away to rest too and I laid with him.

"Tonight we all need some quiet restful time, too."

Magdalen made it clear that this would be the end of her storytelling, and she went to put Sharon down for the night.

Chapter 18

Crosses of Crisis

The next morning Magdalen felt a burning pain when she emptied her bladder. She was feverish and ached all over. The women gave her some herbs, the equivalent of laudanum, and she dozed on and off the remainder of the day. Her new friends cared for Sharon and woke Magdalen only to feed her baby.

The fever broke quickly, but many others were now sick too, some with urinary tract infections others with stomachaches and flu-like symptoms. All had fevers. It was decided that most, if not all, of the water kegs had been contaminated and the contents were unusable for drinking. They would have to go back to Rome to restock water in new kegs. Magdalen and the women attempted to nurse others even in their own misery.

"Thank God the baby is still nursing and had not been given any of the poisoned water."

Magdalen gave thanksgiving to God and Goddess for Sharon's health.

When they arrived back at Rome deck hands and other men rolled the huge kegs of water down wooden ramps and off the boat. They would empty and burn them to avoid any more contamination. The women went to the baths but spent the night on board the ship. They were back at sea early the next day.

Two days out of the Roman port, the grumbling began. Passengers and crew alike, perhaps out of boredom, were finding fault with the captain, blaming him for the bad water incident and resulting illness and delay. When the crew began spreading gossip and rumors of the captain's bad reputation, Magdalen could see that there would be trouble on the ship. A deck hand, obviously intoxicated, shouted in a loud voice.

"Perhaps he means to kill us all and rob the passengers of their purses!"

"Be quiet or I'll have you taken below in chains!" The captain warned, but the deck hand would not be silenced. A second time the captain cautioned him. "Watch your words, man, or you will not live to regret your foolishness."

Still the man continued to shout. "This would not be the first ship lost to the captain's greed!"

The captain's hand went up in a gesture to move and three crewmen overtook the struggling deck hand. As they were forcing him down into the ship's belly, he shouted once more.

"May the Gods send you to the bottom of the sea!"

Now the captain's thumb went down. Just like Caesar at the arena he was calling for the man's life, thought Magdalen. Sure enough the crewmen now pushed their captive up to a viewing perch on the ship's mast. Then they wrapped a large chain around his neck and pushed him from his roost. The captain turned his back on it all and retired to his quarters as if he had no interest in the matter whatsoever.

The man struggled a long time. His face and neck turned blue and then black. He appeared swollen and his tongue hung out of his mouth. The crew made jest of this, since it had been his tongue that had gotten him where he was. People gathered on the deck to watch. Some joined in the crew's laughter, others turned away in disgust. Still others shook in fear of the power that the captain had over crew and passengers alike. It was a horrible sight for Magdalen, this man hanging there in such misery and hopelessness. The justice of the sea did not seem to be justice at all. She began to weep silently and to pray for the man's soul.

She thought of Jesus and how he hung silently on the cross for those hours and wondered if he had felt as hopeless as this man must now. When he had expired the body, along with the chain that had strangled him, was thrust into the sea and sunk slowly beneath the gentle waves. Magdalen whispered a prayer and moved away from the rail where she stood. The ship fell silent. The captain had accomplished his goal, the grumbling among them stopped and things would return to normal by his show of power.

Magdalen cried herself to sleep as she nursed Sharon. This scene had brought back many memories of the pain and suffering of Jesus' death.

That evening Magdalen and her little group of disciples gathered for dinner and after they had shared the bread and wine of commemoration she sat cross-legged in their midst. The story she would tell this night was one of fear, pain and justice gone awry.

"Now" she began, "I will tell you how Jesus died and why my husband was killed and by whose hand the Way was silenced. It was just after that first meal of commemoration. Jesus bid us all to come with him to Gethsemane for prayer and meditation. Upon arriving at the garden, Jesus left all but three of the apostles there at Mt. Olive, and the three he took with him and went on a little further. The hour was late and the wine had taken its toll on all the men. Everyone slept as we waited for Jesus, everyone but his mother and myself, and, of course, John who by that time was wakened from his alcoholic stupor.

"It seemed like a very long time before Jesus returned to us. Then as he stepped into our midst he said, 'The hour has come' and we heard the Roman guards approaching and saw Judas there in front of them. We all knew what Jesus had foretold to John that the traitor would kiss him as a sign. Judas walked to the Master and kissed him calling him Rabbi. And then he left hurriedly. He was afraid that some of the disciples and the other students of Jesus would confront him for his act of betrayal, or that perhaps the Master himself would rashly strike out at him.

At least that's what I thought, because Peter had already armed himself. This was not like Peter. No one among us carried much more than a small knife blade for utility purposes, certainly not an offensive weapon. But everyone was afraid now, for the Jews had been conspiring for some time among themselves about Jesus and his band of disciples. I couldn't really blame Peter for holding his sword.

"As the head of the soldiers approached Jesus, the Master asked, 'Are you looking for me?' And the soldier replied, 'Are you Jesus of Nazareth? If so, then it is for you that we have come.'

"Now the group of eleven or twelve soldiers carried heavy arms, and it was dark so three of them held torches to light their way. Peter, sure that Jesus would be taken and that they would perhaps all be called before the governor and suffer the consequences of Roman law, drew his sword and struck out at the first centurion. The man's ear fell to the ground a ways off, and he barely was aware of what happened it was so fast, until the blood was felt as it came to his shoulder. In the darkness, the others could not see the injury that Peter had subjected the man to and for a minute or two, no one seemed to move. Then, Jesus, almost angrily spoke to Peter, 'Go, get that man's ear and bring it here to me with your own hands.' Peter was shocked, I think. He did as he was told. But now the others had brought the light closer to the place where the piece of the man's ear had been thrown. And Peter could see the blood both on the man and on the ear as he picked it up. He was ghost white and in a minute he had handed the thing to Jesus and then turned to run for the hedge of the garden. Peter vomited for a long time. The wine had not helped, and the humiliation must have been very great, for now the soldiers laughed and jeered and the disciples themselves, while they could not understand the actions of Jesus, were cruel in their response to Peter's weak stomach.

"Jesus, holding the man's ear to his head, said, 'I am indeed, Jesus of Nazareth.' Right then the ear mended itself and the man tugged at it and felt no pain. He answered Jesus. 'You are indeed. And you are one beyond understanding. It is no wonder that the Jews fear you so that they have called upon Pilate to question you. This is an act that no other man has done. The governor awaits your presence, and I will lead you.' Jesus answered, 'I am accused of being a king, let me then walk as I am called. I will lead you and we will arrive at the governor's palace without further incident.'

"They walked away, Jesus at the lead. And the centurions could not understand what had happened or the reasons for this man's behavior. The apostles scattered, but remained in pairs. They always did. Peter went in pursuit of Jesus, but he kept himself crouched even as he walked. He could not bear to have another confrontation with the soldiers. They would have been angry despite the Master's healing actions. Jesus' mother calmly said that she would return to the room where we had had supper and wait. I could not be so calm. I followed also, but a mere woman would not be noticed as easily as the disciple who was violent, so I could follow more closely. But, being a woman, I could only go so far. I did not need to be recognized by one of the men I knew from the temple at Magdala. I shook inside because I too was frightened by all the events of the evening and, of course, of what would happen should I be discovered. There was a sort of storage house near the palace, and I found cover within its porch and there fell asleep on the wooden steps. I prayed that morning would bring news of Jesus' release, but I knew that my prayers would not be heard, for he had told me himself that his death was imminent.

"Andrew shook and woke me. I had not slept long. It was not yet midnight. He pleaded with me to enter the courtyard of the governor's mansion. He knew that my former position within Roman society would enable me to pass the guards with little effort. I knew the grounds, and I knew the men. I could do what Andrew asked but only at the risk of having someone realize that I was no longer Magdala High Priestess of the temple but the bride of the captive Jesus.

"There was a resentment building in me as I agreed to the apostle's request. How could these men ask me the person they had so rebuked for so long to use the very things that they reputed to despise in order to do their bidding? How could they love Jesus and support and follow him one minute and then put my life in danger to protect their own skins? They were sending me into peril and, by their absence, denying the man that they called Master. I could not understand. Yet, I knew Andrew was concerned or he would not have asked me, and I myself was anxious beyond belief. I needed to know what was happening.

"I arranged my clothes and my hair; the night had taken its toll. But now it was important that if I were recognized, it would be as Magdala, the Priestess to the Great Mother and Sacred Lover to the Roman guard, and not as Mary, the bride of Jesus.

"Coming into the courtyard was easier than I had thought. The guards only laughed at my presence, wondering who in the court had summoned me. I passed them shaking inside but smiling for their benefit and my own protection. It was easy to find a place where I could lean against the wall with my face turned downward and simply listen. I had learned long before that listening at court proved most informative. Secrets are not the forte of the Romans. They like very much to brag about their conquests, no matter how large or small, and they talked a great deal among themselves about strategy and plans for political advancement and monetary gain.

"There were three soldiers not ten feet away, three that I recognized from the incident in the garden, when they had taken Jesus away. They were talking about their commander and how he had lost his ear only to have this man Jesus heal it. I wanted to laugh out loud when one told the other that the commander was still shaking when he came before Pilate to present Jesus. And how he had pleaded with the governor to let Jesus go before he pulled the walls down or dropped them both to their own demise of demonic possession or perhaps leprosy. But I could not afford to laugh and have them realize that I was listening. I wanted to hear more. I prayed that they would speak more of where Jesus was at that moment and of what the governor had said.

"One told the other that the governor had called for witnesses, and that none had been there. The Pharisees had promised Pilate that they would produce such witnesses before the morning, and Jesus was being held until such time that those witnesses could be brought before Pilate. That meant that for the moment Jesus was safe and a feeling of relief took over within me.

"I knew Pilate; he had come to me and summoned me to him many times. He was a small man, in more ways than one." Magdalen laughed and the women giggled at her attempt to interject humor into such a dramatic tale.

"There was not a decision making bone in that man's body. He was ever at the mercy of the consort." Magdalen continued once more very somber.

"They made all the decisions for him really. He simply signed his edicts and collected his Roman coin. If Caesar knew of Pilate's inability, then Caesar had no use for Jerusalem. And if Caesar did not know, then soon the consort would see to it and Pilate would find his end, for he was no governor. Realizing all this, I realized something else. At this very minute, Pilate was more than likely seeking counsel as to what he should do with Jesus, and who should be pleased in this matter - the law of Rome or the Jewish Sanhedrin.

"That thought prompted me to move into the court itself. If I was careful, I could seat myself with some of the other women and not be noticed for more than one of the deaf and dumb of the women's quarter. Those poor women had their tongues cut out and their eardrums pierced to keep them from telling government secrets or hearing of Roman plans of war. That custom is one that the Romans had brought from Egypt and this was the first time that I felt it had any value to anyone, but I thought it could serve me well for the moment. And it did. I slipped in and sat with four other women whom I knew could not speak in order to ask me why I was there, and who further would not give my presence away by any gesture.

"I was right about the governor's need for counsel. Pilate had the commander and his chief counsel, Tobias, in front of him. Also there were two Pharisees, Annas and Caiphas, who were still making promises of being able to produce witnesses shortly. According to them, some of their scribes had already been sent to obtain the presence of those witnesses. Pilate was playing dumb, like a fox. He asked over and over again what Jesus was to be accused of within the Roman court. There is a decree from Caesar that prevents Roman law and government from interfering with or adhering to the law of the Jewish people. The Jews are granted the right to practice the law of their religion without interference in return for their tax money and support of Caesar by the Sanhedrin.

"It was obvious to both of the men that there was nothing of which Jesus could be accused under Roman law. The crimes that they claimed against him were crimes only under Jewish law, and even these could not be proved, I knew that. There was talk of Jesus having been born a bastard, a child of Satan himself. But what that had to do with Roman law, I could not understand. Pilate seemed to disregard it too, at first, until the commander spoke up. He was still certainly frightened. And he believed that if Jesus were a bastard, then that would explain his power. He was under the influence of some demon or some God who could be of service or of detriment to the Roman emperor and to Pilate himself. Now the commander knew as well as I how to get to Pilate. Simply tell him that someone else's power could be of service to him either financially or politically. For a moment Pilate was certainly considering that perhaps Jesus was of more use to him than the Sanhedrin. All of the accusations of blasphemy Pilate had to release as mere religious upheaval, and since it had not caused riot or uprising against the empire it was of no consequence in a Roman court.

"It was about that time that the witnesses came in. There were at least ten or fifteen men, but only three spoke. I recognized them from the temple and the synagogue at Nazareth. They were there in Jerusalem, like us, for the feast day. They testified before Pilate that Jesus had healed on the

Sabbath and that he had brought leavened bread and eaten it in the temple, in the very presence of God and their ancestors. Pilate scoffed at that. What difference did all this make to the empire? And further, if a man heals, can this be called blasphemy to any God? Is it not God's way and place to heal? Certainly, the Roman Gods would find this a good work, and he questioned the validity of their thoughts in regard to their divine and ancestral beliefs. For the first time, Pilate was right about something, without any coaxing.

"This went on for an hour or more. Conversation, accusation, and more conversation. Then Pilate asked if anyone would testify for Jesus, and I had all that I could do to keep silent. If I spoke, they would recognize me, and my testimony would mean nothing. If I kept silent, I might learn something more of what was to be done with Jesus. I wondered where Peter and Andrew were by then. My feelings of resentment were renewed. And my thoughts must have been heard, because someone said that even now his disciples were hiding, and that one had been found who had been in the garden. But that one, Peter, had denied that he even knew Jesus. He had denied, the commander said, three times over, three times to three different soldiers. And I remembered that Jesus had predicted that Peter would deny him three times before the cock crowed; poor Peter was probably hiding from shame. He loved the Master more than most, but he was human and certainly as frightened as I, especially after he had done such damage to one of the members of the emperor's army.

"There were a few disciples who did come forth and two that spoke in Jesus' behalf. They spoke of the fact that Jesus had been present during the work of God on the Sabbath, but that always he had said that it was by the act of God and not by his own power that these things were done. And that none had he touched on the Sabbath. Pilate scoffed again. This was as of little consequence as was the accusation. It still had nothing to do with Roman law. Then they testified that Jesus was not a bastard, but that his father was Joseph and that they could, if the governor desired, summon this man from afar, for he was working away from home as he always did. The Jews could not deny Jesus' parent's marriage, for it had been arranged and recorded in the temple at Magdala. This ended any conversation regarding Jesus' danger to the public interest as one possessed or one that, being a bastard, would be of poor influence to the Roman community. Pilate was yet stymied. He called Jesus before him. I held my breath.

"Shortly, two centurions brought Jesus in. He looked tired now, but he was still regal in his gait. His hands were tied with leather thongs and held in front of him and he was dirty from the jail, but he stood like a king there in silence.

"It was harder than ever to remember that silence was my cover and the only way that I could stay this close to him and to the situation. Pilate spoke to Jesus. 'Your own people bring you before me. What do you have to say?' And Jesus questioned the governor, 'Of what am I accused?'

"Pilate stated that he was accused of blasphemy and that he was said to be possessed by the devil and that his mother had no husband and his very life was the result of fornication. He said that these things were not the problem of the state, but that the Sanhedrin had one last accusation that had insulted the empire. Pilate asked, 'Have you said that you are the King of the Jews? Do you question the authority of Caesar? Have you any idea that treason could be involved here and that treason would result in death?'

"Jesus stated simply, 'Caesar is the emperor of Rome.' Pilate asked him then, 'Are you the King of the Jews?' And Jesus responded, 'I am who you say I am.' Pilate was not satisfied. He asked again, 'Do you say that you are the King of the Jews?' And Jesus answered again, 'Who do you say that I am?'

"Then Pilate's wife entered the room and went to her husband, whispering in his ear. I could not hear, but immediately after that Pilate ended the interview. He said, 'Take him out and have him scourged. Then hold him, tomorrow is a new day, and in the light of the sun the Jews will prefer this gentle, and perhaps simple man, to the terror of Barabas. It is their feast. It is their favor. And it will then be their choice. Even the Sanhedrin cannot be so stubborn as to prefer murderers to prophets, holy men, or the insane.'

"And then Jesus was led away into the courtyard. It was easy within a few minutes to move back to where I had been. By this time it was coming dawn, and I was grateful for the increased movement of servants and slaves, which gave me more obscurity in the daylight.

"Jesus was bound to the whipping post, stripped naked and flogged until he was near unconscious. He was bleeding badly and weakened by the pain and the weariness of the whole night. He fell to the ground, unable to get up. The soldiers jeered, Rome is known for training its men to enjoy the shedding of blood and the pain of others.

"I cried silently. There was nothing that I, or anyone, could do here in the court of the governor. I could only watch and keep praying that Pilate would be right and that when morning came they would release Jesus. Then he could heal himself and have time for rest and surely find a way to put an end to all of this and to the people who were at fault. But I was remembering also, Jesus' own prediction that he would die.

"A soldier, one who had been in the garden, threw his own cloak over Jesus, and led him back to the jail to be held until Pilate called him before the people."

"It must have been awful for you Magdalen," Carmel's heart went out to the storyteller. "To watch such pain in the one you loved so much and to be so helpless." There were tears running down Carmel's young face.

"Do not weep for me, Carmel, but for the guilt that Jesus' murderers carry with them now and for the way the world has lost its finest teacher."

Magdalen didn't want to lose her own composer and Carmel's tears made her feel quite close to crying. She went on with her story in a softer voice.

"It is the custom that a Jewish prisoner is set free by the Romans at Passover. Ordinarily the governor, from a list given and recommended to him by the Sanhedrin, selects that prisoner. This edict came down from the emperor as a sign of respect for the Jews, and of course to create good relations politically with Jewish leaders.

"Pilate had a plan to rid himself of this whole thing. For some reason, some reason much deeper than what I knew, Pilate wanted to take no responsibility for the sentencing of Jesus. The Pharisees had pleaded for crucifixion, but Pilate had ignored their request. He had offered to hold Jesus until after the holiday and the Sabbath, when the Jews could lawfully deal with this matter themselves. It is as unlawful to punish crime on the Sabbath, as it is to commit it - another law I never grew to understand."

Magdalen shook her head is disbelief.

"But the Pharisees refused Pilate's offer. They did not want the responsibility for this thing either. It seemed as if everyone was afraid of someone. Pilate was afraid of the emperor, perhaps, but more of the Jews. The Jews were probably afraid of Jesus' power should he continue, but afraid of their God, too.

"Pilate's plan meant that the Jews would have to take responsibility for their own actions. He planned to present to them, as the choice of prisoners, Jesus and one named Barabas. Barabas was a killer, a madman, whose crimes had gone long unpunished and who was now awaiting crucifixion at the hands of Rome. The Jews had disowned the man, not wanting to put him to death themselves, but realizing that he certainly deserved the sentence. They had turned him over to Rome for sentencing under Roman law. Barabas would serve more as an example, not only to the Jewish people but also to all of Jerusalem, of the consequences of violent behavior against either and both societies. The pact had served to put them further in favor with the emperor and it was a decision that had been respected by almost everyone. Now they would have to take not only their own feelings of insecurity into consideration, but they would have to insult the emperor by changing their minds as well. If Barabas were their choice for release, certainly Rome would have something to say. If Barabas were crucified, and Jesus set forth, then Pilate would end the matter with no repercussions from either Rome or the Sanhedrin. The politics of the empire are always the foremost concern."

Magdalen paused with her personal observation.

"You are right, Magdalen." Polaris agreed. "Men make laws, break laws and bargain for the law. Rome is a place where men live in fear of what they have created and the injustice of their own actions."

Now Polaris caught herself in her need to comment on the politics she so abhorred and covered her mouth for a moment.

"Please, dear, do finish your story. I did not mean to interrupt with my judgments."

Magdalen went on with her tale.

"The sun finally began to show brightly and the day warmed to an arid dryness. It always did by noon, but it was hotter than usual. There was no wind to cool you, and the crowd began to gather beneath the balcony of the palace. There were over a hundred people there before Pilate appeared. This was a holiday celebration, and everyone was eager to cheer the prisoner who would be given a second chance. Many though, did not know of Jesus at all. They all knew of Barabas. No one was aware of Pilate's plan and there was a great deal of shock when the centurions brought out both men. Pilate reminded them of the charges. First against Barabas, that took as much as ten minutes just to list. Then he turned his hand toward Jesus, and stated but one charge. 'This man is being accused of calling himself your king. Whom do you choose to be set free?' And he stated their names again. It was unbelievable; they called for Barabas.

"Pilate was as shocked as I was. There was no reason for this except that the crowd, unknowing of all the facts, had made the assumption that Jesus must be a worse criminal and threat to society than Barabas merely by the fact that Barabas, an infamous killer and thief, should even be compared with him. Pilate's short statement was being taken, not as a charge of blasphemy, but as a charge of authority. They thought he was belittling Jesus' crime with sarcasm and that Jesus surely was some unknown thief and murderous villain who had undermined Roman and Jewish authority. Calling himself king meant to them that he had put himself beyond authority or punishment, and surely they felt Jesus must be put to know the authority of the law. Barabas had been imprisoned a long time, and he was already aware of Roman law and Jewish tradition, besides they would catch Barabas again. Obviously, to them, Jesus had been escaping capture, that was why Pilate had referred to him as a king. They called for Barabas again, and Pilate fell to his chair.

"The thief was released to the crowd. Jesus stood there still tied and still wearing the cloak of the Roman centurion and nothing more. His body was torn from the whipping and still bleeding, although not as profusely. Somehow, he looked leaner than I had ever known him to be. He was drawn with fatigue and pain and there was little if any color left in his cheeks, usually so tanned by the sun.

"Pilate called out to the Jews, 'What shall I do then with Jesus?' And shouts rang out for crucifixion.

"Pilate's wife appeared behind him on the balcony. She whispered again in his ear and then stood back, as if she were waiting for a response from her husband. Now this is not the way of things in the Roman court. Women have no public part in politics, and certainly not in the politics of Jewish holiday and law. Pilate called for water with which to wash. A basin was brought, and as a servant poured water over his hands, Pilate rang them together as if terribly distraught. He called out loudly and more firmly than I knew him to speak about anything before, 'I have no part in this; let it be on your hands. I am the governor. Crucify him, but the soul of your God hangs with him. It is your doing.'

"And Pilate's wife began screaming. She went mad. She pulled at her hair and pulled at Pilate's hair, and at his throat, and screamed again. You really could not understand her. She was absolutely stark raving mad, and was hysterical in her cries. The soldiers subdued her and took her out, away from the balcony and the crowds beneath it.

"The centurions led Jesus down into the courtyard. Much of the crowd had dispersed except for a few soldiers, some Pharisees who stayed to be sure that the sentence was carried out, and some disciples who hid along the walls fearing that they too would suffer the fate of Golgotha.

"You know that crucifixion is not uncommon a punishment under Roman law and Golgotha holds six tall poles upon which these men are hung every day. They are raised on cross bars that hold their arms outright to the top of the permanent poles, and there left to rot and show any other proposed criminal the result of Roman authority. The cross bars and the carcasses of these men are removed only when the poles are required again for another execution. The centurions were now holding Jesus in the courtyard awaiting the arrival of two more criminals who were to be executed that day and for the carpenter who supplied them with the cross bars for each prisoner.

"While they waited they made a sign with wood in which was carved, the King of the Jews. Pilate had ordered this as a reminder to the community of Jerusalem that this was not by Roman law but by Jewish request. And he had it carved in three languages so no one would misunderstand or be confused in his meaning. While two men set to this task, two others held Jesus. One, jeering in the usual way of Roman cruelty, pulled from the hedge a branch of thorns and encircled Jesus' head with it. The second soldier did the same and each repeated the process several times until Jesus' hair, scalp, and forehead were filled with the nasty briars and the blood that resulted. They hailed him in mocking. 'Behold the King,' and struck him on the head and about the forehead until the thorns had embedded themselves quite securely into his flesh. I could see his right eye fill with blood and realized that the length of one of those thorns had pierced it.

"The cart arrived carrying both the criminals to be crucified and the trees on which they were to be hung. One of the centurions pulled a pole from the cart and raised it upon the shoulder of Jesus. 'Let him carry the thing. Better he be tired going to hell, than the horse be tired going to market.' And they forced him then to carry the cross bar the mile or more to Golgotha.

"It was a slow procession, getting through the holiday crowds and stopping to eliminate the jeers of children and lepers and criminal sorts of the street. Women cried that knew him, and disciples sobbed unable to do anything to save him in the face of the Roman soldiers. His mother walked along side of him, as close as she dared, and cried not one tear. I walked behind her, wanting desperately to offer comfort, but unable to control my own sorrow and fear.

"My tears flowed quite openly and Jesus fell. They raised him to his feet and pushed him along. He fell again and was offered water by one of the women that lined the road. The soldiers pushed away the cup and offered him a rag tied to the end of a sword, and the rag had been dipped in gall. They brought him to his feet and the procession continued. When he fell for the third time I thought that they had already killed him.

'I cannot see,' he said. 'The thorn has blinded me.' And they mocked him. 'Heal your blindness and move on.' One soldier shouted as he kicked him forward.

I thought that it would be more than I could bear. My fingernails had pierced my own hands and the anguish and fear caused me to shake on the inside."

Magdalen was shaking now on the outside as she told the story.

"Perhaps this story is too much for you." Polaris put her arm around the shaking woman. "We have all had too much violence this day."

"No" Magdalen said. "It is a story that you should hear and one that may renew my grief only to relieve me of it. It is a catharsis that I am sharing with you as well as a lesson."

Polaris tightened her arm around Magdalen's shoulders. "If it will help you and we are of service, then please continue."

Magdalen smiled briefly at the older woman whose comfort was welcomed.

"Thank you, my friend, for understanding.

"I walked near to my mother-in-law and John was near to Mother Mary too, and I could hear him cry out loud. Just a boy yet, I thought he would become hysterical if someone did not talk with him. I tried, but he rejected my effort at consolation. I could not try very hard, though, or I too would go as crazy as Pilate's wife.

"We arrived at Golgotha and there was no longer a crowd. They had left for other celebrations. There was some interest in crucifixion at times, even among the Jews, but this day there were only the few who had gathered in the courtyard when the procession began. I had never seen a crucifixion myself. The first centurion, the one from the garden, was giving the orders. He had the two thieves hung first. Each was tied to the tree that was his by the wrists, and then raised by a pulley system to the top of the pole. Then his feet were tied together, but not secured to the pole. This put all the weight of each man upon himself. It is a tortuous death in which the air is forced from the lungs that cannot expand under the pressure of the body's weight against them. In reality, crucifixion is a slow and painful method of suffocation like the hanging we saw today."

Magdalen's eyes were filling with tears as she went on.

"When both men had been lifted up, the centurion came to Jesus. The centurion said to him, 'Have you no friends, sir? Where are those who would have fought with me when I arrested you? Where has the power gone that returned my ear? Why have you let this happen, and why must I be the one?'

"Jesus had fallen to the ground again and he looked up at the centurion and answered him softly, 'Do what you must, my power is within.' And the soldier knelt and tied securely Jesus' hands to each side of the tree.

"One of the Pharisees cried out, 'He claimed to have the power of God. Perhaps he will get free from your ties.' And another soldier took from the cart wooden stakes, and he drove one of them through each of Jesus' hands into the tree. 'He will not free himself from this authority,' and Jesus gave out with a cry that went to my heart.

"I cried out myself as the second stake entered his hand, and I begged the centurion for his mercy. I was ignored and Jesus was raised as the others into position. They then fastened his feet together with leather thongs and the soldier again drove his stakes into Jesus. This time he fastened his feet, each one of them, to the tree. And Jesus braced himself there, knees bent, holding his weight against the tree. I could not believe that he had the strength for this, and I began to pray that he would release himself, so that this thing might not go on much longer.

"My husband called to me then, 'I cannot see you my sweet Magdala or my mother. Come closer,' and we moved up to the foot of the pole. The pain within me was indescribable as it is now. His body, once so strong and filled with life and love, hung now, naked and bloody, in a weak and lifeless heap upon that pole. Yet he breathed, and even spoke occasionally. He did not cry out in pain, and I felt that he could no longer feel anything at all. Some said that he had worked some sort of magic that had relieved him. Some said he was only waiting for the right moment, and that he would come down and punish those that had raised him up. Mother Mary was quiet as she held John in her arms. She had fallen to the ground with him and sat there with what seemed no regard for the presence of anyone else. I cried until I thought my own breath would stop. Some of the people left. The Pharisees posted two of their own men to stay until the end. The disciples walked off, saying that they could not bear it any longer. Peter had tried to take us away, but we sent him ahead without us. It took a long time for the thieves to die, almost three hours. And in the end, one spoke to Jesus. Jesus spoke back to him, and then the thief died. Only Jesus was left, and still he breathed. The soldiers were shocked, but they continued their vigil.

"It is the custom that after a man is proclaimed dead by the guard, that he be driven through, so there can be no mistake that he is dead and so that other criminals can't contrive an escape for him through a deception. So both thieves were established dead and then the first centurion, whose job it was, drove his sword through their hearts. Now as he did this, Jesus called out. 'Where is my divinity? I can do no more!' And he died. And I begged the centurion to pierce my husband's heart also, so that if he suffered any longer it would end. But the centurion said that it had been Pilate's order that he should not be killed, but by the order of the Jews, and that he was not to pierce Jesus. I cried out loudly and another soldier did as I asked. He said, 'Pilate need not know that I took mercy on this woman, and the man is dead anyway. He's not going anywhere. And I have killed no one.' Then they broke the legs of both thieves, another precaution. But Jesus they did not touch again.

"As all this was happening the earth began to tremor and the sky went black. There was a total eclipse of the sun, and an earthquake that made all look upward begging the heavens for mercy. The first centurion began to cry out. 'What has been done here? What evil have we called down upon ourselves?'

"And the soldiers all rushed from the place. John and Mother Mary were taken by Simon, a family friend who had watched at a distance, to his house to stay until things had quieted. I refused Simon's hospitality. I needed to be alone and in my own place. And it was to my own home that I went, which I had left over two and a half years before. There were rumors in the street that the temple had fallen, the veil torn, and all manner of things that were miraculous and evil. But I ignored all these sayings, for if Jesus had meant to punish or rebuke, he certainly would have done it before his death, not after it. I only wanted to get home.

"When I arrived, the two servants I had left to manage my affairs greeted me with excuses. My home had been ravaged. A great number of my beautiful things were gone, and these unfaithful ones were filled with surprise at my arrival. They tried to persuade me to forgiveness with embraces and pleading, but I pushed them off. It mattered, but it didn't matter. I poured and drank several glasses of wine, cried until I slept once again in my own bed. My mind filled with feelings of frustration and sorrow, as well as grief and loneliness.

"Tonight, I will take to my dreams those feelings once again. I have told you this story tonight for a reason. I want you to understand the grief of injustice and the pain of others. I want you to know how easily fear can create within us demons of our own. Today many were possessed by the demons of fear, of guilt and of blame. Many were possessed by the demons of arrogance, power and control over others. Tonight, many on this ship, even some of you, will sleep as I slept that fateful night – with a shattered heart and despair."

Magdalen wept openly as she ended her story. The women's eyes were filled with tears too. They felt the pain in Magdalen's heart, and they knew that part of the Way would be learning and using some new form of justice within their community. They all hoped that Magdalen would teach them how to do that, but not tonight. Tonight they would comfort her and ask fewer questions than usual.

"Magdalen, you should rest now." Said Polaris. "This story has drained you and you are living again the pain of the past."

"No" Magdalen retorted, "I am living the pain of the moment, for this day has proved to me once again that the world must walk a New Way. We must lead the Way of the Master and bring Love to the hearts of those who are possessed by their demons. But, yes, Polaris, I will rest, for soon our work will begin in earnest."

Everyone retired and Magdalen wept until sleep came.

Chapter 19

Myth and Magic of Gaul

"What will we find in Massilia, Magdalen?" Carmel broke the breakfast silence. "I am still welcome, am I not?"

The other women, including Magdalen, hugged Carmel in excitement. Everyone was excited about arriving in Massilia, but now it was more thrilling to know that their little band would remain together on their journey and on the Way. When the hug broke up Magdalen answered Carmel's question.

"Massilia is a Roman port like any other. We will find the baths first!" she laughed and the others with her. "Then a tavern and finally the market. Once we have gotten our supplies and our land legs back, we will find a caravan with which to travel across Gaul. It is what we will find on those travels that excites me."

"Why, Magdalen, what have you heard? Please, tell us more."

Once again the women coaxed Magdalen into telling them a tale. This time though it was not about the Way but about the ways of others, mainly the Celts and Druids of which Magdalen had only read or heard scuttlebutt.

"Well, I've heard that they go to war naked!"

The group giggled and James moved away from them. He had eaten and these stories were of no consequence to him.

"I've also heard that the Druids, that's their priests, perform human sacrifices offering up live human beings to the fires of the temple. That's what frightens James now. He is afraid for us all; but I think that the stories are only rumors designed to make the Roman army look more civilized than the Celts."

"I don't know, Magdalen." Said Polaris. "Sometimes it is wise to look at rumors as a warning, and while I am not suggesting that we travel in fear, it would be a good idea to let James take the lead here. I've heard that they are deep into slave trade with Rome, and they carry chains and swords of iron as long as they are tall. Perhaps James is right in being afraid."

She gave a false shutter of fear and winked at Magdalen.

"Certainly I'm right." James had overheard Polaris' remark and saw her wink. He obviously didn't find the conversation and its topic to be amusing.

"We will travel the Roman trade roads and with a well armed caravan, too. The safety of the child and her mother are my responsibility, and I will see to it that it is not jeopardized any more than need be. These Celts could be as uncivilized and savage as you have heard. We will take no unnecessary chances then."

"You're building dams again, James." Magdalen couldn't resist.

"I've also heard that they wear beautifully colored clothes and jewelry and that they make wonderful leather boots and ship them to Rome for a very high price. And I've heard that they have vineyards there that produce rich wine. I've also heard that they worship Mercury and the Great Mother and that all women are highly esteemed. Maybe one of us will one day be your mistress, James! Who knows what's to be believed?"

Magdalen laughed out loud at the thought and how it brought the hairs on James' arm to full attention.

"You heard me, Magdalen, we will take no chances with these people."

With that James walked off again. Magdalen turned to the women.

"Would you like me to read to you from Julius Caesar's account of Gaul?"

All heads nodded affirmatively as Magdalen reached into her leather bags to find one of the few remaining books she had. She had kept this one because it spoke of Gaul and of Massilia and all of the things that she was hoping to find there.

"This is how he begins, 'Since we have come to this place, it does not appear to be foreign to our subject to lay before the reader an account of the manners of Gaul and Germany, and wherein these nations differ from each other. In Gaul there are factions not only in all the states, and in all the cantons and their divisions, but almost in each family, and of these factions those are the leaders who are considered according to their judgment to possess the greatest influence, upon whose will and determination the management of all affairs and measures depends. And that seems to have been instituted in ancient times with this view, that no one of the common people should be in want of support against one more powerful; for none of those leaders suffers his party to be oppressed and defrauded, and if he do otherwise, he has no influence among his party. This same policy exists throughout the whole of Gaul; for all the states are divided into two factions.

'When Caesar arrived in Gaul, the Aedui were the leaders of one faction, the Sequani of the other.'

"He goes on about many battles and the Roman's need for assistance. 'Divitiacus urged by this necessity, had proceeded to Rome to the senate, for the purpose of entreating assistance, and had returned without accomplishing his object.'

"I've heard of this Divitiacus in other writings." Magdalen interrupted herself. "He was a Druid priest, I think, and a friend of Caesar's as well. But let me continue,

'Throughout all Gaul there are two orders of those men who are of any rank and dignity: for the commonality is held almost in the condition of slaves, and dares to undertake nothing of itself and is admitted to no deliberation. The greater part, when they are pressed either by debt, or the large amount of their tributes or the oppression of the more powerful, give themselves up in vassalage to the nobles, who possess over them the same rights without exception as masters over their slaves. But of these two orders, one is that of the Druids, the other that of the knights. The former are engaged in things sacred, conduct the public and the private sacrifices, and interpret all matters of religion. To these a large number of the young men resort for the purpose of instruction, and they (the Druids) are in great honor among them. For they determine respecting almost all controversies, public and private; and if any crime has been perpetrated, if murder has been committed, if there be any dispute about an inheritance, if any about boundaries, these same persons decide it; they decree rewards and punishments; if any one, either in a private or public capacity, has not submitted to their decision, they interdict him from the sacrifices. This among them is the heaviest punishment. Those who have been thus interdicted are esteemed in the number of the impious and the criminal: all shun them, and avoid their society and conversation, lest they receive some evil from their contact; nor is Justice administered to them when seeking it, nor is any dignity bestowed on them. Over all these Druids one presides, who possesses supreme authority among them. Upon his death, if any individual among the rest is pre-eminent in dignity, he succeeds; but, if there are many equal, the election is made by the suffrages of the Druids; sometimes they even contend for the presidency with arms. These assemble at a fixed period of the year in a consecrated place in the territories of the Carnutes, which is reckoned the central region of the whole of Gaul. Hither all, who have disputes, assemble from every part, and submit to their decrees and determinations. This institution is supposed to have been devised in Britain, and to have been brought over from it into Gaul; and now those who desire to gain a more accurate knowledge of that system generally proceed thither for the purpose of studying it.

"The Druids do not go to war, nor pay tribute together with the rest; they have an exemption from military service and a dispensation in all matters. Induced by such great advantages, many embrace this profession of their own accord, and many are sent to it by their parents and relations. They are said there to learn by heart a great number of verses; accordingly some remain in the course of training twenty years. Nor do they regard it lawful to commit these to writing, though in almost all other matters, in their public and private transactions, they use Greek characters. That practice they seem to me to have adopted for two reasons; because they neither desire their doctrines to be divulged among the mass of the people, nor those who learn, to devote themselves the less to the efforts of memory, relying on writing: since it generally occurs to most men, that, in their dependence on writing, they relax their diligence in learning thoroughly, and their employment of the memory. They wish to inculcate this as one of their leading tenets, that souls do not become extinct, but pass after death from one body to another, and they think that men by this tenet are in a great degree excited to valor, the fear of death being disregarded. They likewise discuss and impart to the youth many things respecting the stars and their motion, respecting the extent of the world and of our earth, respecting the nature of things, respecting the power and the majesty of the immortal gods.'

"I think these druids might be the ones to fear," Magdalen interrupted the reading again.

"I'm thinking that Caesar would not lie about such things as this." Replied Polaris.

"I hope they can speak Greek as well as write it," said Magdalen. "Language could be a problem once we leave Massilia."

"It sounds to me like we might have more than language borders to cross." James was back and interrupting again. "These druids sound like a secret society of executioners to me."

"Let's read on James, he speaks of the Knights next." Magdalen began where she had left off.

"The other order is that of the knights. These, when there is occasion and any war occurs (which before Caesar's arrival was for the most part wont to happen every year, as either they on their part were inflicting injuries or repelling those which others inflicted on them), are all engaged in war. And those of them most distinguished by birth and resources have the greatest number of vassals and dependants about them. They acknowledge this sort of influence and power only.'

"I'll bet they are the naked warriors you heard of and the slave traders, too."

Carmel interjected with a slight upward curl in her lips. James' glance told her that this was not the time for jest or fanciful supposition. Magdalen went on reading.

"The nation of all the Gauls is extremely devoted to superstitious rites; and on that account they who are troubled with unusually severe diseases and they who are engaged in battles and dangers, either sacrifice men as victims, or vow that they will sacrifice them, and employ the Druids as the performers of those sacrifices; because they think that unless the life of a man be offered for the life of a man, the mind of the immortal Gods cannot be rendered propitious, and they have sacrifices of that kind ordained for national purposes. Others have figures of vast size, the limbs of which (formed of osiers) they fill with living men, and, setting the figures on fire, cause the men to perish enveloped in the flames. They consider that the oblation of such as have been taken in theft, or in robbery, or any other offence, is more acceptable to the immortal gods; but when a supply of that class is wanting, they have recourse to the oblation of even the innocent."

"Glory be to the Goddess! And Her Consort!" Magdalen almost shouted this call on the Divine.

"I can't imagine a human sacrifice! The Jewish bloody sacrifice of animals was more than I could bear! We must bring these druids and Celtic knights the Way and soon!" She looked back at the scroll.

"They worship as their divinity, Mercury in particular, and have many images of him, and regard him as the inventor of all arts, they consider him, the guide of their journeys and marches, and believe him to have very great influence over the acquisition of gain and mercantile transactions. Next to him they worship Apollo, and Mars, and Jupiter, and Minerva; respecting these deities they have for the most part the same belief as other nations: that Apollo averts diseases, that. Minerva imparts the invention of manufactures, that Jupiter possesses the sovereignty of the heavenly powers; that Mars presides over wars."

Magdalen paused and Polaris spoke what everyone else was thinking. "These people must have had a strong Greek influence even before the Romans arrived. They have a pantheon of deities that is much the same."

"Wait " said Magdalen, " in the next paragraph Caesar goes on about their heritage and source.

"All the Gauls assert that they are descended from the God Dis, and say that this tradition has been handed down by the Druids. For that reason they compute the divisions of every season, not by the number of days, but of nights; they keep birthdays and the beginnings of months and years in such an order that the day follows the night. Among the other usages of their life, they differ in this from almost all other nations, that they do not permit their children to approach them openly until they are grown up so as to be able to bear the service of war; and they regard it as indecorous for a son of boyish age to stand in public in the presence of his father.

'Whatever sums of money the husbands have received in the name of dowry from their wives, making an estimate of it, they add the same amount out of their own estates. An account is kept of all this money conjointly, and the profits are laid by; whichever of them shall have survived the other, to that one the portion of both reverts together with the profits of the previous time. Husbands have power of life and death over their wives as well as over their children: and when the father of a family, born in a more than commonly distinguished rank, has died, his relations assemble, and, if the circumstances of his death are suspicious, hold an investigation upon the wives in the manner adopted towards slaves; and, if proof be obtained, put them to severe torture, and kill them. "

Ruth interrupted. "I thought you said they held women in high esteem, Magdalen. These people are far more bigoted than the Greeks."

She who usually was quiet through Magdalen's stories seemed rather frightened now of where this tale that Caesar had written was taking them. Sarah seemed a bit edgy too.

"Perhaps we should leave the rest of the Emperor's account for another time."

It was Polaris in her wisdom who knew it was time to quit this revelry into an unknown future. The book was written before any of them had been born and certainly civilization had entered the ranks and realms of even the Celts. Gaul, after all, was now more than a Roman Province. It was represented in the senate at Rome and highly respected by the government.

"You're right, Polaris," Magdalen began to roll up her scroll. "You don't want to hear about the animals that are bigger than elephants right now either, I suppose"

She laughed at the wide-eyed curiosity that showed in everyone's face.

"I'll read that part to you after supper."

It truly was time to stop this conversation anyway. Sharon was beginning to stir from her morning nap and diapers had to be washed and linen folded.

The women went about their personal chores and helped Magdalen with the laundry. Seawater was a poor substitute for the fresh water Magdalen knew she would find in Gaul. The salt irritated her hands and did no favors to the tender skin of Sharon's body.

"Soon," she thought, "soon we will be where fresh water flows and we will bring so many to walk the Way, and Sharon will grow to be a woman of renown."

A bite of cheese and bread were lunch, and it was the custom that crew and passengers alike rested after this meal. Magdalen took the scroll bag from is covering and found the part about the animals and the trees and the forest of Gaul. After reading it to herself, she turned the scroll to the appropriate column marking her place for after supper.

"I can't read them any more of that fearful description given by Caesar of these people. Yesterday and the story and experience of violent death were enough for a long time to come. I'll just stick to the exciting things like new animals and trees and colors and gold and silver. That they will like to hear." She thought it in a whisper.

The Great Sea was as blue as the sky and Magdalen was sent to daydreaming as she pondered on what lay ahead of them. The baby slept again that afternoon and the warm sun felt good as Magdalen reached for her embroidery. Her thoughts were of the future as she moved her needle back and forth across the fabric she intended for Sharon's wardrobe. The child was growing all too quickly and would soon be a toddler and an infant no more. To remind her mother that the day had not come yet, Sharon let out a loud howl in hunger. Magdalen went to her calling and then the group gathered again for their supper.

There was fresh fish and some small pieces of dried fruit that the ship's cook provided. Of course there was the cheese, bread and wine that made up all of their meals. It was Ruth's turn to break the bread and pass the wine for their commemoration, and Magdalen was pleased with her eagerness to officiate. Ruth and Sarah looked coyly at one another when they were done. The two were ready for Magdalen to read to them from Caesar's scroll the account of animals large as elephants. Magdalen pulled the scroll from its sleeve and began to read. She knew full well that Ruth's eagerness was rooted in the girl's desire to hear the rest of the story.

"There is a third kind of animal, consisting of those animals that are called uri. These are a little below the elephant in size, and of the appearance, color, and shape of a bull. Their strength and speed are extraordinary; they spare neither man nor wild beast, which they have espied. These the Germans take with much pains in pits and kill them. The young men harden themselves with this exercise, and practice themselves in this kind of hunting, and those who have slain the greatest number of them, having produced the horns in public, to serve as evidence, receive great praise. But not even when taken very young can they be rendered familiar to men and tamed. The size, shape, and appearance of their horns differ much from the horns of our oxen. These they anxiously seek after, and bind at the tips with silver, and use as cups at their most sumptuous entertainments."

"Magdalen," giggled Sarah as she noticed some discrepancies from what they had been promised, "you said they were larger than elephants. I think that you have been playing with us."

"Perhaps, I was mistaken," Magdalen feigned a blush of embarrassment. "He doesn't write though of the Unicorn, the animal that is enchanted and cannot be hunted nor held. The women of the temple told me of them. He is a beautiful white beast whose place it is to save those who are lost in the forests of the Celts both in Gaul and in Avalon where he is said to have originated. No one has ever, ever seen his mate."

"Oh, Magdalen," Ruth was grinning "I want to see both the Unicorn and his mate, even if we have to go all the way across Gaul and into Brittany."

Everyone agreed that seeing the Unicorn wouid be the highlight of even a world tour.

"It is myth and meant to entertain children." James was putting a damper on what otherwise was a joyous occasion.

"Myth or not," Magdalen recovered the joy, "let us dream of Unicorns and of fresh water and of all the beautiful things that we will find when we arrive in Gaul."

They would see the shore of Gaul the very next day and hastened off to sleep in hopes of making their dreams come true.

Chapter 20

Roma of Gaul

Morning came with shouts from the crew. The rocky shore of Massilia could be seen from the ship. The white limestone cliffs were decorated with umbrella pines and below you could see the earth's reflection in the water of the Great Sea. The sun shone brightly, and Magdalen thought of this morning as more than a new day; it was to be the first day of a new life.

The others seemed as excited as Magdalen when the ship moored in the Roman port. Tin and salt traders scurried along the docks loading and unloading cargo that would bring the trade merchants great wealth. The ladies scurried too to see what was available for sale before it reached the marketplace. Magdalen made sure that the cover for Sharon's basket-cradle was securely in place and that she was not too warm under its protection. James strode down the dock like a peacock Magdalen had seen in the Roman gardens of Jerusalem. He wanted, she thought, to give an air of confidence and strength, hoping his demeanor would ward off any attempts of thievery or brawling. The police in Massilia would ignore such attempts and their outcome so long as there were no bloody battles.

"Magdalen, you promised – the baths first!"

Ruth was almost squealing with delight. The five-day journey had left everyone feeling sticky, salty and hot. Now the women could indulge once more in fresh water baths and perhaps purchase some of the fine perfumes Massilia was famous for. Magdalen felt her hair and nodded smiling that they

224

would, indeed, go to the baths first. James had other things on his mind.

"I will seek out a meal first," he said. "I'll walk with you to the baths and then find the nearest, cleanest tavern."

James was smiling too. This plan was agreeable to everyone. James left the women and Sharon along with their belongings at the baths and went off on his search for a tavern.

The morning and afternoon went quickly by. The women bathed, and when Magdalen had bathed Sharon and all of them were feeling comfortable and clean, they ate a fine meal set for them by slaves in the courtyard. For all intents and purposes one would have thought that they had arrived back in Rome. Resting and sharing stories of their journey with other women at the baths, they waited for James' return.

That time came too quickly and soon the respite was over. James led the women back to a room he had rented for them. Here they would spend their time until a caravan could be arranged for. Magdalen was sure that this would not be a long wait, because the Roman road was constantly being traveled to and from the capital city of Lugdunum just up the river Rhone. James was not going to be over-anxious though. He wanted to be sure that they would travel with a reputable company and with the utmost safety and protection from barbarians and pirates who had been let ashore unable to find new passage and using their skill as robbers along the Roman highways.

After supper that night Magdalen gathered her band around the table and pulled out the maps that Paul had given her back in Athens. She pointed out the Roman highway that led from Massilia to Lugdunum.

"Lugdunum will be our next stop," she stated quite matter-of-factly. "It is about one-third of the way, and a good place to spend a night."

James interrupted, " We will find a caravan and follow the instructions of the caravan's captain as to where and when we will stop."

He sounded rather determined, but Magdalen ignored his attitude.

"I think that after one night in Lugdunum we will move on to Alesia before stopping again. After that we should be able to make Gesoriacum without any further delay."

James decided that there was no use arguing over Magdalen's excitement and enthusiasm. He would find a caravan captain the next day and make the best travel arrangements that he could. This could be both an exciting adventure and a dangerous or expensive one. With that thought he reached for his purse and began a check of their remaining resources. Five thousand sesterces would provide nicely for their journey, he thought, if he only needed to pay passage for Magdalen, Sharon and himself. What of the other women? Until now they had paid their own passage and expenses as they had planned on this portion of the journey. Would they still have funds with which to travel? James decided he had better discuss this with Magdalen alone and before morning. When he had the opportunity later in the evening, he approached Magdalen.

"Magdalen, what of funds for the journey? Are we to pay passage for these four tag-a-longs?"

Magdalen felt the hair on her head stand on end.

"James, they are not tag-a-longs, they are apostles just as you were to Jesus. Did he ever question the cost of your presence? Everything will be provided for. We will establish a community purse. You will carry part of it and I the other in case of loss or robbery."

With that Magdalen reached into the basket and beneath Sharon's sleeping body. She handed over a purse and in it James counted twenty thousand sesterces. He was shocked.

"Nicodemus did well for me and Paul gave me a gift."

Magdalen never raised an eyebrow. She divided the money between their two purses, handed one to James and tucked the other back under the baby.

"I will ask the others for their contribution in the morning."

With that she was off to bed leaving James both astonished and relieved. Although he was hesitant about telling the others of their good fortune and of the way Magdalen was carrying her purse beneath her child, Magdalen 's strength of character and mind impressed him. She did have the savvy to know what she needed and when.

The next day before they could reach the market, Magdalen asked for the women's donation to the community funds, leaving each of them a personal allowance of one hundred sesterces a piece. To James' relief she never mentioned the amount in her purse and tucked the newly acquired funds into her clothes.

"She is savvy." He thought to himself.

James went looking for a caravan to travel with. Caravans provided safety both by their numbers and by the presence of armed captains and escorts. Most of them provided nothing more. That meant that cart and animals of burden were usually a necessary purchase, one that would later require care and constant attention. James interviewed three different captains before he came upon Gotellius. Gotellius owned many carts and carriages. He rented them to travelers going to Lugdunum who had their own animals and rented them again on the return journey to Massilia. He told James that the group could pick up another caravan in the capital that would take them all the way to the coast if they desired, and a friend of his would rent him a cart or carriage just as he would.

Despite the fact that once again this made Magdalen's prediction right, James booked passage and rented the cart for one hundred sesterces per day for the anticipated two-day journey. He then bought two oxen to pull the cart and a donkey to bear some of the burdens that would not fit in the wagon with the women and child.

Meanwhile, Magdalen and the women did their shopping at the marketplace. This time they would have to provide all their own food and water and Magdalen was careful to prepare the food cupboard for a three-day stint just in case there was a delay. Stopping to sit on a bench in the market and nurse Sharon, Magdalen decided she would have to have a goat. Sharon was getting bigger and perhaps she would wean her soon.

The ladies followed dutifully behind Magdalen as she sought out a fitting animal for her daughter's source of nourishment. She found a beautiful little she goat that had a beard and one drooping eyelid. The goat looked more like a dog than a milking goat, but she fell in love.

"I'll call her Mare," she said, "because she will produce a sea of milk for Sharon when the time is right."

The ladies laughed as Magdalen tethered the goat to her belt and moved through the marketplace collecting food, flasks and fancies. She just couldn't resist another ribbon or two!

When he returned from the stables to join the women, James announced that they would leave in the morning with a rented cart and three beasts of burden. They all laughed when Sarah spoke up.

"And one sea of milk!"

Magdalen explained her purchase and her decision to James and he smiled too. Magdalen was disappointed that it would take two days and not one to reach Lugdunum, but glad she had bought enough supplies to last three days. She had to chuckle on the inside when she discovered that Lugdunum would be the caravan's stopping point.

"Right again, " she thought.

What should have been an early departure turned into a late start. People were having problems with harnesses, animals and carts whose wheels were worn. James harnessed the two oxen to the rented vehicle and helped the women aboard. He raised Sharon, her basket, and their purse up to Magdalen and bound the baggage to the donkey. Through the day of traveling the women sang childhood songs and chattered about Unicorns and wild pigs and even made up stories about suave and handsome highwaymen. James walked beside the cart and every once in a while Magdalen joined him allowing the women to care for Sharon in the wagon and to doze off comfortably and un-crowded. Everyone laughed a lot and Magdalen seemed overjoyed to have begun her new life.

The caravan didn't stop all day; Captain Gotellius felt that they had lost enough time that morning. He, after all, had a schedule to keep, and Magdalen was glad of that. The group was forced to eat in the cart and to settle for dried fruits and nuts, cheese and bread. When night fell, the caravan pulled into a field beside the road and built a huge fire. Now they cooked bits of meat on sticks and ate them from those same tree branches.

"I feel like a Roman soldier in the field." Laughed Ruth.

"Be glad you are not." Polaris retorted.

James laughed. "Neither of you knows the first thing about soldiering."

"I think the fire and the food would be just like this." Ruth insisted.

"Yes, and I'll bet someone tells stories after the supper!"

Sarah was asking Magdalen to tell another tale.

"Let's skip it for tonight, Sarah. I don't know what story to tell." Magdalen objected.

"There's a story teller over here!"

Polaris raised her voice in invitation. Magdalen was shocked at the older woman's brazen approach to committing Magdalen to entertain the others in the caravan. People began to move closer and Magdalen felt surrounded. They were eager for entertainment and diversion. But she truly didn't know what story to tell or how to tell it. She decided on a travel story – that of Mother Mary and Joseph on their way to Bethlehem.

"Let me tell you," Magdalen began, "a story of two travelers who returned from their journey with a gift for the world."

Everyone leaned forward to listen to Magdalen's story.

"In the time of Herod, when dissatisfaction reigned within the hearts of so many, the people, especially the Jews, were anxious for God to intervene, to send the Anointed One about whom it was prophesied would come out of the House of David. At the temple of Magdala, however, the Goddess saw the need through her Priestesses. The Virgins of the temple while lying with their lovers all hoped that they would be the one to bear the Holy Savior. Among them was a girl named Mary who was too young to have taken the initiation of priesthood and was destined one day to wed a man of the community's choosing. She had read the prophecies but had never thought of herself as worthy of bearing such a child.

"One day a scholar arrived at the temple out of the East. Mary, being favored by the others for her intelligence and wisdom beyond her years, was sent to meet with him and learn all that she could from this great and learned man. Days passed and Mary was a worthy pupil. The man became enthralled with her fine features, her childlike simplicity and her love of God and Goddess. Mary admired the man, fell in love with his wonderful blue eyes and often lost herself in his gaze."

Magdalen did a little swoon and sighed to give interest to the story and then continued.

"One day their love turned to passion, and the rite of initiation was hers via this mere traveler to the temple. After he had gone to return to his homeland, Mary had a vision. An angel appeared and spoke thusly, 'Hail, Mary, full of grace, the Lord is with you. Blessed are you among women, and blessed is the fruit of your womb.'

"Now Mary wasn't frightened, angels had appeared to her in many of her meditations and prayers, but she questioned the reference to the fullness of her womb. Being a young one, she had not yet realized that she was with child. The angel told her then that she was to bear a son and that that son would be the long awaited Messiah. Mary was a dutiful servant of the God and Goddess and replied, 'Let it be done unto me according to God's word.'

"Now, when a virgin of the temple becomes impregnated the community must seek out an appropriate husband, one who is older, wiser and wealthy enough to care for the woman and her child. Since Mary was of Jewish descent and since her parents had entrusted her to the temple at an early age, it was decided that she should have a husband from the Jewish sector who could provide appropriately for her and the child.

"The priests and elders met in a council and they decided to call all the widowers of the Jewish community together, instructing each to bring his rod. The high priest took all the rods and went in to pray while the men waited outside for his return. When he returned, he gave each man back his rod, and from Joseph's rod there came a light like the whiteness of a dove.

"The high priest then instructed Joseph. 'You have been chosen to take the Virgin of the Lord and to keep her for him.'

"At first Joseph refused, but he was reminded of his duty to God and to God's deciding power. Then he took Mary to his house, but never did he violate her or conjugate wedlock, for he knew in his heart that she would bear a special child.

"Now shortly the Emperor Augustus called for a census and Joseph and Mary would have to travel the Roman roads, just as we do now. They would go to Bethlehem where Joseph was born to be counted for taxation. Joseph put Mary upon a donkey and led them on foot to Bethlehem. It was not a long journey, but Mary became tired. She was only in her seventh month, but that night she gave birth.

"There was no room in the inn and the couple was forced to find shelter in a barn. Mary had no mid-wife but Joseph delivered the child and shepherds came and saw the boy when they heard his first cries. All could hear the voices of angels singing to the child's glory and a great light shone around them there in that manger. Mary called the child Jesus; for that was the name the angel had told her to give him. They did not return to their home but exiled themselves in Egypt for fear that he would be abducted or killed when his power was discovered. The three had to journey many miles to Egypt and then back again to Nazareth and then he was presented at the temple to fulfill the Jewish Law. When he was twelve, Jesus left his parents and traveled far and wide learning many things and communing with God. He returned to Galilee a man but not a man alone, for he was united with the Source, Our Heavenly Father.

"That child was my husband, and he grew to be a prophet and a miracle worker and truly the creator of the Way about which I will tell you more another night."

This ended Magdalen's tale and the group dispersed without much conversation, to many this was just a story about another prophet. The Jews in the caravan denied that a Messiah had come; the Romans and Greeks could not imagine that the Gods would send such a messenger and then hide him from them. No one seemed to remember Jesus or word of him from Jerusalem or anywhere else in Judah. Magdalen was glad of that, and wondered if her word of secrecy to Mother Mary should have been broken. Her intention was not to shame her dear mother-in-law but to put her in the place of honor that she so deserved. Realizing her intention to be pure she soon dispensed with any self-doubt and went to bed alongside the cart completely satisfied that she was doing the right thing by telling the tales of Jesus' life and teaching.

In that twilight sleep that comes just before one loses consciousness, Magdalen had a vision of Jesus. He told her to be her own person and to teach from her heart and not only from memory. She was astonished at this and had a moment of overwhelming love before he vanished. This brief encounter with his spirit comforted her and yet she had to wonder how she would ever teach as he did – completely from his heart.

The next day was much as the first. Evening came and after a meal of sweet potatoes and beans, it was storytelling time again. Magdalen thought about her vision – from the heart, her own heart, she pondered on what kind of story to tell.

The Way as Jesus taught it was life with equanimity, evenness among all people. Women and children walked the Way side by side with men. In this caravan and in the society of the Roman Empire there was little place for women and children. Magdalen decided on a Goddess story that showed the Way to all people.

Polaris called the others to join them around the fire with a gesture of welcome. Once again eager for the entertainment, the caravan members sat in silence waiting for Magdalen's presentation.

"In the beginning there was God and there was nothing else, for God was as the breath without a body." She began. "Then God breathed out and the breath was as a thought and the thought moved in the breath of God until it found words to describe itself, and then the word moved forth in the breath and it became flesh. This was in the beginning.

"But the flesh had no mind, no thought of its own, and the flesh had no gender and no feeling. It moved within the breath of God but without understanding. Now the breath began to move forth as more thoughts and, Compassion was borne, and Forgiveness, and then Knowledge and Understanding who were like twins born through the breath of God.

"Then these thoughts congealed and they took form and were made female and so Wisdom was made. Wisdom took pity on the flesh that had none of her qualities and breathed these things into it as God had breathed them forth into her. And the flesh became alive with spirit and with mind and its body rose up to see the universe and all its beauty and Adam was the name of the flesh. Now Adam called Wisdom the Divine Mother for she had given birth to his wholeness. He called upon the Divine Mother to bring life to all the thoughts that he might have and Wisdom did as he requested.

"At first Adam thought of his physical needs. He thought of food and of water and so these things became alive by the grace of Wisdom. From these were fashioned the herbs and the plants and all green things. The seas and the fields came out of the thoughts of Adam and the grace of Wisdom. Adam had yet another need, for he was lonely and sought a companion. From his desire Wisdom created Eve, a female, and gave Adam gender, that of male. Through the grace of Wisdom, the Divine Mother, the two could now live happily and procreate and bring goodness to the earth.

"Then a terrible thing happened! Adam began to have thoughts for which he had no need. He thought of hatred, he thought of fear, he thought of lack. The Divine Mother held back her breath, but she was borne of truth and of commitment to her word; so she eventually gave life to these thoughts also.

"Soon Wisdom regretted her promise to Adam for the world was becoming populated with such thoughts and limitations and she lamented her breath. Adam and his offspring began to consider themselves higher than Wisdom, higher even than the Divine Father, the breath of life. Then the day came when Adam struck out on his own, he abandoned Wisdom and began to create chaos. Wisdom was left in the breath without form, but feeling the feelings that God had given her. From Adam's thoughts were created the true demons of the world.

"And Wisdom cried out in a loud voice. 'From the womb that is my breath I have borne the demons of the world. Now I will hide from Adam and from all his offspring, until they will once again honor my presence and teach their children to do the same.'

"It is at the mother's knee that children learn of God. It is from the mother's womb that life is given. It is by man's reverence for her value and respect for his children that a man will return to Wisdom's grace."

"Oh that is a wonderful story, Magdalen," Ruth seemed joyful.

"It is only a story, Ruth, but it is a story that holds truth in its lesson." Magdalen said. "The Way that we walk is the Way of Wisdom and the consort of Wisdom is Love. When each one respects and regards the graces of another as valuable and as a part of the Way, we will see God. In the morning we will arrive at Lugdunum. We will see how much Wisdom lives there and if she has bound herself to Love."

James spoke up, "Fine, but for now we need to sleep. The dawn will bring us more time for stories and myth. We must be prepared to find the Way among savages by being well rested, I think."

"Dams again, James, dams."

Magdalen prepared her bed and placed Sharon next to her. The others retired with her as James sat against the wheel of the cart, one eye open as if watching for robbers and thieves.

They traveled only until noon the next day when they arrived in Lugdunum. This place, thought Magdalen, was not where she would find the true Celtic traditions. Here Rome and even Greece had taken over both religion and politics. Coming through the Roman gates at the city's entrance, Magdalen could see the merchants' quarters. Lugdunum had become the clearing center for corn, wheat, wine, olive oil and lumber. Its full name was Colonia Copia Claudia Augusta Lugdunum; Claudius was the family name of Emperor Claudius, born here. Lugdunum was from a Celtic god, Lug whose name meant light or sun.

Along with the markets and exchanges, there were apartments for travelers, a large theatre and of course the baths. Aqueducts had been erected by the Romans and the city looked like any other metropolis of the empire.

Lugdumum was merely the "Roma of Gaul" and even if Magdalen were lucky enough to spot a Druid Priest coming or going she certainly couldn't expect that he would share any information with her. Everyone else in her party seemed happy and excited to have reached this way station on their journey, Magdalen however was no longer convinced that Lugdunum was to be a transfer station. She was sure that their true mission was not on the Roman highway or in the Roman cities. She was ready to explore the countryside and find real Celtic farms and towns. There she could be sure she would make contact with Celtic women and Druid men who would share information and perhaps even accept the Way.

Once James had procured rooms for what he thought was a short stay and returned the rented cart to the captain, Magdalen made her announcement.

"We will leave tomorrow for the country."

She said it with authority and resolution. Obviously no one was going to overthrow her decision. Ruth and Sarah giggled at first. Polaris looked to James for his reaction. She knew that he was about to object strongly to Magdalen's proclamation. The giggling stopped immediately when James began his argument for safety.

"We will find a caravan and follow the Roman roads as we have already decided, Magdalen. I cannot assure these women or your daughter their safety otherwise."

Young Carmel asked, "Why not continue as we planned, Magdalen? There will be plenty of adventure on the road and not nearly the danger."

Magdalen could tell that the women were frightened at the thought of being outside city walls and away from Roman roads.

"Ladies, we will not find Unicorns on the Roman roads."

She smiled at them all and nodded her head in affirmation. Then, hands on her hips and a stern look on her face; Magdalen looked James full in the eyes.

"James stay with us or return to Judea, but Sharon and I are going into the countryside. The ladies can make their own choices, too."

With that she moved toward the door taking Sharon with her. She looked back to see James' look of astonishment when the women all moved to follow her.

"You've won! Now let's eat." James too moved to follow Magdalen into the street. "Now we'll need to buy a cart! I'm glad we have our own animals still." He was already planning for the work and worry of traveling.

"All right, we'll stay in Lugdunum more than overnight." Magdalen conceded a little.

She gave some consideration to what their needs would be as the group walked to a nearby tavern for their meal. There was a lot of chatter over dinner. The women were sometimes joking about Magdalen's belief in Unicorns and other times seriously discussing what possible danger there would be in meeting up with Druid priests. James and Magdalen were somewhat detached from the women's conversation. They were busy strategizing their campaign into what James considered a savage wilderness.

Magdalen agreed to stay three nights in Lugdunum giving James ample time to purchase a cart and their other needs. While James was fully taking care of their journey supplies, she was going to seek out anyone who could give them information about the Celtic villages and the people in them. Once they had the information and store needed, they would venture into the countryside but keeping to the pathways and minor roads that led from one village to another.

The next day at the baths Magdalen began immediately her quest for information. She struck up a conversation with a woman who looked to be native to Lugdunum. She wore a tremendous amount of jewelry and smelled strongly of perfume and soap, but she seemed friendly and open enough. Magdalen asked about the Celtic villages in the area and whether or not the woman had ever visited them. The response was a wonderful surprise.

"Just northwest of the city walls," she said, "there is a small Celtic village. You couldn't see it from the highway as you arrived, but it is close enough to walk if you use the North Entrance to the city. The Aedui live there. They are friendly enough to Roman citizens and Greek visitors as well."

Magdalen was eager to hear more. "Have you been there?"

"Yes, many times. Although they don't speak Latin, they are really very friendly and a few motions with your hands will tell them what you want. We get our eggs and chickens and sometimes fruit and vegetables from them."

Magdalen was getting excited. If this woman felt safe in the Celtic village then she would too. The other women were glad to hear her news and promised eagerly to watch Sharon the next morning while Magdalen walked out to the village and investigated. They were just as eager to keep their plans a secret from James. Magdalen assured them that she would be back by noon to nurse Sharon and James would think that she was somewhere in the municipal buildings of Lugdunum. By the time he was hungry, she would be back. Everyone giggled a little at their minor deception.

Chapter 21

The Celtic Village

Magdalen had a hard time sleeping that night. She was anxious to see the village and meet its people. She had to wonder though if going alone was really a good idea. James certainly would not approve. Still, better not to risk the life and limbs of the others until she felt safe herself. Sleep was short and the night too long, but now Magdalen could see the dawn through her window. She was up and in the courtyard within the hour. Sharon was quietly resting in her basket on a full stomach and in clean linen. Magdalen could find her way to the North Entrance without a problem. She stood there between the pillars of the gate and hesitated. She looked beyond the trees that surrounded Lugdunum at the fields in which beautiful white horses grazed and meadow flowers bloomed. It was an awesome sight! And there in the distance she could see the village of the Aedui.

Their houses were round and had thatched roofs. The entire village was in the round. Magdalen could see the people moving about, but could not fully describe them. What appeared to be only a few paces from the center of the village was a farm hut. It wasn't round, but had the same thatched appearance. Curiosity filled her to the core.

The first step toward the village was a little scary. Being outside the city walls was scary in itself, let alone the not knowing what she would encounter when she arrived there.

"Fear," she told herself, "would serve no purpose."

She continued her walk enjoying the countryside and its wildlife. She had a plan. She would seek out a farmer who she could buy eggs and fruit from. It would be easier to strike up a conversation with a mercantile purpose, and then she could ask some investigative questions.

There were no walls around the village and no gates to enter. The avenues were as circular as the homes, and they were lined with wooden sidewalks.

"Another trace of Rome," she thought.

She could see no shops or marketplaces, but at the entrance of some of the homes women were setting up vending stations. No one paid much attention to Magdalen's presence. Some of the women did smile at her but they didn't pursue her or beg her to buy. Things were definitely different here than in the city.

Finally, she moved toward one of the vending women whose table held a basket of grapes and another of eggs.

"Your grapes look delicious, and I haven't yet had breakfast." Magdalen opened the conversation. The woman looked at her with a look of ignorance.

"That's right," thought Magdalen, "They don't speak Latin."

She tried Greek, then Hebrew and Aramaic. Nothing was working. Gestures would have to do. She pointed to the grapes and then to her mouth. The woman nodded knowingly and plucked off a branch of the sweet fruit handing it to Magdalen. Magdalen took out her purse and handed the woman a gold coin. The old lady smiled broadly and put the coin inside her shirt. As Magdalen walked away she munched her grapes thinking that if she hadn't gotten information she at least had gotten breakfast.

Deciding to try another vendor, she followed the winding wooden sidewalk until she saw a younger woman with a child who was selling milk. Venturing another try at communications, Magdalen said in her perfect Latin.

"Good morning."

The woman responded. "Blessed Be."

Magdalen breathed a sigh of relief. She had found a Latin speaking Celt. She bought a draft of milk hoping it would make the young mother more comfortable. She talked about Sharon and how quickly she was growing and asked about the child that crawled about their feet.

Proud as most mothers are, the woman began to tell of her son's shooting growth and how soon he would grow to manhood. The two women talked for several minutes before Magdalen queried.

"Why is everything round here?"

"The circle is the symbol of the One. It is the representation of Unity. Homes and families must remain One. We find that round houses make us aware of one another's presence in the family at all times. There are no dividing walls in the round Celtic homes. The village is planned as a circle for the same reason. The tribe is the larger family and must also remain One.

"I suppose our houses are a bit odd to you. At one time we all lived in round houses. They are very easy to build, and keep warm very easily. But further into the village, you'll see how some people have started to live in rectangular houses, copied from the Romans."

"Romanization comes to every bit of the empire," Magdalen responded. "It's too bad, because I think I like the principle of your architecture and planning. It demonstrates the way of your people. I'd like to know more about that."

"About round houses? Or Celtic ways? " The woman laughed and Magdalen laughed with her.

"Both silly. I want to know everything about the Celtic ways especially their philosophy and religion."

"Well then you might want to visit one of the farms. Come, I'll introduce you."

She took her son's hand and motioned with her head for Magdalen to follow her.

"There is a man at the farm who can direct you to a Druid Priestess. She will tell you everything you want to know, save for the mysteries. I'd tell you where she is myself if I knew, but she moves around in the forest. Cedric sells her food and pays her for enchantments, so he always knows where to find her."

They arrived at the farm and the woman commented on the beauty and pleasant atmosphere of the little gardens. Magdalen nodded in agreement.

"Hello! Is anyone home?" The woman called out in a strange dialect that Magdalen had never heard before.

"Oh, good, there's Cedric feeding the hens."

As the man approached Magdalen was glad to have a translator.

"Have you got fresh eggs, Cedric?"

The man smiled broadly to assure them that he did.

"Good. I'll have a basketful, please. You are certainly successful, Cedric. I saw the livestock and the way it flourishes, and your gardens are so fruitful."

Magdalen's translator was making all this small talk as the farmer filled her basket with eggs.

"They are fine eggs, I'm sure you can sell all the hens lay and all the crops you grow as well. You grow good food, charge a fair price, and people are eager to do business with you. She might buy some eggs too."

She pointed at Magdalen and then repeated her conversation in Latin adding a bit of direction.

"You have to compliment and honor him as a person and merchant, then he will give you a good deal and you both contribute to the One. Remember, every act between two people must result in this honor and fair exchange. This is another part of our culture."

Magdalen swooned over the size and color of the eggs, commented on the luster of the home woven basket and complimented the man on his broad smile. Her new friend translated it all for her and the man's face lit up with delight as he took her single coin in return for a full basket of eggs, making the basket a gift. Then she introduced herself to both of them and asked the young woman her name and that of her son.

"I am Cybele, after the Mother. My son is called Regino. You know already that this is Cedric."

She pointed toward the farmer. Cedric smiled and attempted to repeat Magdalen's name. She felt as if they had all been friends for an entire lifetime. When she made that statement, Cybele smiled.

"Perhaps another lifetime long ago."

"You believe in reincarnation, then? And the eternal life of the soul?"

Magdalen was finally getting the information she had to come to Gaul to get.

"Yes, and we believe that all things have soul. But it is not my place to tell you so much. It is the job of the Priestess."

At first Magdalen was disappointed with this remark, but then Cybele spoke to Cedric and he scratched out a map of trails through the forest marking both the farm and the Druid hideaway with large X's. He handed the scrap of bark on which he had drawn to Magdalen and then encircled her with his arms.

Magdalen returned the hug with warmth and the ladies said their goodbyes to Cedric.

"You should wait until the morning to go to her." Cybele warned Magdalen. "She will be resting now and tonight is the full moon, she will be doing enchantments and you will not be welcomed."

Magdalen was almost grateful for this news. She had to get back to Lugdunum by noon or the others would worry and Sharon was surely hungry and getting cranky by now.

She walked back to the village with Cybele and made her excuses. With her basket full of eggs she rushed back within the city walls and made her way to the waiting conclave of worried women. Even though they had all been as excited as Magdalen, they were not as confident as they had wanted to appear. Carmel had been crying and threatening to tell James where Magdalen was off to in hopes that he would find her. The others had held her back, but Magdalen's arrival came only in the nick of time. Everyone embraced her and tears and laughter mixed to express their relief.

After she had nursed her hungry daughter and changed her linen, Magdalen and the others waited only a short time for James' arrival. As Magdalen had predicted, he was hungry and eager to return to the tavern that he had made his favorite. Magdalen handed him the basket of eggs and picked up Sharon in her basket.

"We can have the tavern keeper fix them for us." She said. "I bought them from a farmer in the Celtic village. The Aedui people are wonderful, James. Not at all what we expected. Certainly not what you have feared."

James' jaw dropped, "You went outside the city without me? You took Sharon to that place? Have you gone mad?"

Magdalen just laughed. "I didn't take Sharon and I am back with eggs and information to boot. Just wait, James, tomorrow after I meet with the Druid Priestess, I'll have so much more to tell you. We will be on our way to sharing the Way for certain."

The rest of the day Magdalen went on like a magpie telling the others of her adventure outside the city walls. She talked about the round houses and streets and the flowers, the farm and the way people affirm one another as a matter of course. Everyone listened, but James pouted not wanting to appear in agreement with Magdalen's secret journey.

The next day Magdalen again left Sharon with the women and exited the city at dawn. She found her friend Cybele just where she had been the day before. After sharing a breakfast of grapes and milk and cheese, the two women headed quickly for the farm. This time Cedric was nowhere to be found. Cybele pointed to the trail that was to be Magdalen's route to the hideaway of the Druid Priestess.

"I can't go with you, Magdalen. You must go alone this first time. It is the way we do things. Courage is important."

Magdalen nodded, "When in Rome, Jesus said, do as the Romans do. So when in Aedui, do as the Celts do." She hugged Cybele and set out on her newest adventure.

On her little map the trail appeared clear and well worn. In reality it was covered with underbrush and thickets. Sometimes she wasn't sure which way to go until she cleared away the fallen branches with her sandals. After about an hour she arrived at the clearing that Cedric had marked with an X. There was nothing there and no Priestess either. Tall Oaks surrounded the clearing and she could see another circle here.

"This must be where the enchantments took place, last night," she thought out loud. Then Magdalen called out, "Is anyone here? I've come to visit and to learn." Then she remembered the lesson Cybele had taught her.

"I know that you are wise and have much to offer me. I know too that you are generous with your knowledge and will always walk the way of your people with pride honoring them by your priesthood."

She wondered if she had been complimentary enough. "I will offer you a gift in return or pay you fairly for your tutoring." She had almost forgotten about the exchange required in Celtic dealings.

Nothing resounded back but the titter of the birds and the chatter of the rodents that scurried along the forest floor. Magdalen was sure that she had said everything she needed to, but she had said it in Latin. What if the Priestess couldn't understand? Why hadn't she thought of this sooner? Surely the Celts would make exceptions for those who did not speak the language and allow Cybele or someone else to accompany visitors as translators. Magdalen was just about to try another language when there came a voice from the forest.

"I understand every word, you have done well to praise a fellow traveler and to offer a fair exchange. "

Magdalen wondered if the female voice had read her mind.

"I know why you have come and what you want to learn. I also know that you have a daughter who may be in jeopardy and you have left her behind on this journey to protect her from any unknown harm. I know, too, that you are a willing walker on a spiritual quest and that you have other women as companions."

Now Magdalen was sure she was reading her mind.

"Build a fire in the center of the clearing. And we will begin."

There was still a voice without a person, but Magdalen began to gather tinder and kindling from the edges of the clearing. She had never built an open fire in the forest. It had even been a long time since she lit the fire for her oven. Still she had been watching James and the others every night of their journey. She would simply imitate what she had seen them do.

"You were a spoiled child, a Priestess of Honor, and now a Prophetess with caretakers. Do not be ashamed, you are willing and you are able to build a fire fit for honoring the Great Mother and the Divine Father."

Once again the voice was revealing Magdalen and it was rather frightening to have this unseen one move into her mind. On top of that she had no flint. Just as quickly as Magdalen thought it, a flint and iron fell from the trees and landed in the clearing where she stood.

Without looking up or saying a word, she lit the fire. When the smoke started to move up through the draft caused by the wind in the clearing, the voice and its body dropped down. Magdalen wasn't even startled. The flint's arrival had made her realize that the woman was perched in the trees above her; she had expected her descent to come at any moment.

"I am Baera, Priestess of Lug and Mithra. And you are Miriam, Priestess of Magdala."

"Is there anything about me that you do not know?" queried Magdalen.

"Only what I do not wish to know." The voice had a smile in it this time.

"You wish to exchange my way for your way. You are here to learn and to teach. We shall have a fair exchange, for you are a righteous teacher. As a matter of fact, I will name you now, The Righteous Teacher."

Magdalen blushed. "I am not so righteous" she said. "My errors have been many, and my lessons hard."

Baera smiled again and motioned for Magdalen to sit by the fire. She brought a piece of wood from the forest and placed it atop Magdalen's effort at fire building and then sat down herself.

"First I will teach and you will learn. Then you will teach and I will learn. That is a fair exchange. Tomorrow we will initiate one another into a New Way, for together we will form it with our thoughts and from our learning."

The woman's words sounded very exciting to Magdalen at first. The idea of a New Way was tempting, but what of Jesus' Way, wasn't it why she had come here? As much as she was eager to learn about these people she did not want to become one of them. She wanted to convert them to the Way that she had been given. Baera immediately picked up on her thoughts.

"Magdalen, no way is without flaw. Philosophy is like a tapestry that is put together by many hands and using many threads. When one finds the inevitable flaw, the thread is pulled free, tossed aside and a new thread is put in its place. That is our job. It must be completed before you can show anyone the Way."

Magdalen liked what she heard once again and this time nodded in agreement.

"The tapestry was planned by Jesus," she said. "But the disciples are the many hands that are putting it together, and their thoughts, sometimes fearful ones, are the threads with which they weave it. Yes, now there are flaws."

"Baera, do you think that we can find them all? And correct them?"

Baera wisely replied, "My Righteous Teacher, you cannot find all the flaws but you can correct all that you find. This is true of life and it will be true of the New Way."

Magdalen was eager now to get started. "You said that you would teach first, please go ahead, I am anxious to learn."

Baera looked up to the sun above the clearing.

"It will soon be noon, you must return to your child. Go now with my blessing, muster up your patience, girl, and tomorrow bring the child and the other women with you at dawn. I will be waiting. I will teach you all the healing arts. To you alone I will teach the mysteries to share one day with your daughter."

It wasn't like Magdalen to forget Sharon for even a moment and she blushed in shame at her lack of responsibility. Dutifully she rose from the fire and was quickly met with a hug from Baera who assured her that she was yet a good and responsible mother.

"You are the grail that held the blood of the Avatar and you are even now the blessed keeper of its future. Go to her and Blessed Be."

Magdalen all but ran the way back to the Celtic village. Somewhat out of breath, she stopped at Cybele's little vending table to rest. Cybele was anxious to hear everything, but Magdalen let her know that there was no time.

"Take the horse, Magdalen, you can return her tomorrow."

Cybele offered a wonderful solution to her haste. Magdalen accepted the offer with gratitude and rode back to the city and the waiting group. Everyone was surprised when Magdalen asked James to stable her horse.

"Where did you get a horse?" Ruth was anxious to know.

"I'd like to know that myself," said James, "before I put up some stranger's beast at our expense."

Magdalen told them of her hurried trip home and Cybele's kind offer. James went to tend the animal feeling that perhaps in this case the stranger had been a true friend.

Once he was out of earshot Magdalen began telling the women about her adventure into the forest and how the Priestess had addressed her and read her mind. When she got to the part about returning the next day with all four of them and Sharon the room filled with the aura of expectation and excitement.

"We can't take James with us," warned Magdalen, "and he isn't going to be happy about it either. But this time I will tell him where we are going and why."

"Why are we going?" Polaris questioned Magdalen.

"She is going to teach us the healing arts of the Celtic people, Polaris. We are going to learn to heal using Love and the gifts of the Earth Mother. We will become physicians of the wood."

Magdalen's voice was as filled with excitement as was the room.

"Well," said Polaris, "for this I am anxious. The surgeons of Rome have taken the women's place as Physicians of Light. The magicians of Rome have used their magic to interfere even in child birthing. It is time for women to learn to care for the sick, the injured and their sisters who are giving birth. We and we alone know what is needed for health."

"Baera said that there is no way without flaws. We do not know it all and perhaps there is even something to learn from Roman surgeons and magicians. Together they have created a tapestry of healing philosophy, but the tapestry is flawed. It is up to us to find the flaws and replace the threads of error with truth. Likewise, we have woven our tapestry of healing and it too has flaws, those flaws too must be repaired. That will be part of our mission and Baera is willing to help us all she can."

Magdalen thought about Berea's wisdom and how she had already learned from only the brief encounter she had that day with this Celtic Priestess.

Telling James was not as difficult or upsetting as Magdalen had anticipated. It was obvious that he really didn't want to be one man among all these chattering women. Now that he felt Magdalen had a true friend waiting for her in the village, he was more confident about the women leaving the city with its walls of protection.

"Go without me, then," he stated simply. "I'll be here when you return at noon."

"No," said Magdalen, "We won't be returning to the city until dusk, James. We will see you for the evening meal."

"All right, meet me at the tavern, then." He walked off without further comment feeling that he had retained his manhood and respect.

Chapter 22

A New Teacher

In the morning Magdalen packed a leather bag full of things for Sharon and some food to share with Baera at their midday meal. Breakfast she had decided would be with Cybele when they returned the horse. She was hoping that Cybele might come with them into the forest this time, perhaps even join them on their quest for the New Way and a way to share it.

The group walked through the streets of Lugdunum, Magdalen leading the horse by its bridle. She didn't want the others to feel badly about walking while she rode. When they reached the gates of the city Carmel gave Magdalen her famous wink.

"We won't feel badly, ride her and have fun!"

Everyone agreed and Magdalen mounted the mare and gave a clicking sound that told her to run. Run she did. Magdalen loved horses and loved riding them even more. This was a rare treat. The mare seemed to be enjoying it as much as her passenger, and soon Magdalen was yards ahead of the others. She pulled up on the reins and dismounted. Stroking the horse's nose she remembered to thank her for her service and beauty. It was something Jesus had always insisted upon. He really didn't like the idea of using animals for burden, but he had admitted that some horses truly enjoyed sharing the freedom of a good ride with a loving rider.

When the others finally caught up with her Magdalen led the mare and her friends right into the Celtic village and up to Cybele's vending table. All of Magdalen's exuberance and confidence had rubbed off on everyone in the group. No one had even thought to be frightened, not even Carmel who was usually the first to shiver over a new experience. Magdalen made the introductions and offered her fair exchange and compliments of affirmation with Cybeie. Then together they ate a breakfast that pleased them all, eggs that Cybele had bought from Cedric with fresh bread, cheese and pomegranates.

"Come with us, Cybele" said Magdalen, pomegranate juice running down her chin.

Cybele reached out to wipe away the red juice from Magdalen's face.

"Cybele, you are so caring, so compassionate, you would make a wonderful healer. Please do come with us."

Magdalen was truly impressed with the humble and loving way that Cybele treated her; she wanted this woman to be among the many she knew would come to the Way.

"I would have to bring the boy," Cybele seemed hesitant. "I don't know that it is allowed. But I do want to learn and to know you and your Way better. Still, it would be better to ask first. Magdalen, ask Baera today and perhaps I will go with you tomorrow. You can let me know what she says on your return this evening."

Magdalen wanted to insist and leave the rest to God and Goddess, but she was certain that would be breaking an unwritten law of the Celtic tribes. They seemed to have only unwritten laws but they were somehow sacred and carried more merit than most of the written laws of Rome or even of the Jews.

After their breakfast the women headed for the farm and then for the woodland clearing where Magdalen knew she would find Baera. Magdalen had the women form a circle around the remains of yesterday's fire and then having remembered her own flint ignited the blaze. It was like a call. The smoke went up and Baera came down. This time there were some startled faces and screams of shock. Polaris grabbed her heart. Ruth and

Carmel threw their arms around one another and Magdalen and Baera laughed out loud. No one had prepared the group for Baera's grand entrance, and their looks were a joke to be sure.

When the laughter subsided it was apparent that Baera was in charge. She motioned everyone to sit and they sat right where they had been standing and with no hesitation.

"May I ask a question?' Polaris had something on her mind.

"Not until we have blessed the fire, my dear. Then you can ask all the questions you like. That is not to say that I will give you all the answers that you desire."

Polaris held her tongue. She could sense that although there was some jest in this woman's voice, there was also a call to respect and reverence. Baera took a packet of herbs from the leather purse that hung from her green sash. She sprinkled the herbs on the flames and a delightful odor arose. Then she called on the Goddess Mithra to be present and to bless them with the graces of understanding and wisdom in their counsel. She sprinkled more herbs and the scent became stronger, white smoke rose from the fire and everyone watched it curl skyward.

"She has blessed us. Blessed Be, our counsel is right and divinely guided by our Mother the Earth and our Father the Spirit."

Baera closed the blessing by putting away her herbs and sitting down in the circle of women.

"Now you can ask your question." She opened the floor for Polaris.

"I didn't know that women could become Druid Priestesses. I had heard that only men were ordained."

There was no response. The circle was silent waiting for Baera to give some explanation. No explanation came. Finally, Magdalen got it.

"Polaris, I think you have not asked your question. You have shared what you have been told, but you have not asked for Baera's knowledge. You have to ask for a fair exchange."

"All right, would you please give me your information because even if it differs from my previous knowledge I know that it will hold the value of your wisdom and experience in this matter."

Polaris had remembered what Magdalen had told them about compliments and honoring one another in a Celtic circle. She smiled at her own good judgment and waited for Baera to respond.

"Yes, women can become Druid Priestesses, and frequently do. Many Druids are women; in fact Celtic women enjoy more freedom and rights than women in many other cultures, including the rights to enter battle, own and inherit property, trace her kinship through her mother's family bloodline, and choose and divorce her husband.

"Celtic law identifies up to nine different types of marriages, they are based on the property brought to the union or on how the bride and groom meet and cohabit. Of course, these ways all protect children from being called bastards and losing birthrights.

"Many of the most powerful Gods in Celtic traditions are female. Celts do not view gender as the most defining attribute of a deity. With their shape-changing powers, perhaps species is not a definitive attribute either!

"Thus there is no good reason to believe that Druidism is strictly a male oriented practice or philosophy."

Baera was quiet again and apparently felt that she had given her fair share of knowledge to this point. Magdalen could see that someone would now have to share some idea of her own before Baera would go on. Carmel's fear made her the next to speak.

"Do Druids really do human sacrifice? I mean I've heard that they do, and I would like your wisdom and knowledge about this because you are closer and more experienced than any I know regarding this matter."

She had done a good job of practicing the Celtic art of communication. Baera answered immediately.

"Druids have sacrificed condemned criminals. Such victims are tied into huge wicker human-shaped effigies and burned alive. There are also some forms of punishment in Celtic law even worse than death, such as banishment from the One of the tribe. Some traditions describe one person's life being sacrificed so that a terminally ill noble would survive, because we believe in a balance of cosmic forces. To the Celts, death is not the frightening final thing it is to most people. Human sacrifice is a very special and powerful ritual, performed only in the most serious of circumstance.

"The Romans kill people in gladiatorial games, for the entertainment of the people. The Druids, when and if they do offer human sacrifice, do it for sacred reasons."

Tears filled Magdalen's eyes. She remembered how she could not even sacrifice two doves for the sake of the Gods. Even though she had promised a fair exchange and that Baera could be the first to teach, she now felt she had to speak up.

"I think we have found a flaw in the tapestry of religious rite. May I share with you my knowledge in exchange for your rebuttal? Your wisdom on these matters is great and I would like to hear your opinion of my own."

Right now the compliments and need for fair exchange seemed tedious, but having conceded to the Celtic way Magdalen did feel less emotional about the matter. Perhaps there was something to this way of communicating your opinion and needs.

Baera gave Magdalen the floor by complimenting her on her ability to adapt and to see into situations that required change.

"I have offered sacrifice to many Gods and Goddesses. I have offered grain, and the grain was wasted. I have offered birds, and the skies became more barren. I have offered lambs, and the sheep cried out for their young. I have offered gold, and the hunger in the street was left unsatisfied. But in the temple of my heart I offer love, and my hands are guided to help another. In the temple of my spirit, I have offered prayer, and my prayers have been answered. In the temple of my soul, I have offered truth and another has accepted me. The sacrifice of life and living things gives darkness, the sacrifice of the non-animate things responds with social paralyses. It is not wise to sacrifice to a living God what we have destroyed. It is wise to use with good stewardship the gifts of the Gods and to honor them with praise and thanksgiving for those gifts. I can see no plausible reason to take life in hopes of gaining good living. If your wisdom surpasses my experience, please won't you share it with me?"

She said her piece and looked to Baera for her opinion. Magdalen was amazed at her ability to speak so openly and without emotional outbursts. This system did work, and was worth learning and using. Now Baera spoke again.

"In the temple of your mind, you have offered up a new idea and you have brought a learning to my mind. This has indeed been a fair exchange. Let us make our Way free of sacrifice that is tangible. Let us offer only our love, our prayers, our good works and our ability to change. We shall celebrate as we eat a good meal."

It was noon and time to feed Sharon. Not only the baby was hungry, the women unpacked the food that Magdalen had brought and spread out a good repast on the ground around the fire. Baera had brought food too and added it to the feast. The two flasks of wine that she set out brought a thought to Ruth's mind.

"Magdalen, let us share our commemorative meal rite with Baera."

"That's a wonderful idea, Ruth." Magdalen was excited to share the ritual with her new teacher. "Baera, I know that you are a women of great learning and that you appreciate the ritual and magic of other cultures. I would like to offer you the experience of the commemorative meal that Jesus has given us. We do this every day to bless our life and remind us of our spiritual and physical union, much as you bless your sacramental fire."

"Yes, an exchange of practices is as appropriate as an exchange of ideas. Let it be so."

Baera seemed anxious to participate in the rite. Magdalen did the honors this day. When the meal was over she explained the meaning to Baera just as she had to the others. Her teacher seemed thoughtful but said nothing for the moment. After the food had been cleared and all the wine consumed, Baera spoke up.

"I have decided what I can offer in return for this sacred rite," she said. "I shall teach you all an enchantment tomorrow, one that will heal fevers, remove demons and eliminate fire in the belly. I offer this because I know that all of you are compassionate women who seek to heal the world and any in it who are diseased."

The women expressed the honor they felt at Baera's offer. They spent the rest of the afternoon gathering herbs at Baera's direction. These would be used as tools for healing both for their medicinal value internally and for the aroma that they gave off which Baera insisted was healing also. They gathered: Devils Dung, Witches Herb, Roman Laurel, Wishing Thorn, Cat's Wart, and Eyebright. They also gathered Wolf Claw, Horse foot, Ass Ear and Swine Snout, Horse Tongue, Black Maidenhair, Hair of Venus and Fairy Fingers.

"You can see," said Baera, "why the Greeks and the Romans think our magic is so filled with witchcraft and violence.

They take our names for these plants literally. In fact, we have named the herbs for the things that they resemble. Each plant has a soul of its own, and to us they are in truth reflecting the essence of their soul by the way they look and the effect they have upon us. Tomorrow, I will show you what some of these things are used for by our Celtic physicians and healers.

"When the time is right, at midsummer, I will gather the Mistletoe or All Heal. It is our most venerated herb and the soul of the Oak Tree. If you are still here you will gather it with me, Magdalen, because you are indeed a fine Priestess and healer of all wounds."

Baera was again using the Celtic method of compliment and exchange. Magdalen blushed a little but was honored indeed to be counted among the Druids as a Priestess.

Dusk was coming upon them, and Magdalen was now concerned that they should arrive back in the city before dark. But she had not yet asked about Cybele and whether her son would be welcome the next day. Just as Magdalen was about to ask, Baera, knowing her thoughts, offered a solution.

"Bring your friend and her son; the boy will act as our emissary with the male principal. He will be an asset to our enchantment."

Magdalen smiled in satisfaction, she truly wanted to share these experiences with her new friend. Everyone said their goodbyes with warm embraces and Baera shouted as they set out down the path.

"Blessed Be Your Journey and Your Souls!"

In return Magdalen called out, "So mote it be. Blessed Be Your Dreams."

She knew that Baera would appreciate her blessing on the dreams that would guide her the next day according to Druid belief.

The women hustled back to the Celtic village. There wasn't much time left for chatting with Cybele, but Magdalen gave her the good news and prepared her for tomorrow's adventure in the clearing. Then they were off again to the city walls and the hungry and awaiting James.

Magdalen first fed and cared for Sharon while the others freshened themselves before dinner. James led them to the tavern listening to the women's tales of their adventure. He still was unsure of the association between them and this Celtic Priestess, but he had to chuckle at the herb names and the common Roman and Greek belief that these herbs were really some ghoulish potions made from body parts of animals and even fairies. He wondered whether fairies really existed. James didn't realize that he had wondered aloud until Magdalen answered his internal question.

"Fairies, I think, are souls that are here as tiny helpers, perhaps they were people once who felt useless and in such a small form feel they are now capable of fulfilling someone's dream. That's my thought, anyway, but I am going to ask Baera about them tomorrow. Thank you, James, for bringing this up."

Magdalen was resolute in her decision to find out more about the fabled woodland creatures. After they had eaten, everyone settled in to rest before the next days' newest adventure. They dreamed of magic and fairies and Mistletoe. Each one of them was wondering what sort of philosophical tapestry they were weaving with their teacher, Magdalen most of all. She was certain that there was some deep and profound purpose in all this, but as yet she couldn't determine precisely what that could be.

Chapter 23

The Sleeping Are Awakened

Cybele and her son were waiting for them when Magdalen and the others arrived at the Celtic village the next day. Together they ate a breakfast of fresh fruit and bread and then took off down the path to Baera's clearing. As usual the teacher dropped from the trees with a flourish when the fire had been lit, but this time no one was surprised. Even Cybele knew what was coming. Baera stroked the boy's hair and complimented Cybele on his manly image. She flattered the young man with her remarks on his power and strength, but then warned him against vanity. Of course, she got away with the admonition because she had preceded it with a compliment. Magdalen and Cybele both laughed out loud at Baera's display of authority dressed in kindness.

"Baera, you are a teacher of teachers to be sure, for from you I have learned the greatest lesson ever. You have taught me to light another's lamp and then to help them polish the lantern."

Magdalen winked at her teacher knowing that there would soon be another exchange required.

"What can I give you in return?"

Wrinkling her brow and cocking her head, Baera acted as if she had to think about that, but you could see by the sparkle in her eyes that it was just an act. Baera knew exactly what she wanted from Magdalen.

"In exchange for the greatest lesson, I would like the greatest story. For the others have told me of your storytelling and how your voice and tales can move the soul and enlighten the spirit."

"What story would you consider to be the greatest, Baera?"

Magdalen had no idea what tale to tell. She was hoping that the women had shared a story that Baera might like to hear from her. Baera's shoulders went up and told her that she was open to Magdalen's decision.

Then Sarah made a suggestion. "Tell her about Lazarus and how Jesus brought him back from the grave. You haven't even told us that story yet."

"Ask nicely, Sarah," Ruth was worried that this outright demand would offend Baera.

"I'm sorry, " Sarah apologized. "I'm simply too excited to be so proper. We haven't heard one of Magdalen's stories for days, and she is such a good storyteller, and the stories are so wonderful. I love the magic in them. Please Magdalen, tell that story, the one about Lazarus."

"This sounds like a grand tale, one that I must hear."

Baera had seen a lot of magic but raising people from the dead was an impossible feat even for a Druid Priestess.

"All right," Magdalen began. "The tale of Lazarus it shall be."

"Some friends of Jesus', that by this time had become good friends of mine, lived in Bethany. Lazarus was a disciple of Jesus and devotedly followed his teaching. His two sisters, Martha and Mary, were endeared to him. They were like sisters to me, for I had no family of my own and often welcomed their company even as I welcome yours. There were many women, even though I lived with Jesus, who would have nothing to do with me, because of my former life. But Martha and Mary, especially Martha, were the closest friends I had aside from Mary the mother of Jesus. Any way, Lazarus was very sick. He was faint, looked very pale, and breathed only shallow breathes. Mary and Martha sent word to Jesus that he was gravely ill, and

Jesus sent me ahead of him to their home. He remained with the disciples. He had told me to tell Martha and Mary that Lazarus would not die, that this sickness was for the glory of God and that it would not take his life from him as they feared. However, Lazarus did die. In my mind I sent the message to Jesus that Lazarus had died and that he ought to come right away, for there was much distress in the house. I wondered why he had not known and why he had waited to come. He could have healed him, I knew, and now it was too late, and even before I sent for Jesus Lazarus was laid in a tomb in the side of a hill. It was a sort of cave that Lazarus himself had once selected, and he had a large stone cut to cover the opening of the cave.

"Now, as I was sending my mental message to Jesus, we also sent a runner to fetch him. Jesus was still with the disciples, and he informed them that Lazarus was sleeping and that he was needed in that house. He said that they should go to Judea. But they did not wish to go at first. They remembered the stoning attempts and feared, not only for Jesus, but for themselves as well. They suggested that Jesus travel after dark and by back roads to avoid any assailants. But Jesus said, 'Are there not twelve hours of the day? Should I not, therefore, use all the hours as God has given them? I cannot stumble so easily in the light of day. This is an opportunity, a light that shows me the way, and it is mine by the grace of God. And I must use this light of my Father. I see in it the light for the world. If I wait and walk forward only in the darkness, in the time when there is no light, no opportunity, then I will fall and stumble. For in the darkness one stumbles, because he cannot see the things that are in his way. That darkness is the time when one seeks to find light. Seeks, that is, to make opportunity. I will use my time while it is yet light. I will go and awaken Lazarus.'

"The disciples objected, for if Lazarus were sleeping peacefully then surely he would recover. But Jesus finally said, 'Lazarus is dead.'

"Now he knew that his first statement was the correct one, but he felt he needed to impress upon them the gravity of the situation, and this mourning that they thought he was feeling was something that everyone respected and understood. So they voluntarily went with him then. It had already been close to four days since we had laid Lazarus in the tomb when Jesus arrived. Martha and I went out to meet Jesus, but Mary, Martha's sister, remained at home. She was secretly angry with Jesus for not having been with her brother and there to heal him, and Martha outright accused him of abandoning Lazarus. But both relented when he arrived. And I wept at seeing Jesus weep for what I thought was the death of Lazarus. But it was not for Lazarus or in mourning that Jesus wept. He wept for the feelings of Martha and Mary and the lack of faith in his love for the man he had so often called brother.

"He said to them, 'I am the resurrection and the life. He who believes this, though he seems dead, lives. And every one that lives, and believes this that I say, shall live forever. Can you believe this?' And before anyone could answer or understand he asked, 'Where have you laid my brother? Where have you put him to sleep?'

"And they took him to the grave site in the side of the mountain. And Jesus demanded that they roll away the stone. But they refused at first, thinking that he was so deep in mourning that he did not realize what he was asking. Mary and Martha feared the opening of the grave and they told Jesus so. They did not want his body disturbed. And they argued that he would already be filled with vermin and unfit to look upon. But Jesus cried out the name of Lazarus in a loud voice and they conceded and two men rolled away the stone.

"Then Jesus called again, 'Lazarus, my brother, come forth, I wait here for you.' And from inside the tomb came the muffled sound of a voice that was weak and harsh. 'Lord, unbind me and I will come to you.'

"Everyone gasped in shock. Martha and Mary went white and clutched at their breasts in disbelief. Mary then fell to her knees and wept in gratitude at Jesus' feet. Then two men went in and loosed the binding that had been placed on Lazarus, as is the custom for burial. And Lazarus came out from the grave praising God. He was not even weakened by the ordeal. Now, of course, everyone was amazed. Even Lazarus himself felt that Jesus had brought him back to this life and that he had indeed been dead.

"Everyone went back to the house of Lazarus in celebration, because he was back among them. Jesus had conquered even death, which was something never before known in all the scriptures and prophecies. But I was not comfortable, and I awaited the opportunity to ask him about all this when we were alone. My time came when the feasting was done and Jesus and I retired to our room for the night.

"Jesus explained to me that Lazarus had only been sleeping really. That his shallow breaths had become so shallow that they were unseen. His mind had left this place and his body and put itself outside the pain of illness, and Jesus knew all this from the very first and would not have come at all had it not been for my message that said he was dead. For it was with this message that he realized that we would bury Lazarus and that time then could take him really to death. The stone allowed some air to pass into the cave, and in the state that Lazarus was in there was little, even no need, for nourishment or water, for he used nothing from within his body but what is required to live in such a passive state. This could not have gone on much longer, he said. And he was grateful for my message and my faith.

"While we lay in sleep, some of the Jews took all this news to the Pharisees. They feared Jesus now, more than ever, for they were being told that this man had power even over life and death. And they feared for their own lives and for the position and power that was theirs, but was obviously subject to his. And they planned then to find him and to see to his death. Now these things came back to us in the morning via some of the Jews that yet believed in Jesus, but had professed loyalty to the Sanhedrin in order to protect themselves. They could not, however, bring themselves to be part of this act of deception and violence that was being planned. And so from that day on, we made no public proclamations or teachings. Jesus did not hide, but neither did he seek an audience as he had in the past. And they found fault even with that, as he did not appear for the Feast of Tabernacle. All of his teachings then were done in the privacy of our home or a rented room, or the houses of friends. His words were not for the people at large, but for the disciples, apostles, and his mother and myself. It was a private and quiet time that began that day."

"Then he did not raise Lazarus from the dead but only from the tomb." Baera made her comment with some disdain.

"But there is a lesson, Baera." Magdalen went on. "The sleeping are called to awaken, and the spirit is revived in the light. For no one really dies, but the soul sleeps in those who have lost faith in life. When awakened by the call of the Divine Power, we are again faithful and we live on eternally."

"It is a good lesson, Magdalen. It is a very good lesson." Baera's disdain had left and she understood. "Those who live in spiritual darkness, those without faith, are like the living dead. They must have the light restored to restore their goodness and life. This is a tale that I will repeat many times, I am sure. For eternal life must be part of our tapestry. The Way never ends, for we live eternally in spirit."

Once again the women felt it was time for a celebration and Baera was asked to preside over the commemoration meal. For the first time, Baera blushed. She was flattered with the honor that the women had bestowed on her. She promised that after their meal she would teach them the enchantment as she had promised.

True to her word, when they had cleared away the food, Baera brought out the herbs the women had gathered the previous day. She carefully selected only a few and put the others aside. Those she selected she ground with a stone and mixed together in a small clay bowl. Setting this aside, she began to explain the enchantment.

"This enchantment is one that heals and restores. It is done in honor of the God Lug for whom the city is named. It is like one of the Greek or Roman plays, really, but with great power for it honors Lug and calls for a fair exchange between the world of humans and the world of the Gods. The boy will be our hero."

She smiled and patted Regino on the head. This was certainly an honor to him. Then Baera began to set the stage and direct the little play.

"A wren offers to help protect a farmer's crops, but he is immediately challenged by a mouse, who of course wants the harvest for himself and his kind. The wren musters an army of all the birds of heaven, but the mouse gathers together an equivalent army of rodents and creeping things. A great battle is fought, and the hero of the tale, the King's son, decides to attend it but arrives when it is almost over, and the only combatants left are a raven and a serpent."

Baera handed a wooden sword to the boy.

"He chooses to aid the raven, and in exchange receives magical aid in defeating a giant and marrying the giant's daughter."

With this the child indulged in a game of make-believe, slaying giants and grabbing Ruth as if to carry her off in marriage. He waved his sword as if he was magically transforming everything in his path. Baera continued.

"Just as the adventures start, the raven turns into a handsome young man and gives the King's son a bag filled with magical treasures."

With this Baera handed the bowl of crushed herbs to the boy.

"Spread them about the earth and on all of us so that we might accept and honor the graces of the Gods sent to us this day."

The boy did as he was commanded and the women and the earth were covered with the sweet scent of the herbal mixture. Baera made certain that some of the sweetness was saved for the fire, for their imaginary hero was becoming a little too exuberant in his play-acting.

The smoke from the herbs rose to the opening in the trees and Baera exclaimed her joy.

"Blessed Be!"

Then she burst into song and Cybele and the boy sang with her. When the song was finished Baera explained.

"The battle between the birds and the creeping things is the battle between Above and Below, the Tribe and the Land, over the ownership of the Harvest. Both the wren and the raven have ties to Lúgh, and he fulfills his usual role by restoring the rightful ruler and pairing him off with the woman who is the fertility of the land.

"The wren serves to remind us of an aspect of Lúgh he is lú, "little", easily dismissed before his powers have been revealed. The wren, too, despite his tiny size, is a "King", the King of all birds. In a folktale known throughout the Celtic lands he gains that title through trickery, stowing away on the eagle's back during a contest of which bird can fly the highest, and then when the eagle has exhausted himself and can go no higher the wren soars high above him. The symbolism of the wren represents Lug as the Mistletoe, who is the smallest of all trees, yet grows at the top of the tallest tree, the Oak, and is thus closest of all the trees to heaven. It is also green in winter, when the Oak itself is bare, so that it manifests life even in the midst of death."

"This is another tale of eternal life, Baera."

Magdalen was delighted to see the theme in their day of learning and teaching. Baera grinned widely; she had pleased her star pupil and was obviously pleased with herself.

The enchantment and the music had taken much longer than any of the women anticipated and it was again growing dark when they parted. Baera said that the following day would be the day of initiation. Magdalen would learn the first of the Druid mysteries and she would then be expected to share a mystery of her own with Baera. The other women would come as witnesses to the rites, but the boy would not be allowed. Cybele was a bit disturbed and Magdalen could see her disappointment.

"I will bring James to the village with us, Cybele. Your son can spend the day with a man for a change, and it would do James good to have an experience in fair exchange."

Everyone laughed large and long. Poor James was about to have his first encounter with non-Romanized Celts.

The trek back to the city was quick with all the joking about James' new mission. The women dropped Cybele and the boy off at the village and hurried on to the city wall. Walking up to the gates of Lugdunum, there was a new reverence, they now knew the God for whom the city was named and the power that could be called upon in his name. This had been a day of discovery. Stopping just before they entered each of them said in a quiet voice, "Blessed Be, Lug has united the All."

Chapter 24

The First Mystery Revealed

An unhappy but compliant James was left to watch over Cybele's son the next morning. When the women arrived in the clearing and lit the fire they expected that Baera would do her usual drop to the forest floor, instead she walked out from the woods with the pomp and circumstance of a true royal.

Her hair was piled in strong thick braids at the top of her head. She wore a long white tunic belted with a deep forest green sash and she was dripping with gems and jewelry. There was the strong smell of herbal soap in the air about her and in her hand she held a golden sword. With the sword she motioned for everyone to be seated.

"Today I will reveal to Magdalen the first of the mysteries and the history of our heritage. In a fair exchange, she will share a mystery and her heritage with me. Together we will be initiated, ordained, into the priesthood of the New Way. All of you are witnesses to our initiation. You today become disciples, apostles, even novices in the new rites. Druidism has its flaws. This Faith of Jesus has established flaws also. Upon this we have agreed. We have come together to find a New Way not by destroying the old, but by mending the flaws and adding to its beauty."

With that said, Baera too was seated.

"The mystery that I will reveal only to Magdalen is the mystery of the Water and the White Horse Goddess. But with all of you, because you are devote and reverent in your search for truth, I will share the history of our heritage and its fundamental rites."

"The universe is without beginning and without end. It is eternal. It is full of life. Each soul takes many forms of life throughout the universe. Life, for now, is in the form of our Mother the Earth. The task of a Druid is to remember that each soul is one with the soul of all life - that we contain the eternal universe. Through remembering our place in the whole we benefit all life."

Baera paused here. She was waiting for her exchange. Magdalen knew that she must reciprocate at this point.

"Jesus also said that the kingdom is without beginning and without end. Life is eternal and the kingdom is filled with it. This then is a truth and part of each one's way. So mote it be."

Magdalen had not truly finished her summation but thought it a good idea to find a first similarity in their philosophy.

"Jesus also said that all forms of life have soul. He said too that we must come to know our Source, which is the kingdom, our Father, which is the spirit, and our Mother, which is the earth. He said that we are in the kingdom and that the kingdom is within us. So we are to keep this in mind and realize that what we do to one another we do to all. That is to say that we heal the all by healing the individual. Likewise we injure the all by injuring the individual. Here again we agree. So mote it be."

This time Magdalen had reached a conclusion and Baera simply nodded and began again.

"For us there are three realms of life."

Magdalen ventured to interrupt.

"Jesus said too that from the kingdom there emanates three other realms."

Ignoring the interjection, Baera began to explain.

"The first realm is The Land of the Living. This is the realm of youth, of women, and the Blessed Ones. It is the dwelling place of the eternal soul when it is not in a body. This realm infuses, surrounds and contains the Other World and the Human World. It is vast and knows no limits. It has no beginning and no end."

"For us this emanation is the Father, the source of life and the spirit which brings life."

Magdalen nodded to indicate that she was agreeing with her teacher on all counts. Once again Baera went on.

"Second realm is the Other World, the Land of the Sidhe, Gods, Goddesses and ancestors. The Other World infuses the Human World at all times with its power and grace. It can be seductive and dangerous. It is the view of the Land of the Living through the physical senses."

Magdalen was nodding affirmatively as she stated her own belief.

"This would be the Spirit, the mind, the world and realm of thought."

Baera too nodded and then continued.

"Finally, there is The Human World. It is the embodiment of the life of the universe in nature on the earth. A body in this world accompanies the soul and the physical senses of the body determine its perceptions. It is possible to journey to the Other World or the Land of the Living from here, or be visited by beings from there. Druids can learn or remember awareness of the eternal soul and thereby gain some understanding of the Other World and immortal existence in the Land of the Living while they live on earth, but full memory does not return until death."

"This would be the Son, the offspring of the Father, the son of man and the Son of God at one time. Capable of visiting and revisiting the realms of mind and consciousness, of knowing spirit and of knowing self."

Magdalen agreed with her new teacher once more.

"So mote it be! We have One that emanates as three. Blessed Be!"

Baera heard the baby beginning to stir and motioned that everyone should take a break. She forced her sword into the ground and moved toward the food that was hidden away in the wood. Magdalen went to Sharon and the others set out their midday feast.

After they had eaten it was apparent that Baera was immediately ready to get back to the matter at hand – formulating a Way that they could all walk. Up until now things had gone well and everyone expected that perhaps they had fewer differences than they had realized.

"What I will share now are not articles of Druid dogma or belief, but are four tenets of faith. These things we cannot fully understand or explain but believe fully in: multiple lifetimes, the presence of soul or spirit in all things, reverence for our ancestors in their continued presence, and multiple worlds.

"We believe in reincarnation, that the soul comes and goes in an eternal cycle of lives. Between lives in this world, the soul dwells in the Land of the Living. The soul may take life in any form, animate or inanimate. At death, the soul loses memory of the details of each lifetime but carries the result of the experience across the worlds in the form of wisdom. This wisdom expresses itself as inspiration, as music or poetry, as the Truth of Sovereignty, or in other ways. The beauty of death is that it erases memories of painful lives, while leaving the soul with the wisdom that the lessons of the life have imparted."

Baera was finished.

"Please finish all of your tenets before I begin, Baera."

Magdalen wanted a whole picture to draw from because she had a story to tell.

"All right then, next is soul or spirit in all things. The whole universe is alive with Divine presence. Water, rocks, fires, hills and rivers, even thoughts, shouts, waves and the wind are alive with soul or spirit. The spirits of place and especially the Goddesses of Sovereignty represent this power in the land. The Druids revere the earth and all of its landscapes, worship within it, and let nature be their guide and teacher. Their task is to nourish the Soul of Life with the life of their own soul.

"And then there is reverence for ancestors. The awareness or wisdom that each soul brings into existence is both individual and collective. The life of each person, the life of the village, and the life of the land, is all the same life. The lineage and tradition into which the soul chooses to take a body shapes a mind's workings. The Druids honor the ancestors and their traditions by honoring the tribe and its symbols. The community of the tribe is made up of the dead as well as the living. There I have finished the tenets, Magdalen, please tell me what you have to share."

Magdalen began delicately.

"I would share this in the way of another story, Baera, if you please?"

Baera nodded once again and Magdalen went on.

"Feeling as though I needed time to myself, I had walked ahead into the desert leaving Jesus and his disciples to their own conversation. He had been speaking all morning of the right to life and its recurring nature. Suddenly, I was aware of pain at my ankle, and the warmth and pressure of the snake that was now coiled there. At first, too startled to be calm, I pulled at the creature, but the nature of his teeth curved inward and forced into my flesh in a way that it made it near impossible to free myself. James ran to me at once and took from his pocket a sort of half-round blade without a handle of any other sort. With that peculiar little knife he cut the creature away. Then he threw the snake aside, farther from us, and quickly slashed twice at my ankle so that the wound would bleed and cleanse itself. By that time Jesus reached me, and he touched very lightly the place where I had been bitten. When he removed his hand the bite, the slashes of James' knife, and all the pain had been removed.

Then he walked over to the snake quite calmly and killed the thing with a rock.

"He sat with me and turned his conversation to the thoughts that had driven me to be alone in the first place. I was concerned with the idea that only those with the innocence of children should ever attain the kingdom, because I felt myself to be anything but childlike and lacking in purity.

"His voice was loud enough for everyone to hear as he said, 'Born again as children, over and over, we arrive evenly among humankind. Each time we are born it is a new beginning without guilt or blame. Only innocence comes with us because we have removed from our bodies and minds the things that had caused us pain. It is only by this rebirth as children that we come to grow in favor with God.'

"He went on to say that pain, even scandal, needed to be here in this world so that we can learn to leave behind its causes. But if the person is the source of pain or scandal, that one is helpless upon the earth, drowned in a sea of sorrowful emotions and weighted down by guilt for injury to others. So that he is like the man who is thrown into the sea with a millstone around his neck and has no hope of survival.

"And if we choose not to see the pain of others or hear their cries for help, in the next life we may be born blind or deaf.

"And then he went on to say that we are not alone here in our learning, left to the mercy of circumstance and events. We always have with us a helpmate or a keeper and protector. For from the world beyond this world that we know, each is sent such a guide, one whose nature is as holy as the angels, and whose presence assures us the right to the knowledge of God's will. He said that this one would follow us about on our journey here and guide our steps as he or she has been directed. He likened it to the snake's bite, the pain of events and life experiences. James was like the protector who acted quickly to assure my life. And his own presence, by my faith and love for him, brought me back to health and wholeness. So this was the pattern of lifetimes, if we retained that faith and love. And as I learned not to walk into the desert alone and unaware, so humankind would learn that even though we walk through life here in blindness to its dangers, by faith and love, Providence provides for us protection and intercession, so that we can continue our journey with more care. In that way, the day will come that our guides and angels could rest, and we would be spared the pain of experience in scandal or what we call sin.

"I think that we have found the Way that we seek, for we are more alike than we might have imagined. Let us set aside any minute differences and concentrate on the sameness that we have found."

"So Mote It Be!"

Baera was delighted in the common ground and understanding that came from Magdalen's story.

"Once again you have proved yourself a worthy teacher Magdalen, today we shall initiate one another into the New Way, the Way of The Righteous Teacher, your Way."

"Let us make a pact among us then that when a flaw is found we will pull the thread together and replace it together. No idea will come from only one mind but instead from The Mind."

Magdalen put her hands out and the others did the same. A pact was formed and the women danced about to one of Baera's songs. Then Baera beckoned Magdalen to come with her into the wood and the two walked off together down a little worn path for the revealing of the secret of Water and White Horses. The others waited feeling a bit put out but nonetheless glad for Magdalen.

When they came to another clearing with a large rock in its center, Baera motioned for Magdalen to take a seat upon the stone.

"This stone is the throne of enlightenment, Magdalen, please sit and listen to me."

Dutifully, Magdalen perched herself atop the grand piece of granite. Baera walked around her making nine circles. Each circle, she explained, was the completion of one power. As she walked, she revealed the nine-fold secret of the White Horse Goddess.

"No one understands why the Divine has chosen them to be the recipient of this nine-fold burden or its attending powers. That is why it is called a mystery. You will never know, Magdalen, why you were chosen, but the Goddess of the White Horse will come to you and she will bring you nine paths to follow. These will be set beneath your feet and you will know that you must one day walk them all. Likewise there will be nine rivers in front of you that will carry you on the watery whirlwind of waves to the emotional places that your heart has yet to understand. You will know these too because they cannot be misunderstood. There will be nine more rivers that will hover over you; these are the rivers of moving water that are not of this earthly life. These rivers you will feel streaming over you and you will not understand them until the Goddess has delivered all your gifts."

As Baera paused, Magdalen thought of the paths she had already followed. First, the path of the temple, second the path of Jesus, third the path of escape and hiding, fourth the path that led her here to Baera and the initiation into Druidry. What paths could be left to walk, she wondered? Baera knew Magdalen's thoughts.

"The five paths of the Goddess are left, my dear. You will meet them all. The mystery of the White Horse Goddess is that she delivers these opportunities only to a chosen few and as they accept the tasks she gives them the boons required to achieve good in this world. It is an Avatar's Way to ride the White Horse of conquest and bathe in the Water of all emotion until Love is found. In turn the Avatar is given nine transformations of fire, nine wells of sustenance, nine kernels of wisdom, nine specific talents, nine great gifts, and nine super-human strengths."

"Why is this such a secret, Baera? And what is an Avatar, really"

"An Avatar or Avataress is one chosen by Destiny to deliver change to wholeness. The mystery is kept secret because others become jealous or fear the powers of the Avatar or Avataress. Still others find emotion to be a hurdle rather than a blessing to encourage the discovery of Love. I cannot tell you where your paths will lead or what set of emotions will bring you to your gifts or even what those gifts will be. But I am honored to be in the presence of an Avataress with such high standing."

Baera bowed to Magdalen a deep bow. Then she went to the edge of the clearing and retrieved a bundle she had obviously planted there. She handed it to Magdalen.

"A gift for your initiation."

Magdalen unrolled the bundle and donned the new clothes that Baera had given her. While she dressed they continued to talk about the new life that was ahead of Magdalen and how they would achieve an initiation rite that would be befitting the White Horse Goddess and the Water.

When the two women returned to the clearing Magdalen was dressed just as brilliantly as Baera. Her robe of initiation was white as snow but the nine sashes were filled with color and added excitement to the ensemble. Chains of gold hung from her neck and bands of copper were wrapped around her ankles and wrists. On top of her head was a wreath of dried flowers that crowned her like the May Queen. Magdalen's smile made it apparent that she was delighted with Baera's gifts.

Each of the women carried an urn of water and a golden basin. As the others watched reverently, they spread herbs upon the fire and created the now familiar rising white smoke. Then Baera poured water over Magdalen's down-turned head into the basin and repeated an incantation.

"Nine waves before you, nine waves above you, nine paths beneath you, nine fires transform you, nine wells sustain you, nine wisdoms open you, nine gifts given you, nine skills given you, nine strengths given you. All nine fold are the blessings of the Goddess."

When she had finished the women reversed roles and Magdalen too recited the incantation. With that they both emptied their bowls on the fire extinguishing its life and the ceremony of initiation was over.

"We discussed it," said Magdalen to the others, "and a new baptism or a rebirth was agreed upon. It is a rite common to both ways and now to our New Way."

"The New Way, Magdalen's Way." Baera added.

"So mote it be!" The others responded.

Magdalen was quiet on the way home and seemed filled with some melancholy, but everyone knew that this was not the time to ask about White Horses or Water. They joined James at Cybele's home and ate her home-cooked feast before leaving. The remainder of the journey back to their apartment in the city was almost silent. Mirth had left them now and they could only wonder what Magdalen had learned and when or if she would share anything more.

Chapter 25

Initiation in the Grove

The days passed and the women continued to visit with Baera and to share knowledge and camaraderie. More than a year had gone by since Sharon was born. Her basket long ago set aside, now she romped in the woods with Cybele's son who had become her overseer. Her hair had grown long and she was the image of her mother. And like her mother, Sharon wanted to learn everything.

She investigated the forest with a sleuth's eye for evidence of woodland creatures, seeking out nests and lairs so that she could, if even for a moment, watch a deer or an elk or perhaps a cat.

"I should have called her Freedom. I hope she can remain ever free as she is today."

Magdalen referred to her daughter's demeanor but also her intelligence and eagerness for learning. Sharon could say as many Celtic phrases as she could Latin ones. Baera had been tutoring her since she spoke her first words. Magdalen herself found the dialect difficult and she was glad that Sharon was growing up comfortable with this new language. While her mother still nursed her, the little girl was eating heartily the fruits and vegetables that the women shared each day and drinking Mare's milk more and more often. She was growing up strong, healthy and intelligent. No mother's pride could have been greater than was Magdalen's.

"Sharon is actually Magdalen in miniature."

Baera commented one day. The ladies all agreed that the little girl was very much her mother's replica in attitude and interests as well as beauty. Her eyes though were a constant reminder to Magdalen of her father's influence. One minute they were filled with fire and the next with deep concentration.

As the children played at the edge of the forest, the women exchanged information and both Magdalen and Baera told stories, not only for amusement but as a source of knowledge and philosophy. Soon the Winter Solstice would be upon them. Baera had promised that after the Solstice Magdalen would be ready to gather the Mistletoe with her.

The Druids held Mistletoe in great reverence. It was believed to have all sorts of miraculous qualities: the power of healing diseases, making poisons harmless, giving fertility to humans and animals, protecting from witchcraft, banning evil spirits, bringing good luck and great blessings. In fact, it was considered so sacred that even enemies who happened to meet beneath Mistletoe in the forest would lay down their arms, exchange a friendly greeting, and keep a truce until the following day. A sprig placed in a baby's cradle would protect the child from faeries. Giving a sprig to the first cow calving after New Year's would protect the entire herd.

Druid Priests went out to the forest clad in white robes to search for the sacred plant, and when it was discovered one of the Druids ascended the tree and gathered it with great ceremony, separating it from the Oak with a golden knife. Two white bulls would then be sacrificed amid prayers that the recipients of the Mistletoe would prosper.

The Mistletoe was always cut at a particular age of the moon, at the beginning of the year or Winter Solstice and again at mid-summer and it was only sought for when the Druids declared they had visions directing them to seek it. When a great length of time elapsed without this happening, or if the Mistletoe chanced to fall to the ground, it was considered an omen that some misfortune would befall the Celts. The Druids held that the Mistletoe protected its possessor from all evil, and that the Oaks on which it was seen growing were to be respected because of the wonderful cures which the Priests were able to effect with it. They sent couriers and assistants around the village with branches of the Mistletoe to announce the entrance of the New Year.

The name of the plant came from the belief that Mistletoe grew from bird droppings. This belief was related to the accepted principle that life could spring spontaneously from dung. Druids had noticed that Mistletoe would often appear on a branch or twig where birds had left droppings. "Mistel" is the word for "dung," and "tan" is the word for "twig". So, Mistletoe meant "dung-on-a-twig".

Baera had taught all of this to Magdalen and the others but today she decided to tell them the story of the Mistletoe and even the children sat in the circle and listened as she revealed its origin through her tale of the Gods.

"The story goes that Mistletoe was the sacred plant of Frigga, Goddess of Love and the mother of Balder, the God of the Summer Sun." Baera began the story.

"Balder had a dream that he would die, which greatly alarmed his mother, because if he died all life on earth would end. In an attempt to keep this from happening, Frigga went at once to air, fire, water, earth, and every animal and plant seeking a promise that no harm would come to her son. Balder now could not be hurt by anything on earth or under the earth.

"But Balder had one enemy, Loki, God of Evil and Loki knew of one plant that Frigga had overlooked in her quest to keep her son safe. It grew neither on the earth nor under the earth, but on Apple and Oak trees. It was lowly Mistletoe.

"So Loki made an arrow tip of the Mistletoe and gave it to the blind God of Winter, Hoder, who shot it into the air, striking Balder dead. The sky paled and all things in earth and heaven wept for the Sun God.

"For three days each element of the earth tried to bring Balder back to life. Frigga finally restored him to life through enchantment. It is said the tears she shed for her son turned into the pearly white berries on the Mistletoe plant and in her joy Frigga kissed everyone who passed beneath the tree on which it grew.

"The Goddess then put out a decree that who should ever stand under the humble Mistletoe, no harm should befall them, only a kiss, a token of love."

Baera was quite obviously finished with her story. The children applauded her and danced about as if celebrating the happy ending to her tale.

"Baera, I think this story holds a lesson: Love conquers Death. It is the same lesson that Jesus taught us by his death and resurrection after three days when he returned to show us a New Way, the Way of Love."

"Indeed!"

Baera raised her eyebrows not convincing anyone of her surprise.

"We have found a tenet for our New Way. Love conquers all, for there is nothing, not even death, which can subdue it. Blessed Be!"

The children applauded and danced again and the women all shouted.

"Blessed Be!"

"Simmer down, now." Baera pleaded. "I have something more to say."

The group stood still waiting for Baera's next words.

"I have had the vision in a dream that the time will be right to harvest the Mistletoe. On the sixth day of the moon after the

Winter Solstice Magdalen will accompany me, she will carry the golden cycle and wear the garb of a Druid Priestess."

Everyone applauded Magdalen. She blushed a bit and then bowed to her teacher, honoring her decision.

In the days that followed the women fashioned a new white robe for Magdalen. It was made of fine woven flax and was soft as down. From the same flaxen fabric they made large catching cloths. These they would hold under the trees to catch the Mistletoe and keep it from touching the ground.

Magdalen spent the days before the New Year in meditation, purifying her mind and heart before her initiatory experience. She would have to spend three days in front of the fire with little or nothing to eat seeking the enlightenment of her soul before the Winter Solstice. Only on the New Year could a Druid be initiated and only a Druid Priest or Priestess fully initiated was allowed to cut the sacred plants from the Holy Oak Tree.

Magdalen wondered what sort of an initiatory experience she would have to endure under Baera's authority. She had heard stories of Druid initiation rites. Some said that the candidate was buried alive in a coffin symbolic of the Sun God's death and resurrection. Some told of being sent out to sea in an open boat. There was no sea here, so Magdalen had little fear of this dreadful ordeal. She thought about Lazarus being buried alive and about the lesson her story had taught. Jesus was dead and then lived. Lazarus had appeared dead and then lived. And then there was the very story of the Mistletoe and how his mother had resurrected Balder.

Knowing that all initiations must remain secret, she couldn't ask Baera what to expect. She would just have to wait for that fateful day and accept whatever the Gods had in store. If she had to, Magdalen decided, she too could endure the test of death and become one of those "born again" like the Gods and Goddesses of legend. She would simply meditate on becoming still, silent and calm. The Spirit would help her and the Great Mother would resurrect her too.

There was something bothering her though. It was the idea of the animal sacrifice of the two white bulls beneath the Holy Oak. She and the other's had made a pact that no sacrifice was necessary and now would she have to break her word and carry out this Druidic tradition in order to complete her work as a true Druid Priestess? She vowed to ask Baera about it before her initiation.

Magdalen realized that her mind was not being purified with thoughts like these and returned to her meditation. She wanted a vision, a dream, a sign that she had succeeded in meeting the necessary purity of heart to don the white robes of priesthood. Her mind strayed again as she wondered whether Sharon would be all right without being nursed before bedtime. Dusk was falling on the first day of her retreat and she was accomplishing very little that she could tell. Her mind was still wandering to thoughts of the mundane. She knew that her friends would take good care of Sharon. There was nothing to concern her but her own fears. With that she dismissed her worry and returned to contemplating the Goddess and the Sun God.

The forest was growing quiet and then an owl called out. It was a magical voice that called her name.

"Magdala?"

Magdalen looked up to the tree limbs above her. Was she hallucinating? Baera had warned her about hunger and sleep deprivation causing horrible visions and nightmares, but she wasn't even hungry or really tired yet. She heard the voice a second time.

"Magdala."

It was like a whisper at first, but then strong and lovingly the owl called out.

"My beloved, Magdala!"

It was Jesus' voice! Could it be? Could it really be him? Magdalen rose to her feet and turned her head upward. There in the trees she saw the owl. He was golden in color with a white ring of down about his neck and he glowed like a dying ember in the fire. His eyes were wide open and he looked full at her. Then from the owl's heart there came a great light that bolted to the ground like a streak of lightening. As it exploded on the forest floor the lightening was transformed before her and Jesus held out his arms to her.

"Wisdom is visiting upon you this night, Magdala."

The vision spoke in Jesus' familiar voice.

"Thy Way is my Way. Sacrifice nothing but your fear. Love all beings. Harness your inner power and restore the world to its greatness by your light. And remember that I love you still."

Before she could embrace it, the vision was gone. Magdalen wept. Had Jesus really come to her through that golden owl? Had she imagined his presence, or fallen asleep and dreamed it? She stoked her fire, wrapped her cloak about her tightly and wept silently.

The cold chill of the night and the memory of her vision kept Magdalen awake. By morning the pangs of hunger were setting in but she chose to save the few berries and nuts that she was allowed for a time when hunger was more unbearable. She did have a sip of water and a bit of bread saying her commemorative prayer of thanksgiving.

"This is my body. This is my blood."

She said the words out loud and bowed her head in gratitude. Just as she finished, Baera dropped down from the trees. She had come to check on her prodigy making sure that no wild thing had attacked her in the night. Baera remained silent however, for she did not wish to disturb Magdalen's meditation process. The women smiled at one another and Baera, being satisfied that Magdalen was all right, vanished into the forest.

Magdalen then went back to her contemplation of the previous night's vision. Rather than concentrate on its reality or unreality, she decided to ponder on the vision's message.

"Wisdom has visited me." She thought. "Sophia has told me that my decisions have been wise to eliminate the bloody sacrifice, to love all beings and to spread this Way of mine as light."

She gave a long thanksgiving for the presence of Wisdom and then decided that supplication for Love would be appropriate. She pleaded mentally for the Goddess of Love, Frigga herself, to open her heart to love for all beings.

She chanted in front of the fire and then meditated in silence for long hours. As dusk returned she ate three of her berries and took a sip of water. This, she thought, would be enough to stave off hallucinations until morning. Still it was cold and she brought the fire to a full roar. Her attention was fully on the blaze. She stared at it until her eyes burned and teared. Though she could feel the cold in her body, her face was hot from the heat of the flames.

The dancing, yellow gold and orange tongues that leapt up toward her from the circle of rocks mesmerized Magdalen. A trance seemed to be falling upon her, and she vowed mentally to let it happen. Perhaps there would be another message or better yet, Jesus would appear again. It didn't matter if it was real or not, his presence would bring that feeling of love that she intended to create this night.

No owls, no voices, no Jesus. Magdalen stared harder into the fire. Surely something would happen if she concentrated on Love long enough. She began thinking about the day of the Holy Spirit, the Paraclete, and the initiation granted them all that day. There had been tongues of fire, not unlike these flames, above the head of everyone there. Then she remembered how they had debated the presence of the dove and its reality or unreality.

At that moment, a white winged horse rose from the flames! It wore a bridle but no saddle. From the center of its forehead there grew a single horn.

"Love visits upon you this night, Magdala."

The voice of Jesus came from its mouth as if it belonged there.

"The flame of Love goes out when it is not fed with good works, kind deeds and compassionate kisses. The flame of Love consumes these things to bring brightness and light to the World of the Living. The flame of Love is smothered and dies out when those seeking to warm themselves indulge in greed, gluttony and boastful philanthropy. You will continue to keep the fire of Love burning by the goodness in your heart and the good works that constitute your Way. Your Way is my Way. And remember that I love you still."

With that the wonderful winged creature flew up through the trees in the misty smoke that rose from Magdalen's fire. Again, she wept. Again she stoked the fire. This time she thought of it as the source of all light and the symbol of Love. It warmed her as Love did. It illuminated the earth as Love illuminated her heart. It raged as the Way itself raged - to be spread, and above all the fire of Love needed to be tended. She watched and tended the fire throughout the night without, she thought, even dozing off.

But when morning came she realized the truth. She had been asleep, possibly for hours. Again she broke her fast and said her commemorative prayer. Baera appeared and disappeared as she had the previous morning. Magdalen was once again alone with the fire and her thoughts. She smiled to herself.

"Wait until I tell Sarah and Ruth about the Pegasus. It was truly a Unicorn with wings! "

Magdalen quickly caught herself, creating jealousy or being vain were not fuel for Love's fire. She would remain humble, truthful and compassionate when she shared her vision with the others encouraging them to go on their own vision quest. But for now she had yet to complete this one.

This time she closed her eyes in meditation and chanting. The fire burned down to almost nothing before Magdalen felt the dew settling on her face, arms and neck. If she had slept all day, she wasn't aware of it. It she had been in a trance, she remembered nothing of its outcome. These blackout periods were something else that Baera had told her about. She gathered wood from the edge of the circle and built her fire up again.

She had received a great gift from the Pegasus, hallucination or not. She gave thanksgiving for its visit and message. Then she began to contemplate the truth of it all. What was the truth? Had she dreamed all these things? Had they been hallucinations? True prophetic vision? That was what she wanted now from the Gods and Goddesses a sign of the Truth.

She gazed into the fire hoping to achieve another apparition. Nothing came. She listened for a voice or an animal call that could be sending her a message. The forest was silent. Far into the night it began to rain. The cold drops made hissing noises as they struck the rocks around the fire. Steam rose from the fire itself and Magdalen covered her head with her cloak to keep warm. Only her eyes peered out from the veil she had created and she watched the raindrops fall around her.

She watched the steam rise and the water fall. It was icy cold and soon became small crystals of lacy white snow.

"Water, water is three fold," She thought out loud. "It is water, it is ice and it is also steam. So the truth comes in many shapes but remains the truth within itself. What's more, the Divine is like water. It is itself – the Divine. It is its manifestation as Earthly Life-the Divine with form, like ice. It is its spirit, the Holy Spirit, the Divine being vapor, breath or steam. The Truth is all is ONE."

She put out her hand to feel the snowflakes. She tasted them.

"They are yet water," she thought.

She looked up at the snowy sky.

"They do not appear as they are."

Her mind continued and the snow became a giant flurry of star-like lights that spun about in the night wind. Then in the midst of these starry illuminations there came one great light. It was so white, so hypnotic, that Magdalen couldn't take her eyes away. She could no longer feel the cold or the wet or the hunger. The light took her breath away and put her in the same awe filled state she remembered from the day of Pentecost – only more powerful than that. Then she heard the voice again.

"Magdala, my sweet Magdala, Truth from inside is more powerful than Truth given by another. Seek always your Inner Truth and respect the forms in which others see it. And remember, I love you still."

The light went out and Magdalen was left lying in front of the fire in the rain, but she felt nothing other than the Warmth of Love, the Power of Truth and the Way of Wisdom.

"Three Gods have visited me in three nights. Now I am the Righteous Teacher."

She whispered the words to herself, gave thanks and fell asleep. When Baera arrived she covered Magdalen's frigid body with warm blankets. Letting an exhausted new Druid sleep she stoked the fire and made tea and soup to break Magdalen's fast when she awoke. This was the first day of the New Year, the Winter Solstice, and the other women would arrive by noon. Baera was relieved when Magdalen stirred of her own accord, she knew from experience how exhausted she must be and truly did not want to wake her but did want ample time before the women arrived to prepare Magdalen for her initiation. She had brought warm, dry robes for Magdalen. The garb was a deep green color, like Baera's own sash. Magdalen felt of the warm fabric and smiled.

"You are a thoughtful teacher, Baera, and a wise woman."

She said it with gratitude for Baera's friendship and concern.

"When you have bathed and changed, you can tell me all about it and then I have some gifts for you."

The teacher helped her pupil to her feet. Baera walked Magdalen to a hot springs that seemed magical. She had not been into the forest before, not really. She had always stayed on the path and in the clearing and this wonderful warm pool had been a well-kept secret.

"You will find pools like this all over Avalon, Magdalen."

Baera had never spoken of Avalon before. Magdalen perked up but was more interested in telling Baera about her visions than using the perfumed soap that her teacher had set out for her.

"Get bathed, dear, its essential."

Baera was coaxing Magdalen to hurry now. Magdalen drew her consciousness back to the task at hand and realized how wonderfully warm the water was and how sweet smelling was the soap. After a short but wonderful bath she donned the deep green finery complimenting Baera on her good taste and thoughtfulness. When they arrived back at the clearing Baera poured tea and soup for them both.

"Don't eat too fast, now. Your stomach will rebel."

There was an "I've been there done that" attitude in her voice as she cautioned Magdalen against breaking a fast too quickly or too fully.

Magdalen sipped her breakfast delicately, not wanting to create a stomach upset. When they had eaten Magdalen told Baera everything that had happened and together they wept with joy. Then Baera opened the large leather bag, the same one she had brought Magdalen's robes in. From it now she took a pouch of purple velvet and handed it to Magdalen.

"These I now pass to you." she said.

Magdalen accepted the heavy pouch and opened it with care. Inside were the things of a Priestess. The golden cycle for cutting Mistletoe, a golden and engraved halo like headdress and a breastplate that looked like golden armor. There was also a belt with a great white stone in its buckle and a scepter of gold with a gem at its tip. Magdalen began to cry again.

"It's over Magdalen," Baera embraced her. "The initiation is over. You are a Priestess now, the High Priestess, not of Druids but of the Way."

Magdalen was astonished.

"That's it? No animal sacrifices, no being buried alive? That's it?"

Baera was laughing hysterically. Magdalen had obviously listened to too many rumors about Druids.

"You have been visited by the three-fold Divinity, Wisdom, Love and Truth. You have received and honored them appropriately and it is done. You do feel reborn, don't you?"

"Yes, I do! And the birthing was a pretty intense ordeal, I'd say!"

"Blessed Be!"

They both shouted as the other women arrived and entered the sacred spot.

"Blessed Be!" came a unified greeting.

Sharon ran to her mother's embrace and everyone sat around the fire as sisters would. Of course Magdalen had to tell the story of her three-day ordeal all over again. She was careful not to make the women jealous over the winged-unicorn as she preferred to call it and said that it was merely a vision. Ruth shook her head rapidly in disagreement.

"I still believe!"

"The truth comes in many forms, little one."

"This truth," interrupted Baera. "Is one of great power."

"Are you going to tell us about the winged-unicorn, Baera?" Ruth was excited.

"I will tell the tale as it was told to me. See what truth you find in it."

Baera was about to begin her story. Everyone applauded, this was after all a day for celebration and a tale, legend or fact, was a great way to rejoice.

"The Unicorn was the first animal to emanate from the Source. For this reason its meat was made bitter, too bitter to eat so that man and beast would avoid killing it. But it was discovered that its horn was magical and that drinking from the horn of a Unicorn would protect one from all manner of disease and even demons. So people did hunt the Unicorn and some kings had cups made from the horns that were encircled with gold to honor it. The Unicorn was strong, a fierce fighter and filled with courage, no hunter could kill or capture it unless by deceit. Because of this the animal became vain and self-centered.

"When the great flood came and the animals were taken two by two to the ship the Unicorn was among them, but the vanity of the male animal was so great that no one wanted him among them. Yet, it was not right to drown the Unicorn and his mate so the Gods intervened. The Goddess Athena of the Greeks gave him wings, and the male flew off to be among the Gods. Athena tamed the horse with a golden bridle. And he remains without a mate to this day. It is the mission of the Pegasus to deliver messages and to inspire people to goodness and humble compassion, the true pride of any God."

"What of the Unicorn?" Ruth was more than curious now.

"The Unicorn lives still, for the female was with foal and mated with her son in secret. The males are still hunted sometimes, by kings and noblemen, but it is seldom that they succeed. The Unicorn has learned its lessons well and now comes in innocence and complacency, seeking a virgin for refuge from its former vanity and warring nature. The white horses of the Sidhe are the descendants of the Unicorn who have lost the horn that caused them so much grief. The Pegasus and the Unicorn are the embodiment of Unconditional Love and Carnal Love, of purity and of pleasure in Divine form."

"I knew it! They do exist."

Ruth was ecstatic. Even with all this excitement the women were growing cold and it was decided that they would move their circle to Baera's cave. No one had been there, not even Magdalen, and they felt honored to be invited. It was a short walk down the path past the hot springs to the rocky entrance of the cave. Inside the fire only needed to be stirred to be revived enough to warm the inner chamber quite nicely. The women watched from the cave entrance as snow began to fall and danced in a circle together, singing the songs of the Baerds from whom Baera had taken her name. The children played with little dolls and with jacks and ate as much of the sweet things that Baera had provided, as the women would allow. It was a grand New Year's celebration and a great celebration too of Magdalen's rebirth.

When it was getting dark the women set out to return to the city, but Magdalen and Sharon remained for the night with Baera. There was so much Magdalen still wanted to know about the gathering of Mistletoe and the secret of the Water and the White Horses. Baera, however, made the decision that Magdalen needed to rest and that any further teaching would wait until morning.

Chapter 26

Tales of Avalon

"You have to go to Avalon."

Baera began their breakfast conversation.

"There the women of the land practice their spiritual and religious rites without hesitation. There is total freedom there for everyone. It is just the place to continue raising Sharon."

Magdalen munched on her fruit and cheese thinking about such a move. She had grown attached to Baera and felt she had so much yet to share with her that a move now would stifle her growth.

"I don't know, Baera," she began. "I think this Avalon sounds wonderful for Sharon and for me, but I am learning so much here. And the other women love you and this place too."

"The others will be here soon, we will talk with them."

Baera was going to try to mold Magdalen's decision by popular demand. She would create that demand by telling them all about Avalon and its wonders. But there was sadness in her voice when she spoke again.

"Magdalen, I will miss all of you, too, especially you and the child. Sharon is like a granddaughter to me, you know that. I will gladly give up our time together if someday I would be able to see Sharon as a Priestess of Avalon. She would flourish there, and you could learn and teach so much more than ever you could here. I would visit, of course."

"I'd feel better if you went with us, Baera. We could share the teaching and the learning and remain together as we are now, all of us."

Magdalen was hoping that Baera could be convinced by this invitation to join her if she chose to go to Avalon. But Baera would not think of it.

"As tempting as it is, dear, I have my position here and my duties to the clan. I cannot leave, not even to see that you get there safely. But do go and explore this wonderful land. Avalon is the right place for you, my spirit guides have confirmed this in my dreams."

"You've been there, to Avalon?" Magdalen wanted more information.

"Yes, and I will tell you all about it." At that moment the others came into the cave.

"It has stopped snowing." Polaris was rejoicing; the cold and wet were uncomfortable to her.

"Shall we go to the clearing then?" Baera wanted to return to their sacred space.

"Why not stay here, warm by the fire?" The older woman's arthritis forced her to object but only with a question. Baera took pity on her.

"All right then pull up a chair and stay warm here by the fire. I will tell you all about Avalon and then together you can help Magdalen decide when you should go."

Baera pulled Sharon up into her lap as she began her tale of Avalon and its wonders.

"It is magical there. Truly it is magical. There is a veil of mist that covers the isle. This misty veil divides the world of humans from the world of the Goddess, The Lady of the Lake. When the moon is new and again when it is full, the veil thins and you can pass safely between the two worlds. At the Summer Solstice you will be able to cross the sea and enter the isle with welcome awaiting you. That is the best time, Magdalen. You should arrive there before the Summer Solstice and cross the sea to the isle just at that time."

Baera was looking Magdalen in the eye and giving what sounded an awful lot like a command, and Magdalen was listening.

"The Tor, the highest spot on the Isle of Avalon, is reached by the Pilgrim's Path along its spine. When the veil is thinned enough, you can see the mountains from there. The Tor is covered with trees and undergrowth, hermits live in the caves and cells on its summit and slopes.

"In certain lights it can be seen plainly that terraces have been carved around the sides of the Tor. These terraces form a huge labyrinth that encircles the hill and leads to its summit.

"By walking the labyrinth, an initiate prepares to enter the Other World through a sacred and hidden entrance to the hollow interior of the hill. But few have found the entrance and gained access to the Tor's inner chambers, where the ancient mysteries are celebrated. You will all take that walk, Magdalen, many times, but only the first time will it be dangerous. For you will be well-known by the fairy kingdom and the dark inner core will be opened to you in light."

Baera appeared to be quite finished with her description of the Tor and its labyrinth walk, but the others were eager to hear more.

"Go on Baera, please tell us more of Avalon and its wonders, and about the fairy kingdom too." Ruth was like a child eager for more stories.

"In Avalon you will find the Blood-Well, but not until you have been accepted by the Lady of the Lake and know the mysteries of the Five Goddesses. One day you will join the Nine-fold Sisterhood. You will become aware of their shape-shifting and the many ways that they can reveal themselves. The Lady of the

Lake will direct you to the Blood-Well with its rich healing waters of Divine Essence."

Baera smiled a soft smile remembering her own experiences at the well.

"The fairies will tend you and make you comfortable. They will fill your hearts with joy. But be wary for beyond the mists of Avalon are also the worlds of the giants and the gargoyles, those fears of smallness and ugliness that create dark enchantments within the mind. Keep your focus on the Goddesses.

"All Gods are One God, and all Goddesses One Goddess.... but on Avalon, there are five faces of the Goddess that the Priestesses work with, although many continue to honor the Goddesses of their homelands as well.

Blodeuwedd is the Maiden Goddess, revered on Avalon as the Goddess of new beginnings, independence and empowerment. She is made of Nine Flowers and created by the great magicians Math and Gwydion, to be the Bride of Llew, the Sun God. She chose another lover, who attempted to slay her husband, but Llew instead turned into an eagle. Llew was found and restored by Gwydion, who transformed Blodeuwedd into an owl as punishment for her deception. The name "Blodeuwedd" means "Flower Face."

"The Goddess Arianrhod, is one of the faces of the Mother Goddess looked to in Avalon. She was Mother to Llew and Dylan, God of the Sea. Her Name literally means "Silver Wheel". Arianrhod is the embodiment of the Mother who is Ever-Virgin, She Who Bears Fruit, yet is beholding to no man. She lays our tasks before us as the wheel of our lives spins on.

"The Goddess Rhiannon, "Great Queen", is the other face of the Mother. She is the White Mare, the Queen of the Other World, whose birds can soothe the souls of the most troubled of mortals. She is the Nurturing Mother, devoted to her children, who gently guides us so that we may learn the lessons before us. She understands hardship and pain, separation and loss.

But always, although she had been wronged, her love is unfaltering, and her honor unwavering. She is the Great Queen Mother of all the Celts.

"Cerridwen, the "White Sow", is the revered Crone Goddess -She who is the Dark of the Moon, into whose Cauldron we must enter to be reborn. She is the Washer at the Ford, the Dark Hag. Those who do not understand her regenerative nature fear her. Yet, from her comes Inspiration.

"Great Branwen, the Embodiment of Sovereignty, is the Chief Goddess of Avalon Meaning "White Raven", this Sister of Bran the Blessed, became Queen of Ireland and was sorely mistreated by her husband. Sending starlings she had trained, she called the King to help her. After battles, the appearance of the Cauldron of Plenty, which restores life, and the beheading of her brother, Branwen was returned to Britain where She died of grief for all of the death and destruction. She is very concerned with the welfare of her realm, and is a Goddess of great depth and complexity.

"That's enough for now. You have to decide soon if you are to arrive in Avalon by the Summer Solstice."

Obviously Baera would no longer be coaxed into telling stories, she wanted to give directions instead.

"You should leave right after we cut the Mistletoe, the very next day. That would give you plenty of time to cross Gaul and arrive at Morlaix in time to sail to Britain and from there travel by land again to the sea that surrounds Avalon. Your journey may be hard, but you will discover many things and encounter many spirits as you cross Gaul."

"I am convinced we should go, Magdalen."

To hear Polaris in such a positive state concerning such a big decision with all its dangers surprised Magdalen.

"I can feel my heart being pulled by the Goddess to Avalon." Polaris went on to finish her thought.

Magdalen could feel the tug too. She could just see Sharon growing as a member of the Nine-fold Sisterhood and being filled with empowerment by the Goddesses and their priests.

"Yes, we will go!"

Magdalen nearly shouted her affirmation. The others chorused in response.

"Blessed Be! So Mote it Be. Blessed Be!"

Baera's smile was wide now and she prayed in song.

"Blessed be the journey and the travelers. So mote it be."

That night Magdalen had a lot to think about. She had visions of the White Mare Goddess and wondered what mysteries surrounded her. Could it have been the White Mare Goddess that had visited her that night during her initiation? She felt it was. She wondered too whether James should be included in this journey to Avalon and decided that she would leave the decision to him. Then she fell asleep and dreamed a wonderful dream of her daughter's growth in a place of such beauty and reverence, a place where the Way would flourish and all people would form a mystical community of godliness. It was a wonderful dream, and she hated the morning to come and end it.

Still, this was the sixth day of the moon, the night when Magdalen would, as the High Priestess, cut the Mistletoe and distribute it to the people of the Celtic village. She wanted to look her best Celtic self for this occasion. As soon as she could attend to Sharon and have some breakfast she went to the hot springs to bathe with Baera. Their preparations would take until dark.

After they had bathed the women took turns braiding one another's hair into many long braids and piling it atop their heads. It reminded Magdalen of the hours that she and her mother-in-law had spent doing much the same. She was glad that it had grown back so profusely. Then they took small amounts of pumice stone ground fine into a powder and polished their teeth until they were a pearly white. Baera showed Magdalen how to dye the nails of her fingers and toes with a crimson dye made from sheep's blood and fat. They lightened their faces with a covering of chalk applied with a rabbit's foot. They shaped their eyebrows by pulling out unwanted hairs and then dyed them black with berry juice. They reddened their cheeks with a plant called ruam.

Tonight Magdalen would be adorned with the white robes and golden attire appropriate to her new position. Baera laid out the clothes and jewelry for after their evening meal. Together the two women ate a simple dinner and waited for dusk to clothe the clearing in shadowy splendor. When the time was right, Baera helped Magdalen dress. Then together they went out into the clearing. Soon the others arrived and each was handed one of the catching cloths that had been prepared. Magdalen looked splendid, as did Baera in her own robes of priestly grandeur.

The group set out in search of the Mistletoe. Baera and Magdalen seemed guided by the Goddess as they moved deliberately off the path and into the forest. Everyone chanted as Magdalen climbed the Sacred Oak and severed its holy soul letting it fall freely. They were quick to use their catching cloths and preserve the Oak's Soul from touching the earth. Magdalen moved quite easily from tree limb to tree limb despite the encumbrance of heavy jewelry, flowing robe and of course the golden cycle.

When she returned to the forest floor in the same fashion as Baera had always used, Magdalen separated the Mistletoe into small twigs quietly blessing the fine herb for its sacrifice. Then they were off to the village where a huge bonfire awaited them. The people gathered about and Magdalen carefully handed each one of them a sprig of the white berries on a stalk of green. There was dancing and singing, harps played and no one questioned this new Priestess. That was much to Magdalen's surprise. Baera offered reassurance.

"They would not insult me by questioning my judgment in these matters. Particularly not in public."

When the ritual and its celebration were over, Magdalen and Baera gave thanks, shared a commemorative meal according to Magdalen's Way and shed themselves of the heavy garb and makeup. Releasing the others to return to their city apartment, they relaxed in silence for a while. Then Baera went to her cupboard and took out a small scroll of bark upon which she had drawn a map for Magdalen.

"This will guide you to Avalon."

As she handed it to Magdalen her eyes filled with tears. She was missing her even before she had left. Magdalen's arms went swiftly about her teacher's neck and she kissed her on the mouth.

"I love you." She whispered.

"And I you." Baera said in her ear. "One day I will visit you in Avalon. I will see Sharon grown. I will see you as Grand Priestess and Goddess in your own right. So mote it be."

The women knew that this was the only goodbye there would be. Magdalen slept lightly that night. Her thoughts were of Avalon and its wondrous magic. She woke early and left without disturbing Baera. It was better to hurry off to the others and get a start as soon as possible; she wanted to be sure that they arrived in Avalon before the Summer Solstice.

By noon Magdalen had given James all the information that he needed to make a decision. He would travel with the women of course; it was his duty to protect them. Polaris, Ruth, Sarah and Carmel were extremely eager to get started. Cybele, however, had not come to the city. Magdalen decided that they would try to meet her and Regino on the road or pick them up at the village. Quite authoritarian in her language, she sent James off to get the needed supplies, animals and cart. What she once thought was going to be a three-day visit had turned into what now seemed a lifetime of learning, but it was over and they once again had needs to be met as sojourners.

By mid-afternoon they were on the road again this time without the safety net of a caravan. Cybele and Regino joined them as Magdalen had planned. As a token of her esteem for his courage, Cybele had made a gift to James of a fine steed and Magdalen and her group traveled now as a rich family with James being the only man. The road was well paved and easily traversed but James was extremely cautious about any passerby or fellow traveler making Magdalen extremely edgy. She was desperately seeking to live the philosophy of love and trust, not the thinking that contributed to fear and uneasiness.

If they stayed on the Roman highways the trip across Gaul was about four hundred and fifty miles, which would be a journey of only fifteen days if the oxen drew the cart full of women and children. James, of course, would ride the horse that Cybele had given him when they left the village. Calculating all this in her mind, Magdalen was sure that not only would they be in Avalon by the Solstice, but they would also have time to explore as they went and still be early for the sacred event. She was eager to learn about some of the things that Baera had told her she would find crossing Gaul. Her plan was to be halfway across Gaul by the Spring Equinox, still almost three months away. The group could stop if they liked for even two or three days in an area of interest, if there was learning to be found there or someone to share the Way with.

Chapter 27

Crossing Gaul

Magdalen's mind was always on the Solstice. Baera had told her of the ritual circle and the great fires that the Celtic people built on the Summer Solstice and she could see it all in her mind's eye. It was the night of fire festivals and of love magic, of love oracles and divination. It had to do with lovers and predictions of love. She could see loving couples jumping through the flames of the bonfire for good luck. She could almost taste the delicious honey that would become these couples' favorite food after their wedding, for this was the full moon of June, the honey moon, and the honey was now right for harvest. Honey, it was said, provided for fertility, prosperity and health.

These thoughts of Midsummer and the Mare Goddess were nice, but it was not yet spring. Days were rainy, cold and sometimes snowy as the little band moved along the Roman roads. Daydreaming was a fine pastime for such gray days, yet Magdalen knew she would have to stay focused on her objectives if they were to actually be in Avalon in time to see the reality of the fires.

Just three days into the journey and she was moved by the weather and the mood it delivered to leave the Roman highway. Magdalen knew that cutting across country the group would move more slowly, but she thought that they would cut miles off their route as well. Grumbling about the danger, James went ahead of the women onto the dirt roads and paths that were scrawled on Magdalen's little map. Truly he felt they were more likely to encounter savage Celts or robbers in the wilderness than they were on the well-traveled roads of Rome. Still he led the way at Magdalen's command.

After several days of hard travel and of cold nights beneath the cart for cover, they eventually came upon a small village comprised of grass huts and a large central fire pit. It was a Celtic village all right, but not at all Romanized like the one near Lugdunum. There were no wooden sidewalks and no marketers or vendors. The natives were dressed in skins and feathers with large headdresses that reminded Magdalen of animal heads with human faces. Despite their monster like attire they were a friendly and joyful people who welcomed the group with a hearty celebration. Being invited to stay indoors for the night was a treat and venison was a welcome fare.

These people might not be walking on wooden sidewalks, but they were true to the Celtic tradition when they asked for a fare exchange and Magdalen offered to entertain with a story. A loud announcement was made and the people gathered around her like school children eager to hear her tale. Magdalen stood up in the center of the circle. She was a bit unsure of herself; she had never been before such a formal and large group for her storytelling. She decided on a story of demonic possession – her own.

"My story," she began, "is not a tale of the Gods and Goddesses but of the enemies of the Divine and Human worlds. It is the story of seven horrible demons that inhabited a woman's mind and body torturing her very heart.

"The first demon slipped into her quite accidentally through her right eye when she saw the suffering in the world all about her. The demon ate at her compassion and her caring. Her right eye became closed and she could no longer see the good in this world but was plagued with visions of crime and cruelty. The first demon's name was Blame.

"Blame called to the woman, 'Let my brother in for he will shut your other eye so that you no longer see the errors of the world but only what can be done to change it.'

"So the woman looked hard out of her left eye and the second demon entered therein. Now her vision was filled with sights of her own making, horrible sights of her past transgressions. She was tormented by her past, for everyone has injured another, made wrong choices, or entangled life with self-created sadness. And the second demon's name was Guilt.

"Guilt and Blame screamed from inside the woman's mind, 'Open your mouth woman, allow our sister to come in. She will make right what is wrong. She is the motivator to change. She is the one who will remind you always of the wrongs of the world and your self, so that you will become wise and penitent.'

"Now the woman, thinking that penance might indeed undo the wrongs of the world opened her mouth and the demon called Regret entered her mind. This demon would not let her rest, Regret kept reminding her through her dreams and her daydreams and her nightmares and her meditations and even her prayers that the world was and always had been a sinful place.

"Now the woman was not only blind to the goodness of the world, for both eyes had been closed by Guilt and Blame, but also she could not sleep finding no hope in the future, for Regret would not let her rest.

"So the woman cried out to the demons in her. 'What can I do? Where can I go? What end shall there be to this torture?'"

"And Regret showed herself in a dream and spoke back to the woman. 'I have two sisters, reach out your hands to them and they will give you hope.'

"Now the woman was desperate and the torture was intense, she reached out her hands in an open gesture and through each palm entered another demon. Through her right hand entered the demon called Idolatry. Through her left the demon called Sloth.

"Idolatry crippled her hand in a horrible grasping position. She sought after all things physical and thought them to be a

306

source of hope. She lusted after money, sexual affairs, position and even food. But the demon kept her from attaining these things. Her grasp was impaired. Each time she reached out for something it dropped from her hand. She became impoverished, lost her lovers and status, she could no longer hold down her food for the demon had eaten away at the pit of her stomach.

"Sloth made the woman's left hand limp, like a wet rag. She could do nothing for herself or any other. She was powerless to change the world for her zeal had been crippled and left lifeless. Her heart was sick with the pain of knowing no hope and she called out to the demons again.

'I have nothing left but the awareness of your presence. I have no vision, no hope, and no zest for life. What can I do now?'

"Well, the demons had her bamboozled because they now controlled most of her mind.

"They answered her. 'Your heart, woman, open your heart, bare your bosoms and allow our brother to come in. He will make your heart stop aching.'

"So the woman tore her garment and into her heart entered the demon called Despair. Despair was a quiet demon. It said nothing and at first eased the pain as the demons had promised, for it emptied the woman's heart of all feeling. She no longer craved after the things of the world. She no longer had dreams of a better tomorrow, or a need to act. Instead she was complacent, empty and stared silently at the world about her. But soon Despair ate so deeply into the woman's heart that pain returned. It returned ten fold and she clutched her chest in agony calling out to the demons.

'What is your source of might? From what mother were you born that you could be so powerful? What Goddess has given you your authority over the mind?'

"In one loud voice from inside her head the demons shouted, 'Fear is the Mother of our Might. It is she from whom we have all come.'

"With that the woman drew in a long breath and she could smell Fear as it entered into her through her nostrils. Fear paralyzed the woman. She could not move. She could not even call out to the demons for help, because now Fear would keep her from doing anything about her situation at all."

Magdalen paused her story there and sipped from her wine cup.

"What happened to her?" called out one of the men.

"You can't leave her like that!" shouted a woman.

"Please, go on with your story," Polaris in her wisdom encouraged Magdalen.

The storyteller raised her arms in a gesture of openness to God's grace and shouted, "She was saved by God."

A hearty laugh came from Magdalen, "I will tell you how, but wait. The demons had yet more work to do."

"More?" someone murmured.

Magdalen nodded, "Yes, more. They mated one with another, like animals they mated among themselves and the female demons gave birth. Out of them came Anger, Hatred, and Bigotry. Out of them came Greed, Avarice, and Vanity. Out of them came Lust, Envy and Jealousy. Nine children of the demons came out of them. These demons turned the woman into a demonic thing herself and she had Fear within her to preside over them all.

"Then one day a man came by, he was a godly looking man, tall and handsome. He didn't wear fine robes or jewelry but was clad in a simple cloak of purple with a tunic of white linen. He had a tender look in his eyes as he gazed upon this demonized woman so tortured by her soul. His name was Jesus, he said as he reached his hand out to her and touched the place where Fear had entered in.

'The children and the grandchildren will follow their mother,' he said. 'Let Fear be gone and all the rest will go with her.'

'Love is the only fitting foe of Fear. Love is the Way to expel her. Love is the Way to keep her from returning. Love is the Way to Life Everlasting. I Love you.' With that Jesus embraced the woman and squeezed Fear out through her heart.

"Instantly she was whole again. Her eyes were opened and through them entered the children of Love. Forgiveness and Compassion entered and she saw the world in a new light. Her hands returned to normal and the children of Love entered in. Temperance and Ability entered through her hands. She opened her mouth in gratitude, and the child of Love entered in. Wisdom came in. The woman embraced Jesus to show her love and the child of Love came into her heart. It was filled with the life of Peace.

"The children of Fear took with them their offspring for they could not live without their parents and the Mother that is Fear. And the woman was healed of all her infirmities. She followed the man Jesus on his Way and comes tonight to share that Way with you. Let there not be Fear among you, that is my lesson and my blessing this night. I know you are a wise people who enjoy the story and seek its gifts."

Magdalen went back to her place in the crowd and seated herself. There was a lot of murmuring and talking from the group and she could feel the positive response to her story as they began to leave and return to their homes. Perhaps, she thought, they are not yet fearless, but they have found a New Way.

Magdalen sat by the fire contemplating the past night's presentation. She was hoping that someone would tell her what they thought of the story and its lesson. Soon women began to join her. It didn't take long before she got the feedback she was looking for.

"If the grandchildren are present does that mean that Fear is also within us?"

"Can anyone have enough Love to ward off Fear? Or only this Jesus?"

"Is there an enchantment against Fear?"

The questions came rapidly and gave Magdalen little time for answers. Instead it was agreed that there would be another exchange, an enchantment today for another story that evening.

At this point Magdalen realized that no men had joined the circle around the fire. She wondered why and apparently out loud, for a woman answered.

"Men do not admit the presence of Fear."

Magdalen realized then that she would have to choose this evening's story carefully if she were going to reach the men and the women both. Meanwhile the others prepared for the enchantment.

They blessed the fire as Baera had always done. Like Baera they believed in acting out their enchantments, soon several men and women appeared wearing masks and carrying weapons. Magdalen and her friends, especially James, became a little nervous. These were not wooden swords like Baera had used and this was not to be a child's game. They all hoped that it would remain a play and not become a true battle. Their minds were still infected with the stories of Druid cruelty and Celtic battles in the nude.

The High Priestess came out of her hut with the same flourish and flavor that Magdalen or Baera would have and did at the Winter Solstice and again when they cut the Mistletoe. That was already over a month ago. This was the Moon of Ice, and the feast of Imboic or Brigantia. The newborn lambs began to nurse this morning; winter was ending and spring was arriving. Buried seeds were beginning to stir within the earth. This was also the beginning of the third of the year that belonged to the

Maiden aspect of the three-fold Goddess. Some called her Brigantia, others Brigit and still others, those in Avalon Baera had told Magdalen, called her Blodeuwedd. This enchantment would bless the new season and honor the Maiden Goddess.

The High Priestess relieved their minds about battles and wars as she disarmed all attending, swept the area with her broom as if to make the earth clean and lit the candles she had neatly arranged. With the first candle she chanted.

"In the darkness the Goddess is stirring, gently she wakens from her frozen dreams. All the world has awaited this moment, the return of the Maiden, and her promise of spring."

From her urn filled with herbs she took a handful and sprinkled them upon the ground around her. Then she lit another candle and her chant continued.

"Powers of the Earth, the Maiden awakens! Come join us in prayer and share in the light.

Everyone in the audience moved inward in the circle and the Priestess lit a third candle.

"Powers of the Air, the Springtime awakens! Come join in her breath and share in the light."

Again everyone moved inward. An aromatic scent was added to the fire. Another candle was lit and another chant followed.

"Powers of Fire, the Goddess awakens! Come join in the Love and share in the light."

The Priestess poured a flammable liquid on the fire and the blaze burst upward. Another candle was lit.

"Powers of the Water, the Maiden awakens! Come join in her Wisdom and share in the light. "

Again the group got closer. The Priestess held her arms high as if invoking the Goddess.

"Be with us now, oh ancestors of yore, hear now our prayers, our hopes and our dreams. The Goddess has been wakened, once more as the Maiden by loving caresses from the Strengthened Sun King. The Earth now grows warmer, it is seeded with life, the Maiden moves forward and into the Light."

Now a mortal maiden appeared out of one of the huts. She was dressed as a bride and made a gesture of submission in the direction of the Sun. The Priestess shouted out.

"Behold the God and Goddess, the Lord of the Land and his Bride."

After this cakes and ale were brought out and there were many cheers. The make-believe bride remained in her wedding garb the entire day, as she was the symbolic union of Sun and Earth. The celebration didn't end until sunset when the Priestess called a halt to the merriment and disrobed the bride, while paying her great homage as the symbol of life renewed.

With that the Bride disappeared back into the hut from which she had come and shouts rang out.

"Blessed Be the Spring! Blessed Be the Earth, the Sun and the Moon! Blessed Be the Light and the Dark! Blessed Be the One."

Well Magdalen hadn't thought that the enchantment would last all day and she hadn't given any thought to her story selection. But now everyone was asking.

"Will you tell your story now? Perhaps you can make it one in which the Maiden Goddess is the heroine?"

Magdalen didn't know where she would find such a story in her head and certainly had no recollection of any that Jesus had told. But then it struck her; one of Mother Mary's stories out of Jesus' past would do quite nicely.

"There was a woman named Mary, she had given birth to the hero of yesterday's story, Jesus. She is our heroine."

Magdalen paused, how would she make the words come out right? How would she link her mother-in-law to the Goddess of Spring? In her head was the word, "Trust" and she continued.

"When the days of her purification according to the Law of Moses were accomplished, Mary and her husband brought Jesus to Jerusalem, to present him to the Lord. This is written in the law of the Jews that every male that opens the womb shall be presented to God at the temple. Now Mary was to offer a sacrifice, according to the law of the Jews, a pair of turtledoves or two young pigeons.

"Now there was a man in Jerusalem, whose name was Simeon; and he was just and devout, waiting for the salvation of Israel. Spirits talked to this man and spoke wisdom and prophecy through him. And it was revealed to him by the Spirit that he would not die before he had seen a New Light for Israel.

"Spirit sent him to the temple that day, on the feast of Imboic, a day much like this one has been. When his parents brought in the child Jesus to present him and to offer the sacrifice, Simeon held out his arms and took the child from Mary.

"Then he called out 'Blessed Be, now I can leave this earth with peace of mind. I hold in my arms the New Light! He will be the One light to enlighten the Gentiles, and bring a New Way to the people of Israel.' Mary and her husband Joseph marveled at Simeon's words.

"But Simeon blessed them, and said to Mary, 'Behold, this child is destined to change the world. The Light you have borne will be the Light of the World and you have arrived here like the Bride of the Sun, spring has brought new light into the world, indeed. Blessed be your womb and blessed be the gift you have given us!'

"Then a dark and troubled look came over Simeon's face and he revealed something else to Mary. 'The spring, Mary, fades to the darkness of winter. Blessed be the broken heart that you will suffer then.'

"Now Mary didn't know what to make of this last statement. But she was not afraid, because she knew that the child's light would warm many winters. Jesus grew to maturity and he brought the Way to many. When you celebrate Imboic in the future you shall remember my story. For Imboic is a festival of Light, of Purification and of Presentation. The Light returns to warm the earth. The Maiden Goddess, purified of earth's painful winter, presents new life and light to us all.

"Mary lit many candles that day in memory of the light of her son's soul. One day her heart was broken when he was crucified for the illumination that he sought to deliver. That was the day that winter returned, but spring erupted again as Mary's granddaughter, my Sharon was born. Blessed Be! A New Light and a New Way has brought the Circle of Life to completion!"

Everyone shouted after Magdalen, "Blessed Be the Light!" and applauded.

One of the men scooped Sharon into his hands and held her high in the air. The child laughed and giggled as the people engaged in complimenting her and honoring her grandmother as the heroine of a spring long past. Magdalen laughed too, she hadn't planned on this demonstration of endearment, but delighted in it.

Soon they began to hail Magdalen, too, for she was the new heroine, the new bearer of the Light. At this she blushed and sipped a bit more ale. The party died slowly but eventually like the fire it was burned out and the village returned to the silence of another cold night.

Chapter 28

The Purification at Bath

The next day, Magdalen decided to move on again using only the animal trails and footpaths through the woods. Such large woods they were. It would be a long time before they reached anything resembling civilization and after weeks of travel Magdalen was beginning to doubt her decision to take this way after all. The roads might have been faster as well as safer.

There were cool, clear springs along the paths though, because the animals had made their way to water while paving the road with their hooves. Each night they camped by one of these springs and washed themselves and Sharon's soiled linen. Then ate a meal of hunted meat, some of the herbs they had learned to use and sweet spring water. Then they slept with James keeping watch half the night and Magdalen the other half. Sharon made a good alarm to sound the changing of this little guard since she demanded to be nursed about midway through each night.

Slow and tedious as the journey had become, the group was still going to reach Magdalen's goal of being halfway across Gaul by the Spring Equinox. The Moon of the Winds would be full soon and she was hoping for a clearing in the trees that would allow her to see it. She had mentally decided that the Spring Equinox which tied closely with the Jewish Passover and of course the anniversary of Jesus' death and resurrection would be exactly the right time for new beginnings and for the New Way to begin to shape itself in ritual and rite.

This would be the day that she would finally wean Sharon. She and the other women would establish a Wind Moon ritual and make this the New Way's New Year. It was not Celtic. It was not Jewish. It was not even Roman. It was a New Way holiday and would be celebrated as such, honoring the Gods and Goddesses that dwelt in all people. It would also be a holiday that included enchantments against the demons that attempted to possess the minds of everyone, the very ones she had told about in her story at the Celtic village. They could be warded off, she thought, by Living Love as Jesus had taught her.

When the Spring Equinox and the Moon of the Winds arrived, Magdalen found her clearing. As the sun set she had her private ritual with Sharon. This would be a passage for the little girl. She was no longer to be considered an infant and this would be the last time that she would taste her mother's milk. Magdalen found tears in her eyes as she fed her daughter. The days of infancy were gone and she could see that time would pronounce that she was a Light to the World, a Light that had come from the seed of the Great Light. But in Avalon she would be safe, and free to shine among the stars.

After she blessed Sharon and put her down for the night, Magdalen called the others to her.

"We have learned much in the villages that we have visited on this journey. We have shared a great deal and always in the Celtic tradition of fair exchange and honor. This was perhaps the greatest lesson of all. It is one that we will keep in our New Way. And we will keep the commemorative meal as our Rite of Remembrance. This Jesus gave us so that we would never forget that flesh and blood are just bread and wine but the Spirit is Life. Our greatest tenet of faith was found with Baera, that Love conquers all. This we will always believe. Another tenet is that we offer up only our good works, prayers and meditations and harm nothing in the name of God. Now, tonight under this full moon, we will begin our New Year. After this night our only goal will be Avalon and the Way."

"So Be It!" they all responded.

Even James had given the cheer. He liked the idea of a single mission much better than moving from village to village in search of something illusive but extraordinary.

The women decided that this night would require many lights.

"Candles and lamps everywhere!" Ruth delighted in the idea.

"Candles will have to do."

James was being practical. There were no lamps in their cart. Ruth set out the entire store of candles but for three that James had set aside for an emergency. Carmel went off to gather flowers. She returned with large white wild flowers and set them near the lights. James built a wonderful fire in the center of the clearing and Polaris made sure that the herbs for aroma were finely ground. Cybele unwrapped the vestments and golden finery that Baera had given Magdalen for such an occasion as this. She polished the gold and brass so that it would sparkle and shine in the candlelight and the rays of the full moon. Sarah brought out the bread and wine for the Rite of Remembrance as Magdalen was now calling her nightly ritual. She created an altar from a flat rock and a bucket that had been turned upside down. Reverently she spread one of the Mistletoe catching clothes over it and placed the loaf and a clay cup in places of honor upon it. Before she could pour the wine Magdalen called to her to wait.

"I have the cup we will use this night!"

Magdalen reached into her leather bag and brought out her most prized possession.

"This is the cup that Jesus used. Now we will share it in remembrance of his resurrection and our future New Life."

She poured the wine herself and went into the woods with Sarah as her handmaiden to dress for the ritual. When she returned the golden cycle was hanging from her belt. She had not braided her hair but instead let it flow freely. She blessed the earth, the fire, the air and the waters. She called upon the Father Divine and the Great Mother to bless the coming year and their endeavors. Then she asked each of the others to state an intention for the new season.

James called of course for a safe journey. Ruth and Sarah both prayed for Unicorns, White Horses and even the appearance of a Pegasus. James couldn't help but snicker. Polaris, wise as always, asked for direction on their journey. Cybele, a Celt to the core, prayed poetically that the seeds of the Way planted this night would flourish under the growth of the Mother Moon and be harvested as souls returned to sanity. Carmel was last and a bit shy to follow Cybele's flowery affirmation. She quietly asked that the misty veil of Avalon be very fine when they arrived so that they could pass quickly through to the other side and meet the Goddesses and fairies. Magdalen commented on the poetry in Carmel's prayer, for she knew that the girl was shy and in need of support.

Then Magdalen broke the bread and they shared the loaf and the cup with great solemnity. When it was over Cybele broke into a beautiful Celtic song to which they all danced. James swung Carmel about with such zest that she all but lost her balance. Everyone laughed and teased the couple about being swept off their feet. They all were truly wondering if there was a bit of a romance brewing and encouraged them to jump through the flames. Both of them denied any intention of romance and refused the fire, but the women weren't going to forget the look of love in their eyes. Magdalen ended the teasing and innuendo by putting out the candles and ushering everyone to bed. Tomorrow would be a new beginning that would require energetic sojourners to say the least.

The journey did require some energy. They continued as they had been along the paths and trails and stopping at dusk each day. Now they were all walking except for the children who rode in the narrow cart. James led the animals ahead of them and they often had to struggle to make even fifteen miles progress a day. But no one grumbled and they never failed to have their Rite of Remembrance in the evening. Sharon and Regino participated in the ritual now too and took their meal with the adults. Magdalen and the women had decided upon a full practice of evenness. James had some reservations at first, he still harbored a bit of resentment at this policy of equality between men, women and children.

Spring brought with it new birth in the forests. Sharon was always bringing some small critter back to her mother. Magdalen of course released the poor creature but only after having honored her daughter's love for animals. Buds turned into leaves and, although the density of the woods often hid the sun, they could feel its warming affect on their bodies. They spoke of Avalon, of the misty veils and of the Goddesses that they would find behind them. Regino pretended to hunt until James decided that the boy was old enough for the pursuit of food in the forest. With James as mentor, he became a fine hunter of smaller game.

Sometimes the group would come upon a little village that had been erected at a hot spring or spring fed lake. They would spend a day or two with the people there offering once again their fair exchange of learning and teaching. Magdalen repeated many of her stories now. She told time and again the stories of Lazarus and her release from the demons. She offered the villagers the Rite of Remembrance and always wore her ritual garb when she broke the bread in public. The cup, though, she kept for only the most solemn and holy of occasions; there were not too many of those now. But Magdalen knew that they would be in Avalon for the Summer Solstice and then would share that Holy Grail with a sisterhood she had yet to meet.

Two weeks before the Solstice James looked once more at the little map that Baera had drawn. He suggested that he could lead the group back to a Roman highway and on to the coast quickly so that they would have time in the port to refresh before venturing to Avalon. Everyone seemed to think that the easy travel and a rest at Isca on the Sea of Britannicum was a fine idea. Even Magdalen was growing weary of the hard travel and eager to arrive somewhere civilized before going to the enchanted isle.

In less than a week they arrived at the Roman port of Gesoriacum and boarded a vessel bound for Isca. They arrived with ten days left until the Summer Solstice and plenty of time for rest and renewal as well as preparation. Magdalen had decided that each and every one of them would use the last three days for spiritual grounding. A clear head and a devout sprit would assure that the crossing would be blessed by the Goddesses, fairies and whoever else would welcome them and lived beyond the misty veils. That gave them one week's time for merriment and rest.

They shopped, went to the baths daily, ate meals under the warming sun and even went to the theatre several times. Wherever they went Magdalen asked every stranger about Avalon and what they had heard. For the most part, however, the isle seemed to be shrouded by mystery and what she considered to be superstition. Still some of the stories peaked everyone's excitement and the crashing ocean waters that they could see from their upper apartment beckoned them with their intrigue.

Magdalen declared the last three days to be a period of retreat from earthly things to those things that were purely spirit. They would quest after visions and prophecy, oracles and messages, just as she had done during her initiation by Baera. The grand finale, the initiation for them all, would come at the moment that they crossed into Avalon. It was a quick day's journey from Isca to Bath. Its hot springs and Oak groves would be just the place for such a retreat.

Bath was founded by Bladud, the eldest son of the renowned Celtic King Lud, or so legend told. As a young man, Bladud contracted leprosy and was exiled to live as a swineherd at Swainswick. One day as he watched his pigs, he saw some of them wallowing in thick black mud and went to investigate. The mud was hot; he found that the marsh was fed by a copious hot spring. Noticing that the pigs' scurvy had been cleared by the bath, Bladud himself tried bathing in the mud. His leprosy was cured. He returned in delight to his father's court and in time became king. In gratitude he built a temple by the hot spring and founded the city of Bath. In a Druids' grove by the hot steaming spring, the Goddess Sul was worshipped as the guardian of the gateway to the Underworld. Through major gateways such as Bath's hot spring, the Celts believed that deities and ancestors could be approached. This would be the perfect place for their spiritual endeavors.

Cybele's presence in the group was well appreciated when they arrived in Bath. Although Rome had taken into its empire many of the southern portions of Britain, they had not yet assumed this part of the countryside. With few Romans making use of the healing waters, finding someone who spoke Latin or Greek was a rare occurrence. Cybele and Baera had both taught Magdalen and Sharon the dialect most used in Gaul, but here the people were harder to understand. Cybele was as fluent as the natives and that made finding out about the springs and the Oak grove much easier.

They all indulged in the healing waters as preparation for their retreat. The hot springs warmed their bodies and relaxed their minds, making them open to whatever would come during the time of meditation and fasting. Aside from Magdalen herself, no one had ever experienced such a durable fast and period of contemplation. Carmel was frightened, but the others gave her encouragement and support. Magdalen told them all again of her adventure in the forest and the visions and messages that she had received during her initiation.

"It is a quest for guidance," she said. "It is a quest for a dream that will come true."

Nods of affirmation came from the group, but they really weren't sure if this was a good idea when Magdalen handed each of them a small bag of nuts, seeds and dried berries along with a flask of water. This was to be their only source of nourishment. They would separate from one another in the woods and each would cast a personal circle and build a fire in its center. Sitting beside the fires they would contemplate, meditate and pray for guidance.

Magdalen realized that Baera had come each morning to check on her safety and wanted to be sure to give the group the same feeling of security that Baera had given her.

"We need help with this if I am to search for guidance too. Cybele, please find us a priest who can check on our well being each day."

Cybele left hurriedly for the town. There she found an old Druid Priest. He wore a long beard and his hair was braided as Baera had braided her own for ceremony. Cybele explained the nature of the retreat and put forth her entreaty.

"Can you come each morning and see to the health of each of us? It would be a service to us and to your Gods."

The Druid said nothing but agreed by holding out his hand to make it a contract. After briefly retiring into his private cell, he followed Cybele back to the waiting aspirants.

Now he handed each person a small tin bell. Cybele explained that the bell was to be used to call for help if necessary. Carmel held hers close to her heart and James put his into his leather purse almost as if to say that he would not need any help. The others followed Magdalen's lead as she placed her bell into her food bag and tied it to her belt.

Then the Druid, still not saying a word, motioned them to follow him. Dutifully they did as he requested. Arriving at a clearing he pointed toward the ground and then at James. This was to be James' place of retreat. Moving through the woodland he continued this practice of selecting for each person a space to be his or her own. When he motioned to Cybele that her place had been selected, he took Regino's hand and led him away with him. Cybele raised no objection; the boy was old enough now to be away from her for this short retreat. Magdalen's place was selected last and the priest held out his hand to Sharon as he had Regino. Magdalen's eyes filled with tears. She had never left her daughter with anyone other than the closest of friends.

"I will care for her and teach her."

The priest spoke in Greek. Until now, Magdalen had wondered if he were mute. The softness in his eyes told her that Sharon would be fine and perhaps even have a holy adventure of her own with this man. With that the priest and the children disappeared into the forest.

As she built her fire Magdalen wondered about frightened Carmel and about the younger women, Sarah and Ruth. She wasn't sure that they were ready for this, but she was sure that they needed it. James she was sure would be fine, he would take this opportunity to prove once again his male superiority. With that thought she laughed.

"And we will prove our evenness," she thought out loud.

She sat to begin her meditation and await the guidance she was sure she would receive. As night fell, Magdalen focused on the Summer Solstice and its meaning. A deer walked through her circle with a slow and meandering gait. Magdalen was silent trying not to frighten it away. As she watched its graceful movements, the doe came toward the fire.

"Move through life with grace, be always alert and forage unceasingly for the food your soul requires."

The deer had spoken to her! Magdalen was shocked. She had not been fasting or meditating long enough to be suffering from delusions or visions caused by hunger and cold. Still, she heard the words and she had to assume that they were a message from the Divine. She decided to change her focus from the Solstice to the message.

There were actually three messages, she thought. Move through life with grace. Be always alert. Forage unceasingly for the food of the soul. Now she began to contemplate only the first message. Move through life with grace. The doe was moving through the forest so gracefully. She was a fine example of grace. Every step appeared planned, determined, poised and yet relaxed. Magdalen wondered if she could move that way and got up to walk observing her own gait. Then she realized this was a very shallow way of looking at a message that was surely meant to be profound. She sat again cross-legged by the fire.

She said the word grace to herself in as many languages as she knew. She defined it in as many ways as she could. Grace was honor, dignity. Grace was also a blessing received from God. Grace was poise under any circumstance. Grace was beauty and it was also mercy and too a prayer. To walk through life with grace would mean to move with confidence and with dependence on God. Magdalen continued her meandering thoughts on grace.

This night would not grow cold as it had when she took her initiation. The moon was nearing fullness and the sky was clear. Overhead she could see the stars through the clearing in the trees. What a wonderful, graceful, show of God's creative power, she thought. Yes, grace also equated with power, a special power that comes from within. To walk through life with grace would be to feel the power within you and know that you are capable of handling whatever comes your way, but capable by the grace of God. With that thought, Magdalen drifted off into her dreams.

Aware that she was dreaming, but somehow insisting to remain asleep, Magdalen welcomed her subconscious vision. She was somewhere else now. The deer stood beside her and they were both watching the stars above them. Out of the black and glittering sky a light appeared. At first Magdalen thought it was the moon rising, but soon she could see that it took the shape of a white and luminous dove. She held out her arm and the dove landed at her wrist.

"I am Faith," said the bird. "I am Faith and the keeper of grace. If you allow me to live with you, I can assure your peace of mind and guide your steps so that you will always walk in grace."

Magdalen sensed that this was a request more than a statement. "Where would I keep you?" she ventured a question. "I have no home of my own now."

The dove replied. "I will live in your heart. Open the door and I will enter."

Magdalen thought of her demon story. But this was no demon, she thought, this is a Goddess to be sure. "Faith, will you live with me forever then?"

The bird cooed. Magdalen opened her garments and the spirit moved in. The dove and its light were gone and the dream was over. Magdalen stirred for a moment and thought aloud again.

"Faith lives in my heart forever. I will walk through life with grace." It was a peaceful thought on which to return to sleep.

In the morning she took some seeds and berries from her bag and then stoked the fire. The Druid arrived in silence and then disappeared apparently satisfied that the woman was doing well. Magdalen thought about the presence of Faith and put her hand against her heart as if to acknowledge that it was still there. Then she decided to contemplate the second part of the doe's message, be always alert. Going through the same process she spoke silently the word alert in as many languages as she could, defining and redefining it to herself.

Alert was also aware, and it was a warning. It was an alarm and it was conscious and it was watchful. Magdalen wondered if there was an element of fear in the idea of being alert. Fear, she knew, was the enemy, a demon that must not be allowed to live within her. To always be alert could not possibly mean to be always afraid, that would not, indeed, be a gift but a curse. Magdalen didn't want thoughts of curses or fears to enter her mind or disturb her retreat. She quickly put these thoughts aside calling upon Faith for peace of mind and renewed grace as she continued her adventure here.

Ever before she had prayed for Faith now she found herself praying to it as if it were indeed an ever-present Goddess within her. She remembered now that the Goddess's of Avalon and of Rome and Greece, the Goddess's she remembered and honored in her youth were always of a threefold nature. Faith she decided was the youngest, the girl. She had not lost her innocence or been violated by fear. She was the first face of the Goddess and that face ruled peace and war, harmony and chaos. Called upon, Faith found ever the power over disharmony.

Magdalen realized that this retreat was taking a pattern much as the first. There would be three visions and each would bring her a Goddess this time, she thought. She began to contemplate again the idea of always being alert. What possible lesson or gift was hidden in that message? What form would the Goddess take as the maiden? What did all this have to do with Avalon? Her mind raced through the list of Goddesses that Baera had given her. There were five, she thought. Which three would arrive to give her guidance? Which one of the five was Faith?

Faith had to be the Goddess Rhiannon, the White Mare. She had sent her bird as a representative, perhaps because Magdalen was not yet pure enough to see her in her sacred form as the White Horse. Baera had told her that Rhiannon sent her birds to sooth the souls of the most troubled of mortals. Certainly she had done that for Magdalen by her now heartfelt presence.

Magdalen decided to forego breaking her fast as evening came. Instead she used some of the herbal seeds to put aroma in her fire and watched as the smoke rose in the clearing. She chanted over and over again the subject of her meditation.

"With Faith is there any need to be alert?"

It became like a song coming from her throat to the ears of the forest creatures. It was a psalm of entreaty that she sang to the Goddess for hours. Then the doe appeared again.

"Mount my back and I will carry you to the Goddess."

Magdalen knew she was dreaming again. She mounted the doe and wrapped her arms around its neck for security. The doe ran off with the woman holding on tight into the depths of the forest. They stopped in a small clearing and the doe turned to face Magdalen still perched on her back.

"You will find Cerridwen beneath the brush."

Magdalen dismounted and lifted the drooping branches of a pine tree. In the darkness she could see a small White Sow. It was Cerridwen, just as Baera had described her. Magdalen was in the presence of the Great Crone. The pig would not move out into the moonlight but beckoned Magdalen to join her under the brush. Magdalen remembered that she was the Goddess of the Dark of the Moon and complied.

"This is the cauldron of change." She said, and motioned with her head toward a huge pot beneath the brambles. "Get in."

Magdalen could now understand why some feared this Goddess, but she stepped into the pot willingly remembering that Faith was present within her.

"In my cauldron things are changed through opportunity and inspiration and become Hope. Those who have Hope will always see opportunity in challenge and be inspired to create. Drink the soup."

Magdalen made a cup of her hand and took in some of the vile mixture that surrounded her.

The Goddess spoke again, "Just as your Jesus claimed that a body is what it consumes, so a heart is what Faith has invited to be its nourishment. You have consumed Hope and you will create and change as Faith demands for your peace and fulfillment."

The dream ended and Magdalen felt a growing pain in her stomach. Hunger was real and the food of the dream had not satisfied her body. She ate a few nuts and went back to sleep.

The morning brought again a silent watchful Druid to check on her and then disappear. Magdalen stoked her fire and drank a bit of water. She then put some of her herbal seeds on the fire once more. This was her thanksgiving for Hope and for Faith in her heart. Then she thought about another Goddess, Blodeuwedd, the Maiden and Goddess of new beginnings and independence. She was turned into an owl. Magdalen remembered that she had met an owl in her first vision quest. Had she actually been introduced to Blodeuwedd? Surely that initiation had been a period of new beginnings. She decided that she would think about that later and concentrate now on the third part of the message.

How would one forage unceasingly for the food of the soul? She had enjoyed her chant the day before and set up another.

"What will I eat and where will I find it?"

She chanted over and over again the psalm of a hungry soul. Twice she stopped long enough to stoke the fire and to break her fast just a bit. Evening came with a drizzling rain. It wasn't cold or uncomfortable. Instead it added a refreshment and glistening beauty to the forest and the night. Magdalen's circle was wet with glittering drops of summer rain and the moon, though hidden by the clouds, cast a glow around her.

She watched the fire and chanted again her psalm of entreaty. Then she dozed off to yet another dream. Magdalen was high atop a mountain and very much alone. She could not rid her mind of the horrors of the world and many of her own troubles as well. She was faced with the tribulations of the past and the pain of the present for the people of the earth. Trying to chase away these thoughts was useless it seemed. Then Magdalen heard the cry of a raven. Looking up to the sky she could see it approaching her. Its white wings were flapping wildly as if they could not rest. She stretched out her arm as she had done for Faith in hopes that the raven would land.

Instead the White Raven circled and seemed to pause in the air long enough to beckon Magdalen to follow her. She cut her bare feet on the rocks but she followed. She felt the hunger in her belly, but she followed.

The bird coaxed her on "You will find food and medicine on the mountain."

Magdalen didn't understand how such a barren place could possibly hold any nourishment or healing for her. Still she was willing to look. The dream continued and she was repeatedly disappointed. She found no food or water, no medicine for her bleeding feet.

Finally she climbed upon an altar-like rock and there found another cauldron. This one was filled with all good things. It had in it foods from the earth, fresh water, salves and ointments of healing. Not ten feet away lay a guile and gruesome looking old man covered with sores. The cauldron filled with relief was just out of his reach; he hadn't the strength to move toward it.

"Eat, drink, and anoint your body." The raven commanded Magdalen.

For a moment Magdalen was afraid that this was some sort of demonic trick to make her lose sight of her mission, but Faith spoke from her heart and Hope let her imagination soar. She made gruel from the grain and fed the man from her hand. She washed his sores with the clear water and anointed them with the oil.

"You have shared the cauldron of plenty." The man said and vanished.

"What have I done?" she asked the raven.

"Now, feed me and anoint my body," the raven demanded.

As Magdalen held out a hand full of grain from the basket the raven was transformed. There was in its stead a woman. She was beautiful in her white robes and colorful headdress.

"You have come to the barren mountain alert to what it offered. You came gracefully and with peace. You were aware that what was offered to you would nourish you. You have fed another first. You have healed a soul, the soul of the Goddess Branwen. Now eat from the harvest of your heart and you will have the unceasing Love that is called Charity. It will nourish your soul always." The Goddess disappeared.

Magdalen was famished. She devoured the food, drank heartily of the fresh water and then gently caressed her feet and hands with the healing ointments. She felt so renewed, so refreshed and alive. It was as if she had been to the Roman baths and eaten a hearty meal at her favorite tavern. But it was more than that. Her good works had satisfied her soul. Now she had the three faces of the Goddess within her, Faith was Rhiannon, Hope Cerridwen and Charity the Chief Goddess of Avalon, Great Branwen. She was sure now that the owl from her last vision quest had been Blodeuwedd. That left only one, the Goddess Arianrhod who would show her the Silver Wheel and guide her on her journey. As she had this thought the doe reappeared beside her.

"I am Arianrhod, I am the Mother who will give you all that you need and from you I will demand much. I am your Humble Pride."

The Goddess vanished and Magdalen awoke to the sounds of the others approaching. The Druid Priest had the children with him and he brought baskets of food and flasks of wine to break their fast. The mothers embraced their little ones with open arms before thinking of food. Finally the priest interrupted the reunion by handing each one a portion to eat. The women remembered to eat and drink gently. Even James was careful of gluttony. The priest offered a blessing in a dialect that Magdalen could not understand but everyone knew that this prayer was one of thanksgiving.

As they began to exchange stories of their quest they realized that there was little difference in the messages they had received or the gifts that they had been given but for one thing. Magdalen was the only one who had met the Goddess Arianrhod. They believed that made Magdalen more the leader on this journey than ever before. It was she and she alone who had the direction required to keep the spirits of Faith, Hope and Charity alive on the Way. Magdalen would lead them through the misty veils of Avalon into a new life. Today was the Summer Solstice and tonight would be the moment of entry into that paradise.

The priest said his goodbyes with but a wave. As he moved down the path toward Bath the others moved toward the entrance of Avalon, the Oak grove at the edge of the tiny sea that surrounded the "Isle of Glass."

Chapter 29

Through the Veil

Dusk brought with it the misty veils just as everyone expected. As the fog rolled in, you could see within it small golden lights each with a halo around it. They darted back and forth in the mist as if they were players in a child's game of catch the firefly. These were the fairy lights that Baera had told them about.

The moon shone brightly when it came up. Even with the dark mist surrounding the isle, the moonlight made its shores visible. The sea was calm and seemed to be waiting for the arrival of any travelers searching for safe passage. As the moon rose higher the mist began to thin and in the distance across the water they could see the Tor standing erect and foreboding.

"Blessed Be!" exclaimed Ruth. "The veils are thinning."

Magdalen put up her hand as if to signal silence. Ruth covered her mouth in apology. Everyone said a silent prayer calling upon Faith, Hope and Charity to be with them.

Magdalen prayed a fervent supplication to Humble Pride for guidance. She didn't want to be too self-satisfied, but she had arrived safely at this shore by the Summer Solstice. And she had passed her purification twice. Now she had only to cross over to the beautiful Isle of Glass. Magdalen could see where that name came from. The island was fully reflected in the water shimmering as if made of fine crystal. It was just as beautiful as Baera had described it.

As Magdalen had this final thought there appeared a flat-bottomed boat upon the water and it was coming toward the waiting group. James was about to hail the boatman when Magdalen put out her hand again. He fell silent and waited for her direction.

She raised both her arms into the mist and quietly called out toward the little craft.

"Divine Mother, ferry us to the safety of your land."

The boatman moored his boat on the shore long enough for everyone to come aboard. The ride across the sea was smooth, so smooth that they seemed not to be moving at all. But within minutes they had reached the shores of Avalon. The dancing lights that they had seen from the other side were bigger and brighter now and even more present and mobile. The foggy mist remained, cooling their skin and leaving them damp. They all stood, huddled around Magdalen, waiting to see what she would have them do next.

Magdalen knew that waiting patiently was the only guidance to be followed just now. The Priestess of the Isle would have to come for them. They were uninvited guests and had arrived safely only by the grace of the Goddess.

"Grace," she thought, "I must move through this with grace."

There wasn't time though for a plan. A Druid Priestess stepped on to the sandy shore and motioned for them to follow her.

"I will take you to the Tor" she said. "Your first act in Avalon must be to honor the Divine Mother."

Magdalen gathered her cloak about her and walked behind the Priestess. The others followed in a procession through the orchards of apples and darkness that lasted about an hour. They were at the foot of the Tor when the Priestess stopped the pilgrimage.

"Wait here until morning, then follow the labyrinth to the top of the Tor. The Goddess will greet you there."

It was more than a request. This was a command to be sure. Even James knew that this woman had the authority here. He moved to build a fire and the Priestess was gone down the winding path ahead of them. The women looked at each other in amazement. Here they were without supplies on completely foreign soil and nowhere to stay but out in the open.

"I guess our fasting was good practice."

Polaris was peeved. She was used to the idea of hospitality from the Celts in Gaul and not at all prepared to be treated so brusquely.

"It will be all right," James assured them.

Magdalen was delighted to hear James' positive attitude. By moonlight they picked apples, delicious golden and red apples and made a meal of fruit that enchanted them. As the fire dried their clothes and skin, they prayed a prayer of thanksgiving.

Magdalen thought that it was good to have Humble Pride with her because she fully expected to be included in a Summer Solstice celebration and now she was on the outside looking in. Morning, she thought, could not come quickly enough. They all slept with dreams of what might come with the dawn.

When they rose the sun was already up and warming the countryside. Now they could see the beautiful golden apples hanging like ornaments from perfectly shaped trees. The sea was beyond the horizon and out of view. The top of the Tor, which stood high above them, could hardly be seen from their vantage point at its base. Birds flew about singing and carrying small pieces of nesting material and feed for their young. Sheep roamed in the rocky pastures and an occasional deer walked in their midst. Avalon was indeed beautiful in the daylight. Magdalen, however, was not satisfied to feast her eyes on the island's countryside; she was eager to begin the journey down the winding path as the Priestess had directed. She didn't want to miss one more moment of summer's celebration than she had to.

The fire had hours before burned itself out, but James parted the cinders with his boot anyway. They ate a breakfast of apples and in the daylight could even find some sweet black berries to feast on.

"I've heard," said Carmel, "that eating fairy food would keep you from ever leaving the island again. I hope that fairies are not fond of apples and berries."

Everyone giggled, but beneath the jokes was a tinge of fear. Would they ever leave here? Would anyone of them ever go home? Carmel was especially concerned. Magdalen decided to alleviate this one fear of imprisonment by revealing one of Baera's secrets.

"Fairy food," she began, "is not food for the body, but food for the soul."

Carmel moved closer to Magdalen hoping to find comfort in her explanation and in being close to her leader.

"Knowledge of the spirit world is food for the soul. The Druids and Celts here believe that the fairies share special spiritual secrets with those who deserve them and that once you have been enlightened you will not leave. Instead you will stay and share with the Divine, and humanity as well, in the blessings of this place by choice. You cannot be a prisoner here, but you can find leaving impossible by your own will. Avalon is more than a place. It is a placement of consciousness on the Divine Will and Workings."

She wrapped her arm around Carmel's shoulders and moved toward the entrance of the great labyrinth. Polaris put one arm around Ruth and the other around Sarah.

"Let's follow the leader to the Goddess as sister's."

"Yes, sisters in Faith, Hope and Charity."

Ruth ventured a comment, something everyone hesitated to do when Polaris made a suggestion. She was easily offended and often thought the young women's remarks to be frivolous. But today she grinned a motherly knowingness at them all. Magdalen stopped them before they could set foot on the path.

"We must pray first. Sadly we did not have our Rite of Remembrance last night, it is absolute that we pray now before we embark on another adventure."

They all knelt where they were as Magdalen said the words of their Remembrance Ritual and passed around an apple to take the place of bread. James handed her the water flask from his belt to take the place of the usual wine. When it was done they rose with a chorus of "Blessed Be the Goddess and Blessed Be the Gods." Magdalen was satisfied now and took the first step upon the sacred path.

Single file the others followed behind her. This pilgrimage would be a ritual journey, even a rite of passage. The spiraled pathway circled around the Tor moving upward toward the tower at its top in a backtracking maze-like action. Still there didn't seem to be any stops or impasses along the way. They walked practically unimpeded for hours, when suddenly the pathway stopped. It had ended before reaching the top or the foot of the tower.

The place where it suddenly disappeared was marked with a large, smooth, oval-shaped stone. There were very few big stones on the Tor, and from their positioning they all looked like deliberately placed markers. To Magdalen this one looked ideal to be used as an altar. She felt that by honoring this stone with the offering of prayer they would be calling upon the Goddess for entrance into the tower.

Magdalen put her veil over the rock as an altar cloth. The women picked wild flowers with a heavy scent to decorate their offering table and James set out apples and water for another commemorative meal. With James' knife, Magdalen sliced an apple. Then they said the usual offering prayers and distributed the sacred food. Magdalen held the knife upward to the sky.

"Lady, we leave all violence and pain as our dowry, we offer our prayers and our good works and our kind thoughts as a New Way of life for all. Let us come before you as pilgrims must, to honor you and to share in fair exchange the gifts the Goddess has given us."

The rock seemed to be vibrating! Magdalen put her hands palms down upon it and was shocked at the warmth within it. They heard what sounded like a chant coming from beneath their little altar when, as if by magic, the rock was rolled aside. It wasn't magic, it was the power of the Priestess, the one who had led them to the labyrinth last night. She had pushed her way from beneath the rock and into their midst. The children laughed and giggled at the women's startled reaction to the moving rock. Polaris, however, didn't think this a funny gesture. Eventually, everyone but Polaris joined in the merriment with Sharon and Regino. James was laughing at himself quite heartily and Magdalen slapped her thighs with delight. They had all been duped into believing in the magical removal!

It took a minute for everyone to catch their breath and regain composure. Even Polaris had belatedly given in to the laughter and now found it hard to stop. Then the Priestess motioned for them to join her as she went down into the Tor through the opening beneath the egg shaped stone.

"This," she told them, "is thought to be the entrance to the other world by some, to the fairy kingdom to others, but in truth it is the underground channel to the tower in which you will have your audience with the Lady of the Lake."

Beneath the Tor's surface was a whole set of caverns and catacombs much like those beneath the city of Rome. However, these were not used for burial but for escape when necessary and for return to the tower unnoticed by enemies or suspicious strangers who had not paid homage to the Goddess. Following the dimly lit caverns it was only minutes before they found themselves in the tower's massive center room.

"No more make-believe magic here," the Priestess smiled at them.

The children joined hands and danced in circles in the great hall. Both mothers looked embarrassed by their children's exuberance. But the Priestess soon joined them in their choreography letting everyone know that celebration was most welcome.

Relieved, Magdalen was now wondering if no "make-believe" magic meant that they were about to see the real thing. She felt it would be impolite to ask questions before introducing herself.

"I am Mary of Magdala, they call me Magdalen. This is my daughter Sharon and her friend Regino who is Cybele's son."

She extended her arm and pointed to each member of the group as she said their names.

"What shall we call you?" she inquired respectfully.

The Priestess bowed, "I am the keeper of Anwyn. My name is Aine; it means Happiness. Happiness will be your guide and teacher while you are here in Avalon."

"Well, I am sure that Happiness is just what I need on this journey." Magdalen smiled at the woman who seemed more like a girl. "We could all use your namesake as a guide through both troubling times and enlightening ones."

Now Aine bowed again as if to honor Magdalen's little piece of wisdom. "The Lady of the Lake will join us shortly," she announced. "You should know that she is a real person, a High Priestess, who personifies for us the Spirit of the Lake that surrounds the Tor. She is not a spirit but a spiritual leader."

Magdalen had long understood that the Celts and Druids honored and worshipped the spirit within each person and thing and were not worshiping idols or creations of nature. She hoped the others were listening to Aine and realizing fully the importance of this fact in sharing with them the Way. There was no time to point out the lesson. The Lady of the Lake arrived with grace and a quiet smile.

"Welcome, Magdalen. Welcome all of you. And Welcome especially to the children." She bowed but not as low as Aine had. It seemed appropriate for everyone to return the bow and Sharon led the way. She bowed deeply to the Lady.

"Thank you for your hospitality, my Lady" she said in perfect Gaelic.

Everyone took his or her turn in honoring the woman as the Goddess within her. James bowed with such flourish that Aine had to wink at Magdalen, and Carmel looked a bit jealous of his chivalrous manners. The Lady picked up on Carmel's feelings.

"I am vowed to both the Virginity of the Temple and the celibacy of human life. Here in Avalon and especially within the Tor and its tower you will find that we pay a great deal of attention to both sides of life, the form and the soul which takes it." She reassured Carmel.

"I am honored that you stopped at the center to worship and to pray. You had a rite that intrigued me, your communal meal and the words you say. I would like to learn more about it and what magic it carries. In return I will share something with you – a trip to the Blood Well."

Carmel swallowed hard; it was obvious that her jealousy had been revealed. Sarah and Ruth clung close to Polaris and Cybele. The words "blood well" made them skittish. Once more the Lady was aware of their concern.

"The Blood Well is a place of initiation, healing and ritual passage, especially for women. There is no blood flowing from the springs here, only fresh pure water of the most sacred kind. It is alive with the female spirit. You will see. There is nothing to fear in Avalon."

Feeling that the Lady was quite finished, Magdalen offered a suggestion.

"I do want to see, and I know that Aine and you will be fine guides as we learn about the well and the ways of Avalon. Tonight I offer to show you my Way in exchange for a lesson from you both tomorrow."

"Good," the Lady responded. "Tonight we will return to the rock so that you can do your ritual again and show me how. For now, you must have something more to eat and drink than simple fruit and water. We will dine on venison, potatoes, vegetables and sweet things and drink the honey wine made here."

James grinned from ear to ear. He was always hungry and could almost taste the venison and heavy gravy. The dining room was set and the feast prepared while the travelers were allowed to bathe and given clothes to wear. After dinner, Magdalen asked her hostess for bread and wine to be used in the commemorative meal. She explained that the apples and water worked very well but that the tradition called for the traditional foods. Without hesitation, the Lady of the Lake ordered that Magdalen be given whatever she needed.

Magdalen knew that this was the proper time to use the special cup and wear her special garments. She had hidden them all in a leather bag beneath her skirts when they left Bath and she was glad to be rid of the extra weight when she had changed clothes. Now she went back to the women's quarters to retrieve them.

When she reappeared she was wearing her ritual garb and carrying the Holy Cup. Now the Lady bowed deeply to her recognizing her position in Druidry by her vestments. She motioned toward the catacombs and Magdalen led the way. Once outside the group set up the altar rock again this time with the bread and wine as well as the sweet fragrant flowers and some candles that Aine had brought to share.

Magdalen explained each act and word of the Rite of Remembrance and then went through the ritual with reverence and devotion as she had always done. Handing the Lady her first communion she spoke to her in a low and healing tone.

"Eat of the food for the body and remember that the food of the soul is harvested within. Drink the wine and know that the soul requires watery wisdom, mutable and intoxicating to the spirit."

The Lady of the Lake received the bread and wine with the same deep bow she had bestowed on Magdalen earlier. Ceremony completed, the group waited for a response from their new acquaintances. The Lady spoke as quietly and reverently as Magdalen had.

"My soul is nourished and my body at rest."

They followed her as she returned to the tower. In the great room her authority and interest revealed themselves again.

"We will speak of this Way of yours tomorrow. I will show you the sameness of our cultures and our paths. You will show me our differences and we will strive to eliminate them. Now rest."

James was escorted back to a special place for male visitors and the women returned to the women's quarters. It had been a long day and they fell asleep quickly.

Chapter 30

Blood Well and The Mysteries

Even before the sun had fully risen they were called from their beds. Magdalen could hear the sounds of chanting as she entered the great hall of the tower. There were both male and female voices coming from beneath her, from the depths of the Tor. It was as if there was a great breathing going on. The Tor, or the earth itself, was breathing and she could hear its breath. What's more, she could feel its pulsating heart beat. The floor beneath her was vibrating with a throbbing rhythm that made it seem as if the earth had a heart as well as lungs. Before she could identify the source of these phenomena, the Lady of the Lake arrived.

"Today I will share with you the Blood Well and its mysteries." She said. "James is welcome to tag along but I must warn him, this is a woman's well and a woman's moon cycle is at the heart of the mysteries."

The women blushed and so did James. The Lady offered a solution.

"You could choose to join the Druid Priests instead."

James nodded with obvious relief and motioned to Regino that he should accompany him. The Lady had an escort lead them away.

"I had a feeling he would choose as he did." the Lady smiled. "Let's go now to the well."

They descended into the catacombs and left through what Sharon now called the rabbit hole. It took almost three hours to walk the labyrinth back down to the base of the Tor. As they arrived at each new level the Lady paused to praise the Great Mother. It was a very reverent walk, a true procession of pilgrims devoutly walking a walk of prayer. Magdalen and the others desperately wanted to ask about the maze and its winding shape, but it would have seemed sacrilegious to query the Lady while she was engaged in such sacred activity. When they had completed their journey to the bottom, Magdalen was comfortable asking her question.

"What is this path that we have just taken?"

"The path can only be explained after you understand fully the nature of our philosophy."

It was apparent that the Lady was about to explain many things and the women were anxious to hear. She continued as they walked toward Blood Well.

"We believe that all life comes from the process of birth. The Great Goddess is the Mother Goddess. The earth was borne from her womb and she in turn gave life and birth to everything here. For this reason the woman is considered the creator. But just as woman cannot become pregnant without a man, so the Great Mother Goddess had her consort. He impregnated her with his Divine Spirit. That Divine Spirit is the Semen of Life, the Great Father. From the two of them came Mother Earth who was impregnated by her brother, the Sun, our Sun God."

Magdalen was forced to interrupt. "This is much as Jesus said."

The Lady looked to her to go on.

"He said that his Divine Father was Spirit and that it lived in all things as a soul"

"We do have some sameness, don't we? But just as life must be conceived in the presence of both man and woman, woman alone holds the womb and the portal to physical life. The Spirit, the Father, need not be seen again but is ever present.

The Mother, however, is the birthplace eternally remembered. That is why we worship the Goddess, hold women in high esteem and regard the Priestess as the embodiment of the Creator. It is by a woman's power that all things have life. Her power is in her blood. What man can bleed so much and not die from his bleeding?"

They were coming to the blood well and the Lady turned to describing its value.

"The water from the spring that feeds this well has always run red, as if tinged with blood from the Great Mother's womb. It is here and with its water that we celebrate the Blood Mysteries. In our sisterhoods we honor every mystery of each other's lives because they are also the mysteries of the universe and the Great Goddess. We celebrate our birth, which is the first blood mystery. We celebrate menarche, defloration, birthing, and menopause and of course last blood or death. Men of course celebrate birth and death as mysteries, but only women can experience the full cycle of life."

She stopped to watch Sharon kneel at the well to drink.

"All of you drink with her, the water is extremely good, healing and filled with Sacred Energy from the Earth Goddess."

The Lady knelt to drink with them. After satisfying her thirst she continued.

"The well symbolizes also the Cauldron of Life, one of our great symbols. Another, to be sure, is the labyrinth on the Tor. It represents the Mother's Yoni and the opening to her womb. When we return to the Mother we return to ourselves, our center, or as your Jesus would say, to our soul."

"Perhaps one day Sharon will make her first rite of passage here when she experiences her menarche."

The Lady looked first at Magdalen and then at the little girl now playing in the water with her hands. Magdalen looked fondly at her daughter but could not imagine her coming of age, not yet.

The women sat in a circle around the well and rested, waiting to hear more about this Avalonion way of life. This was truly a beautiful place to accept stories of the energy of this Great Goddess the Earth Mother. Birds flew overhead, the area was filled with wildflowers and the land was a bit terraced to make sitting quite comfortable.

"Please, go on dear Lady," Magdalen encouraged the Lady of the Lake to continue her lesson. "I have celebrated these passages myself, in the temple at Magdala and Bethany and I am most curious to see both our likenesses and our differences."

"We come to the Blood Well, as I said, to celebrate the Blood Mysteries and to heal and nurture as well.

"Birthdays are very important in Avalon, because our birth is the first rite of passage experienced by all that is living. When a child is born we have great merriment both for the mother who makes a birthing passage and for the child who makes the passage into new life. The anniversary of one's birth is a time to celebrate too. It is a time to be filled with gratitude for your mother's labor and to honor her with flowers, song and food."

Magdalen thought about Sharon's umbilical cord still held in the Holy Grail. This she decided was how she had celebrated birthing and Sharon had celebrated first blood. She decided, though, that she would keep this a secret for the moment.

"Young maidens coming into their first moon blood are considered the embodiment of the Maiden Goddess and the huntress. They are no longer children but considered fully contained, whole women. The maiden is attended by her mother and when possible her grandmother. She is honored as the full Goddess for the time of her first moon blood. She prepares her own moon lodge when her mother directs her and then on the first day of her mooning, she goes into the lodge to be honored and cared for. The older women unbraid her hair and comb it to remove the tangles and knots in her life. They bathe her feet with water from the well and prepare warm and delicious foods for her to eat. She is kept warm and allowed to contemplate quietly and undisturbed by any of life's entanglements until the moon has passed. Then there is a celebration and she shares the stories of her dreams because the moon brings with it the gift of prophecy and messages from the Goddess for members of her family and others in the community.

"Each moon cycle a woman moves into a special lodge with the others that are mooning. They drink the waters from the well and sometimes fast. They bathe themselves with the water too to keep themselves clean and pure. Their blood is collected and later returned to the Great Mother's womb. It nourishes the fields and provides for future harvests. The male guardians stand outside the lodge keeping anything from disturbing the dreams and prophecies that the women experience. These are shared when they return to normal life until their next cycle."

"Sacred blood!" Polaris almost shouted it. "Women do have sacred blood! Why then do the Jews think so badly of this Divine source of all life? Why all the purifications and taboos?"

There was more than a bit of anger in her voice, and the others murmured in agreement with it. Magdalen agreed too. "I think we should incorporate at least these two mysteries into our New Way."

She looked at the others for consensus and it was forthcoming, so she went on.

"Jesus honored men and women as equal and respected birth, mooning and motherhood. He honored my time as sacred and his mother's as well. We shall do that and more for one another. I want Sharon to know and understand her womanhood one day and all of your daughters as well.

"We had similar rites in the temple at Magdala and when I explained them to Jesus he thought they were most useful and comforting, compassionate ways that would be approved of by the Divine. But the next ritual came when we were ready to be lovers, the breaking of the hymen what the Lady calls defloration.

Jesus found it to be cruel. What do you think of that rite, dear Lady?"

Magdalen knew to ask a question rather than making statements of judgment. The women turned to the Lady with expectation.

"We do have a rite defloration. Our sisters do it gently in a pool of the blood waters the night before our first love affair. We do this to honor ourselves and the man with whom we will lay. It also assures that the lovemaking will be painless and open to a true achievement of union between Goddess and God. We believe that a man who lays with a woman before her defloration dishonors himself and her. He robs her of her right to a perfect completion and he makes of himself a God of violence."

Carmel was ghost white. She had never thought of anything like this before. "It is frightening to think of such a thing," she finally commented.

Magdalen put her arm around her.

"Carmel, my sisters opened my womb with love and affection. It would be that way for you too. I myself would help you with this rite."

Carmel took Magdalen's hand and squeezed it tightly.

"This is a controversial ritual" the Lady went on. "But it is truly a helpful one. It honors your womb and the soul that will one day reside there when you make the passage into motherhood. It honors your soul by removing the fear of lovemaking."

Magdalen actually approved of this ritual having experienced it herself with gratitude, but she could see that the others were not so sure.

"Let us keep this rite," she said, "not as a command but as a choice. We can make this decision for ourselves, one at a time in the New Way."

Since they were all still considering the value of this mystery, they agreed that it should remain at least for the moment the choice of the individual. The Lady spoke up in response to their decision.

"I think that perhaps you are right to allow a woman to make her own choice. Perhaps the ritual instills more fear in some than it relieves. Let it be so!"

"Blessed Be!" the others stated.

"What of motherhood?" Cybele asked the question.

"From the moment a woman conceives, her womb is honored as the Cauldron of Life. She makes pilgrimages to the Tor and meets with the great Mother Goddess learning from her the secrets of birthing and regeneration. The child's father honors her by bringing her here to the well each month when it would have been her time for mooning. He bathes her and oils her belly and adorns her head with a wreath of flowers. When her labor begins she is taken to the well again and the midwife delivers the child while the womb is enveloped in the comforting waters. That way the child is honored too. It is gentler don't you think, to be born into new water while releasing the water of the womb?"

"It does sound more comforting." Cybele agreed.

"After the child has shouted out its presence to the world, the whole community celebrates. The woman is brought to the fire and there introduces her new son or daughter by the name she has given the child. Then the father takes the child from her and parades the wee one around the village for all to see. Men and women alike bring flowers, food and clothing to the new mother in honor of her labor. For three days she rests and nothing is expected of her but to nurse her child.

"All of those who have given birth are then trained in the art of midwifery and some become physicians to the community as well. Women here learn many of the healing arts as well as astrology, oracle and Priestess craft.

"None of you is ready to be a crone, but when your menopause does come you will have been well prepared for the place of the Great Goddess, the woman through whom all teaching and guiding of the community's spiritual life is done. The Crone has a subtle but definite passage. When her mooning does not come for the first time, its absence tells her and she takes the children and cares for them while the others of her cycle remain in the moon lodge. That is a signal to all that she has achieved the Wisdom of the Great Mother. When the cycle days have gone by and the women come out from the lodge they share their stories and then bring the new Crone here to the well where she scrys into the water and receives guidance for each of the women who have shared her cycle. Then she is carried to the Tor to meet for the first time the Morgens, the Nine Sacred Crones who are the Great Council of Avalon. The Morgens dress her in finery and put out a huge feast and the women dance circles around her with song and the playing of the flutes and wind instruments, the music of these symbolizes the harmony of wisdom moving through life.

"Death is the last mystery. The body of the dead is prepared for burial here at the well. And when it is buried in the earth the village sings songs of encouragement to the spirit that now returns to the womb of the earth. We are not afraid of death here. Those who mourn are sad for themselves and we all comfort them, but we know that the dead are not dead at all, but only living in another realm. They remain present as shadows of themselves within our minds and hearts and can reappear at any time in many shapes. After burial we often come back to the well to mourn and to look for our loved ones as we scry into the water."

"I like all of these mysteries and their rituals, Magdalen." Ruth turned toward her leader to see how she felt. Magdalen smiled.

"I think Jesus would approve and that we should keep these in our Way, too"

The Lady of the Lake was pleased with Magdalen's decision especially when the others celebrated by shouting.

"So mote it be!"

The summer sun was very warm as noon approached. So when the Lady proposed that they bathe together in the stream that fed the well everyone agreed that the refreshment of a dip in the sacred waters would be most welcome to both body and soul.

The stream flowed with some force, its redness making it appear magical. The banks were lined with Apple trees and bright yellow and lavender flowers. The women disrobed and found their refreshment. The waters were soothing as they swirled about them. Sharon clung to Magdalen's neck so as not to be carried away but laughed and splashed until her mother suggested lunch. Apples were both the available food and the finest. The meal reminded Magdalen of their first commemorative meal in Avalon the day they were left feeling so alone here. She was still feeling badly about having missed the Solstice celebration.

"Great Lady, my teacher Baera had made it an imperative that we arrive in time for the Summer Solstice, I cannot help feeling that we have not accomplished our goal."

Magdalen decided that she would find out why she and the others had not been invited to the celebration.

"You arrived just in time, Magdalen." The Lady smiled, "You see you arrived on the night of the full moon of June the time when the veils are the thinnest between the physical world and the world of spirit. The celebration that you felt you had missed will not come until tomorrow. We do not keep a Roman calendar here, my dear, but a Celtic one based on the stars and the moon and the sun and the seasons."

Magdalen was excited, "Really? We haven't missed anything? We can be at the celebration?"

The Lady of the Lake took Magdalen's hands in her own and swung her about.

"You can be with us and join in as a true Priestess. You will be one of the sisterhood tomorrow. The celebration lasts four whole days from sunset to sunset is one day. It will be grand!"

She swung Magdalen around again and the others coupled up and did their little dance with them. Then it was time to dress and head back to the Tor. They wanted to be back for the evening meal and Magdalen was anxious to hear what kind of adventure James and Regino had in her absence.

Magdalen was invited to do the Rite of Remembrance before dinner that evening. Having completed the ritual they dined and the table talk was terribly interesting.

James told of his new understanding of manhood. Men in Avalon were called Guardians. They reached their highest honor as guardians, fathers and sages, protecting the Moon Rath or Oracle and their families. They were protectors of home and family. Warrior honors went mostly to those who fought the enemy within, which he understood now to be fear. Druids did this through what they considered Shadow work. They engaged in a withdrawal to the deeper self and found the Shadows present within the conscious mind, the spirit, and then purified themselves through long and arduous work to subdue the Dark Forces by calling on the Goddess to help them in their interior battles.

As James went on, Regino politely waited for his turn, but his patience was limited by his age. The minute James paused long enough he blurted out his manly intentions.

"I will be a man someday, a true Druid, with no fear. I will study hard and I will be fearless!"

It was easy to see that the day's activities had impressed the boy. His mother smiled and nodded showing her approval of Regino's enthusiasm.

The women were curious to know more about the shadow work but James said that the mysteries would have to reveal themselves to them through the Gods. He was sworn to secrecy for now. When he looked toward Magdalen and asked what they had learned on their journey to the well, Magdalen smiled a knowing smile.

"You really don't want us to tell."

James laughed, "You are probably right, at least for now, Magdalen."

"But dear Lady of the Lake," Magdalen was changing the subject. "Please tell us about the Summer Solstice and why we have come to this place for its celebration."

"We will spend all day tomorrow getting ready." The Lady began her reply.

"The men will build huge fires to be lit at dusk. They will prepare the wheel of fire too. One Druid will be chosen to be the sacrificial King of the Oak. The men will polish their swords and their shields in preparation for the mock battle and the burning of the Sacrificial Oak. The women will gather heather for the aroma of the fires and prepare a crown for the Oak King made of roses that still boast their thorns. Of course we will prepare food – lots of it!"

The Lady looked to James and laughed as he was still devouring his venison and strong gravy.

"You see," she went on. "The Summer Solstice is mid-summer when the sun is at its highest point and its light remains with us the longest. It is the time of Death and Rebirth. The Sun God will reign for but a moment and then succumb to his symbolically sacrificial death in order to assure continued life on earth.

"The men will set the fires ablaze to light his way into the New Year coming and at the moment of the sun's rise to fullness they will set the tree afire with flourish. As the tree burns the pilgrims will watch the play that shows the sacrifice of the Sun. The Druid Priests will be in great form for this. Some will dress like serpents that drop their skins at the mid-summer. When they drop their robes they will have been renewed. They will shout that their heart has changed, that they have been reborn. This is a sort of initiation for them."

Magdalen had to interject something, "That is what John the Baptist and Jesus both called for – a change of heart! Their baptism ritual was a rebirthing. We have more sameness, dear Lady!"

"We differ only in the way that we observe this rite, then." the Lady commented.

"Yes," said Magdalen "our baptism has become tainted with guilt that has bled into our Way from the Jewish philosophy and others. I think that this is a better ritual, really. But we will see tomorrow."

"You, my dear Magdalen, had best get plenty of rest." The Lady was taking her leave. "We will all have many preparations to make. Oh, and please, prepare a story for us, Magdalen. We have heard so much about their worth, they will make fine entertainment during our celebration."

It was getting late and everyone was ready to retire. As Magdalen tucked Sharon in she thought about the Blood Well and what her daughter's first moon might be like. Then she too went off to sleep.

Chapter 31

Summer Solstice a Mid-Summer's Night

The day was as busy as the Lady had predicted. By sunset everything was in place. With great flourish the Druids rode in on their white horses. They were wearing headdresses with large animal horns and armor that sparkled in the firelight. The young man who had been selected to play the Oak King was especially dazzling, brandishing a wide blade sword and riding a white stallion that had to be seventeen hands high. Magdalen's equine interest caused her to admire both the stallion and its rider for their stance and speed.

In mock battle the Oak King slew each man while the villagers cheered him on. They threw heather into the myriad bonfires that now blazed in the fields and sang songs to entice the Oak King, Lord of the Sun, to remain standing. There formed a constant procession on the Tor labyrinth. Each pilgrim carrying a large torch symbolized the waxing and waning light as they ascended and descended the hill.

This would have seemed almost frightening, a play in which the audience was also the cast, for there was no stage. But through it all the children played their make-believe games of Sun God and Moon Goddess, and villagers, Priests and even warriors stopped to eat the fine delicacies that had been prepared. Minstrels played flutes and stringed instruments and sang psalms of battle and victory, life and death. People would stop to listen and sometimes join in the song or dance to the tune hand in hand.

The last warrior met his feigned death just at noon. As he went down the Oak King shouted out his victorious call.

"The Light has won."

With that the villagers hushed a little at a time until they were silently gathered around the central fire. From the forest the Lady of the Lake rode in appearing to be extremely pregnant and representing the Fertile Earth. She too rode a great white horse. Her hair was flowing without restraint and was bedecked with heather. Magdalen thought her to be the most beautiful woman she had ever seen.

In her lap she held a wreath of roses whose thorns were very apparent. She dismounted and approached the King who removed his headdress to accept the crown that she engaged with some force. A drop or two of blood oozed from the Druid's forehead and Magdalen ran for the forest. James ran after her.

"I cannot bear it!" she shouted out as if in great pain as James caught up with her.

"It is but one of the men's blood mysteries, Magdalen. He has not been hurt really." James tried to console her.

"Leave me to myself." She pleaded with him. "I need to be alone for now."

James gave her a rich hug and walked back to the fire. Magdalen sobbed for a long time. This reenactment of a crowning with thorns had aroused old and painful emotions.

"They have crowned him and now they will kill him." She thought out loud.

Just then the Lady of the Lake approached and put her arms around the mourning Magdalen.

"Hush, my dear Magdala." She whispered. "It is only make-believe."

"To me it is real." Magdalen argued. "To me it is very real."

She told the Lady the story of Jesus, his crowning with thorns and the crucifixion.

"He was, indeed, this Jesus, the personification of the Sun God or the Oak King."

The Lady had a tear in her eye as Magdalen concluded her story.

"We believe that humans have occasional lifetimes as the personification of the Great Power. Your Jesus was having a lifetime as the Son of God and the son of man. It is a rare gift that he delivered here, the Light of the Divine."

She stroked Magdalen's hair with a gentle compassion that healed her.

"The crown of roses and thorns symbolizes the paradox of pain and pleasure that is inevitable in the Light. The King will wear the crown for but a short time, just as we wear our bodies for but a little while. At sunset the King will hang the wreath in the branches of the Oak. He will disrobe and mount his horse. When he rides into the forest the serpents will appear. They will shed their skins also and take on a new life. They will be transformed with freshness and innocent beauty. At midnight we will set the great Oak ablaze and the wheel of fire will be rolled down the hill to show that the Sun is waning. It will be a new year and we will have yet another chance to plant and to grow and to harvest, both in the fields of Avalon and in the fields of the soul."

The Lady stopped to see if Magdalen truly understood the rituals. Magdalen was becoming more philosophical than emotional now.

"Jesus too descended down into the shadowy places after his death. He told me that his Light waned those three days that he was not with us. Then he rose again in a new light, a new skin, I suppose. You are right to say that he is the personification of the Sun God."

The women walked back to the fire. The Oak King danced with the maidens as the minstrels played their songs. The villagers drank mead and ate heartily from the long tables that had been set out as buffets. Now merriment was the most delicious dish on the Solstice table. It didn't take long for Magdalen to lose her melancholy and join in the festivities.

At sunset a Druid Priest blew on a large horn the call to attention. The Oak King climbed the waiting tree and hung the crown of roses and thorns high in its branches. Right there in the crotch of the huge old Oak he disrobed and then dropped to his waiting horse below. As he rode into the forest about twelve or thirteen druids appeared. Each had donned a robe that covered them from head to toe. The robes were dark and shadowy looking and the men did a winding sort of dance that actually reminded the people of coiling snakes. Soon they were all clumped together winding around one another. James tapped Magdalen on the shoulder to get her attention.

"They are creating a ball of powerful energy. It is yet another one of the mysteries. The ball is called the egg stone or the snakestone. When they part it will appear as a ball of light. It is meant to keep the earth protected during the Sun God's waning."

Magdalen nodded as she watched the ritual dance. When the men parted, just as James had said, Magdalen could see the huge ball of light that their energy had constructed. Then with the light in the middle of the circle that they had formed the men dropped their robes. Beneath them they were naked and their bodies were painted in great detail with symbols of transformation and rebirth.

"That's the symbol of freshness that the Lady spoke of."

Magdalen was commenting to James quietly. The men shouted over her as they ran about in a circle.

"I have shed my skin! I have shed my past and am born again. I am a serpent of great power!"

When the last man had disrobed and shouted his affirmation they ran into the forest and the light from their energy went out.

"One thing about Jews, they keep their clothes on. All this nakedness reminds me too much of Rome and Greece."

Polaris had found Magdalen and James and greeted them with her attitude of distaste.

"I found them to be quite handsome, really." Magdalen's retort was rather matter of fact.

"And I find the entire celebration and ritual to be an honor to my manhood." James was relishing in the first male oriented rite he had seen in Avalon. "Let's find the others." He looked about for Ruth, Sarah, Carmel, Cybele or the children. "They must be here somewhere. I saw Sharon and Regino dancing with Cybele before the serpents came."

The three soon discovered the rest of their party at one of the buffets. Together they took large plates of food off to a grassy spot to enjoy them. Magdalen noticed that Sharon was picking bits of food off of everyone's plate and adding it to her own.

"Sharon, why are you doing that? Don't you like your own food?"

"It's not for me, Mama. It's for the fairies." The little girl walked a little ways off and set the plate on the ground. "They will come to eat it, and I will catch one."

The adults giggled at her resolve. A fairy hunt was part of the tradition of this holiday, they had been told. The children all had a grand time catching fireflies and making wishes for the New Year.

They rested and watched Sharon on her hunt until midnight. Even in the midst of the music and laughter it was easy to nap with such full stomachs and long days. But when the horn blew everyone gave a loud cheer that brought even a napping James to his feet.

"They will light the Oak now." He said as he jumped up to consciousness. "And the wheel will be rolled down the hill."

Everyone assembled at the giant Oak still bearing the King's crown. The Oak King had returned now fully clothed but without horns or crown. The Lady of the Lake joined him at the base of the tree and together they set the oil soaked branch on fire. Loud cheers rang out and everyone turned toward the Tor. The people waiting at its top for the first sign of the blaze lit the wheel and with huge poles rolled it through the labyrinth having to run to keep up with the wheel's momentum. The Sun God was descending into the shadowy winter of darkness, as was the natural way of things.

The ceremonies and rituals were over and the villagers went back to their joyful celebration. The Lady of the Lake, holding her plate of sweet delights, joined Magdalen and her disciples in their grassy spot near the fire.

"We will not feed the fires anymore. They will slowly burn themselves out and then the celebration will be over. Can you tell a story about the light and the dark, or the Sun God and his waning and waxing power, Magdalen?"

"I can, but it will be a play, and you must all help act it out."

A thought of what Magdalen perceived as pure genius proportion had just entered the storyteller's head.

"James, you will be the Sun God and Regino you will be his servant, the Keeper of the Light. It is an important role. Are you up to it?"

Magdalen smiled at an eager Regino.

"Ruth, Sarah and Carmel you will each play a Goddess, one be Faith another Hope and another Charity."

Leaving the women to make this decision on their own, Magdalen pointed at Cybele.

"You, Cybele will be the sister of the Sun God, the Moon Goddess. And you Polaris will be their Mother, the Great Creation Goddess."

It was obvious that Polaris had been honored for her age and wisdom.

"Sharon, little one, you can be a true Fairy Princess."

That left only Magdalen and the Lady of the Lake to be cast.

"Please, dear lady, join us in our play and be the Fairy Queen."

"I would be honored' the Lady bowed her head. "But who will you be, Magdalen?"

"I will be the Avataress, the one who bears the light and saves the earth and her people."

Everyone clapped violently. This sounded like a good play, indeed.

"Save the applause until after the performance, please."

Magdalen laughed as she said it. They spent a little time in rehearsal with Magdalen assuring them that she would narrate and coach them as the play progressed. Magdalen gathered her props: a table set by the fire, her precious cup, bread and wine. Next came costuming. She decked herself out in her priestly garb, put flowers in the hair of the Princess and Queen and a crown of bright yellow flowers representing light on the heads of the Sun God, and the Moon Goddess, and the Great Mother she dressed in one of the leftover Druid snakeskin cloaks. To Sarah who had chosen to be Faith she gave a cross fashioned from branches and vine. To Ruth who was now called Hope she gave a small boat anchor obtained from the Lady of the Lake. To Carmel she handed a rose with a long and graceful stem.

When the costumes and stage were set, the Lady of the Lake announced the opening of a great epic as Magdalen had described it, about the Light and its Guardians. The people gathered around the fire to enjoy the entertainment. Little did audience or actors know that Magdalen was formulating a ritual of Light for the Way that would please both her followers and the people of Avalon for many generations to come.

"There is an invisible world," Magdalen began her story. "Where the Great Mother of all resides."

Polaris entered entirely hidden by her cloak and stood in the midst of the gathering.

"The Great Mother is neither spirit nor matter. She is a Cause, which gives life to all things. The Great Mother gave birth first to the Sun God."

Polaris grunted from beneath the cloak and there were giggles in the crowd as James dashed comically unto the stage.

"Now the Sun God was born a Spirit and had no form or matter. He was only Light. The Great Mother labored again."

Polaris grunted once more and Magdalen paused for the chuckles to subside.

"This time she gave birth to the Moon Goddess, who was born as her brother was, a Spirit only. She too was but a light."

Cybele danced unto the stage in her yellow crown of light.

"Now the two lights could not see the Great Mother, their source, but could only recognize one another. They became enamored with one another and collided in a huge and powerful energy."

Cybele and James embraced. Magdalen wondered if she should have put Carmel in this role instead of Cybele. But she went on.

"Sparks of light were scattered across the universe when they collided and the Fairy Queen was born."

The Lady of the Lake moved to the center.

"The Fairy Queen was a spirit also, like her sources the Sun God and the Moon Goddess. She had but a fraction of their power, but because of her small size she could move about quickly and gracefully."

The Lady did a fairy dance around the fire and the God and Goddess. The people applauded her and she bowed deeply.

"There were many fairies born that day, including the Fairy Princess who came from her mother when she collided with another fairy."

Sharon danced her fairy dance with such innocence and grace that everyone cheered and stood for her. Magdalen had invented this part of the story to give her daughter an active part and wondered now what symbolism it would hold.

"Now the fairies spread themselves throughout the universe and their power was undeniable. Each spirit light was moving quickly at first but as their energy wore down their speed decreased. They moved slower and slower until they became very still. When they stopped a wonderful thing happened. The stars of the sky were born!

"The Sun God and the Moon Goddess stopped to look at the new stars and they became the light of the daystar, our Father Sun and the light of the night, our Mother Moon. The Sun impregnated the Moon and Mother Moon gave birth to the Earth and then the spirits of the fairies exploded with delight and some descended to live here as the spirits of all living things.

"Yes, within every living being there is a spirit, a fairy that is empowered with great potential. But slowed down by these new bodies as they were the spirits became filled with fear that their power would no longer work. From their fear was born guilt, blame, regret and shame. Humans began to bicker and to wage wars and struggles over possessions. They enslaved one another and they mistreated children and women. They forgot that the Divine was living within them and kept looking for their Source outside themselves. They began to call the Sun a God and the Moon a Goddess forgetting that it was the spirit of the invisible world that was the true Source of all Power.

One day the Spirit of the Sun saw the havoc men were making. He called to the Spirit of the Moon.

'We must come together to make a new light for people to see."

James made a calling gesture to Cybele and again they embraced. Magdalen returned to the story.

"We have conceived a thought. And it shall be called Love and it will be the mother of many children." Said the Spirit of the Moon.

"But with whom shall this thought conceive?" The Spirit of the Sun questioned.

"Our daughter, Love, will wed with human hearts. Because of her, human hearts will conceive compassion, caring and respect and honor. With these thoughts present, humans will couple because of love. They shall conceive one among them, an Avataress who will have a Divine Spirit and a Human Body and who will follow the Goddesses of Faith, Hope and Charity."

In danced the three women with their props.

"And then the Avataress was born."

Magdalen came forward and took a deep bow and the audience cheered and applauded.

"To keep the Avataress safe and unharmed by the darkness, the Sun God sent his aide to attend her. He was the Keeper of the Light and would remain with the Avataress all her life making sure that the Light of Love never left her."

Regino bowed low to Magdalen with an adoring glance and held high the candle that she had given him.

"The Avataress honored the Goddesses, and they found her to be in their favor."

First Magdalen bowed to the waiting women and then they returned the bow.

"The Goddess Faith gave the Avatar a gift. She placed in her heart the eternal knowing that where she stood was exactly where she needed to be and that what she was doing was exactly right for this moment in time. To remind her of her knowledge, Faith gave the Avatar a cross. One arm pointed to the sky, another to the earth, another to the past and another to the future. The point in the center where the arms met, this Faith told her, was the center within, the seat of the Divine Spirit. It was midway between heaven and earth and at the moment of now."

Sarah handed the cross to Magdalen who took it with a deep curtsy to the make-believe Goddess.

"The Avataress cherished her knowledge of the eternal moment and her place in the universe and she placed the cross upon an altar in honor of Faith."

Magdalen placed the cross upon the buffet table that had been set aside for the play.

"Not to be outdone, the Goddess Hope gave the Avataress a gift too. She brought a beautifully carved iron anchor to the Avataress. This, she said, was to remind the Avataress that she would always have another chance if she remained anchored in knowledge that the Divine Spirit that brought her into being was Love. The Avataress set this upon the altar along side the cross. It would be her way of honoring Hope and her sisterhood with Faith."

Magdalen placed the little anchor upon the altar.

"Charity, the youngest of the thoughts to have been born from Love, wanted to give her gift to the Avataress as well. She picked a lovely, long stemmed red rose from the Garden of the Fairies and brought it to the Avataress. This she said was to make the Avataress always mindful that the purpose of Love was to share itself. Like the rose, Love must be seen to be appreciated. To be a thought was good, but it was not enough. Love must blossom into the roses of good works, kind deeds and soothing words. The petals and the scent of the rose were to remind the Avataress of the need to share her Divine Spirit through action in the earthly world."

The storyteller placed the rose beside the cross and anchor.

"These, the Avataress thought, will be the marks of my life and my Way. I will share them with everyone I meet. And she did until one day when Love's only enemy, the demon Fear, attacked the hearts of those who were listening to the Avataress and because they were filled with Fear some returned to the old way of violence and to silence the Avataress, she was crucified, hung on the cross of Faith. But Hope's anchor reminded her that she would live again. Like the rose of Charity in the spring she was resurrected and returned to share yet more of this Way of hers."

Magdalen made a gentle leap to the center of the "stage" and stretched out her arms as if to preach. Her audience was delighted with her return from the dead.

"Now the Avataress called those who loved her to a special feast. In her absence from Earth she had made some observations and wanted to make an announcement. As they were about to dine she told them Faith, Hope and Charity must be honored, but above all Love must be our great Goddess."

The villagers interrupted with applause and shouts of "Long live Love."

Magdalen waited for a moment and then went on.

"Ignorance is the breeder of Fear. Fear is the enemy of Love. We will not be ignorant but forever learning. This is how we will honor Love herself. We will honor Faith by living in the moment. We will honor Hope by forgiving others and ourselves. We will honor Charity by sharing what we have in every way that we can. We will honor each other by sharing knowledge, asking and answering questions and a fair exchange of ideas. We will honor the presence of our own Divine Spirit by affirming our presence and purpose in front of one another. We will always remember these things: The body is but bread, the wine is but blood, but it is the Spirit that is the Source that we share and it will never die. Then the Avataress asked her friends if they wanted to ask questions or to give an opinion. Some of them did and the discussion went on for a long time.

"When the table was quiet, the Avataress held up a loaf and blessed it."

Magdalen held up the loaf of bread and blessed it solemnly. Then she broke it and handed it to one of the villagers who followed suit. She continued with the Rite of Remembrance and the audience dutifully participated. When it was finished and everyone had received their first communion, Magdalen held up her golden cycle to the sky and proclaimed.

"This is how Love's Way will defeat the enemy called Fear."

Magdalen bowed and the audience cheered and threw things into the air as if to celebrate the Avatar's victory over Demon Fear.

The storyteller had almost forgotten Sharon and her part as the Fairy Princess.

"The Fairy Queen sent her daughter, the Princess, to earth. The tiny fairy entered into the minds of everyone at the meal as the Holy Spirit that would bring a warm flame of wisdom that could unite with the love they already held. This would be a comfort, a Paraclete, that would keep the flame of love alive."

Sharon did a little dance about the actors throwing flower petals from her crown and the villagers applauded and sent kudos her way. When Magdalen took her hand and the others joined in to take a bow the play was over. But Magdalen wasn't finished yet.

"I want to share my Way with you, the Way that the Avatar Jesus brought to me and which has evolved from my experience here and in Gaul. Each evening I will offer you knowledge, hear your questions and opinions and of course share the Rite of Remembrance. If you would like this then in a fair exchange, please come to me tomorrow evening."

Now she was quite done. Magdalen took her place around the fire next to the Lady of the Lake. There was some murmuring in the crowd but it all seemed affirmative and the Lady smiled at Magdalen as if to tell her that she would indeed have disciples come the next evening.

Chapter 32

First Moon

The following evening and the evenings to come found Magdalen traveling throughout the British Isles putting on her little "mystery" play and teaching her Way. The people had come to call the band of missionaries the Culdees, which means "certain strangers." Magdalen's Way was quickly becoming the Culdee Church. Wherever they went people gathered to hear the Priestess' stories and participate in the Rite of Remembrance.

The years went by quickly and Sharon was growing closer to her womanhood with each passing season. Magdalen decided that she would soon have to be putting down roots that would ground her daughter both in the Way and in family and permanent friendships. Constant traveling like troubadours was not a fitting lifestyle for a young girl.

Word had come to Britain that those following the Way in Rome were being persecuted for their faith. Magdalen was sure that a return to the mainland was not safe for them and that perhaps she would have to make her home in Avalon itself for a while longer. One day she could return home, but not until this persecution of believers had subsided. Her fear for Sharon's safety, even her life, was growing again and Magdalen was often melancholy or agitated.

James knew Magdalen's distress, for he was afraid himself. Still, he wanted his Priestess to feel safe and secure, happy and filled with joy. Perhaps this is why he insisted on waking her one morning far before dawn to give her the red mare that he had captured. Magdalen was delighted with the horse and so was everyone else.

She was a red mare very many hands high with a definite five-pointed star on her brow that was as white as snow. The mare readily allowed her new mistress to mount and ride bareback and the growing group and even some of the natives celebrated with races and jumping contests. Magdalen's horse won every time. The natives felt that this was a mystical mare and meant especially for Magdalen who then must be mystical herself – a prime candidate for a Priestess. The beautiful mare, now named Mystic, changed Magdalen's attitude completely, just as James had hoped.

Returning back to Avalon, riding on the back of Mystic, Magdalen was sure that this new home was the answer to her prayers for inner peace. Now wearing the colorful garb of the natives, allowing her hair to fly free and riding like the wind that blew her locks, she was finally happy. There was a sense of freedom in this land that she had never felt before. Guilt and burden seemed to have been left far behind in the land of the Jews and Romans. Here she could be herself, truly her self, as Jesus taught her to be without repercussion or fear.

Magdalen and the Culdees were soon accepted as permanent fixtures in the community. The villagers even built her a hut made of grass and mud that when dried in the sun appeared red in color as the water of the red fountain did. That water carried with it a great fascination for Magdalen and she went to the Blood Well daily to watch the falls and to bathe in the pool and then sit on the rocks and meditate, not seeking God but instead truly communing with Spirit and with Jesus in a mystical presence that she could not easily explain when James asked what she did so early and all alone.

Magdalen knew that she wanted Sharon to grow up in this place where a woman was thought to be powerful by nature of her femininity and she also wanted her to learn the healing arts and the rituals but most importantly she wanted Sharon to always be herself and to feel the freedom of empowerment from within and to know the presence of God as real love rather than another power under whom she might be forced to live a life of mental and emotional slavery.

While Magdalen watched her grow, Sharon studied the Jesus teachings with her mother and the Celtic and Druidic culture under the Lady of the Lake's directions. Sharon was a quick study and justifiably proud of her progress. Each birthday brought her closer to womanhood, but her next would be celebrated with great flourish, for her grandmother was coming to visit.

As this year's Autumn Equinox approached, and Sharon would be ten, she was looking forward both to Mother Mary's visit and to her menarche. Each day she prayed fervently that her time would come while her grandmother was with them. Magdalen had assured her that the blood time was soon approaching and the girl did not want it to pass before Mother Mary arrived.

Some of the older women, including her mother, helped Sharon to built her own moon lodge. Like her mother's hut it was red inside and out. Sharon furnished her lodge with warm wrappings, a fine hair brush, wood for the fire and pillows fashioned from fine fabric and filled with aromatic herbs and goose down. The pillows would be fine seats for her mother and grandmother. She herself would sit upon the moon rock to collect her blood during the day and at night she would sleep on a mattress of down and straw, later to be burned returning her night blood to the earth and honoring the moon. It was a fine hut, and Sharon took great pride in its construction and furnishings. Now all she had to do was wait for grandmother and her menarche.

The girl's prayer was answered; Mother Mary arrived just as the moon was full. Of course, grandmother didn't know about the customs and cultures of Avalon and the Way that the Culdees had adopted as their own. She was astonished at the ingenuity and mastery of Sharon's moon lodge. Mother Mary looked in awe at her granddaughter as she greeted her first in Greek, then in Hebrew, and finally in Gaelic. Sharon was bright, well educated and beautiful. This did not surprise her, but it did please her. She knew that whatever Magdalen had derived from the Celts, it had been good for them all.

Sharon was beginning to feel the pains of womanhood, and she was eager to explain the blood mysteries to her grandmother before her time came. Magdalen led the way to the Blood Well as Sharon chattered on telling Mother Mary exactly what would take place during her mooning.

"My friends have braided my hair this morning, and picked flowers to put in my moon lodge. Now we will gather water from the Blood Well and take it to the hut to be used for my cleansing later. At the first sign of blood I will call you and mother and we will go into the lodge together. Mother will build a fire to keep us all warm and outside the same friends that braided my hair will play their flutes for me. But they mustn't play too loudly or the Guardians will shush them."

"What are guardians?" Mother Mary questioned her granddaughter.

"The men, grandmother, the men stay outside the lodge and keep away anyone or anything that would disturb me or keep me from getting the psychic messages from our ancestors, or from the Goddesses of Faith, Hope and Charity, maybe even from my father. Oh, I hope I get to know my father Jesus during my first moon."

Sharon made this last remark almost as a pleading to Jesus himself.

"Somehow, I can't quite imagine my son standing outside a moon lodge, Sharon. But perhaps in your heart you will know him."

Mother Mary looked lovingly at the granddaughter whose youth she had all but missed.

"Do you think he would be proud?"

Sharon wanted her grandmother to say the words she feared she would never hear her father pronounce.

"He is already proud, I am sure, darling."

Mother Mary said just what Sharon had hoped to hear and the girl's eyes filled with light and joy.

"Anyway, while my friends play the flutes, softly that is, you and mother will take the braids out of my hair and brush out the tangles. This is to symbolize my release from the entanglements of physical life. Mother will use the water from the Blood Well to wash me and the fire will be kept high to keep me warm and comfortable. I will spend my time eating when I am hungry, all the good and delicious things that you prepare." Sharon paused to laugh and wink at her grandmother, "sleeping when I am tired, and meditating and praying for the most part. It is a special time, grandmother, the others have all told me how wonderful the visions and the journeys of light can be on your first moon."

Mother Mary smiled knowingly. "It is, indeed, a very special time in a woman's life and a psychic one that can lead us to great discoveries within ourselves."

When they arrived at the well, Mother Mary looked into the water in contemplation. Magdalen watched her mother-in-law for a moment and then addressed her.

"You are already a crone with great wisdom, Mother, and I honor your presence during my daughter's first moon."

"Thank you, I think."

Mother Mary laughed a little in response to Magdalen's obvious compliment. She did not yet fully understand the culture or tradition behind this ritual, but she did appreciate the honor and respect with which women and their life passages were treated here. Following their direction, Mother Mary helped her granddaughter and Magdalen carry water from the Blood Well back to the moon lodge.

Reverently she sat through Magdalen's evening service and commemorative rite, taking communion with them and listening attentively to the questions and answers that came from the villagers. She marveled at the feast that had been prepared in her honor and indulged her granddaughter with stories of her father and mother before she was born.

They were up late and Magdalen was surprised for a moment to have her daughter call her so early. It was not yet light, but then she realized that Sharon had seen her first blood. Sharon called her grandmother and the three women went into the lodge. Eager to begin this experience, she had already called her friends who had summoned the Guardians and gathered, flutes in hand, at the door of the hut.

Magdalen lit the fire and Mother Mary took her place on one of the pillows that Sharon had made for her comfort. Sharon wrapped herself in one of the warm covers and sat in her place on the moon rock. As Mother Mary released the braids from Sharon's hair, Magdalen bathed her daughter's feet and hands with water warmed on the fire. Mother and Grandmother took turns brushing the tangles out of Sharon's long locks and singing her lullabies from childhood. The young woman soon drifted off to sleep and Magdalen prepared a special sweet tasting soup for their breakfast.

"I dreamed of him, of you and my father, in your own kitchen."

Sharon was eager to share what she had seen in her dreams. As she took the hot soup from her mother's hand she beamed with delight.

"It was just as if I was right there with the two of you. Grandmother, you were there too!"

The girl went on with her dream telling.

"Mother, you awoke before dawn, bathed and dressed in a robe of white tied with ribbons of many colors, knowing that my Father, Jesus, intended to teach that day, as he always did on the Sabbath. You began to pack food for the day. All the things that had been prepared the day before were placed in three baskets to carry with you to the temple. This was not the temple of fame, but a smaller synagogue that you frequently attended.

"Father must have risen long before you and was at prayer and meditation by himself outside the house. Coming in, he had you unpack one of the three baskets and refill it with leavened bread. This was not in accordance with his religious faith, and you questioned whom the bread was for. He said that he intended to teach today of the law. The bread, he said, was a tool with which he would show the Pharisees the folly of their faith in a God who would bring down the temple walls as a result of a person's appetite for food.

"As all three of you prepared to leave for the temple, you covered your head with a veil. Father removed the cover and said that God's beauty was not to be hidden. As you went out of the door, you reached for the cloth again and said, 'For the temple only, I will not bring disgrace upon myself.' He laughed a bit and you proceeded to walk to the temple in near silence.

"In the temple, there were gathered thirteen people, including my father, grandmother and you Mamma. Among these were three Pharisees and six scribes. The scribes began to write all the words of the priests. They spoke a great deal about the lack of attendance at this Sabbath, and of the sinful ways of Jews in neglecting the Law of Moses and of God. All this was being written down, and each elder was given opportunity to venture his comments and opinions. Then one, the High Priest, turned to father and asked his opinion on this matter. Grandmother stood by the side, her head covered, listening intently to father as he spoke.

"He asked them. 'Is it lawful for these that are not here to harness the oxen to drive their cart to the temple on the Sabbath? Was it even lawful for you to have driven yourselves here? Or to break the rest by walking the distance that some might have come? Is it lawful for my wife to have carried goods for us to eat on today's journey? Is it lawful to do any physical thing according to the Law of Moses? For all these things that we have done here, there has been no crack in the walls of this place. Can you see in the ceiling the punishment of the Lord God? And have the homes of those who are not here crumbled to the ground? Seek the answer now from these proofs. If the Lord God thought poorly of our presence here, would this building yet be standing, by the Law of Moses?

"'There is no reason either then why the homes of those who have not joined us still stand, not under that law. You mock the ways of other men. You stand righteous in your indignation with those who do not come here to hear your opinions. Let me suggest that they, in their temple, find indignation with your refusal to rest from the work that is yours this day.

"'I do not venture an opinion on the Law of Moses, for I am not that man. I do not venture an opinion on the law of the Lord God, for that law cannot be changed, and is without flaw or need of anyone's approval. I do not come here to venture an opinion but to seek truth; to speak words of law is not a wise one's way, for the law is subject to change. To speak words of God and his way isn't a wise one's mission, for God is known in truth only in a person's heart and not in one's head. You cannot think of God and his law, but you can only know these things in your hearts. The law is not my place. This is the job of the Pharisees, the Priests, and even the scribes, who now break the law as they write there on the Sabbath. They, not I, have ventured an opinion as to the folly of the Law of Moses. I beg them not to break their own law, and speak as hypocrites during their writing.'

"And he gathered up from all the scribes their sticks and broke them, scattering them across the floor of the temple. He did this in surprise to them, but with no haste or anger. They murmured amongst themselves, but could find no lawful reason why these scribes should have been allowed to work. And among the group was a man whose hand was useless. It appeared to have no scar of injury or no mark of other disease, but he could not hold even the weight of his food in that hand. It was his right hand. The Priests sent this man to sit beside my father. They hoped that Jesus would make comment now about this man's need for healing. The law forbid even this work on the Sabbath, for God was believed to be resting with them, and would not heal on that holy day.

"But my father knew that they were testing him and his opinion. He ventured no statement, but only asked a question. 'Do you wish that I heal this man's hand on the Sabbath day? Do you intend to entice me to break the Law of Moses before you? I ask you, is it lawful for God to choose to heal on the day of the Sabbath? Is God capable of evil doing? Or is doing good considered to be evil when it is done in the temple on the Sabbath?'

"There was silence among them as they waited. And then my father told the man to move away from him, and to put himself in the center of the circle of the men. He did so. Father said, 'Stretch forth you hand for these men to see God's goodness on the day that is his by the proclamation of Moses.'

"And the man did what Father asked. As he turned his hand for all to see, my father threw to him a loaf of the leavened bread from the basket. The man caught the bread, held it there, and realized his healing had been completed. Father then rose, took the bread from the man, and biting off a piece, he said, 'I am not the law. I am not in opinion of the law. I am not even the Priest and caretaker of the law. Neither am I the judge of the law. I am not breaking the law by this healing, for I have not touched this man. I break bread, not the law of God. For even now the ceiling has not cracked, the walls do not crumble. Go man in peace with yourself, for you have no sin as a result of this miracle.' And he moved to leave.

"As he set the bread back in its basket, he spat out the piece yet in his mouth and said, 'I leave for you the bread of human life, it does not taint my mouth, my miracles, or your temple. Only know that the law of man is not the decision of God, your Father. Know also that I have not, even now, broken your law this day. I have not consumed the bread, but spat it out. It is for you to spit forth the folly and consume then only the truth.' And you all left and walked to a grassy place where you ate the food and drank a great deal of wine with many others. All ate and drank until they were more than full, and there was a lot of laughter and joy among the people there.

"Father talked and explained the healing. This man only had to relax all of the parts of his hand and his body in order to release the nerve that kept his hand useless in its unnatural position. It was the man's faith that had allowed him to do that. The miracle was in the mind of the man, a mind that had come to know God's goodness. That must have been a wonderful day, Mother."

Sharon looked to her mother in complete confidence that her dream had revealed a true story of her father's life. Magdalen wasn't surprised at her daughter's experience.

"Sharon it was truly a good day, a day before the tragedies of his life, a day when we were happy and safe."

Mother Mary stroked her granddaughter's hair.

"You are a remarkable woman, Sharon, a whole woman whose spirit is filled with your father's wisdom"

"Thank you, grandmother, I think so too."

Sharon was feeling the fullness of her Goddess nature and was proud of who she was. Her first moon lasted just three days. Magdalen had to wonder if her daughter had used some enchantment to make her reentrance into the community just in time for her tenth birthday. There would be twice the celebration in the village, and twice the storytelling. Sharon's dreams and visions would be enough entertainment for three days, to be sure.

Chapter 33

Birthday Gifts

Sharon's friends, many of whom had not yet had their first moon, eagerly awaited her return from Blood Well. They were anxious to hear her stories of initiation and to shower her with birthday greetings and gifts. The village itself was preparing for the Alban Elued or Harvesthome. This day marked the last harvest before winter would claim the earth and it was a time with powerful energy for magic of all kinds. Sharon was blessed to be born at such a powerful time and blessed twice more to have had her menarche now.

The girls had strung garlands of Muin, her power tree, all around her hut. Today, Magdalen would bake a round cake and decorate it with candles. The cake symbolized the moon and the candles its light. When Sharon prayed over the cake her prayers would ascend to the heavens, to the Goddess, to be answered quickly. Her friends would clap loudly, slap Sharon gently and bang on drums. This would assure that no evil would befall her simply because she was left unaware. It's hard to be unaware of the moment when you are being pinched, slapped and shouted at!

Birthdays were meant to honor the first blood mystery of birth, coming alive, but they were also a celebration of motherhood. Sharon would give her mother gifts today and honor the great service Magdalen had performed through her labor of love. Mother and daughter would both drink water from Blood Well and share the cake that Magdalen would make.

The anniversary of birth is the beginning of a new year and so there would be prophecies of good fortune and guessing games that symbolized knowing the unknown or the future. But all this would have to wait until after Sharon had shared her dreams and prophecies from the moon lodge. The mystery of menarche and the valuable information that it revealed for the village would take precedence over Sharon's birthday celebration.

When the women returned from the well refreshed and renewed Sharon was all-aglow. She was dressed in white and wore ribbons in her long tresses. Magdalen had helped her to paint her face for the very first time, and she wore a crown of Muin around her brow. The young woman held a cup that contained her first moon blood. It was a precious gift to be given back to the earth, especially powerful at this time of Harvesthome when the people prayed for a renewal of the field's abundance in the spring.

As Sharon walked through the village and out into the communal fields the villagers gathered and followed behind her. They cheered as she poured the blood out onto the waiting furrows. Then for the first time publicly Sharon prayed, using a song of the earth and a psalm that she had created during her visit to the moon lodge.

"From the womb of the earth, we are borne
From our mother's womb we come forth
From the breasts of the earth we are nourished
From our mother's breasts we are nursed
Praised be our Divine Mother, our earthly mother
And all who are fertile with life and filled with love to nourish
   it!"

Sharon paused just long enough for the villagers to herald their approval of her words and wishes. "Blessed Be the Mother!" they all chorused.

"Until now I have known my Mother solely,
But now I also know my Father.

His spirit has visited me
His blood has flowed from my womb
This is my blood, shed in order that another might live
Spilled on the earth to demonstrate my love for all
What my father has done I have also done
And greater things I will do
By the blessing of the Mysteries of the Goddess.
So mote it be!"

The villagers shouted a loud "So mote it be!" Magdalen beamed with pride as everyone returned to the central fire to hear her daughter's dreams and prophecies.

"Tell us, Sharon," an enthusiastic Ruth encouraged the young woman to begin her tales. "You must have some of your mother's storyteller's blood still left in you"

The women and girls giggled, but James pretended not to have heard this remark. Sharon sat at the head of the circle and a hush fell over the group.

"I will tell you of my father," she began, "for he visited me in my dreams and left me knowing his true nature, and the nature of all things. All of you are loved and all beings are worthy and deserving of that love. This is what my father said:

'Whoever does not accept the kingdom of God as a little child will not enter into it. When the children came to me for attention or when they approached an altar, they came in their innocence and faith with no notion of fear or unworthiness. But their parents, who were afraid that they are not worthy of God's love, attention, or touch, pulled them away or removed them from the altar. Those who chose to protect me from such innocence and faith or to keep silent the altar place would have done better to find themselves to be so faithful in their love and so trusting in their worth as the children.

'Live a chaste life. Honor all life. Share willingly. Speak only the truth. Be fair and honest in your dealings with one another.

Honor your father and mother. Above all else share what you are and what you have and you will have treasure in abundance, for your heaven will be in a heart of generosity. Yet, if you do none of these things, you are loved. For you are spiritual children and loved by the Father and the Great Mother, no matter what.

'Once a man asked me the way to heaven saying that he had kept all the commandments since his childhood. And I looked upon him, and loved him, and I told him, one thing is lacking in your life; go, sell whatever you can, and give the money to the poor, and you shall have treasure in the heaven of a generous heart; and then come, follow me.

'That man came to me, saying with his words what most say only in their minds. He felt unworthy in himself. He knew himself to be abiding by the Law of Moses and the law of Caesar, yet he needed to be made worthy. On my word, he made for himself a place in the eternal thoughts of the poor, and this he could call heaven. He became immortal by their memory of him. He was not satisfied with the immortality of soul, so for him the memory will extend his person in time. The children would not ask for such recognition. The children would not feel that they must do more than be children, good children. Our bodies grow in size and our minds in information and only then do we find the shrinking of our faith. This man followed me only to learn that he could have both goods and charity.'"

Sharon wanted to make the lesson clear in her own words now. "People exclude themselves from God's love by the thought that others are more loved and more worthy of loving. They make one another feel less than loved. Trust is what makes man and woman dear to one another. Trust in God is what makes us immortal."

The Lady of the Lake smiled at Sharon as she ended her story.

"Your father has taught a valuable lesson and sent a message to us all from the Goddesses of Faith, Hope and

Charity that reside within our hearts. You have grown in heart with your body and mind, Sharon."

"I had yet another dream." Sharon was ready to go on and they all fell silent again.

"As many as fifteen or seventeen, including Jesus and my mother were gathered to hear him speak. The weather was excessively dry and hot. There was not one tree under which to find shade, and the disciples had draped a cloak up over a frame made of willowy branches to make shade for the Master. It looked rather comical really, to see him sit there with the cloak overhead in its weak attempt at covering such a large man. The grass was tall in some areas, and it was absent in others. The wind was calm that day, and you could hear him quite clearly. Often the sound of the wind had to be shouted over, but not that day. These were his words.

'The search for the kingdom of heaven is like the search for great treasure hidden in a field. He who finds it hides it, and in his joy, goes and sells all that he has and buys the field. Or the search is like the search of a merchant for fine pearls. When he finds one of great value, he goes and sells all that he has and buys that single gem. Again, the search is like setting a great net in the sea, and when it is filled with fishes of all kinds, it is hauled out. And then when they can see them all, the fishermen sort the fish, the good fish from those that would make them sick. The good fish, they keep, to be sold or shared or eaten. And the bad, they are thrown into the furnace so that no one can eat them, lest the fever and the blistering of the mouth and lips cause them pain. So it will be in the end. The good things in life shall be kept and used, and that which causes you pain will be thrown as if into the furnace, lest these things cause you weeping and the gnashing of teeth.'

"There was then a long, very long, pause. Then my father asked, 'Have you understood all these things?' They answered, 'Yes.' But he knew that their minds were filled with confusion, and he explained once more. 'Every person of wisdom and knowledge, like the scribes who study and write about the kingdom of heaven, is to be like the householder who has stored up many things, and when they are needed, the householder brings forth both the new and the old.'

"They all reclined then, on what grass there was, to eat and rest for the night. My mother asked my father why they answered yes to his question of understanding, when even she knew that they had no knowledge of his meaning. He answered that time would pass, and with its passing would come the realization of the need for both the new and the old in law and language. He said that for the moment they saw him as the new, the valuable thing, the only thing. But with the passing of time people would come to see that all things were of value and learn to sort the fish of philosophy in the net of their mind. Mother said she felt that perhaps they would be very old people before they knew all this, especially if they were afraid to ask. Father laughed and said, 'even older than Moses is now.'

"Jesus' intention was to show the foolishness of hiding what we know to be valuable, for it can do no good when resting only in our mind. It is like the treasure in the field. He showed that in our searching we can find many singularly valuable gifts or tools. But when these are the only things left in our lives they will not feed us nor clothe our children. Nor will these things give us spiritual growth. It is only by learning and experiencing all the things of life that we can sort out what is useful to us and what has caused us pain or has the potential of causing pain. To understand you must be aware that there were particular fish, which when eaten caused fevers, blisters of the mouth, and even eventual death. These fish were sorted from the edible ones and burned in order to dispose of them without danger and to reduce their population in the waters." Sharon paused here leaving the floor open for questions or corrections.

"You are, indeed, a hill of poetry as your birth month claims."

Sharon's grandmother had gotten that information from the Lady of the Lake and now wanted to compliment her granddaughter and let her know that she approved of the Celtic Way.

Sharon blushed a little at her grandmother's compliment, but smiled just the same. Then she told the group about her first dream, the one that recalled the healing of a man's hand and heart. When she finished she whispered a prayer of thanksgiving as an indication that she had completed her tales. The group began to sing and dance in thanksgiving for the harvest of the heart that they had just received.

Harvesthome would not begin until sundown and Magdalen and Mother Mary took this opportunity to bake Sharon her birthday cake. Sharon went off with her friends to tell them all about the moon lodge and what it was like to be a woman and sit at the head of the circle telling the tales of wisdom.

As evening approached Magdalen called the young woman home. Her cake was ready and it was time for their prayers. Sharon and her mother prayed quietly over the cake with its burning vigil of request and then went out to share the rich dessert with Sharon's friends. But before they ate, Sharon broke off a bit of cake and scattered it about for the creatures of the woods just as she had done many years before. Magdalen smiled to think that some things might never change, even with our growth. That thought delighted her.

Sharon presented her mother with some small gifts then, a necklace she had made from clay and nuts, a bouquet of brightly colored flowers and a ribbon of deep purple that she had traded for a parchment. She thanked Magdalen quite publicly for the labor of her birth and for nursing her as a child. Magdalen bowed to her daughter in recognition of her gratitude and then Sharon and her friends played their flutes and sang songs, dancing about obviously still children at heart.

As the sun sank beneath the horizon and the mists closed in around them, the people lit the harvest fires and carried the last shaft of wheat to the top of the Tor.

"The last shaft of wheat symbolizes our hope for the future." Magdalen explained to her mother-in-law. "We will allow it to dry and not be burned until the spring fires are lit. It will remind us all winter that the light will return, and our hope for the future makes the present more pleasurable."

Harvesthome was more a celebration of life than any kind of religious holiday. The fires burned, the people made merry and very little time was spent in prayer. Because it was less serious than Samhain, now only another six weeks away, it gave the peasants a period of rest after the toil of the summer and its harvest. So without too much structure to interfere with the merriment, the people were focused now on Sharon and her birthday.

The Lady of the Lake gave her a flute. Her friends had polished stones and engraved them with the symbols of divination. The runes were in a velvet bag that the girls had made, James had fashioned a fine pair of boots for his "niece". Certainly he had become a spiritual uncle to Sharon who had come to adore him. Magdalen had made her a wonderful dress with a cloak of many bright colors that would keep her warm through the long winter to come.

As she watched the fires burn down, Sharon became quite serious. Magdalen asked if anything was wrong and the girl simply smiled and told her mother that she was growing up and needed some time alone. Honoring her daughter took some restraint because Magdalen found more than a little humor in Sharon's complexity.

Sharon went into the woods holding a small lantern and was gone for over an hour when Magdalen decided it was time to interrupt her solitude in order to assure her safety. James and Magdalen found the girl in a small clearing not far from the circle. But she was not alone. Lying with its head in Sharon's lap was a beautiful white stallion.

"Father has given me the most wonderful present, Mother!"

With that the girl swung her leg over the horse's back and he rose with Sharon astride him.

"Where ever did you find him?" James questioned.

"I told you, my father gave him to me for my birthday." Sharon was rather abrupt at having been made to repeat herself.

"You had a vision, then? And the horse appeared?" James questioned again.

"No, Father led him in himself. He was not a vision, but I don't think he was human either." Sharon looked a little perplexed about what had occurred.

Magdalen smiled. "Jesus came in his risen body, not as a man and not as spirit only. He came to you in his body of convenience as I called it."

"Well, it was a fine body. He is so handsome Mother, no wonder you were in love. And he held me close and gave me the horse so that I could ride like a Goddess on the wind."

Both Magdalen and James knew that it was as she had said and never questioned it further. For the next three days the merriment continued for the village and Sharon spent much of the time on the back of her stallion. Ruth, Carmel and Sarah all called the horse Sharon's Unicorn, which seemed to make her very proud.

When the Harvesthome celebration finally ended Mother Mary announced that she would have to end her visit as well. The apostles would be in need of her counsel and she was ready for the journey home. To Magdalen's surprise, James had an announcement too. He would accompany Mary back to Jerusalem. Sharon had tears in her eyes as the two travelers started out at dawn, but by lunch time her attention was drawn back to her horse and riding through the fields. She called her horse Magic, because of the way that he had come to her. Together Magdalen and Sharon road bareback on Mystic and Magic every morning and life in Avalon continued to grow in pleasure and beauty.

Chapter 34

Destiny & Love

Just before Sharon's sixteenth birthday, with the tin trade at its peak, Avalon was getting many more visitors than ever before. Among them were the merchants and tinsmiths from Rome who often brought messages from the apostles. Magdalen and Sharon always looked forward to their "mail" and word of Mother Mary and her ministry.

The two women rode their horses into the meadow to read the long scroll that had arrived that day. As Magdalen began to read her eyes filled with tears.

"Sharon your grandmother has gone on to be with your Father."

Sharon's eyes too welled up.

"How, Mother? And when?"

Magdalen unrolled the scroll still further and read out loud for her daughter's sake.

'My Dear Magdala, Bride of Christ and Grail of the Way,

You know that since the ascension of our Lord Jesus Christ the most Blessed Virgin Mary continued to pray day and night. On the third day before she passed away, an angel of the Lord came to her, and saluted her. "Hail, Mary, full of grace! The Lord is with you." And she rejoiced saying, "Thanks to God." The angel of the Lord told her, "Your ascension will be in three days." And she rejoiced again. "Thanks to God."

'When the third day came we were all gathered with her and heard the angels sing and her soul was lifted up to the Lord. Her body too soon joined him, but this is a tale I cannot tell from experience or set to writing. I will save it for another time. Only know that she was not defiled by the crypt but ascended, as did the Master Jesus into the kingdom.

'It is from here, in Jerusalem, that I send you this news and the recollection of the ascension of our Holy Mother Mary from my own attendance and Mother's own words. Here Roman and Jew alike call for the mutilation and death of those that follow the Way. It is a horrendous time, Magdala, Please pray for us.

Faithfully, John'"

The women mourned the passing of the Mother of Jesus, but for their own sake and not hers. They knew that the final Blood Mystery had been fulfilled for Mary on Earth but that the future would be filled with mysteries of spirit. That night they burned incense as she had done so often and prayed in veneration of the adorable Mother. She was, indeed, they agreed, a Queen and a Goddess who would one day reign supreme over the New Way from the spirit realm.

Many martyrs were to join her court that year. The persecutions in Rome and throughout her empire were violent and ardent. Magdalen was happier than ever to be in Avalon and to know that she and her daughter were safe.

Sharon's birthday and the Harvesthome came and went. As winter approached, the Roman wars raged on. The New Way was spreading as fast as the empire was growing, but somehow, nestled within Britain's mists, the Culdees and their Bishopess remained untouched by either war or persecution. Perhaps Rome had thought it best to let a sleeping dog lie. The Celts could be fearsome warriors if provoked, but they were not apt to make war for its own sake.

By Samhain Sharon would be fully ordained in the New Way and able to cut the Mistletoe this year. The maiden had flowered into her father's footsteps, making appearances and disappearances as she pleased and healing with but a touch. Sharon, who had been drawn to the woodland animals all her life, went about healing wounded birds and beasts of every kind. Just as she was pulled to these helpless creatures, she was also attracted to children and to the elderly who had become as helpless as children. There was an innocence and joy about her that in and of itself was healing to mind and spirit.

Magdalen watched as her daughter grew into her priesthood. Perhaps, she thought, Sharon would soon take her mother's position and Magdalen could return home. Rumors had reached the isle that Magdalen was believed dead or in hermitage ending her life in penance and sacrifice. Those rumors were laughed about but welcomed, for if the Jews and the Romans believed her dead, Magdalen would not have to fear returning to what was once her home. Although it saddened her to think of leaving her daughter, Sharon would have to remain here in Avalon. Here she would be safe, and here she would fulfill her father's mission. Magdalen believed that her own mission would take her away from Avalon one day, and home was the obvious place to go.

The winter was long and dark, but spring arrived with the promise of a new beginning, especially for Sharon. As she went out on the morning of Beltaine to wash her face with the dew, a group of travelers was arriving at the village. They had blonde hair and fair skin. This was rather rare and it intrigued Sharon. She walked up to the horsemen and offered a bit of potato to one of the mounts. Looking up into the face of a fair-haired stranger she was mesmerized by his deep blue eyes. He looked to be about twenty years and was strong, handsome and well dressed.

A polished sword hung from his leather belt and he wore no breastplate but instead a vest of fine lamb's skin. His trousers came only to the tops of his knee-high boots, which carried within them sabers with handles of ivory. The stranger looked down at Sharon with scrutiny. Could this wonderful girl possibly be approaching him so openly? Sharon was anything but shy.

Her approach to strangers had always been one of acceptance and hospitality. Introducing herself, she told the man that he was in time for Beltaine and the festivities of the day and night to follow. He thanked Sharon for her hospitable greeting and led his horse to drink. The other six men did the same and Sharon ran back home.

"Mother, I am in love!" She rocked Magdalen to consciousness.

"And what or whom do you love today?" Magdalen woke with laughter in her question.

"A man, mother, a man from far away, I think."

Sharon was almost breathless with excitement. It was love at first sight for her. Magdalen went out to wash her own face with the morning dew. The holy water of Beltaine's dew would preserve the skin and Magdalen wasn't getting any younger, she thought, as her daughter proceeded to talk of her meeting with a stranger who had not even told her his name.

"You met father and went with him immediately, perhaps this man is my destiny as Jesus was yours."

Sharon was arguing against Magdalen's caution about getting to know at least a man's identity before you declare your love for him.

"You would do well to put your attention on your position as Queen of the May, my dear. When I crown you I would like to have your full attention."

Magdalen laughed at her daughter's enthusiasm for destiny and attempted to draw Sharon's attention back to the high holyday. The villagers had selected Sharon to be their May Queen and Magdalen, being the spiritual leader, would crown her after a long procession from the Blood Well up the Tor. There Sharon would lead the hymns of praise as the sun rose with the dawn. With some coaxing from Magdalen the two were soon dressed for the occasion and proceeded toward Blood Well.

"It is Beltaine, and the visitors can participate at the well. I am going to invite him." Sharon was adamant and decisive.

"Be sure you get his name then."

Magdalen laughed again as Sharon ran toward the stables where, she assumed, she would find the travelers tending to their horses and finding food and lodging.

The stable came with the traders. Celts seldom stabled horses this way, but merchants required inns and stables if they were to trade with the village. This establishment served both horses and riders. There was always something ready to eat for both, and a place to wash and refresh yourself after a long journey.

Sharon's hunch proved right. The seven horsemen were sitting about one of the long wooden buffets wolfing down large bowls of porridge and drinking mead. She walked up to the handsome stranger and made her invitation. With a slight curtsy she backed away and then turned and ran to catch up with Magdalen.

"Mother, he will be here at sunset, at the well I mean."

Once more Sharon was breathless both with excitement and from running.

"And his name is Levi. That's a Jewish name, isn't it? But he doesn't look Jewish at all. He is fair and so handsome."

Magdalen took a motherly tone, "Look at you! Fix your hair now and your cloak. You are the May Queen, after all."

Magdalen didn't often worry about appearances and Sharon was rather surprised by her mother's tone and attitude.

"What's the matter, Mother? Why are you so skeptical?" Sharon knew that this new Magdalen must be the result of her love announcement.

"I love my daughter and I want only your happiness, but these men could be here to seek us out or to persecute those who follow the New Way. We must be careful about strangers and the reasons for their arrival."

The Roman persecutions laid heavily on Magdalen's mind these days and her otherwise confident and secure demeanor left her with each new arrival and each rumor of martyrdom.

"His eyes tell me, Mother, that he is honorable, compassionate and loving. Just as you said my father's eyes told you."

Sharon was very sure of her faith in Levi's good nature. Magdalen only nodded with concern and then took her place at the well. Villagers came and went from the well all day each bathing in the waters and drinking from their hands. Some threw coins into the well for good luck and fortune. Magdalen sat with Sharon beside her as the village's spiritual leader and sometimes acted as an oracle for those seeking prophecies of the new season.

At sundown the villagers went quickly back to their homes to put out the hearth fires and then assembled at the central bonfire the men had erected for the occasion of Beltaine. Magdalen and Sharon remained at the well; it would be up to them to lead the procession to the Tor but not before they had prayed and meditated on the sun's return and the rebirth promised to all.

Before they could begin their meditation, Levi arrived. He dismounted and allowed himself to be introduced to Magdalen who could now see for herself what Sharon had described. His eyes and his stature captivated her too. Politely, Magdalen honored the visitor's presence and invited him to participate in the village celebration.

"There is deep tradition here, Levi." Magdalen began to explain procedures. "A visitor is allowed to come to the holy waters and experience their power on Beltaine. In complete silence we walk around the well three times. Then a coin is thrown into the water and while thinking of our wishes and prayers for the new season we drink from the well using our hands as our only cups. When you have done that then you are to tie a bit of your clothing in one of the trees, this is to be sure that your energy remains here in a place of reverence for the entire season. We must all be out of sight of the well before sunrise. You can follow us in procession if you like to the Tor where I will crown Sharon May Queen and she will sing praise to the sun as it rises."

Levi looked a bit confused by this ritual practice, but, wanting to please Sharon, he dutifully made three passes around the well in reverence and silence. Taking a silver coin from his purse he threw it into the water and bent to drink with his hands. Then he walked over to a nearby Oak and removing his neckerchief, tied it on one of the branches. Returning to Magdalen he waited for her to speak first.

"You can talk now." She assured him that silence could now be broken. "I will contemplate your questions if you desire, and act as an oracle to give you answers from the world of sacred spirits." Magdalen offered her services.

"Will your daughter marry me?" Levi asked the question without embarrassment or levity.

"I will!" Sharon didn't give her mother a chance to respond.

"One doesn't need an oracle to see the future for your love." Magdalen knew that this was going to be the way that Sharon would have it no matter what.

"With your blessing, I hope."

Levi's entreaty went to Magdalen's heart. He might not be Celtic, but he knew the need for honor and she approved and blessed the couple by holding out her arms to Sharon who returned her embrace with glee.

People were arriving now for the procession to the Tor. In the distance you could see the bonfire burning but there were no torches or hearth fires lit. When everyone was assembled Magdalen led the way through the labyrinth to the top of the Tor. She crowned her daughter with a crown of willow branches and fern still curled within itself.

As Magdalen stepped back Sharon stood alone and sang loudly and clearly a song to the rising sun. Sharon was again true to her poetic nature. The words were wise and beautiful; she had become a bard of high quality.

> "The wonders of the Universe are surpassed only by the miracle of light that enables us to see them. The glory of the heavens is mere ceiling for the profound manifestation of the earth life below.
> The Robin's trill echoes the voice of Divinity as the sun rises and we are aware of the Light present in all."

She repeated her psalm three times and then turned toward the people behind her who broke into Celtic songs of praise to the Light. When they had finished the procession went back down the Tor and to the central fires. Here Sharon distributed light among the people who then went home to light the hearth and make merry.

The solemnity of the feast and the winter vanished together and couples jumped over the fire forcing their cattle to do the same. This was said to protect them from evil, but Magdalen and the Culdees had decided that what it really did was prove that fears, any fears, could be conquered and jumping over the fire was an exercise in faith.

Sharon took Levi's hand and nudged him toward the bonfire. Together they jumped into what Magdalen knew would be a new and blessed future. The couple danced announcing their betrothal to anyone and everyone who would listen. Sharon's friends whispered about her stranger and giggled about the look in the couple's eyes. Magdalen was eager to know more about Levi and so was anxious for the celebrations to end.

As she and Sharon left the party to return home, Magdalen invited Levi to dine with them the next day. This would give her an opportunity to find out more than the man's name, she hoped.

Sharon's education in hospitality and home economics hadn't been neglected. The next day she prepared a wonderful meal of venison and vegetables and baked both sweet breads and dry to soak up the gravy. She set a fine table covered with a linen cloth and decorated with the young green shoots that she could find in the still cold forest. Magdalen made a pie from berries dried the year before and brought out both mead and wine to wash it all down.

Table conversation was truly an interrogation of poor Levi. Where was he from? What work did he do? Why was he here in Avalon? Who were his parents? Magdalen went on hardly waiting for the answers before asking another question.

As it turned out, Levi was from the Roman County of Holland in Western Germania near Belgia. He and his men were on a mission of sorts. His parents had sent them to Britannia in search of Joseph of Arimathea who was supposed to hold the Holy Grail from which a great Rabbi had served up his blood. They were following a Way that this Rabbi had taught, and wanted to preserve and protect this relic for eternity. When and if the men discovered Joseph or the cup they were to return to Holland with it and it would be put in a safe place of honor.

Levi himself was not yet a follower of the Way, but was very interested in it. He was particularly interested in why it frightened the Romans enough to murder its followers. He said that his parents were wealthy merchants who had found the Way while in Rome and actually beheld the beheadings and some of the miraculous ways in which the martyrs had escaped death from the lion's jaws in the coliseum.

Sharon could hardly keep from laughing, but the look on Magdalen's face told her that she had better wait for her mother's reply to all this information. Magdalen was dumb with shock. How could this be, she wondered. Surely, the followers back home didn't believe that Joseph was here or that he had the cup. But maybe they did believe it. Rumors abounded throughout the empire regarding Jesus and his disciples.

Regardless of what the truth was or was not concerning Joseph, Magdalen could see that Levi was brought to Sharon through Spirit and this was the arrival of Destiny. She was ready to share the Truth and the New Way with her future son-in-law.

"Joseph is not here, Levi. I have the cup from which Jesus served." Magdalen said it and then fell silent.

"Mother is the Holy Grail and I am the blood of his line that was held within her when Jesus left for the world of Spirit."

Sharon felt safe now in revealing everything to Levi. Her mother had taken out all the stops and she babbled on about her father and the New Way of the Culdees. Levi asked to see the cup and Magdalen obliged.

"It seems such a simple cup to have held such precious blood."

Levi commented as he held the grail. Then Sharon proceeded to explain the Rite of Remembrance and Magdalen offered up the bread and wine as she had done so many times.

After Levi had received his first communion at Magdalen's hand the three planned a wedding for the next month and with long embraces of love and trust the evening ended.

Chapter 35

The Wedding

It was time now for Sharon to make a decision. Would she choose the initiatory Rite of Defloration at Blood Well or would she instead wait for her wedding night and Levi's love to move her from maiden to womanhood? The New Way did not demand a sacred rite but encouraged maidens to make a decision based on their personal spiritual beliefs. Many of them would meditate or vision quest before making the decision, thus allowing the Goddess to reveal her choice for them.

The word virgin came from vir the Latin for man and gyne the Greek word for woman. When put together this way the words meant a man-woman or androgyny, a complete person. A virgin symbolized the whole potential of the total original human being. The true virgin was believed to be unique, and recognized by her behavior, her voice, her walk, her looks, and the shape of her breasts, her urine, her smell and various other characteristics. Whether through sacred rite or through the lovemaking of marriage, Sharon would never loose her virginity; she was born and remained a whole person. Sharon realized all this, however her defloration would be the end of maidenhood and the beginning of womanhood; the transition from 'maiden flower to fruit-mother.'

Some believed that at the moment of defloration a powerful impulse of psychic energy was released. A maiden represented an untapped source of sacred energy, and the spark that flashed forth at the moment of defloration could be used to empower magical enchantments. For this reason Magdalen had encouraged her daughter to consider ritual defloration and offered to assist her if that was her decision.

She recalled for Sharon her own defloration at the hands of her sisters within the temple of Magdala, and assured her that this Blood Mystery was both sacred and painless. Magdalen suggested that Sharon opt to seek answers from spirit before she made her choice.

At her mother's coaxing, Sharon went off to the woods to meditate, pray and fast. Levi couldn't quite understand the secrecy and solemnity with which this was all being considered. He was of the belief that man and woman uniting sexually for the first time was sacred rite enough, and for the most part Sharon had agreed. There was, however, the element of the psychic energy that should not be used frivolously or without forethought. Before she went on her quest she had told Levi that she would let her future unfold in a dream.

In Sharon's absence, Magdalen sent word to James of the couple's intention requesting that he return for the wedding and stand in the place of her father to give away the bride. She began to sew and embroider Sharon's wedding dress. This was a talent that she had used all too seldom recently, she thought. But her hand and her needle were as adept as they had always been and the gown would be fit for the Goddess that her daughter would always be.

After three days, the traditional period of questing, Sharon arrived home to the open arms of both Magdalen and her fiancé. They gave her little time to refresh herself before asking about her adventure.

"Well, what will it be? " Levi asked with consternation. "Another woman? Or me?"

"Please, Levi," Sharon pleaded with him. "Let me tell you the dream and the revelations I have had. Be patient and respectful of my place, I beg you."

"I'm sorry, Sharon, I feel jealous of this rite and unsure that it serves any sacred purpose." Levi's tone changed to one of contrition.

"Your feelings are not warranted, but they are valid and common to most men, Levi." Magdalen intervened. "Sharon's dreams are of value, with this I know that you agree. And I know too that your honor and love for her will not allow you to interfere with her decision."

Wise woman as she was Magdalen was once more using the Celtic techniques of conversation.

"When she has finished you will give us your opinion please, as a fair exchange of ideas."

Levi nodded and Sharon wiped away a tear from her eye. Then she began her story in a soft voice.

"While I was in the deepest part of the forest," she said. "A large and beautiful Unicorn came and laid his head upon my lap. I stroked his horn and he laid there quite contently all notion of battle or rage having been removed from his spirit by my gentle touch."

"Then a warrior rode up, a big man in full armor. He held a spear in his hand and was ready to do away with the Unicorn who was so vulnerable now."

Sharon gave a sort of shiver as if the event had frightened her.

"I held up both my hands, as if to stop the fierce attack. The horseman put down his spear and waited to see what I would do. I think he was perplexed by my refusal to allow the kill. Then he told me that he only wanted the Unicorn's horn so that he could complete a magical cure for his beloved who was direly ill. I held the Unicorn's organ in my hand for a moment and smiled at it waiting for approval. Finally the animal whinnied, like a horse would do, and I knew the time was right. I lifted the horn from his head and handed it to the horseman who threw down to me a golden coin."

Sharon looked into Levi's eyes wondering what he was thinking of her dream and its significance. Levi gazed back at her lovingly.

"Go on, my darling, finish your story, please."

He wanted to be as respectful as Magdalen who was completely silent and waiting for her daughter's interpretation and decision.

"The coin," Sharon was about to finisher her story. "Bounced off of my belly and flew into the sky becoming a beautiful white dove. The Unicorn raised his defrocked head and looked at himself in the pond where we were. Then he sprouted wings, like the bird, and flew to the stars. Then I heard my father's voice say, 'Sacred energy is released through Love, but ritual and rite empower it. Together heal all things.'

"I knew what it meant, Levi." Sharon looked intently at her husband to be. "The Unicorn was content in my lap as love is content in one's heart. Its horn was the symbol of defloration and the power of rebirth or healing. You, Levi, are the fierce one filled with fear that you will not get what you want but you are disarmed by my presence long enough to see that I can hand over the power to you willingly for Love's sake and in so doing transform sexuality into sensuality soaring to spirit. The coin is your willingness to give in lovemaking and marriage, and those traits transform a union into the sacred and holy marriage like in the Song of Songs in Jewish scripture. We must do this together Levi, just you and I, as a sacred act and the power will be released as it should be."

Sharon looked to her mother and Levi for understanding. Levi gave a sigh of relief and Magdalen smiled.

"So mote it be."

Plans for the wedding continued. Magdalen sewed relentlessly on Sharon's gown. Each of her many exacting stitches represented to her another moment in her daughter's long and abundant future. This was her way of making this a sacred dress. When Sharon donned the wonderful cloak and gown she would be donning a new stage in her life and her mother meant it to be as safe, secure and comforting as her clothes would be.

A messenger was sent to invite all of Magdalen and Sharon's friends. This included Ruth, Cybele, Sarah and Carmel as well as Sharon's lifelong friend Regino. The group would stand as witnesses to Sharon's wedding and make a fine bridal party. Even though they had all scattered throughout the isles, they remained close in spirit and this would be a great opportunity for a reunion and sharing. They sent word to Baera too, of course, and to the Lady of the Lake. Levi sent two of his men back to Holland County to inform his parents and family. Although he didn't think that they could make the journey, he wanted them to be with him in spirit on this special day.

Uncle James arrived days before the wedding bearing gifts fit for his Queen niece. He was proud of his "little one" and honored to serve in her father's stead at the altar of marriage.

Magdalen was honored too, to be officiating at her daughter's wedding. She would tie the decorative Celtic knot that would bind them forever. Sharon and Levi had elected a forever contract between them. Some couples opted for a trial marriage that would have to be renewed in a year and a day, but the loving couple was sure that a marriage so divinely guided would last for all of their lifetimes.

The mother of the bride was pleased that they had chosen this commitment to their love. She was equally pleased that her daughter's wedding would be a public and formal rite of marriage and not simply an elopement into sexual union. While union's like her own with Jesus were accepted, they were never really as revered by the community as one that was publicly and with reverence witnessed by family, friends and neighbors. Sharon would be a wife of joint authority as Magdalen had been. She and Levi would be considered of equal rank and status within their union and they would contribute evenly to its success financially and emotionally.

Summer Solstice arrived and with it her wedding day. Sharon was in seclusion with her mother and the female members of the bridal party until just before dusk. Then the women made their way to the Blood Well where Levi, James and the others were waiting. Levi looked upon his bride with pride and wonderment as she approached her betrothed.

Her gown was exquisite. Magdalen had put every stitch in just the right place. Its white folds cascaded to the ground and the knots and decorative designs told the story of her heritage. Over the gown she wore a cloak of royal blue. Beneath a crown of flowers her veil, soft and light like the very mists of Avalon, flowed over her shoulders down to her unshod feet. Both ankles were adorned with bracelets of gold. She held a bouquet of summer flowers in front of her like an offering to the Goddess.

As harps and flutes played softly in the background, Magdalen led the group in prayers for fertility, womanhood and for the bride as wife and mother. The psalms were like poetry and the music like an audible aura of love.

When the prayers here were ended both bride and groom were given water to drink from Blood Well before moving on to the standing stone. This station of prayer honored the groom. The stone itself was a phallic symbol for fertility, manhood, husbands and fathers. This was a place of male power and the group prayed for his future success as a husband and father.

With Magdalen leading the way the entire party moved in procession to the altar that had been erected in the community circle. Here three circles were formed one within another. Magdalen, Sharon and Levi formed the interior circle around the altar. The invited guests formed a wreath around them and then Sharon's friends scattered flowers in a circle behind them. The last circle was representative of those that attended the ceremony in spirit only, like Grandmother Mary and Jesus himself.

Here the couple pledged their love and commitment and asked for the blessings of the Mother and the Divine Father. Some of Magdalen's precious and delightfully colored ribbons had been braided to form a soft and lovely cord with which she tied Sharon's right hand to Levi's pronouncing them husband and wife, lifelong partners on their future journeys. She then lifted Sharon's veil to symbolize that she needed no further protection from evil; Levi would be her lifelong protector now.

Just beyond the altar was the sundial and when the formal ceremony was over Levi untied the cord, allowing Sharon her freedom to move to the carved stone timepiece. She passed the cord through the hole in its center and made a wish for the future, and then Levi did the same. Family and friends each took their turn passing the lively bond through the hole and making wishes and prayers for the newly married couple. Then everyone joined hands and danced in a circle around the sundial, just as the sun moves around the earth, this was to bring everyone into harmony with the cosmic rhythms of life. The party could now begin and the music became loud and lively.

The long buffet tables had been set with cloths and flowers. Then piled with food. The men and children ate, the women served continuously. From early evening, the onset of the day, until late into the night they ate venison, wild boar and mutton washing it down with gallons of ale and mead. Sharon and her bridesmaids went off to whisper about women things and Magdalen listened to the girls as they joked and teased. Levi enjoyed the festivities thoroughly but being careful not to over consume the honey mead that he had come to like so well. At one point a man dressed like a bull appeared doing a suggestive dance in front of the groom and Levi laughed heartily when the man offered him a cup of milk spiked with Bull's Blood, a rich red herb that was supposed to enhance sexual performance. He drained the cup in merriment and expectation.

That being done, the best man, one of Levi's favorites from Holland County, sent word that it was time for Sharon to make her appearance. The bride danced into the community circle and Levi literally swept her off her feet and into his arms. Laughing and singing the group followed the newlyweds to their waiting hut where Sharon was carried over the threshold as the party pelted them with wedding cake and rice.

The couple closed the door, but the others did not leave. They remained outside making noise and singing loudly so that the sounds of lovemaking could not be heard from within. At dawn, Levi threw Sharon's waste girdle out the door and they knew that a marriage had begun.

Chapter 36

Church in the Round

As the nights grew colder, fewer and fewer people came to the central fire for Magdalen's sharing each night. Despite the fervor of the Celts for a good story, the weather was getting far too inclement to sit outside when warm wattle homes were waiting. Magdalen decided that she must find a way to move her "church" indoors. In winters past the group had been small enough to move into someone's home or one of the animal shelters. Magdalen feared that if she moved to one of these buildings now she would have to turn people away and they would be discouraged from coming back. What she needed, she thought, was a special building, a temple large enough to house her entire congregation of followers with room to spare.

Magdalen was a dreamer. She could envision just what the temple would look like, not at all like a Roman or Greek place of worship or like those erected by the Jewish community. She would have a house of worship, not a house of Gods. Wattle would have seemed the building material of choice. Her own home was constructed from this mixture of mud and straw. But Magdalen wanted something more substantial, something befitting a strong faith. It would have to be wood, she concluded. However then would she be able to keep the building round and circular as it appeared in her mind's eye? She decided to take the question to her new son-in-law. When Levi heard Magdalen's vision he was completely intrigued.

"My grandfather makes furniture from wood that has been steamed to hold its curves." He told Magdalen. "It might be possible to heat the wood while it is green and bend it to a curve, with one log meeting another".

Taking stylus in hand he drew on a child's palette a perfect circle. Within the circle he placed a square.

"We would have to soak the logs in the river first. Then build fires both inside and outside the square of wooden walls. Each day we bend the walls a bit further until the straight wood becomes curved enough to create the round."

Magdalen was impressed and even though Levi himself was somewhat doubtful of the outcome she now had a plan.

"I'll take this to the Lady of the Lake and talk to her."

Magdalen was off and running to the Tor. Levi looked after her with amazement. There was more energy in this now aging woman than he had realized. When the Lady of the Lake pointed out a grassy knoll and told Magdalen that her church could go there, the project was off to what Magdalen and Levi thought was a very good start. Along with the land the Lady also gave the pair hands and materials, as they needed them. The entire village seemed to want to be involved and to contribute wherever and whatever they could.

First Levi traced the pattern of the church on the ground with a stick. Trees were felled and cut lengthwise to make two boards from each log. The boards were fastened end to end with iron spikes until the square within the circle pattern fit perfectly. Then the fires were lit, inside and outside the frame. Villagers, men, women and children kept the logs wet by pouring water on them. The steam rose and the wood gave way to the heave ho of the men's strength a little at a time. They would drive wooden stakes into the ground on both sides of the board to hold them in their new curved position. When one row of the frame was complete another was begun.

It became harder with the second row. The wood had to be held up on stilts so that it could be bent to fit perfectly atop the row beneath it. The third row, Levi decided, would be practically impossible. He contrived an idea. With the first circle complete and fastened to the ground with spikes, he used it for a pattern for each following row. When the next ring was completed the men set it aside and created another. When enough rings were finished the men of the village raised the church with pulleys and levers. They chinked the crevices between the boards with wattle to keep out the wind and cold.

The work went on throughout the winter. By Beltaine a hollow tube of a church had been erected. At Magdalen's direction a thatched and braided roof was then raised. She wanted a roof that would rise to the heaven's, she said, and the villagers obliged her. The A frame roof resembling praying hands came clear to the ground and was thatched and braided to resemble a piece of sculpture like damask fabric or embossing on fine parchment. The thatching and braids had symbolic meaning and were not merely design but meant to tell a story of the good news of our human nature as seen by the Creator.

The women braided and knotted the grass so that it revealed the truths in which the Culdees believed. There was a three-looped trinity knot that represented the three-fold nature of humanity: body, mind and spirit. There was a six-pointed star with a sword which represented the coming together of the three fold nature of man and the three fold nature of the earth: sea, sky and land. The sword was the blade of unification forged strong in the fires of fear and separation. There was a four armed cross, each arm looking much like the letter L which represented the presence of Luck, Light, Life and Love imposed upon one's life by the Divine. There was a hammer and cycle arranged in an X fashion upon the cross, which symbolized the presence of building and harvesting life's richness. And an X shaped cross upon the Latin cross which was a sign that we are, even in our present place, radiating our light to the universe in more than four simple directions.

Magdalen's round church with it's A shaped roof was a wonder to be sure. Where the fire pit in its center once burned to heat the steaming wood, there was now a fountain of the purest water. The fires that burned continuously outside the circular walls were now mere lights for the pilgrims who came here every night to hear the word.

Each night these Celtic Christians arrived for a period of worship, celebration and learning. Magdalen wore robes of deep purple now, symbols of her age and wisdom, but she couldn't give up her ribbons and scarves of bright red. These were, she thought, symbols too, signs of the youthful life within her heart. Her menopause and croning approached, but she remained filled with zeal. She began each service by addressing the group with assignments and announcements for the next day, and then set aside the earthly concerns of the community in favor of more spiritual endeavors.

On the first night she had made an address of thanksgiving and celebration, now each night the program began with a reading from her own works, her gospel. A dissertation followed, an explanation of the reading and always, always an example from the life of Jesus, the Rabbi who shared not only his love but also his life and learning so intimately with her. Women and children sat on the floor surrounding her, men were reclined on the couches, like that of Jesus, made of stone and ornately carved with designs similar to those on the roof that created shelter and shade for their place of worship and learning.

After a long homily, Magdalen would open the floor not only to questions but also to rebuttal and a kind of Tibetan exchange of argument and apology concerning the principles she had taught. This could and did go on for hours. Once both her opposition and her support had agreed that Magdalen's postulate was the most plausible, they all moved, one at a time, to set ablaze the fire prepared earlier to warm the night, light the church and cook the evening meal. First though there must be the sacrifice, not the bloody ones of the Jewish tradition that so angered and upset both Magdalen and Mother Mary, but a bloodless surrender through a pledge of allegiance to community and Creator and the symbolic offering of a personal gift to be contributed to the fire. Some brought wood from a tree that for them carried a great spirit, some offered the bones of a woodland kill that has served as their food the day before, still others put corn or meal, seeds or bits of hand woven wool into the fire as a piece of their life was offered for the benefit of the community's evening celebration.

Now the women prepared the communion meal. There was pan bread without leaven, wine that had been diluted with water from the central fountain, and meat roasted earlier in the day over an outdoor spit and fire.

When the meal was ready, they served Magdalen. She accepted the single piece of pan bread and a cup of wine. Breaking it off and passing it around the room, she repeated the affirmation of her beloved.

"Take and eat, for this is the body."

Drinking from the cup, she again made the affirmation.

"Take this and drink, for this is the blood."

It too was passed about the room and maidens were ready to refill it each time that it was drained. When all had shared their repast, Magdalen loudly and without hesitation once again affirmed.

"This is your salvation, that you are body and blood, that you are what you have consumed, choose wisely the nourishment of your spirit and the sustenance of your body, for these affect your mind."

Everyone proclaimed in loud voices their agreement with this principle and rose to the occasion of celebration. Music became the entertainment of the evening as the feast continued with meat, bread and wine and a few vegetables. Rattles, drums, flutes and harps made a noise that was joyful unto the Lord. Singing would break out as bellies were filled and children played games among themselves until they were carried off to their homes and a bed of dreams.

Now without light for her writing, Magdalen would retire to her own bed and her private dreams of what the future might hold. Life was growing shorter and home was a long way off. She often thought of returning to Jerusalem, but dreamed of how it used to be and the fear and guilt that yet lived in her homeland. To dream too soon of going home would be to expect too much from Sharon and her new husband. They must be ready to keep the fires warm each night, and to keep the light bright on the truth that these people sought before she could leave them. Nothing should be allowed to deter the continuance of Jesus' work; this was Sharon's heritage, her birthright, and her dharmic task. Magdalen would not take this opportunity away from her by moving too quickly to her own dreams of recluse and returning home.

Perhaps, she thought, tonight's dream will be tomorrow's written word. As her eyes closed to the present her mind opened to remember the Master and a love that had never faded.

Greek letters moved right to left across the page as Magdalen scratched out her story on the rolls of parchment made from birch bark. She knew that back in Jerusalem they were still speaking of her release from the seven demons from hell. Oh, should they know the truth! That the demons of fear within her were seven times seven and that love, faith and hope are what freed her from the terrible curse of despair. Jesus had shown her that love, given her that faith and hope required for salvation from the ravages of guilt, regret and the paralyzing fear that comes from past abuse.

There was no supernatural demon within her, but only the demons that all must slay. They were demons of people's own making, helped of course by the religious zealots who preached unceasingly in temple and synagogue the need for sacrifice. The sacrifices they suggested were the bloody, senseless killings of many of God's treasured creatures. The sacrifice that Jesus asked of Magdalen and of everyone else was simply the surrender of fear in favor of faith. She wondered if those that would one day read these scratchings on parchment would ever truly understand that earthly life was the salvation they sought.

Jesus had shared more than love and lust with Magdalen. He had shared his mind and spirit, his deep understanding and wisdom were gifts that he had meant for her to share. Share them she would, she thought, before her own life was over.

Some already thought that Magdalen had died, possibly in childbirth. Others thought that perhaps she had gone into a self-imposed exile to ponder on the teachings and to repent of her sins. Sins, she queried her mind, were they the acts of outrageous girlish behavior once thought to be prostitution and the weakness of the flesh? Or were sins really the emotional reactions of guilt, fear, blame and regret that had made her sorrowful for so long and caused others so much pain? Jesus had found no breaking of law, Judaic or Roman, to hold a person to punishment by God. The Father, he had said, was all forgiving, wise and without any need for human sacrifice or repentance. Pleasing the Father could be assured if your conscience left you without these negative responses to life and its experiences. The Father promised all of his children peace and happiness. All people needed to be assured of these gifts and to accept them from the Father's own hand.

Thoughts like these continued to run rampant through her mind as Magdalen continued with her gospel script.

"In the beginning was the Spirit, and the Spirit was like a thought of God, and God was what the Spirit was. It was with God in the beginning. All things happened through it, and not one thing that has happened, happened without it. Within it there was Life, and the Life was the light of the world. And in the darkness the light is shining, and the darkness never got hold of it."

"There was a person sent from God, and he had the name John. He came as a witness to testify about the light, so that all would have faith through him. He wasn't the light himself, he was to testify about the light.

"The light was the true light that comes into the world and shines for every human being. He was in the world, and the world was created through him, and the world didn't know him. He came to his own kind, and his own kind wouldn't accept him. But to those who did accept him he gave the right to become children of God if they had faith in the nature of Spirit, they who were born not of blood, nor the flesh's will, nor a man's will, but of the Divine.

"And the Spirit turned flesh and lodged among us, and we witnessed his glory, the kind of glory a father gives his only son, full of grace and truth. John testified about him . . ."

Magdalen set down her stylus and began to think about John and his teaching and the baptism he offered to symbolize a rebirth, a change of heart.

Many would believe and have a change of heart. They would wash themselves clean with a shower of their own tears of relief, joy and gratitude for the Father's goodness. Others would find freedom reason to fill their conscience with yet more guilt and blame. Still others would read these words and find within them sacrilegious and heretical theology against both the Judaic and Roman religious hierarchy.

The governors of both had beheaded John the Baptist and crucified Jesus, now they would fear strongly the effects his words might have on their control of the people. They would seek to bring death to Sharon if possible. This was Magdalen's greatest fear, that her daughter would pay the price of pain and death for her father's greatness. Perhaps it was Sharon and not Magdalen who should retire to recluse and build a life of contemplation rather than oration.

Each day long hours of writing would continue into the evening and those words would be shared at that night's gathering. Sleep came with the darkness and with daylight came more work. Soon the stories would be written, but there was yet this question that plagued Magdalen's mind, should she truly pass to Sharon bishopric of this new and fragile faith?

Magdalen's obligations to the Master outweighed the worry of her motherhood. Sharon would be trained if that was her choice, and she would follow in her father's footsteps but with the gentle and quiet approach of the Goddess. Sharon quiet? The notion made Magdalen laugh with pride!

It was time for bed she decided, only to be awakened with great exhilaration by her daughter before the dawn. Sharon shook her mother into attentiveness.

"I am with child," she shouted. Joyously she bounced on Magdalen's couch and belly. "I am with child!"

Magdalen so wanted to be happy, she held her daughter close and shed tears of joy and of concern. Now there was a larger family to be considered and safety would have to become even more of a worry. A decision had been made by fate; now she could not leave her daughter and return to Jerusalem or Rome.

Chapter 37

Holland County

Levi was extremely excited to learn that he would soon be a father. His blue eyes filled with tears when Sharon told him and he gave thanks to the Divine for blessing him so fully in so short a time. Then he immediately began to think of home and of his parents. He hadn't seen them for months and he so wanted to share this good news with them. He proposed a visit to Holland County to Sharon, saying that the sooner they would leave the better for her health and the child's.

Sharon was doubtful that she could leave Avalon and especially her mother at such an important time. She was not afraid of the journey or of childbirth, but she wanted to share the pregnancy and delivery with Magdalen according to the Blood Mysteries. She had envisioned herself giving birth at Blood Well with her mother acting as midwife. Still, she could fully understand her husband's desire to go home, at least for a little while. It would be exciting, she thought, to see where Levi grew up and what his parents, family and friends in Holland County were really like.

As they discussed it, Levi suggested that Sharon invite Magdalen to accompany them to Holland County and be with them for the birth of her grandchild. Sharon thought this a wonderful idea and went immediately to her mother's home to make the invitation. Magdalen was hesitant at first.

"Sharon, do you really think that this journey would be safe for you and your child? These people who sent Levi here for the grail may be well intended, but what of those that persecute them? Any whisper of Jesus or of the grail or of me for that matter will raise suspicion and you may be endangering us all, including Levi's parents and family."

Magdalen had a mother's concern in her voice. Sharon's eyes were wet with emotion. She wanted to please both her mother and her husband and above all to keep her baby safe from any harm.

"We will travel as you did, Mother, keeping our lips sealed and our behavior unobtrusive. You brought me here to safety by the grace of the Divine One and with the blessings of the Divine Mother we can bring this child to safety too."

Magdalen could hear the pleading in her daughter's voice and her heart melted.

"We will go then as Levi said as soon as possible. The sooner we arrive in Holland County the better for the health of my daughter and my grandchild."

Sharon's eyes lit up with delight and their watery pools turned to dewy expressions of joy.

It took several days for Levi to make all the arrangements necessary. Sharon and Magdalen would ride Mystic and Magic. He and his men would be mounted on the same horses that they had arrived with, but there was still the matter of a cart to put their supplies in. When he had come to Avalon he did not have need of such things. The men had lived on what they could find and carried any personal needs in their own purses. Now he had a wife, mother-in-law and an unborn child to provide for. His thoughts of home and family were clouded a little by the anxiety he had over Sharon's safety and a journey that might take her into peril.

When he had completed all of his preparations, Levi announced that they would leave the next day. Magdalen and Sharon went to the Tor to find the Lady of the Lake to express their gratitude and to say their goodbyes.

"Will you be back, ladies, after the child is born?"

The Lady of the Lake knew that she and her community would miss both of them and too the stories and services that Magdalen had always shared.

"Avalon will always be home." Magdalen assured her. "One day you will see the child and celebrate his richness with us, for you are indeed a Goddess Mother to him."

"How do you know that the child is a boy?"

Sharon looked at Magdalen who had a slip of the tongue when she said him.

"Is that a prophecy?" the young woman was looking for confirmation of her suspicions.

"It will be a boy," Magdalen said, "one whose destiny it will be to instill pride in the hearts of those who have followed and will follow the Way."

Sharon put her hands to her belly and whispered to her son.

"You have a Divine Destiny and Love will be the finest sword you will ever know."

The Lady of the Lake blessed them all and their journey, she called for their safety and return as well as the child's success. Then mother and daughter returned to a waiting and packing Levi.

In the morning Magdalen put her leather pouch in the cart that Levi had provided. She had thought that it would be best to take her ritual belongings with her on this journey. Levi's parents had waited a long time to see the grail and Magdalen wanted very much to please them.

As Sharon mounted her horse, Levi warned her to ride sidesaddle. He didn't want anything to disturb his unborn child.

"Our son is as safe in my womb as within the belly of the earth, women are made just right and babies know exactly how to ride within us."

Sharon laughed at Levi's concern and Magdalen smiled a knowing smile at the young couple and their jest.

It was a short journey from Avalon to the Straights of Dover, only four days ride. There they were ferried across to the mainland. Levi found a room for them that night and in the morning they went by Roman roads to his home at Cassel. Stopping, as Levi insisted they must do for Sharon's sake, this journey took another four days. It was not a complicated journey, nothing to compare to Magdalen's adventures while she was with child. Still, she appreciated Levi's need to protect them.

Arriving in Cassel at nightfall, Levi ushered the group right to his father's house. His mother ran from the doorway with open arms to greet them.

"Blessed be God, my son is safe!" She was filled with obvious joy at Levi's return home.

"My new daughter, how beautiful you are!" She wrapped a warm and wonderful embrace about Sharon's neck.

"You are Magdalen, blessed be the womb that bore the daughter of the Master."

As the woman reached Magdalen she fell to her knees expecting to be blessed, but the Priestess covered her mouth with her finger as if to quiet the over zealous follower of the Way.

"Please, your words jeopardize us all." Magdalen warned.

The woman was embarrassed to have lost control of her tongue and quickly rose to her feet.

"My heart is so filled that my mind has been emptied." She apologized to Magdalen. "Please, come into the house, meet my husband and I will give you a meal of stew to warm you."

It was cold and the entire group was eager for something to eat and a warm bed in which to sleep.

"You are more than kind." Magdalen accepted the invitation for them all. "Let us share something with you then, after we eat."

The Priestess had not left her Celtic manners in Avalon and she felt that once everyone was within the safety of Levi's home she would have them look at the grail and perhaps tell a story and share the Rite of Remembrance.

After the hot stew had been consumed and the fire stoked to keep them warm, Levi was eager to oblige when Magdalen sent him for her leather pouch. Secretly he felt that he had now completed the mission on which his parents had originally sent him. He had returned with the cup that they so treasured, more importantly he had brought them the Grail, Magdalen herself, and the Blood, his beautiful and precious wife, now with child, an extension of the bloodline within her.

Levi's father had remained fairly quiet throughout the meal, now he was a fountain of rhetoric. He wanted to know all that he could about Magdalen's Way and the Way that Jesus had taught her. The Priestess and her daughter gave him his way. They talked for hours, telling many stories and sharing the wisdom of the Way in Avalon. When the night was drawing to a close, Elizabeth and Ezekial received their first communion at Magdalen's hand and vowed to live the Way as she was showing it to them. Levi was pleased to have been the one to unwrap the Holy Grail and place it in his mother's hands. She wept as she drained the cup and her husband's hands shook as he took it from her.

"This," he said, "is the cup from which the Master consumed the wine that celebrated our liberation from fear."

Magdalen filled the cup for him and he too drained it in tears.

In the days that followed, Magdalen was introduced to many of the followers of the Way who often worshiped with her hosts.

Soon the evenings in Holland County were very much the same as they had been in Avalon. A small group of friends and neighbors would gather in Levi's home and Magdalen would tell her stories and share the rite, giving each an opportunity to drink from the Holy Grail for which they had all been searching so diligently.

In exchange they told her stories of the martyrs for the Way, those who had died and those who had escaped death by the grace and protection of the Divine. Each time she heard one of these stories of beheadings, crucifixions or the Roman practices in the coliseum, Magdalen cried out.

"Blessed be the blood of the martyrs for it has nourished the earth with its richness and sacred energy!"

This too, she thought, was a blood rite, an example that humankind produced from within itself Divine Life through faith in Spirit.

The remaining six months of Sharon's pregnancy passed quickly for everyone. The Way was being shared and there was now a church of sorts in Holland County. It wasn't safe, Magdalen had decided, to build an edifice as she had in Avalon, but the church was really about those who participated and followed the Way, not about the building or the gathering place. Levi's parents had a large barn and as the nightly group grew the celebration of Jesus was moved to its bigger headquarters there.

Elizabeth and Ezekial were very proud to have been selected by the Divine and destiny itself to have the bloodline of Jesus carried on through them. They honored Sharon and her mother everyday with blessings and gifts. They had given Levi a piece of land and upon it helped him to erect a home for Sharon and himself during her pregnancy. Of course, they were anticipating that the couple would remain with them in Holland County. Levi knew that Sharon expected to return to Avalon after their son was born, but he was settling in quite well at home. His heart was here, and he was beginning to contemplate staying with his parents and the new church. Sharon liked it well enough, but never mentioned staying. Magdalen, realizing Levi's longing, brought up the subject of their return.

"Sharon, I see now that it is safe, quite safe for you and your son to be here in Holland. Your home is wonderful and you would make a fine Bishopess of Holland County. Perhaps, since Levi and his parents are so good for you and the Way, you will want to remain here with them after you give birth."

Sharon was very surprised at Magdalen's suggestion. She had never even thought of not returning to Avalon.

"I know that Levi is happy here among his friends and relatives. Our son would have great support with them, but in Avalon we have had our roots, you and I."

She was giving the idea some thought, Magdalen could see.

"I've thought that now that I am older and you are well off, I might return home to Jerusalem."

She brought up the idea of an eventual separation from her daughter very cautiously.

"They will not recognize me now, and I could return to the places that I shared with your father. Too, I would be able to help the apostles and those that are attempting to follow the Way amidst the chaos of Roman persecution."

Sharon was just about to object when she felt her child leap within her.

"Mother, it is time!"

The conversation came to an abrupt halt as Magdalen helped her daughter prepare for the child's arrival. She called to Levi and sent him to get his parents. Then she prayed with Sharon for a pain free delivery and a healthy child. The young woman drank the herb tea that her mother prepared and then immersed herself in the birthing tank that Magdalen had ready and waiting.

Just as they would have done at Blood Well, the women birthed Sharon's child beneath the water to ease his transition into the world of physical reality from the place of security within his mother's womb. Magdalen wrapped the baby in a piece of fine cloth that had been decorated by Elizabeth just for this occasion. She wiped the blood from his face and blessed him with water from Blood Well that Sharon had brought with her. Then she handed her new grandson to his mother.

"What will you call him?" she asked.

"That will be Levi's decision." Sharon looked into her husband's eyes as he took the baby from her.

"We will call him Christen, the son of the Anointed One." Levi said his son's name with deep reverence and looking at his wife he stated.

"You are the Anointed of Spirit and you have given birth to a large destiny for the world. Blessed be the womb within you."

He cradled Sharon and the child in his arms as he sat beside her.

Magdalen and the others left the couple with their new son and went out from the house to spread the news of his arrival. All those who had been following the Way with them had been eagerly waiting this day, and a grand celebration was planned.

"It is as wonderful as it would have been in Avalon, this celebration of motherhood and birthing."

Sharon was delighted at the gaiety and love with which friends and relatives prepared the ritual and its celebration. Levi held Christen high above his head as he displayed him to everyone in attendance.

Certainly, from the moment Sharon had announced her pregnancy, her womb had been honored as the Cauldron of Life. She could not make pilgrimages to the Tor, as she would have in Avalon; but she and Magdalen had been preparing spiritually together for this day. Levi had honored her in body, mind and spirit, wreathing her head with flowers and anointing her belly with oil every month at her mooning time. Her son had been born into new waters with his grandmother as his midwife.

Now she sat by the fire having introduced her son as Christen to the whole community and they were celebrating his birth according to the mysteries. She watched Levi parade the baby around the village for all to see. Men and women alike brought flowers, food and clothing to Sharon in honor of her labor. She was satisfied now that staying here with this new family would be good for them all.

Magdalen waited for Sharon's three days of rest to be accomplished, cooking and cleaning for Levi, bathing the child and keeping the house. This was her duty and pleasure as the maternal grandmother. For Magdalen it was an honor.

When the time had passed she began to share many of the healing modalities and ways of the oracle with Sharon, those mysteries that were reserved for revelation until after a woman had given birth. Together they studied the skies and the meanings of the stars and their positions. Magdalen coached Sharon in the ways of storytelling and the ability to prophecy at will.

After six months of these studies Magdalen announced that she was returning to Avalon. What she thought once was a home in Jerusalem now seemed distant from her mind and she was being drawn back to the Tor, the Lady of the Lake and her own round and wonderful church.

Sharon and Levi, although sad to see her depart, recognized Mother Magdalen's need to follow her heart's longing. Levi arranged for a three-man escort and all the supplies that they would need. Within the week, Magdalen was home again in Avalon. The very first night she began her evening services again. The Lady of the Lake embraced her warmly and Magdalen knew that she was home and home to stay.

Chapter 38

Return to Avalon

Magdalen and the Lady of the Lake sat over tea exchanging stories and news. Of course, the Lady wanted to know everything about Sharon and her new son. Magdalen was, indeed, the proud grandmother and went on for a long while about the boy's strength, beauty and quickness to learn. Then she realized that this was anything but a fair exchange.

"Lady, please tell me what has transpired while I was gone. I'm sure that you too have news to share and I do enjoy your tales. It was not my intention to monopolize the conversation, I am a bit overly proud, I think."

She ended her apology with a giggle.

"Have you heard of Paul, then?" The Lady looked inquisitively at Magdalen. "His name was Saul, but since he had an enlightenment, an epiphany he calls it, he is called Paul."

Magdalen shook her head no and the Lady went on.

"He is bringing the Way to the gentiles, he thinks only Jews have heard the Good News." The Lady laughed. "He is setting down rules different for Jews than for gentiles, and he is setting down lots of them. I think his "Good News" has become tainted by his need to control."

The Lady looked to Magdalen for approval of her last statement. It was, after all, a bit negative and judgmental.

"I haven't heard of this Paul and his ministry to the gentiles. But if he is putting words into my husband's mouth, then he is not teaching the Way."

"He is putting his own words to the Way. He accuses others, especially those in Crete and those who have been circumcised. He calls them liars, evil beasts and gluttons. He advises women to be obedient to their husbands, Magdalen, for to be disobedient to them is disobedience toward God. And he condones slavery in the same way."

The Lady seemed to have a need to get her concern off her chest, and Magdalen was listening intently. She didn't know what she could do about the blasphemy of this man, or even if it were true at all. The Isles were filled with vicious gossip about the Way and its followers. But she thought it her place to somehow dispel these attacks or express her dissatisfaction if they were indeed not false accusations but truth.

"Tonight, I will write this Paul a letter. I will send it by courier quickly to him in the hope that he will respond with the courier's return."

"I have other sad news, my dear Magdalen."

The Lady and her voice declared true sorrow.

"Some of Jesus' apostles have already been murdered at the hands of those that would stop the Way from spreading. Philip, the one testifying in Heirapole at Phryga was crucified. He left behind three daughters and a wife. They will mourn him long, I would think. And in Great Armenia, Bartholomew was murdered. By some it is said that he was flayed alive; by others, that he suffered crucifixion. Some say that he was beheaded after a severe beating. How cruel are the works of those that judge. And Thomas, who traveled all the way to Corehandal in the East Indies was run through with a lance."

Magdalen was openly weeping and the Lady held her to her breasts.

"I am sorry to bring such tidings, Magdalen. Oh, that I would not have been the one to tell you these sad tales."

She comforted Magdalen, stroking her hair and wiping away her tears.

"Thomas, doubting Thomas, strengthened our faith by his questioning." Magdalen sobbed as she remembered how Thomas had questioned Jesus' resurrection. "And Philip, yes he will be mourned. His wife and daughters were devoted to him and to the Way. They must not lose their faith because of this. I will also write to them this night."

As her tears subsided, Magdalen thought of Bartholomew.

"Bartholomew sent himself, not by the command of any other, to the most barbarous places of the earth to share the Way. He has come to a barbarous end, but he will be with Jesus now and will from that place look down at the savages with compassion."

Magdalen wiped away her remaining tears and forced a small and gentle smile.

"Lady, please share with me some good news."

The Lady of the Lake returned Magdalen's smile.

"We have had two rich harvests while you were gone. And the people have used your church each night and shared the Rite of Remembrance. I have been privileged to have the honor of filling your place during your absence. You would be proud to have seen the reverence and the good will among them, Magdalen. They shared both their thoughts and their faith. They satisfied one another's doubts and always with fair exchange and honor. The women have been following the mysteries and great prophecies have come through them. One said that the oracle shared with her the outcome of the Way that it would eventually be diluted in the waters of many ways but would never be truly lost. I can believe that fully."

"As do I."

Magdalen was firm in her faith that her Way would remain forever a Way rich in spirit and truth but would evolve as all things must.

The women continued their conversation until the evening service, after which Magdalen retired to candlelight and parchment. She was determined to write her query to Paul and to send her condolences to the family of Philip. Slowly she scripted the Greek letters:

"To Saul of Damascus, now Paul who has found the spirit within him.

From Magdalen, the Bride of Jesus and Keeper of the Way, High Priestess of a New Way.

I send greetings and the blessings of the Divine upon you and yours.

Let this letter be an inquiry to which you respond with haste. My courier will wait for your reply.

Let me first say that word has reached me of the martyrdom of the apostles Philip, Bartholomew and Thomas my heart goes out to them and those who mourn them. Let your prayers for consolation join my own. If you are unaware of these things, let me say that I am sorry to have been the bearer of such news, but I realize that your devotion would demand that you know.

Now to my questions. I have heard through rumor and gossip that the gentiles are being wrongfully accused and judged by you. That you have been purporting obedience of wives and slaves and that you have begun name-calling and accusing others of blasphemy without regard for their honor. Should this be true, you have tainted the Way of Jesus with the way of control and I, Magdalen the Bride of Jesus, beg you to stop so that your Spirit may be at peace with that of all. If this is not true, then I, Magdalen the Bride of Jesus, apologize for the question and offer you my true contrition. You can see, I am sure, that as the Keeper of the Way I must come to know what is true among us all."

Magdalen paused, she wasn't sure if it would be safe to expose her daughter and grandson, but she couldn't resist the urge to share some truly good news. She wrote again

"To share with you good news. Jesus' daughter has given birth to a son and his name is Christen, the son of the anointed one. I am his grandmother and share this news in a great cry for secrecy as he may be endangered by his heritage. Still, I offer you this in order that you may share our joy. Please reply quickly.

Mary of Magdala, Bride of Jesus and Keeper of the Way in Avalon"

With this letter out of the way, Magdalen turned to her second task. How could she possibly encourage a family who had lost a husband and father to the Way and its philosophy? Her tears stained the parchment as she wrote.

"To the widow and daughters of Philip, Apostle of Jesus and care-taker of a holy family, I send my condolences. I send also a blessing that you might know that your great husband and father was likewise a great friend and companion to the Master and to me. Philip has not left you but only been removed from your sight. He lives in your heart and walks there still the Way of Spirit. Walk with him now and do not lose faith for you are safe by your goodness from any true harm. The body lives to be destroyed, but the soul lives to live forever. Bless the day of his passing and mark its anniversary, for it will be remembered as a day of mourning for you but a day of joy for him that has left you, for he has reached awareness beyond understanding. Let the tears I have shed upon this document be waters that wash you clean of regret, guilt or blame. Let our sorrow be comforted by our faith.

Mary of Magdala"

Not wanting to reveal anything to the grieving family for fear that their sorrow might make them enemies of the Way; she did not share the news of Christen's birth or the whereabouts of her family. She sealed both documents and laid down to rest.

In the morning Magdalen sought out a courier to deliver her letters. She gave him firm instructions regarding a reply from Paul. He was not to leave Paul until a letter accompanied him and he was then to come straight back to Avalon with the reply. Now that her obligations were fulfilled for the moment, Magdalen could get on with re-establishing her life in Avalon. She went to the church to pray for those departed and to meditate upon her decision to write to Paul. She had done this, she thought, with some negative feelings and with a resolve that had not allowed for the input of Spirit. She did not regret her decision but only the way in which she had made it.

As she was contemplating the purpose of her resolve, James entered the church.

"Why are you hiding here?" he asked with some obvious agitation.

"I am not hiding anything, James, only finding something – my soul."

Magdalen felt her privacy had been violated and her motivation to prayer questioned without regard for her honor. James swiftly realized what he had done.

"I did not mean to interrupt, dear, but I have missed you and you have not taken time to meet with me."

The now elderly apostle was feeling hurt by what he thought was Magdalen's rebuff. She was quick to ease his mind.

"James, I have missed you too. And Sharon misses you tremendously. She hopes that one day you will visit and see her son. I know that you have done a good job here in Avalon and I am most appreciative of your wisdom and sharing, as well as your concern and friendship. You have been a protector to us as Jesus asked of you and it was always you that I could rely on. The bad news of the murders of the apostles and the rumors of

Paul's attacks on others have taken my mind away from my gratitude, but only for a while. I did not mean to slight or hurt you. Please sit with me now."

Magdalen pointed toward one of the couches as she invited James to join her.

"Perhaps I should visit Sharon and her family soon." James began. "I feel a calling to return to Jerusalem. Now that some of my brothers in faith have left the earth, there is a great deal to be done on their behalf. I had thought that on your return I would journey homeward and maybe see Sharon and the boy along the way."

He paused to see what kind of reaction Magdalen would give to his suggestion.

"James, last night I made a decision without inquiring of spirit. I sent a letter to Paul of Damascus inquiring of his gospel and my negativity was revealed in my script. I do not want to answer your thoughts without first finding my spiritual guidance. Let us pray and meditate on this together. The final decision must be your own, of course."

Magdalen was not about to have another decision to ponder with doubt. James agreed and together they prayed and burned aromatic herbs in the fire. After about an hour James rose to his feet.

"I will drop the herbs upon the flames. If I am to go the smoke will rise white as snow. If I am to stay it will be blackened by spirit's disapproval."

He took a handful of the herbal mixture from its urn and threw it upon the fire. The smoke was white and billowing to the sky.

"You must go then when you are ready."

Magdalen rose to stand next to him and hold him tightly against her.

"Take good care of yourself, my protector and friend. And carry with you my love and a letter to Sharon."

"I will, indeed."

The old man smiled down on Magdalen who had wrapped her arms about his waist, as a child would do.

"I love you, Mary of Magdala. Only Jesus could love you more. Remember that in my absence."

In but a few weeks James was gone. He had taken a letter of good tidings and bad to share with Sharon.

The seasons came and went and still no word from Paul. Yet another harvest was taken in and the Mistletoe cut once more, and she had not heard from Sharon or from the apostle to the gentiles. Magdalen wondered often and prayed hard for the safe return of those she loved. She continued in her nightly services and told her tales of the Way that Jesus taught and that Way's evolution through her experiences with the honored Celtic clans.

That spring a courier delivered a letter from Sharon. James had made his way there and she had received Magdalen's news. The child was growing fast and James had moved on to Jerusalem to do his good work there. Sharon and Levi were still very much in love, and Levi's parents were doing well. Magdalen shared the news with all the others and they gave prayers of thanksgiving and joy that night during the service.

But that joy lasted only until the Winter Solstice. The cold brought with it a frigid feeling in her heart when she learned of Matthew's death. He was slain by the sword in Ethiopia.

Her heart bled and her weeping would not cease when only months later a courier brought news of James' martyrdom. Herod Agrippa had ordered his beheading by the sword. The old apostle had joined his Teacher and Rabbi at the hands of another Herod with equal zeal for persecution as his predecessor who had sought the infant Jesus to kill him.

Magdalen sent the news to Sharon with her tears once again upon the letter.

Through prayer and meditation, the Bride of Jesus gave up her grief finally and was satisfied with James' spiritual presence. She had obligations to fulfill here and she took direction from spirit now without hesitation. She would write her book in order to dispel the rumors and gossip and the attacks of Paul, which she now believed to be true since he had not replied with a rebuttal.

She had started that gospel many times, but each time she had been interrupted before it could be completed. Now, she thought, with her menopause approaching she would be free to devote her life to sharing her wisdom through her words and the book would be completed. Then it would be time for her to see her daughter and grandson again before she would join the others in the presence of her husband in spirit.

Chapter 39

Final Farewell

Just before Beltaine, there was a pleasant interruption in Magdalen's life and way. An uncertain but determined group of Christian's arrived with Joseph of Arimathea leading them. Magdalen was ecstatic to see her old friend. Joseph was just as surprised and elated to see her. He had heard the rumors of her hermitage and death and long lamented the loss of the sweet Magdala that he had once tried so hard to care for. He could hardly believe it when Magdalen told him of Sharon's marriage and the birth of her grandson.

Magdalen had always remained grateful for his help with financial and business matters then, but she was especially endeared to him because he had provided a sepulcher for Jesus and assisted in getting the Master's body back from the Romans. It was Joseph who had retrieved the cup from the upper room of the last supper and he that had given it to Peter to be a gift for Sharon one day.

Joseph had anticipated coming to Avalon with something new to teach the Celtic people here. He was not surprised, after seeing Magdalen, that he had little new to teach. Instead, he had a great deal to learn. Magdalen was brimming over with her good news. She told him about the Blood Well and the mysteries that the New Way kept regarding women and children. She asked about Paul and expressed her discontent. She told of healings, visions and journeys within that brought about great enchantments that enlightened and illumined the people. She talked of the method of fair exchange and honor that had developed so fully among the Culdees. When she was quite finished. Joseph made an entreaty.

"Magdala, please may I see the cup?"

He was pleading. Magdalen went to her leather pouch and retrieved the chalice and handed it to Joseph.

"We celebrate the Rite of Remembrance each evening and receive the cup remembering the blood that is life and the spirit that provides it."

"Others are saying that the rite is a miracle that transforms the wine into blood and the bread into the body of Jesus." Joseph sounded concerned. "Some Romans have started rumors that the Christians are cannibals and eat true flesh washing it down with true blood. It is a dark heart that would spread such gossip."

Magdalen agreed but could see how this kind of rumor might have started. She thought of the things she believed of the Celts and the Druids before she came to Avalon. Sharing some of that information with Joseph led to laughter at the folly humanity engages in when the imagination takes control of the tongue.

That evening Joseph was the guest of honor at the service and took communion with the others using the Master's cup. He was as honored to be there as the Culdees were to have him. Magdalen wanted to tell a special Jesus story this night, for Joseph would appreciate it from a personal viewpoint and it would honor him.

"When Jesus had died," Magdalen began her story. "And as the day of preparation for burial was drawing towards evening, Joseph, a man well-born and rich, a God-fearing Jew, found Nicodemus, and said to him, ' I know that you loved Jesus when he was alive, and gladly heard his words, and I saw you fighting with the Jews trying to protect him. If you would like then let us go to Pilate, and beg the body of Jesus for burial, because it is a great crime for him to lie unburied.'

"Nicodemus was afraid to go because Pilate knew that Nicodemus was a follower of Jesus and his Way and Nicodemus was wise to fear him and his reproach."

Magdalen paused for a moment to look at Joseph's face. He appeared honored but humbly so. He was not used to having this much attention focused on him. Magdalen was ready to continue.

"Joseph went to Pilate alone and fell at his feet pleading for the body. And Pilate took pity and said he should take it then and do what he wanted with it. He bought a new tomb for Jesus and with Nicodemus and the rest of us Jesus was buried properly. When the Jews found out about this, they were enraged. They threw him into prison, and said to him, 'If we had not tomorrow the feast of unleavened bread, tomorrow we would have crucified you too; but we will keep you until the feast has passed. Then you will die for sure.'

"They sealed him in that prison to be sure and then they went back to Pilate and told him that Jesus said that he would rise after three days and they wanted a guard to keep someone from stealing the body and pretending that his prophecy had come true. Based on this, Pilate gave them soldiers who sat round the tomb to guard it, after having put seals upon the stone of the tomb.

"On the Lord's Day they sent a guard to take Joseph out of the prison, in order to put him to death. But having opened it, they couldn't find him. And they were astonished at this. How, with the doors shut, and the bolts safe, and the seals unbroken, Joseph had disappeared. But Jesus himself had set Joseph free by the work of angels because he had treated his body with such respect and had such compassion for Nicodemus and the rest of us who mourned. I know all this to be true because the angels and saints have declared it to me. And today he honors us, this man of God, by his presence in our place of worship."

Magdalen stretched her arm out toward Joseph and the applause and joyous cheers rang out. Joseph was a little embarrassed to be made the center of attention this way, but as Magdalen knew he would be, her friend was honored to hear his story told.

Joseph spent the night at Magdalen's home and she instructed him that courtesy demanded he pay a visit to the Tor and to Blood Well and to get the blessing of the Lady of the Lake before embarking on any mission, Christian or otherwise. He vowed to make his pilgrimage in the morning.

At dawn Magdalen walked the labyrinth with him and showed him the way into the womb of the earth through the great stone. Joseph's audience with the Lady was brief but she blessed him fully for his part in preserving honor for the Master Jesus and acting as protector to Magdalen and Sharon so long ago. She couldn't deny this hero of the Way any request. Joseph expressed his gratitude and was on his way to spread the Way of Jesus throughout the isles. One day, he promised Magdalen, he would make his way to Holland County to see the family of the Master.

For all the years that the Priestess had been in Avalon she had gone each month to the moon lodge. This month her time did not come. Magdalen had arrived at another passage in life and went instead to Blood Well to bathe. She dressed herself in fine clothes and tied ribbons in her hair. Looking at her own reflection in the pure water she thought of the freedom that aging had brought her, but she thought too of the past and the many lessons she had learned throughout her years. Now that wisdom had the freedom to be expressed fully.

The Priestess had been well prepared for the place of the Great Goddess, the woman through whom all teaching and guiding of the community's spiritual life was done. Her sisters immediately became aware of Magdalen's absence at the moon lodge. After her bath she had taken the children to care for them while the others meditated during their moon cycle. Magdalen had now achieved the Wisdom of the Great Mother.

When the cycle days had gone by and the women came out from the lodge they shared their stories and then brought Magdalen, the new Crone, back to the well where she scryed again into the water and received guidance for each of the women who had shared her cycle. For each of them she had a message from the Goddess and to some of them she expressed her love with a kiss on the mouth.

On a chair-shaped litter Magdalen was carried to the Tor to meet for the first time the Morgens, the Nine Sacred Crones, the Great Council of Avalon.

Just as Baera and the Lady of the Lake had promised, the Morgens dressed her in finery and put out a huge feast and the women danced circles around her with song and the playing of the flutes and wind instruments, symbols of the harmony of life as wisdom moves through it.

It was a gala that surpassed any of the celebrations that had gone before it. Magdalen was now honored as one of the Great Ones. She was, in effect, being called the Great Mother Goddess. On her return to the village circle the men too honored her as they passed by, dropping flowers into her lap and greeting her as Holy One.

The remainder of Magdalen's life would be spent in teaching the maidens and making community decisions with the council. She would not be obligated to any household task or to work of any kind that was not of a sacred nature. Except caring for the children during her sisters' moon cycle she would have no responsibilities to childrearing. Her wisdom was free to express itself through prophecy, teaching, healing and giving guidance.

Mary of Magdala was coming to the end of her lifetime in Avalon. As the years passed and she fulfilled her duties as the Great Mother, she began to look forward to the final mystery of this life. Death of her body would reunite her spirit with Jesus and with his mother, Mary. She would know again her brothers, Jesus' apostles, who had gone before her to be with him in the Kingdom of Heaven.

She was content with the idea of her return to pure energy and did not fear death. The Way had prospered as had been predicted by so many. Magdalen knew that she had contributed to its incline and to preserving the goodness and to hastening its evolution through experience. Still, she wanted one more time to see her daughter and her grandson. She sent a courier to Holland County to request Levi to bring his family back to Avalon for her departure.

When the courier was gone to deliver her entreaty, Magdalen set her hand to completing her gospel. This, she thought, she would put in Sharon's hand before she breathed her last.

Magdalen's hands were old now and she was slow to form her letters. Resting on her bed she would formulate the words in her mind attempting to assure that the stories of Jesus and the truth of the Way would be preserved for her grandson and so many others. Christen would be a man soon, taking his own rite of passage. This parchment would be her gift to him from beyond the earth. She finished just before her family's arrival.

For several weeks they visited, shared stories and meals. Each evening the Rite of Remembrance was given by an aged and weaker Magdalen. Each night she prayed for her passing to arrive swiftly. Just before the final hour arrived, Magdalen asked for the Holy Grail to be brought to her. Levi brought the cup in its fine cloth covering and handed it over to the High Priestess of the Culdees.

"This cup will be yet another mystery of Avalon." She said. "Many will seek for its secrets. Little will they know that the womb within me held the true blood of Christ or that Christen walks among them, the bloodline of the Holy Grail."

Magdalen unwrapped the Holy Grail and removed its contents before she passed the cup to Christian.

"Let it remain a mystery, grandson, a secret that will protect you and your grandchildren as it has protected mine."

Christen took the cup from his grandmother with reverence. Sharon and Levi had shared with their son the stories and mysteries of Avalon and the Culdees. He knew his grandmother's importance to the entire community of Christendom. Now twelve the blonde-haired, blue-eyed boy was growing into a fine man. His gaze had the piercing compassion in them that his mother's had and his heart was large with love.

"Wise One, my grandmother, you are a true Goddess, one to be worshiped and obeyed out of our love for you. I will honor your request and keep safe the mystery to be shared with those that follow the Way. It is my honor to be your messenger to the people."

Christen truly was an honorable man. He held the cup close to his heart as Magdalen motioned for Sharon to come closer. From under the bedclothes, the old woman produced her scrolls. These she put in her daughter's hand as she had planned.

"I have written down the stories of Jesus and the Way so that they will never be forgotten. Teach from them, but do not forget that evolution must continue. Your mother has not written in stone or on it, all ways change, but the truth of Love will never change."

Sharon accepted the gospel from her mother's hand and kissed her on the forehead and then on the mouth. Now Magdalen looked at Levi.

"To you I have given my dearest gift, my daughter. In fair exchange you have cared for her and returned my trust. Thank you, Levi; whatever else I have is now yours. Wear my sword with honor and my breastplate with courage. Bury my body beside Mystic and look for my spirit in the wind."

She squeezed Levi's hand tightly and he bent to kiss her.

Sharon cried out "Father has come for you!" and with that Mary of Magdala, Bride of Christ and Great Mother Goddess, the High Priestess of Avalon left with her beloved.

A Journey with the Bride of Christ

In Magdalen's hand was clutched a small cloth bag tied with a red ribbon. Sharon opened the bag and took from it the fragments of her own umbilical cord. There was a brief note of farewell tucked in with it.

"Through the mystery of birth we became
bound together for life. Through the cord of Love
we remain tied together for eternity. I Love you,
Sharon, and always will. Mother"

The family did as Magdalen had requested and the village mourned for their loss with them. When three days of mourning had passed, Sharon went to Blood Well once more before returning to Holland County. She scryed in the water and finding her mother's image she was comforted. Magdalen appeared youthful and filled with life as she spoke to her daughter.

"I have become the grail filled with life for all. I will always love you and ever be with you in many forms."

With that the image disappeared. Sharon opened the scrolls that Magdalen had given her and read for the first time the Gospel of Jesus Christ through the words of Mary Magdalen

"I, Mary of Magdala, Bride of Christ and High Priestess of Avalon, write here the truth of the Way as I recollect it from my moments with the Great Teacher and High Priest of Heaven, Jesus of Nazareth, the Anointed by God now departed husband and father."

Sharon's eyes welled with tears of mourning and pride as she read her mother's descriptions of the Jesus stories. She read Magdalen's history of her life with the Precious Prophet recalling how she had told those stories with such emotion and reverence.

Then she came to the deeper subjects of life, the things her father had tried so desperately to explain while he was on earth and that Magdalen had found revealed through her Celtic travels, her ties to the Goddess and to the Earth and the evolution of the Way.

439

Magdalen's gospel went on with the teachings that Jesus had shared with only her. Here at the end were the teachings of the Goddesses of Faith, Hope and Charity. Here were the songs of the seasons and their eternal cycles. Here were the explanations that her mother had shared through her New Way. She had long ago revealed them to the apostles just as she had revealed them to the people of Avalon.

Then Sharon came to something more, something that her mother had not shared with her as a story. She had no idea of the conflict between Magdalen and the other apostles regarding Jesus' teachings.

"When I had said all this, I fell silent since this was all that Jesus had shared with me.

"But Andrew answered and said to the others. 'Say what you will about what she has said, but I for one do not believe that Jesus said this. For certainly these teachings are strange ideas.'

"Peter answered him and spoke. He questioned the others about Jesus. 'Did he really speak privately with a woman and not openly to us? Are we to turn about and all listen to her? Did he prefer her to us?'

"Then I cried and I said to Peter. 'My brother Peter, what do you think? Do you think that I have thought this up myself in my heart, or that I am lying about my husband and your Teacher?'

"Levi who is called Simon answered my question and said to Peter, 'Peter you have always been rash and hot headed. Now I see you attacking his wife like one of his enemies would. If Jesus found her worthy, who are you indeed to reject her? Surely Jesus knew her better than you?'

'That is why he loved her more than us. We should be ashamed and put on the precepts of his Way and go off to preach as he has asked us to, not laying down another rule or another law beyond what he has said.'

"And when they heard this they began to go forth to proclaim and to preach. And I Mary of Magdala, Bride of Christ and Keeper of the Way fled to escape the anger of those who were jealous of what I held within me and I have kept it safe as I had promised allowing it to grow into fullness of heart.

Now the Grail has been drained but the Blood has gone forth to nourish the earth. "

Sharon rolled up the scrolls, vowing to honor the New Way and to watch the grandchildren of Jesus and Magdalen perpetuate its growth.

She shouted aloud affirming her oath.

"This is the Good News. Blessed Be!"

Bibliography & References

Caesar's account of Gaul first and second Books

Gospel of Nicodemus

Gospel of Mary

The New Testament Book of John

Many Celtic and Druid Internet Sites

All these confirmed my dreams and added depth to this work.

About The Author Dr. Arlene J. Colver ND

Director of Lifelight University, Arlene is a teacher and a counselor with a personal grasp of what it takes to reach happiness and health. Her clients range from psychologists and ministers to anyone concerned with life values. She has studied body chemistry, human nutrition, iridology, homeopathy, herbology, and other life sciences, theology and preventive health care. She is a minister of the Society for Universal Concordance and a Doctor of Naturopathy.

Arlene Colver is the author of two self-published books channeled to her by the Master Sinat Schirah: <u>Accounts, Designs & Roses</u> and <u>Placements</u>. She also writes for periodicals and produces Letters from Consciousness, a monthly contribution to the Internet experience that offers thoughts on spiritual living.

Arlene Colver has lectured on many topics. In addition to natural health care her subjects include: forgiveness, women's issues, relationships, and the link between Christian doctrine and 20th century philosophy. Dr. Arlene Colver is available for counseling, lectures and free lance writing on any of these topics or those related to them.

You can contact Arlene by email at: <u>Schirah@cheqnet.net</u>
Or telephone: 715-794-2638
Write: Lifelight University, 44030 Dodd Dr., Cable, WI 54821
Visit her website: http://lifelightuniversity.org

Other Works by Arlene J. Colver ND

Accounts, Designs & Roses

Channeled through direct conversation with the Master Sinat Schirah, was originally dictated to the author as a twenty week program of study designed to give the reader a progressive and rewarding but simple method of obtaining awareness and control over physical and spiritual life.

Placements

Placements is a study prepared by the Master Sinat Schirah through the channel, Arlene Colver. Its workbook style and suggestions for Consciousness Placement have been likened to A Course in Miracles. The journal pages that have been provided assure the student both the space and the time to savor the progress that is theirs as they complete each week's study program. The channel has described this work as the closest exercise given to the daily experience of living with the Master himself.

I Send You Roses (Ebook)

A collection of inspirational letters from Love to your soul.

We have compiled some of our past letters from consciousness and arranged them for meditation with corresponding pages containing prayers, affirmations and blessings for each letter's topic. This is a great book to have by your bedside after you've printed it or right there on your hard drive to access in one of those trying moments.